Saving Fiction

Liam Moran

Copyright © 2018 Liam Moran

All rights reserved.

ISBN-10: 1723136077
ISBN-13: 978-1723136078

To Jennifer McConahy, who always taught me to keep an eye on the future (no matter what the other one was doing). And to Mike Carter, whose advice has helped me more than he will ever know, even if I never did take him up on the advice he gave most often: to settle down and say a prayer if I wish to.

AN INTRODUCTION BY THE AUTHOR

The Hindu philosophy teaches that the Atman (the soul or self) can reach the Brahman (God or everything existent in reality) through the process called 'Moksha.' The theory that we can achieve a higher level of consciousness or enter a greater plain transcends all religions.

Many Native American tribes believed that when they died they would become one with nature. Everything whether plant or animal had a soul that was shared universally. You could catch a glimpse of becoming everything and reaching that higher plain through a spiritual journey. At a certain age when the child is believed to be ready to enter this stage of adulthood, they would take peyote or other hallucinogens and starve themselves for days on end until they had taken their journey and experienced their greater consciousness.

Even the Judeo-Christian religions have a similarity—while much milder—akin to this process. They pray and either thank God for all that He has given them or ask for help in a troubling situation. This is communicating with a deity on a higher level than us through the only means that we can feasibly do on earth.

Yet this task is not exclusive to the religious. Even an atheist or an agnostic can meditate with the hopes of getting a better understanding of their inner self.

As for me, I don't pray. I don't starve myself. I don't have a drug-induced spiritual journey. I don't go through Moksha. I don't even meditate. I write.

A writer is constantly living in two worlds: the world of reality (the tasks you do in life, the social interactions you have, the rent you have to pay, the deadline you have to worry about) and the fantastical world of the story. All the time we have one side experiencing life's mundane tasks, and one side in a state of constant search of how we can improve our story, what lines we can use, and what we will have our characters experience next. One foot in reality and one foot in fiction.

When we go through the task of writing, it is our own form of Moksha. Character development: our meditation. Plot: our spiritual journey. Narration: our prayer. When we write, we are no longer in reality. We have breached the walls of our minds and entered a new world. The story is our heaven and the pen is our ascension.

So once again I leave this world. Once again I am reincarnated in fantasy. The insanity of the story becomes who I am. I place my hands on the keyboard and say my prayer.

—L.M.

Saving Fiction

LIAM MORAN

CH. 1

Richard Sweeney sits alone at the booth, lightly digging the blade in his pocket deeper into his right outer thigh, as he stares in utter serenity at the innocent civilians surrounding him, with the most magnificent images playing through his head. For instance, the family laughing at some rude comment made by the youngest child, are, in his mind's eye, dangling from ropes tied around their necks, swinging back and forth in synchronized harmony. The couple that embrace each other with a warm kiss are naked and in pieces on a concrete floor with their decapitated heads taped together, still locked in that beautiful kiss.

"How are you doing today? Can I start you off with something to drink?" the waitress appearing at his left asks.

Inside his mind he sees quick flashes of him cutting her apart. First he smashes her into the wall. *Flash.* He jabs his knife into her right kidney. *Flash.* He plunges the blade into her heart. *Flash.* He slits her throat as the arteries open and blood comes rushing out. *Flash.* The light goes out of her eyes as he cuts off her middle finger and thumb of each hand. *Flash.* Her middle finger and thumb are draped over each lifeless eye in the sign of the cross. All the while the music of incoherent whispers, mutterings, screams, and whimpers echo melodically in his head.

"I'll have coffee. Black," he says in a pleasant tone. "And I've actually already made up my mind on what I'd like to order."

"Alright. What'll it be?" she responds.

"I'll have the steak and eggs. Eggs over-easy, and steak medium-rare. As for my sides, I'll take hash browns and toasted whole wheat bread." He smiles, looking at what he sees as a mutilated talking corpse. "If I'm going to do as much damage to my body by taking in all this red meat, eggs and carbs, I might as well try to salvage some of it by avoiding white bread," he jokes.

"Sounds good," she chuckles, "I'll bring that out as soon as it's ready."

He nods and smiles as she vanishes from the table. His eyes follow her as she checks up on all the other tables. *A nice blond beauty. Could be a potential client,* he thinks to himself, and then later decides that he likes this restaurant too much to have to suspend his frequent visits for as long as it takes for all the hype to die down.-

The doorbell rings. Damn it, I was finally making some progress on this story. Halfway to the front door I shout, "Who is it?"

"Who else would visit your boring ass at this time of night?" the voice behind the door bellows.

"Oh Jimmy, figured it was you. Who else's life would be so full of meaningless drivel that they would come to visit my 'boring ass' at midnight?" I say. "Come in, it's unlocked."

Jimmy opens the door and walks in. Standing at five ten, and weighing in at around one-fifty, his beard and battered clothing reveal a truly disheveled individual. "You know, at this time of night, you might want to consider locking your door. This isn't exactly Sesame Street."

I laugh, "What are they going to steal? An outdated computer, a broken TV, and a collection of beaten-to-death novels?"

"Well, they could always kill you," he says.

"They'd be doing the integrity of literature a favor," I laugh. "Have a seat. I don't have much. Scotch good?"

"Yeah, that's fine," he says and plops down on the couch.

I take out two glasses, and a bag of ice that had melted previously, causing it to congeal when it was refrozen. In order to break the ice up, I bash it repeatedly against the edge of the counter that comes together to create a ninety degree angle. The ice breaks off into smaller chunks as slight flakes fly away into the air, melting into nothing before they hit the table contributing nothing to anything, besides making the room less than .000000000001% more humid. As significant as a mosquito miscarriage. Or a stillborn sloth. Or a single raindrop. Or mine and Jimmy's contribution to the Arts. I dump the coagulated chucks of ice in the two glasses and pour the scotch over it watching the liquid break apart the ice. I walk steadily over, carefully watching that I don't spill any scotch on the carpet, and hand a glass over to Jimmy while I set the other on the coffee table closest to the sofa chair. I walk back, grab the ashtray by the computer, and sit down.

"You still smoking? What is it? Does killing yourself slowly make you much more of a tortured artist that needs pain to give him inspiration?" he asks mockingly.

"Oh I'm sorry," I overdramatically apologize as I pull out a cigarette. "I clearly am not as strong as the almighty Jimmy Hansen, who has quit for how long again? Three days?"

He mutters a laugh, "Alright, alright, but I'm not going back."

"Oh really?" I say. "Wait...didn't you say that the last time...And the time before that...And the time before that...And, hold on a second, I think the time before that too."

"Ha-ha-ha," Jimmy says sarcastically.

"I'll give you this," I say. "You sure do know how to quit smoking, because you seem to be doing it every week."

Jimmy sighs. He stirs the scotch around with his finger, then removes it to take a sip. The residue on his finger drips onto the couch a couple of times before the hand that directs it reaches to the coffee table to pick up a book. The title reads, <u>The Savageness of the Spirit</u> by Coralline Thomson. Above it says 'New York Times Bestseller,' and the back of it is littered with praise. The cover shows a man cowered in the fetal position against the street with torn up clothes, a bruised face, and a forty in a brown bag being clenched tightly against his chest like a baby with its favorite teddy bear.

"My only reason to question my atheism," I say with reverence, "forty-two novels in twenty years, each one better than the next, countless awards including three Pulitzer Prizes. Coralline Thomson may just be Christ incarnate." There's a long pause out of an uncanny respect for the author.

"Yes and someday people will have a new author to view in awe and wonder," Jimmy says, "and his name will be," he pauses and picks up the book, <u>The Devil's Redemption</u>, sitting on the counter to his right, "Henry Riddick."

Immediately we both burst into laughter so quickly that I choke a little on my scotch. <u>The Devil's Redemption</u>. My one book that was published. What a joke. The critics tore that book to pieces. The New York Times said that <u>The Devil's Redemption</u> was, "the worst thing to happen to literature since the Nazi's book burning." A more vulgar magazine said that, <u>The Devil's Redemption</u> was "only useful as a substitute for toilet paper." What a joke.

Finally my laughter dies down long enough to say, "I think that the literary gods might smite you for saying that."

"Well at least one thing is for sure," he says. "According to what the media says, and the shots of the paparazzi and reporters trying to interview her, you sure are not nearly as ridiculously antisocial as she is." He pauses. "She's like an inebriated sloth with Asperger's syndrome."

"Yeah," I say and pause remorsefully, as if I'm talking about a sacrilegious taboo subject, "but it's kind of strange how in some interviews she seems just as energetic, and full of life and socialness as any other person. Maybe even more so."

Jimmy shrugs, "Maybe she's got undiagnosed manic-depression."

"Maybe," I say spacing out. "Maybe."

CH. 2

It's September 30th, Thursday night. The thirtieth memorial to my exit of my mother's womb. Some places consider this my 'golden birthday.' Apparently on this particular celebration, I'm supposed to celebrate it in full force because my age correlates with the date of my birth. So what do I do to celebrate to my fullest capacity? I spend it drinking at Henry's Bar with the five people who can stand my presence. Excluding my brother, we are all failures. Some of us have fully realized our insignificance. Some of us are just realizing it. And some of us have yet to accept it. All us failures sit around this table sipping our drinks, and spending time to ignore the inevitable fact that we are, and forever will be, nobodies. We are "The Rejects of the Round Table."

My youngest brother and only sibling, Mark Riddick, is the only success out of the group because he followed my only good advice. "Change your major, because the world needs plenty of things, but a mediocre author is something they can do without," I told him when he was in his second year of college. "And they sure as hell have no objection in letting you know that." After that he changed his major to business, and now owns two businesses, is making good money, and has recently become engaged to his future beautiful, kind, intelligent, wife. I used to have some resentment and envy towards his success, but that mainly dissipated as I realized at least one Riddick will be a success. It's also not worth my time to hold animosity towards someone just for not being as much of an imbecile as me.

Then, of course, there's Jimmy Hansen—my closest friend—who has, like myself, chosen to live a life of 'expressing one's emotions in the arts.' And also, like myself, completely failed at it. He chose to dabble in abstract paintings. Sure, he's got some paintings that are hung up in showings sometimes, but the showings barely make enough for him to pay for cheap rundown shelter, and food to feed his shallow, malnourished, skeleton that somehow qualifies as a living body.

Then there is a friend by association—Frank Samson. A mildly plump man, who keeps himself well-groomed and looks fairly presentable as long as his mouth remains closed. If he cracks his smile slightly too much—revealing the corrosion of teeth caused by poor dental hygiene and an infection that, despite the agonizing pain he must feel, he can't fix due to a lack of health insurance and currency—it makes it hard to not be repulsed immediately. He's doing slightly better financially than most of us, with his portraits that he sends to art shows. But try as he might, the money he makes isn't enough to fix his dental atrocities. Jimmy met him at a showing, they started talking, and next thing you know, he becomes an addition to the rest of us artistic rejects.

To my left sits Carl Johnson, the youngest of the rejects. I wouldn't exactly call him a reject; he's more of a reject in training. Not yet has his dreams been shattered by critics, and readers, and bloggers, and all the ignorers. No, not him. He's the cockeyed optimist who can't focus on writing his first novel because he's too busy fantasizing about future interviews when the public deifies him as The God of Fiction. About how his novel wins all sorts of awards, and he's on Oprah, and all of his living literary idols send their praises wishing they had that sort of talent. I don't want to break the kid's ignorant heart, but I can give him the easiest reason why he's destined to sit in honor with The Rejects of the Round

Table: he's picked me as his mentor. I was flattered I admit, but I should have just given him the same advice I gave my brother, "Turn back while you still can."

There's me of course, Henry Riddick. After the horrid display of my first novel, I insult literature once again by trying to create another mangling of fiction. Another grotesque torturing of innocent words set in an unoriginal plot accompanied by one-dimensional characters and littered with clichés. But I think to myself, *even if the pay is shit, it's still pay.*

And finally, to my right sits Hank Wiseman. Just the look of him makes it completely obvious that he no longer cares in the slightest. Not about anything. Not about anyone. Not even about himself. I've been fortunate to only have one failure published. He's on seven. I've seen many people let themselves go, but he does it free of even the most remote sense of dignity or shame. His beard probably hasn't been trimmed in maybe four months, his hair sticks up without pattern, and his body has a smell of at least one week without bathing. Hunched over his whiskey taking large sips, just by smell alone you can tell that he's pretty far into his nightly drunkenness.

The three of us writers sitting here—Carl, me, and Hank—are the three stages of a failed author. Carl is the first stage: the innocent optimist with the world ahead of him, still in the illusion of feelings of future grandeur. Then there's me, the second stage: with my first disgrace published, I've just recently adopted cynicism. Then finally there's Hank, the third and final stage: his cynicism has bloomed into the ever-so-potent pessimism that subsides subtly when he consumes mass quantities of alcohol and wraps himself up in his blanket of self-pity. To my left: my past. Where I sit: my present. To my right: my future.

The difference in how people talk or the actions they take completely changes as you progress through these stages. For instance, when the three of us imbibe alcohol: Carl drinks to feel social, I drink to feel happy, and Hank drinks to feel nothing.

When each of us finds ourselves in bed with a woman: Carl 'makes love,' I 'have sex,' and Hank 'fucks.' The list goes on and on. My past. My present. My future.

"So," I say in a futile attempt to add some levity to Hank's drunken depression, "how are things going with Liz?"

"It's over," he mutters, void of emotion.

"Sorry to hear," I say. "What was the reason?"

Still with no emotion, "Cause she's a fucking cunt."

I see Carl wince as Hank utters this last obscenity. Carl is not usually queasy when it comes to vulgarity, but this last seldom used expletive stings his ears.

One time we were walking home from the bar, Jimmy and I were lightly tipsy, Carl was slightly buzzed, and Hank, well he was too intoxicated to walk with us. He barely even stumbled his way into the cab. Carl asked me why I associate with such a vulgar disgusting man who has no common decency and no respect for anyone including himself. And I said without hesitating, "Cause it's cheaper than a crystal ball." At first he looked confused, and then noticed the smirk on Jimmy's face and nodded accordingly. My future is dim, but I might as well keep an eye on it while I can so I'm not completely off balance when it hits me.

Back in the here and now, Jimmy and Frank are occupying themselves, discussing different painting techniques. I have to admit, I've never really been attuned to art. Jimmy can see all sorts of hidden meanings behind paintings, and can discuss the carving techniques of sculptures, or the subtle strokes of the artist. But it never really fascinated me. I never could quite dive into it to the level that he could. I can interpret symbolisms in novels and laugh at the ironies and whatnot, but the art you look at and put in your house just could never grab me. Carl went to the bathroom, and Hank is way too far gone to probably make a coherent sentence, so I decide to talk to my brother Mark.

"So," I say, "have you picked out a date for you and Sue?"

He shakes his head, "We're still looking. I just want to say screw it and pick the next place we go to, but unfortunately Sue isn't that easy. And to think, this is only the beginning of the exploration for 'the perfect wedding,'" he says in a mocking voice. "I just wish that I can skip forward to the honeymoon." He smiles. "Not that taking time off of my day to walk around with my fiancée and find out which of the fifty shades of the exact same white would make the perfect tablecloth, isn't fun."

I laugh, "Well the wedding and honeymoon will be pretty good, not to mention the bachelor party."

"Alright, I admit it," he says. "That part I am looking forward to. But, come on, you don't really want to sit around talking about my wedding plans. Last time I checked we were still men. And this is your thirtieth. Isn't that the 'over the hill' age?"

"Actually," I say, "I'm pretty sure that's fifty."

"Whatever," he says. "What do you plan on doing now that you hit the big 3-0?"

"Well," I say tentatively, "I would like to actually get a *decent* novel published. You know, maybe one that has at least one critic that doesn't equate it to dog shit."

Hank releases a condescending single laugh, because in his mind there is no chance that I would create anything even remotely bearable to read. Just as Carl doomed himself when he took me as his mentor, I doomed myself when I took Hank as my mentor all those years ago. And besides, who better would know what my potential will lead to than my own future personified?

Mark ignores the drunk's laugh, "Come on," he says, "it wasn't that terrible. I read it and thought it was a decent book."

"Are you kidding?" I laugh, "If I had even half a conscience I'd put the critic's reviews on the cover just as a cautionary warning to the reader."

"It's your first book," he says. "No one expects it to be the greatest novel ever produced. Your second one will be much better. I know it. In fact, I promise it."

I roll my eyes and sigh, creating the universal sign for

'bullshit' and take another sip of my drink as I ask the waitress if I can get another whiskey sour. At this time Carl returns and I start to discuss his book with him. He's overly excited and mentions how he wrote a couple of new chapters and wants me to look them over. I know I shouldn't, for his sake. I should tell him to give it all up, go back to school, and get a degree that he can actually use. Or at the very least, find a better mentor than me. But he's developed a fondness for me, and his eyes are burning with anticipation of my feedback, and I'm too polite to not destroy his life.

Hank takes a large gulp, finishing the remnants of his whiskey, and I see his face make a sign of sickness and without a word he vanishes to the bathroom.

While he's gone, Jimmy looks at me and smiles, "Well it's your birthday, and you know the tradition."

"Oh, please no," I make a futile plea and shake my head.

"Since we were twenty-one we've been doing this," he says, "and we swore we'd never chicken out."

Jimmy goes to the bar and says loud enough for me to hear, "One shot of tequila, one shot of whiskey, and one of vodka." He looks back at me shaking my head, "I'll make it easy on you since you're getting old now." He turns back to the bartender, "And a coke." Then back to me, "See, I'm so nice I'm giving you a chaser."

I let out a groan, but along with the dread there's a little excitement. It was a stupid immature deal we made back when we thought that the epitome of having fun was getting as obliterated as possible, and the less we remembered, the more fun we had. It's juvenile, I know, but sometimes, as long as it's on seldom occasions, it's fun to be a little juvenile. It brings us back to a time when we were young and our lives were ahead of us, opposed to now where it appears our lives are mostly behind us, leaving only the shrapnel of shattered dreams for comfort.

Jimmy puts the three shots in front of me. Then he says, "And even though it's against the rules, I'll let this slide." And he sets the coke down in front of me.

I'm already feeling sick. Unfortunately for me, I forgot about this tradition, and drank quite a bit already not expecting to be taking three shots back to back. I stare down the shot glasses, then I realize that the longer I stare these down the sicker I'm going to feel, so I start it. I down the tequila, then the whiskey, then the vodka. The table cheers. In the spirit of the tradition I decide not to drink the soda. I'm holding it all in and I feel terrible, but I'm still managing it. Then Hank returns to the table with the scent of vomit attached to his stench of liquor and body odor. With all that hitting my nose, I have no choice, I have to chase it with the coke or else the liquid is going to make a second appearance. I take a few gulps of the soda but I still feel queasy.

The conversation continues, and after those shots, I stick mainly to water. The night ends up coming to an end and we all decide to split off. As always, a couple minutes in advance we call Hank a cab. Once again, he stumbles, barely making it to the cab, and falls inside. Ah, my future always haunts me with the ghost of what's to come. Mark offers me a ride, but I tell him I'd prefer to walk, but Carl and Frank take the opportunity and they drive away. At least Jimmy accompanies me. Once outside I light my cigarette, and with that Jimmy pulls out his own pack.

I give him a look of sarcastic confusion, "Wait a sec?"

"Yeah, yeah, yeah," he says. "I cracked. What can I say? I'm human."

"That's debatable," I respond.

He laughs. "I'm surprised that you're still able to keep up on the wisecracks with all those toxins flowing through you."

"Well I guess my brain at half function is about equal to yours normally," I joke.

All of a sudden it starts to drizzle. I look up and the clouds look pretty bad, a storm could break out and we're still about six blocks from where we live.

"I'm starting to think we should have taken the ride," I say

"I'm starting to think you're right," he replies, now cocking his head to look up at the storm clouds.

Of course the thought crosses my mind, *it could be worse,* and I can't help but say it out loud. After a block and a half, as if in reply, the clouds really open up.

Jimmy smiles, "Happy birthday."

CH. 3

I'm at the pool hall with Jimmy as he lines up aiming to put the three-ball in the corner pocket. He's focused hard on the ball, with the anger of a repressed memory of a past ghost dancing in his head. This apparition always haunts him every year on this day, October 6th. He overpowers his shot and slams the table exclaiming, "Motherfucker!"

Understand that he is not often this vulgar in public. But that guilt and anger from his horrible mistake all those years ago, despite his attempts to suppress it with alcohol and monotonous activity, always makes an appearance this day each year. When you screw up as badly as he did, there's no cure for that immense underlying guilt. No matter what you do to take your mind off of it, no matter how much therapy you go to, no matter how many pharmaceutical or recreational drugs you take, there's no cure for that one colossal fuck-up.

Even though the presence of what happened is there, and I know he's almost constantly dwelling on that moment, it's something we made a silent agreement we would never speak of. It's like when you enter a house and there's an unbearable stench that makes you gag but you're too polite to comment on it. And while you're talking to the owner of that house, you try to think of what to say, but all that's going through your mind is, *"The stench!*

The stench! The stench!"

Even though the stench is so intoxicating, and the entire conversation we have is awkward, Jimmy needs someone to bear it with him. He can't be alone with his memories or he'll go mad with guilt. He needs me to be with him. Me: his closest friend. If he would ever talk to anyone about what happened that night, it would be me. But of course, that day when he opens up to me and brings up again what happened is a very distant future, if it will happen at all. But he doesn't have to bring it up to me, because I was there for the event that birthed the stench.

I lean forward on the table, my pool stick in hand, lining up my shot to hit the eleven-ball on the far left side to sink it in the side pocket. I nick it in but unfortunately didn't think far enough in advance, because I end up getting a scratch by sending the cue ball in the corner pocket. I lean back and give an annoyed sigh. I look over and see Jimmy taking large gulps of his sixth beer in an hour. I know he's hurting.

"So," I say, "how's your artwork going? Anything new you're working on?"

He wipes some beer off of his lips and parts of his beard, "The same garbage as always. The same meaningless shit that gets me nowhere." He lets out a feigned laugh, "But it's good enough to earn my spot at the table of rejects." Overpowering his shot again he shouts, "God Damn it!" Then he composes himself again, looking a little embarrassed. "Anyway, how are things going with your story?"

"Well, I haven't had much time recently to work on it," I respond.

Suddenly the stench rears its ugly head once again. This specter dances over our heads revealing to ourselves how utterly uninteresting our lives are. Our jobs are barely worth talking about. Our social lives are a joke. We have scarce communication with our families—well, except for my brother, but the only thing that comes to mind regarding him is the wedding. And there's only so much that men, who are not the grooms, can talk about a wedding and still retain some trace of their masculinity. We don't have wives or children. We don't even have any significant others currently. So the god of awkwardness screams, "The stench! The stench! The stench!"

I pull out my shirt a bit, straightening all the wrinkles, to keep from mentioning any taboo subject. When this is over, I start picking at my fingernails. Jimmy flubs his shot again and shouts another expletive. During my shot, he downs his beer and orders his seventh drink.

I realize that after this game, I should probably head home so Jimmy doesn't pull a Hank and make a fool out of himself by becoming a vulgar belligerent drunk. Jimmy heads back and I tell him that I'm getting tired and want to call it a night at the end of this game.

"Yeah," Jimmy says, "that's probably a good idea. I'm getting a little tired myself."

He spends the rest of the game overpowering nearly all of his shots. Rage manifested inside him, peeking its head out in the abuse of a poor innocent ball.

The entire time, the stench is becoming more and more empowering. The biggest problem is that, for three-hundred-sixty-four days of the year, Jimmy and I have a near telepathic relationship. We have inside jokes formulated on the spot that only the two of us get. In fact, we could pretty much tell an inside joke, or basically communicate an entire conversation by merely sharing a look with our eyes. But on this one day, he's an impenetrable rock of loneliness. Our telepathy is neutralized by the ever-so-potent power of this stench. Nothing is transmitted fully, through either body language, or even the bluntest of acceptable communication: words.

We leave the pool hall, and start walking home. I take out a cigarette and, knowing he must need one too, I hand him one as well. We continue walking and the stench grows more overwhelming with every step. Every block we pass, the stench's potency doubles. The silence only makes it more unbearable with every moment we remain speechless.

Finally after four blocks I blurt out like conversational Tourette's, "You know, it's not your fault." I can't believe I said that. I don't know why I said that. That is a taboo that we agreed we would never *ever* mention in our lives. It may have been a silent agreement, but in many ways, those agreements are the most sacred.

"Yeah, I know," he says, "but it sure as hell doesn't feel that way."

CH. 4

It's five years prior and I couldn't be happier in my life. This is when I was still Carl Johnson. This is when I was still my past. My young, joyful, optimistic, past. In fact, this is probably when I was doing even better than the present Carl Johnson. This is when I got my first book deal. This is when my entire life's dream has finally come true. This is before everything went to hell.

I'm sitting at the table with Jimmy, his girlfriend Molly Idle, and my then-girlfriend Lindsey McClain, in a lake house we rented for the week. Jimmy just got a job teaching art in high school, and a couple of weeks later, a publisher finally makes a deal to pick up my book. Needless to say, this is before the critics tore my book to pieces, and Jimmy got fired for showing up to work in a drunken depression, rambling to his students about how life is completely meaningless and then vomited in the trash bin. No, this is when we were at the top of our lives. And in order to celebrate our accomplishments, Jimmy recommended that we go to a lake house, and party until we have no more energy left. And we did.

I've got my right arm around Lindsey and my left hand straddling a margarita. Lindsey and Molly are laughing as Jimmy tells some stories about our past endeavors while he pours himself another drink. We're all laughing because we've reached that alcohol-induced, mind-numbing, mental utopia, where the only things the brain allows the body to do are laugh and pour yourself another drink. We're all having, what could have been, the best week of our lives. If only things went according to plan, which as all inhabitants of this world know, is a rarity.

"So then he stumbles down the street. No shoes. No shirt," Jimmy says. "So I wake up the next day and look around the house thinking, 'Where the hell is Henry?' So I call him up, and no answer. I call him again, no answer. I call him another five times, no answer. I keep walking around the house thinking, 'Where the hell is Henry?' Then I remember him starting to walk down the street without his shirt or shoes and I start getting really worried. So I'm walking down the street, retracing his steps, thinking where he would go, hoping that I'll see him passed out on someone's lawn and wake him up to bring him home before anyone sees him. I call him up and once again, no response. Now I'm starting to get worried that he was arrested for being drunk in public. So then I get a call on my phone, and who is it? Henry. I pick it up and I hear Henry say, 'Hey asshole, get in the car. We're gonna get food.'" Lindsey and Molly start to tear up a little.

The entire time I'm shaking my head knowing what's to come, saying, "I don't remember this. I don't remember this."

Jimmy continues, "So I'm like, 'Henry? What the hell are you talking about? Where are you?' And then he says in this voice I can't describe but I'll try to replicate. He says-" he pauses laughing so hard at what's to come and then mimics my bizarre voice from that day, "'I *see* you.'" He raises the pitch of his voice on the word 'see' and creates this completely strange voice of mine that makes everyone laugh.

There I am, continuing to shake my head laughing, saying, "I don't remember this. I don't remember this."

Jimmy's bawling with the rest of us, and the only one who's not crying with laughter is me, limiting my laughter due to slight embarrassment and the fact that I've heard this story so many times, even if I only have fragmented memories of it.

Once the laughter fizzles down enough for him to speak, Jimmy continues, "So then I'm looking around going, 'Where the fuck is he?' And continue walking and look down and see a giant pile of vomit on the sidewalk. I look up and see Henry, without his shirt, and with horribly grass-stained socks, sitting on the passenger side of a random car. I open the door and Henry says, 'Get in we're going to get food.' So then I say, 'What makes you think you're going to get food?' He looks confused. And finally, *finally*, he looks like he's starting to realize what's going on and he says, 'Cause I'm in a car.' I ask how he got in that car. And he looks at me confused and says, 'I don't know.' I say, 'Why don't you get out of the car?' And he's like, 'That's probably a good idea.'" Everyone's laughing through the entire story, and Jimmy wraps up the adventure.

"I still don't remember that," I say laughing. "Don't believe him. It's all lies." Everyone just keeps on cracking up.

We sit at the table and continue to swap stories. It's the one positive thing about having a reckless past; you end up having a hell of a lot of entertaining stories. And when you spend a large portion of your reckless past around someone else, you have someone who actually remembers them for you. It's great at parties or any social gatherings among friends. Even some of the stories that were not great at the time are great when you're looking at them in retrospect. My reckless youth may have gotten me into trouble but at least it made way for some funny stories.

After a couple of drinks Molly asks me about my upcoming novel. I'm so fueled with anticipation to talk about it that it's hard to shut me up once I start going. Like I said, I was still the first stage of a failed author; the one where the world is ahead of you and your favorite thing to talk about is your future success. This is, in fact, the pinnacle of the first stage. The one before the world gives your ego a reality check.

"It's called <u>The Devil's Redemption</u>," I begin. "It's basically about a man who soared up the economic latter by stepping over the little people. He became a big CEO of a major banking industry, but had to fire multiple people, and do certain things that were borderline illegal, but certainly unethical. One day a man that he laid off's life goes to hell, and in a complete depression he hangs himself. The main character, Howard, then decides to give it all up and begin to find a way to give back to all the people he had wronged and make amends. Unfortunately he is met with hostility, and sees, in person, all the lives he has ruined by stepping over them in his attempt to get to the top. It is a book that mainly focuses on what people will do for their own selfish benefit, and the hypothetical situation that after all those horrible things we do, we see what it would be like if we saw the result of our sins face to face."

"Wow," Molly says, "That sounds really interesting. I'm just telling you, I would definitely buy that book."

"Thanks," I say a little bashful.

Everyone starts talking about my novel, and my vanity surges. For that one moment, I was an amazing author. Ah, my first critics. Of course these are the critics that never read my novel, and of course, those would be the only good criticisms I get. If only all the other critics only read the concept of the book and not the book itself, I might have had much better reviews. But of course, in the real world, they do, in fact, read the book.

A little later, we play some music, and we all start to dance, taking occasional breaks to sip our margaritas.

After a little bit of dancing, Jimmy says what he says every time I dance, "Wow. There really is no denying your whiteness."

I laugh. It's an old joke that is used every time, but it's very true. I am a horrendous dancer. For this reason, I always stay away from clubs. The only people I dance in front of are people that I have no problem making a fool out of myself with. I cannot stress enough how terrible I am. If you put a man having a seizure and myself in a dancing competition, the judges would have a very difficult decision to make. It wouldn't be so bad if I didn't love it so much. Despite the fact that I'd lose the respect of anyone who didn't know me that well, or who was superficial enough to judge me just based on my sorry excuse for dance moves, I still stand there, jerking around, with my body making spasms that are supposed to be to the beat of the music. But luckily, the people I'm with today are not so superficial that they would defriend me based on my horrendous moves. Still, they have no problem making fun of me.

The night continues and we all gather around to take another shot. Everyone is more than fairly well-lit, and we're all just having a blast, but I have to admit, I'm getting a little tired. However, I'm not going to go to bed if everyone else is still moving about and having a great time.

About half an hour later, Jimmy says, "Let's bring this party down to the lake. Who's coming with me?"

Molly immediately volunteers. Lindsey says that she's going too. I tell him that I'm a little tired and want to get some sleep.

Lindsey retracts her volunteering saying, "Actually, I think I'm going to stay with Henry. I'm a little tired as well."

"Alright Molly, it's just me and you," Jimmy says and turns to Lindsey and I. "But don't complain to me tomorrow at your envy of how much fun we had when you lame-o's decided to sleep."

Jimmy and Molly switch to their swimsuits and run out the door heading for the lake. I lay on the futon and Lindsey lies beside me, her head on my chest and her hand gently resting on my stomach.

There is nothing better than one of these moments. When you're in love with someone, and they lay on your chest, listening to you breathe, as you gently hold each other and talk yourselves to sleep.

"What a fun night," she says.

"Yeah, Jimmy had a great idea to come down here," I say

She laughs, "Jimmy, Jimmy, Jimmy. If I didn't know better I would think you're in love with him."

"What do you mean?" I ask.

She looks up at me, her head still resting on my chest, "Almost every conversation I have with you; it somehow gets brought back to Jimmy. You know what I think?"

"What's that?" I say.

"I think you're afraid to tell anything intimate to anybody because you're afraid that you'll somehow get hurt," she says, still stroking my stomach.

I shrug my shoulders and say, "If there's anything you want to know, just ask. I'm an open book. All you have to do is flip to a page and start reading."

I look down at her and look into the comforting hazel eyes of the most beautiful woman I have ever known–and I don't mean the skin-deep shallow beauty that is ninety percent of all relationships. Yes, she is physically gorgeous—breathtaking in the right dress even—but there is an even deeper beauty inside her.

Jimmy set me up with her. Actually, to be more accurate, Molly set me up with her. Jimmy met Molly through some bowling league, and then she met me and wondered why a guy like me doesn't have someone. After getting to know me better, she ended up introducing me to one of her best friends, which led to the relationship that I can say has been the greatest and most intimate one I've ever had.

"Forget some question that I have to ask. Tell me some genuine intimate detail of your life," she says. "Or even something inside your mind. I'm too tired to dig for your soul, just reveal a little bit of it to me. Just a piece."

"Alright," I say, "let me think." I pause for a moment running through my mind, wondering what to pull out and show. Then I decide on it. It's not a vital detail, but at least it's something. "Alright I got it. It may not be much, but at least it's beneath the surface. It's not something I tell most people. Consider this like a teaser trailer for my soul."

"Alright," she says, "I guess that's a start."

"When I was in school one time, the question was asked in a hypothetical philosophical kind of way; if I were to choose one, either living to be one hundred, or dying at the age of fifty and being remembered for a hundred years, which one would I choose?" I begin, "Now what I told them is that I wanted to live to be one hundred. To get the fullest out of life. That anyone who would trade in fifty years of their life, in order to be remembered in a world where you no longer matter, was a vainglorious scumbag. But," I pause, "in all honesty, that was a lie. If it came down to it, I would be willing to die at the age of thirty if it would guarantee me a century of respect and fame. Hell, I'll die this week if I could be remembered for eternity. But I was scared to say that, because I didn't want to admit to anyone—to myself even—that I was truly that narcissistic. But now I can be here with you, and admit one of my flaws that I try to cover up all the time. I do hope you don't judge me."

She smiles at me and says, "I don't judge you. We all have flaws, and I know that in your heart you're a good man. You're a truly good man."

She reaches up and kisses me. She then lays her head back down on my chest and I stroke her long blond hair as she closes her hazel eyes to go to sleep.

I lay back continuing to stroke her hair as she sleeps with her head softly against my chest, and her warm breath lulls my body to sleep. I wouldn't trade this moment for anything. Not even for an eternity of fame. I close my eyes and drift into the black nothingness.

The door busts open and bolts me awake. I look over to the door mumbling, "What the-"

Then I see it. Jimmy is carrying a motionless Molly, his eyes red with tears, his face looks terrified, and his pupils darting frantically.

"Call the ambulance!" he shouts.

I jump off of the futon, accidently shoving Lindsey so her head hits the corner of the table. She grabs her temple saying, "Ouch! What the fuck?" Then she sees Molly and immediately starts screaming. "What happened?!"

"I-I-I-," Jimmy says through sobs, "I don't know. I fell asleep on the beach. And then Molly, she was in the water, and she wasn't- she wasn't- Call an Ambulance!"

I run to the phone and dial 9-1-1. Jimmy's crying, pounding on her chest and breathing into her lungs in a futile attempt to revive her. In between this he's sobbing, "Jesus Christ, wake up! For fuck sake, wake up!"

I'm on the phone, "Yes, my name is Henry Riddick. There's been an accident." I'm trying to remain as calm as possible but my voice is still on the verge of hysteria. I've never witnessed someone dying right before my eyes, or for that matter, seen a dead body that wasn't in a coffin. I relay the details and give the address. They say to keep applying CPR until they get there and that they're on their way.

Jimmy fell into a drunken slumber on the beach, and Molly drowned. None of us know if she dozed off while in the water, or started screaming for help but Jimmy was too deep in sleep to hear her. None of us know.

Lindsey's in tears and praying to a god she doesn't believe in. Jimmy's shouting, "Christ help me!" as he pounds on her chest and breathes into her lungs. But I can tell that this is in vain. She must have been dead for a while. Needless to say, this will not be one of those stories of recklessness to tell at parties.

CH. 5

My body is shivering, and I'm soaked in sweat. I must have contracted a mild flu and this lack of heat takes its toll. Even though I'm in a jacket, long pants, and have a blanket engulfing me, it's not nearly enough to subside the cold. Shaking as my hand flimsily holds a lit cigarette, I sit at the computer racking my brain for some inspiration to write another chapter in the novel. The entire time I'm thinking of that night all those years so long ago, when one moment I'm drifting to sleep with the woman I love caressing me, and the next I'm being woken by a corpse entering the door. The poetic real-life story of the illusion of peaceful bliss swept away by the inevitable impending sorrow of reality. My "Mid-Autumn Night's Nightmare."

My body is weak from sickness, and my mind is loopy from the cheap knockoff brand of over the counter medicine. Despite these restrictions, I'm determined to write. If it's garbage, then I can adjust it later. But it's been way too long since I touched this story, and if I don't write soon, I'll put it off forever.

I take another drag from my cigarette, cough up a little goo, and wipe it on my pants leg. This is when it's terrible to have that addiction that only worsens your sickness. You can't smoke, but at the same time, you can't not smoke.

I think to myself a little bit, my mind bouncing between

memories of Lindsey and ideas to write in the story until finally some inspiration hits me. I set down my cigarette and lay my hands upon the keyboard to start typing.

>Todd Reynolds tosses and turns in his sleep. The ghosts of the women he didn't save in time burn his thoughts. He sees their corpses, all with the signature amputated fingers shaped in crosses upon their eyes. They cry out his name. "Why? Why couldn't you have saved me?" These visions haunt him every time he attempts to sleep. A futile attempt every time. He's been averaging about four hours a night for the past two weeks.
>
>As a detective, sworn to protect the public, and hunt down criminals like this 'cross killer,' he feels that he has completely failed his city. And he knows that he failed those victims that cry his name each night. At the station, they've been discussing different theories about the motives of this killer in an attempt to find out who they should be looking for. The most popular theory is that he's a religious extremist—this would explain the crosses—who targets attractive blond women who he feels are too full of vanity and pride. Pride being the first of the deadly sins. Another theory is that he was a high school victim of bullying and was rejected by one too many girls, and then finally he snapped. Most of the theories are based on some sort of affiliation with Christianity. But, really, he could just be doing it for shits and giggles. *That's what they never relay in all those detective shows,* Todd thinks to himself, *ninety-nine percent of the serial killer experts' work is guesswork.*
>
>He sits up, pops some nicotine gum in his mouth, and looks at his empty king-sized mattress. Another person he failed. And down the hall in another room, is yet another reminder of his failures. When the victims of

this killer aren't haunting him, these two familiar apparitions occupy his mind.

He walks down the hall and fills himself up a glass of water. Then, he pushes the Nicorette in between his cheek and his gum and drinks the water.

He stares at the empty water glass and thinks about the night he was with his wife and son. They were coming back from Disney world, driving in order to save money. His son, Robbie, was laughing his joyful, seven-year-old, innocent laugh. His wife was smiling at Robbie, playing 'I Spy' with him still giddy with the recent memories of 'the happiest place on earth.' They were all happy. The happiest they've ever been. But as time passed, that happiness led to boredom. That boredom led to sleep. And that sleep led to a tree. And that tree led to no more wife and son.

He can't let himself forget that moment, although a part of him would kill to have that memory purged. But it's a reminder to him of his largest and most important failure. He must remember that to make sure he never fails again. To reinforce that memory, he's left with a token of that nightmare. His knee was severely damaged. Although it isn't bad enough to remove him from the force on disability, after a while of walking on it, it starts to hurt. It hurts, not enough to impede him, but just enough to remind him to never *ever* fail anyone like that again.

Despite a lot of resistance brought upon by the male ego, he started seeing a shrink about three years ago. Last week he talked to her about his inability to catch this killer and what that's doing to him emotionally. She tried to relate it back to his accident all those years ago, but he avoided it with great restraint. He's tried to delve into that subject before. He figured that if he just said everything about that day again, it would go away.

But this did not alleviate any of his depression. A band aid does nothing for a fatal wound.

He spits out his nicotine gum and reaches for the Nyquil. He's not sick in the slightest, but he needs sleep. He *needs* sleep. On the rare occasions that his failures don't haunt him in his dreams and he can finally taste the sweet darkness, he can feel some relief from this cruel world of constant reminders.

He pours himself thirty milligrams and downs the horrid flavor. He walks back upstairs and lies down on the bed in that vain attempt to sleep.

I gaze at my computer, rereading my work, and light another cigarette, still sweating through my sickness. I notice a little recurrent word through what I've written. In this measly eight paragraph beginning to a chapter, the variation of the word 'failure' is written eight times. And then the line catches my eye, 'he can finally feel some relief from this cruel world of constant reminders.' I chuckle to myself.

How true it is that what the author really thinks and knows is translated through his stories. 'Failure,' of course! 'Constant reminders,' how true. The omnipresent truth. The ubiquitous knowledge. I can't help but laugh.

Of course the entire time I'm writing this I know those 'constant reminders.' I know those 'failures.' It's like a gremlin inside my skull hacking away. The mind reveals itself through my words.

This book is going to be a failure. No question about it. That's what I am: a professional failure. That's what this constant reminder is. This is why I avoided writing anything for so long. I haven't been passionate about anything in half a decade, except for avoiding to write this book. That I've been completely passionate about.

I look to my bookshelf for guidance. The wooden

monument filled with my gods. My bookshelf is the cross that I worship. I have a wide range of authors that I love; tons of novels, novellas, collections, and anthologies. My taste in books ranges from the classics, to science fiction, to contemporary, to horror, to thriller, to humor, to fantasy, to collections of short stories and poems. All of these I worship. And my deities decorate the shelf: Twain, Vonnegut, King, Dickenson, Irving, Poe, Dickens, Crichton, Woolf, Huxley, Palahniuk, DeLillo, Ovid, Shakespeare, Tolkien, Orwell. And then at the top of the first shelf, spanning through three of the shelves; all forty-two works by my all-powerful god, Coralline Thomson.

"How do you do it?" I ask her out loud.

Through the silence of her response, I can hear her say through the wind, "By not being you."

I laugh. How true this is. You see, I am of the severe disadvantage of most potential authors by not having that certain je ne sais quoi, or whatever the French word is for 'talent.'

I gaze up at my almighty deity's large body of scriptures and say, "Please tell me. What do I have to do to become a success? Do I have to give up all of my social skills like you? Say goodbye to all of my friends? Give up everything and make people believe that I have a serious mental disability if it weren't for the fact that my writing is a success? Cause I'll do it. I swear I'll do it. I'd give up half of my life for the talent you possess. Anything at all. All you have to do is say what you want of me."

Once again, no response. I puff again on my cigarette and cough up some more goo. My place is not among my gods, not among even the least literary inclined man's gods. My place is here in the pit of my hell. Here in my cesspool of failure.

Oh the omnipresent truth. Oh the ubiquitous knowledge. How it haunts me.

CH. 6

Lindsey and I are sitting in my shabby apartment not speaking. A frown takes command of my face as I reread the reviews of my novel, hoping that maybe this time, when I read it, they'll give me the praise that I anticipated. That I felt I deserved. That, above all, I *needed*. But as any man knows, rereading the same material a second, third, or even fourth time, will not provide a different outcome. They say repeating the same actions over and over again and expecting different results is one of the definitions of insanity.

Lindsey, she's looking at the newspaper while her eyes are darting around the apartment and, every once in a while, when she thinks I won't notice, she glances at me. She's not actually *reading* the newspaper. Why would she? Two hours ago when we started this silence, she was already finished with the entire paper. She just needs to pretend to be occupied in order to feel more comfortable in this unbearably long awkward silence. I'm too grim to say a single word. I'm just fixating on these brutal reviews in order to solidify my self-pity.

I let out a few sighs occasionally in an attempt to appeal to her sympathetic side. But in all reality, there's only so much pity a woman can give. Only so much she can rock you to sleep and say, "It's okay. Everything's going to be okay. Hush baby. Don't cry."

Especially when all you give her is this macho-man resistance in order to say that you're too masculine to need somebody to comfort you. At one side I'm inviting her help. On the other side I'm shoving her help back in her face.

"I'm sorry," she says. "I can't do this anymore."

"Hmm?" I mutter.

"I said I can't do this anymore," she says. "I can't be in this relationship. I can't see you like this. I can't see Jimmy without remembering that horrible night. I just- I just can't take any of it anymore."

"Figures," I say still wrapped up entirely in myself. "The critics insult me, my readers ignore me, God forgets me, and just when I think life can't shit on me anymore, my girlfriend leaves me. The way I see it, it just seems like a perfect ending to the tragedy that is my great fucking life."

"I've got to go," she says. "Understand that I truly *do* love you. But I can't see you like this. I can't see you spiral down into nothing."

And then I make the biggest mistake of my life. I have many regrets in life, but what I say right here tops them all. I should have begged her to give me another chance, told her that I'll do anything if she'll just give me one more opportunity. Told her that I'll change. I'll find a new job. I'll do anything. This is just a passing phase. I'll be a new man tomorrow. I swear it. I should have said that I'll stop moping around and actually make a change in my life. But I didn't say that. No I say, "Shouldn't you be packing then?"

She frowns at me as her eyes water a little bit, and walks to our bedroom. I hear her shuffling through the room and packing her bags, as I look back at the reviews. I hear her leaving. I hear my life ending. I hear my heart being torn to shreds, never to beat again. I hear my smile fading, never to return. I hear my soul being gouged from my body. I hear my emotions saying goodbye, and hightailing it as far from me as possible.

She walks to the door, a suitcase in hand, as she's holding back tears. She looks one last time at me, her lips trembling with sadness, and mouths the words 'goodbye' as she opens the door.

"Don't let the door hit your ass on the way out," I say. And she closes the door, never to return. And I close the door, never to return.

A knock on the door wakes me up from that dream, maybe 'nightmare' is a more appropriate word. If the night that Molly's motionless body entered the cabin was my worst memory, this was an easy second. Some people say they 'live a life free of regrets.' Some people lie. We all have regrets–every one of us—regardless of what we tell others, or even ourselves. And that remorse slowly removes pieces of our soul with each passing day. Some of us are just lucky enough to have fewer than most. And others of us, we're just a little less lucky I guess.

I'm sitting on the couch, with my cigarette in one of the slots on the ashtray creating a long line of unbroken ash—a reminder of an ember that burned out so long ago. An empty glass lies on its side facing downward; the remaining scotch and melted ice is spilled on my stomach. My shirt has a large stain and reeks of alcohol.

I put the glass on the table, rub my eyes, and shout, "One moment." I walk to the door and halfway there I say, "Who is it?"

"Come on," Jimmy says, "we both know you don't have *that* many visitors."

I laugh and open the door, "Come on in. Don't mind my appearance, I just woke up."

He gives me a questioning look, "It's 6:00 PM."

"Yeah, I know," I say with a chuckle. "I just got over the flu, and I'm still pretty wiped out and took a nap on the couch."

"Oh," he says walking in. Looking around, he makes his way over to the couch, and sits down putting his feet up.

"Scotch?" I say, and he grunts in approval.

I walk into the kitchen with my spilled glass only holding the remaining pieces of ice in it, and pull out a second glass for him. I grab some ice, throw it in the glasses, grab the scotch, pour that in the glasses, and make my way over to Jimmy. I set one down on the coffee table closest to Jimmy and then one next to where I'm going to sit and lower myself onto the chair.

"So how's the novel going?" Jimmy asks. "Make any progress since the last time I saw you?"

"Yeah, a little," I say, "Just a couple of chapters. I've been sick for a while but I decided that if I put it off for too long, I'll never give the world the gift of my newest atrocity. Just think of all the fun I'd be depriving the critics of their perfect opportunity to completely eviscerate another of my novels. I'm not *that* selfish."

Jimmy smiles and changes the subject after glancing at my bookshelf. "You see the most recent interview of Thomson?"

"No," I say. "I must have missed it."

"Well, let me fill you in on what you missed." Then he makes his face seem completely emotionless, moving even less than those women who shoot their face up with way too much Botox. His lips hardly moving and his eyes void of any emotion, he says in a completely monotone voice, "'Yes…No…Yes…No…No…Yes…Yes…Okay.'" He laughs. "If she didn't have the talent to be the best author of our time, no one would ever talk to her. She's simply not likeable. It's even hard to tell sometimes if she's actually human and not some android put on this earth in order to pump out ridiculously great stories and nothing else. Why can't she create these stories and still retain some trace of humanity? Hell, Mark Twain is one of the greatest authors of all time, and when he would speak, he would be incredibly entertaining."

"She's better than Twain," I say as I pull out a cigarette and point at him interjecting in my own sentence, "Don't start." Then I continue with what I was saying, "She's better than all of them put together. She's not just the greatest author of our time; she's the greatest author *ever*. I would trade anything for her kind of talent."

"Come on, you're not *that* terrible at what you do," he says.

I roll my eyes, "Give me a break."

"Listen," he says leaning close to me, "listen. Separate, we're nothing. I'm an overlooked artist. You're a scorned author. But if we put our talents together," he pauses looking at me intently, pulling me in close to listen to his big idea, "we could make at least twenty bucks selling a children's book on the street to an idiot."

I tilt my head back and roar out laughter. Jimmy's great at that. Lulling you in so you're hanging on to each subsequent word in anticipation of some deeply profound philosophy or idea, and then once you're hooked, he throws you that curve ball of the absurdity that not in a million years you would have ever guessed. I'm sure that if he actually put his mind to it, he could be a decent author with that unexpected humor. Well, at least better than me.

Here we sit once again. I'm writing a book once again. I'm with Jimmy once again. We drink and smoke and bitch and gripe and talk about nothing but our idols and how much wastes of oxygen we are in our desired fields once again. What was that saying? Oh yeah. They say repeating the same actions over and over again and expecting different results is one of the definitions of insanity.

CH. 7

I hold out this morning's paper, jumping from headline to headline looking for something interesting. "Local Boy Scout Christmas Tree Sale Draws Unexpected Clientele." Too monotonous. "Researchers Find New Possible Damage Caused By Marijuana." Too much propaganda. "Obesity Epidemic Reaches Concern of High Officials." Too meaningless. "Drunk Driver Kills Three in Car Accident." Too common. The only things interesting in the papers anymore are sports and obituaries.

I'm outside the coffee shop holding a medium blend with cream and two sugars and a cigarette to start the day. Jimmy comes out of the shop with the same and sits across from me.

He looks at me briefly, "I only got a couple minutes 'till I have to head to the art studio."

"How's Frank doing?" I ask.

"Alright. He's just getting over the flu," he says. "Maybe he caught the same thing you had."

"Maybe," I say. "There's some kind of bug going around. It seems like everyone's coming down with something."

"Yeah," he says. "You wanna hit the pool halls after I'm done with the studio?"

I think for a moment, "No I'm fine. I feel like I'm liking pool less and less each day."

"First it was bowling," he says, "then it was movies, then it was television, now it's pool. You know losing interest in things you used to like is a sign of depression."

"I haven't lost interest in everything. I still like writing, drinking, and masturbating," I say.

"Yeah," he says, "because I've never heard of a depressed writer that drinks and masturbates."

I shrug my shoulders. He pulls out his phone and checks it, "I should probably start heading out. Maybe we can get together to drink and write." Then he adds, "I'm not sure if I'm ready to masturbate with you."

I say goodbye and go back to browsing the paper. "Local Undertaker Finds Vandalized Jewish Grave." Too uninteresting. "Man Found Drowned to Death in Lake." Too mundane. "Man Murders Wife and Children." Too common.

I go to the obituaries and scan the names for any people I once knew. One hits me, 'Samuel Tracker.' He was an old buddy I met in high school. I only fraternized with him outside of school a few times. One time, I remember, we're sitting on the swings of some elementary school at night and he starts diving into some secret that he never told anyone, "I never really like to talk about this; In fact I never really revealed this to anyone in my entire life," he says, "But I'm different—you know—different than most people." I tell him that we're all different, every single one of us, in our own way. And he says, "No I don't mean that 'I'm some special unique snowflake' bullshit. I mean- can you promise to keep it just between you and me?" I tell him sure. I tell him that my lips are sealed. He looks back at me and says, "I don't know why I'm telling you this, but you just seem reliable." He says, "I think I'm gay." I shift a little uncomfortably in my swing. I know that back in that day I think I'm tolerance personified. I think I'm above the mainstream bigotry. But I'm still suffering from that high school homophobia, and my mind's wondering 'Why is he telling *me* this? Does he think that *I'm* gay too?' But I try to remain calm and say that all of us question our sexuality at some point. I tell him he shouldn't worry too much about it. "No," he says, "it's not like that. I didn't say it right. I don't *think* I'm gay. I *know* I'm gay. I'm passed that phase." I shift a little more uncomfortably in my swing and straighten out my shirt. I tell him in that case he should embrace it. Maybe he shouldn't say anything to his fellow students currently, for fear of bullying, but he should tell his parents. He says he will and we each walk to our separate houses. The next day I see him enter school. He's got a fat lip, a black eye, and a broken nose. The kids are walking up to him and asking what happened to him. He shrugs it off in a tough way—he's got to be tough, he's on the football and rugby team—and he says he got into a fight with his brother. "He got me pretty good," he says. "But you wouldn't believe what I did to him," he lies. Then he walks up to me close enough for only the two of us to hear it and he whispers, "Thanks." Then he walks away and the only other time he said more than a greeting or farewell to me is the next day when he told me what happened. You see, his parents were old school Catholics. Not the kind of Catholics that are accepting and live up to the actual meaning of the word 'Catholic,' which by definition means 'universal.' No these are the conservative Catholics who think that all forms of sexuality not under the legal binding of marriage between a man and woman are perverse and sinful. Homosexuality, premarital sex, and even masturbation are affronts to God. And once he came out to them his mom started crying saying, "Why? Oh Jesus! Why?" But his dad didn't start crying. Oh no, he didn't start crying at all. He started hitting. And he hit hard. Once Samuel was curled up on the floor in the fetal position, screaming and bawling from the pain, his dad said, "I don't give a fuck what you think about, but you're going to marry a *woman*. And I don't give a rat's ass what you think about at all, but you're going to have children. And you'll never mention this to anyone again. You understand?" Samuel's on the floor weeping as his dad kicks him again and says, "You understand me?" And

Sam, he nods and says yes.

Now I can't say for sure if he ever told another person about his secret, but if I had a million dollars, I'd put it on he didn't.

I read the obituary and see that he was in a 'loving' marriage with his wife Susan and had three daughters and two sons. He was a godfather to another two people and went to church every day. I also see that the cause of death was a suicide. He started his car in the garage and let himself suffocate on the exhaust. He didn't leave a note and no one could understand why this churchgoing happy father ended his life so suddenly. No one had a clue. Except me. I had a clue. I knew why. That secret. That lie he led for too long. Truly depressing, but truly predictable.

I go back to scanning the rest of the paper, name to name, headline to headline, taking occasional drags of my cigarette and sips of my coffee. My eyes drift, looking up at the clouds floating in the sky, the streetcars driving by, the grass growing in between the cracks of the sidewalk, the pedestrians crossing the street, and the customers drinking their coffee. All the time, I'm thinking about Sammy and his mashed up face that school morning.

Then my eyes fixate on a woman walking down the sidewalk in the distance, heading in my direction. She looks somewhat familiar. She's walking slowly with minimal movement of her arms. Her eyes stare blankly at nothing. Her face doesn't display any emotional expression. She's got black hair with streaks of grey and a plain white shirt with dark blue genes. *Where have I seen her before?* I think to myself. She looks so familiar. Hold on. Is it-? No it can't be. Oh my god, it is!

Less than thirty feet in front of me walks my deity in human form. My all-powerful god. My omnipotent idol. My supreme being. Coralline Thomson. *Can I withstand seeing her face?* I think. *Is my hair turning white?*

The Jehovah of the pen. The Yahweh of character development. The Allah of plot twists. The Shiva of storytelling.

She's standing less than twenty-five feet away from me and moving closer. *Is she coming to save me?* I think. *Am I worthy?*

My heart's beating in my chest. I'm stuck frozen still. This isn't just a celebrity coming your way. This is Jesus himself heading toward you. What do you say? Do you confess your sins? Do you beg for forgiveness of your first novel? Do you ask for her to baptize you in literature?

I'm sweating. *What do I do?*

I rub my eyes again to make sure that they aren't playing tricks on my. That this isn't a mirage. That this isn't a hallucination. That this is, in fact, real.

I decide that I have to say something. At least express my reverence for her work. Explain to her how much she influences me. Explain to her that anticipation for her next perfection of literature gives me the motivation to continue the inane task of breathing.

First I drop my cigarette and stamp it out; then I stand up and begin to walk in her direction, leaving the coffee and paper on the table, shaking in an overpowering mixture of fear and excitement.

I walk step by step wondering, *what do I say?* Each step bringing me closer and closer to her. Each couple of feet solidifying more and more in assurance that this is, in fact, her.

I'm standing right in front of her, blocking her path to continue where she's headed. I open my mouth but nothing comes out. Only a whimper of air escaping my lungs. I'm star struck. I'm mesmerized in her divine presence. I don't know what to say. Above all, I don't know *how* to say. Making a fool out of myself, I simply stare at her in awe and wonder. My jaw dropped, and I don't know if drool is coming out. Like when you were in middle school. Just recently you hit puberty. Just recently your armpits started getting hairy. Just recently your voice started to crack. Just recently your balls dropped. And you come up to the 'hot girl' in class in an attempt to speak, but you can't say anything. You simply ogle. That's what I am right now. That ogling middle school boy who just hit puberty. That's me.

"Hi," is all I'm capable of saying. I stick out my hand to shake.

Her eyes meet mine—only they don't. They're not looking *in* my eyes; they're looking *through* them. I see her pupils. They're well past normal expansion, even when it's dark out. The bags around her eyes are so vast; they seem to go on for eternity. Her face is absent of color as if she's sick, or, if I compare this with the rest of her facial oddities, she's stoned. More stoned than any drug-induced person I've ever met. And as someone who studied in the arts, I've seen a lot of people under the influence. She looks like she's on something more potent than the most potent poppy seed based drug. More potent than any psychedelic or narcotic or opiate I've ever seen.

She moves her lips less than I thought was possible to formulate a word and says, "Hello." She ignores my extended hand.

"I'm sure you get this all the time," I say with my body still shaking like mad, "but I just wanted to say how much of a fan I am of your work." I wipe some sweat off of my forehead right in front of her.

"Oh," she says. Her face still lacking any physical evidence that she has a working brain.

I'm thinking to myself, *what do I say? What do I say?* Then something passes through my head. I can't say that. But I have to. My superego, filled with all the societal restraints, is shouting, "Don't ask it. She's a giant among the literary community. She won't want to. You'll just make a fool of yourself." My id, free of these social chains, is saying, "Ask it. When will you have an opportunity like this again? When in a million years? When?"

Postponing this mental dilemma, I say, "I'm an author actually. Not like you of course. But I just wanted to say how much you influence my work. I found that <u>The Night of the</u>

<u>Wolves</u> was one of the greatest novels of our time, if not the greatest. The way you combined our society's paranoia and lust for war, and transcribed it in that brilliant wordplay and sentence flow was uncanny." Some sweat drips into my eyes and I wipe it away with my right hand.

"Oh," she says. Her eyes still fixed on the nothingness past me.

My id is bellowing, "Ask It! Ask it! When will you ever have this chance? Don't you see that you'll never have this opportunity again?" My superego warns me in reply, "Don't do it. You'll make a fool out of yourself. You'll embarrass yourself in front of your idol. She's a bestselling Pulitzer Prize winning author. You're a failed kid scribbling random words on a piece of paper and calling it art."

"And the twist in <u>Dreams of the Donkey and the Elephant</u> completely demonstrated the potential horror of our two-party system, and how it could all come crashing down in ruins," I say, still avoiding the question dancing through my head.

"Oh," she says again, still barely moving her lips and emotionless.

Inside my brain, the argument between my id and superego has turned into an all-out war. Neurons are piling up as causalities to this battle. Each one dead makes me less and less able to focus on anything but the question I have to say but can't say. My id shouts, "Ask it! Ask it!" My superego responds, "Don't! Don't!"

Finally the war is over. My superego is defeated, and my id reigns victorious. I say, "I hate to ask this, but understand that I feel that I have to take a shot. You can say no if you want to. But I just need to ask." I'm perspiring even more than before. I'm talking to the greatest author of all time, and I look like I just took a shower with my clothes still on. "Is there any way at all—and remember you can always say no—but is there any way whatsoever that you might be willing to read my story and give me tips?"

I can't believe I just asked that. As soon as the words left my mouth, I was wishing I took them back. Why would I say that? What on earth would possess me to say *anything* like that? Who do I think I am? I'm a nobody. She's a god. Where do I get the gall?

And then to my incredible surprise, I hear her say, "Sure."

I pause for a moment not able at first to comprehend that one syllable response, not able to fathom the fact that she, Coralline Thomson, just agreed to help me, Henry Riddick, with my book. I can't help but smile and move quickly, looking like a fool in love. You know that boy in middle school who just hit puberty and asks that 'hot girl' out on a date who's way out of his league? He's stumbling over his words, barely able to speak. Then finally, after he feels that he just completely set himself up for rejection, that 'hot girl' says yes. And he's overjoyed and can't hide his excitement. That's what I am right now. That middle school boy who just got accepted by the 'hot girl' and can't restrain his excitement. That's me.

I look around not sure what to do. I say, "Thank you. Thank you so much. Here let me give you my number. Thank you for this. Thank you."

I pull out the pen in my pocket and stand there looking at the pen, intently thinking, *what do I do now?* I'm not able to process what's happening. It seems like a dream. Everything is unreal. Coralline Thomson just agreed to read *my* story and give me input. Mine. Me. Henry Riddick.

Once my thoughts become lucid enough to think like a semi-normal human being, I realize that I need some paper. *Paper?* I think. *Oh yes, I need paper. Where do I get paper?* Then I tell her to hold on one second as I run to the table I was sitting at, tear off a corner piece of the newspaper that doesn't have any words on it, and write down my name and number. I run back to her as though if I didn't come back soon enough, she would disappear.

"Thank you so much again for doing this," I say a little too loud from excitement, "Feel free to call me up anytime. Day, night;

whatever works best for you. Tomorrow, a month, a year; I'm at your disposal."

"Okay," she says, and walks away.

Is this real? Will she really call me back? Will I really be taking on Coralline Thomson as my mentor? It's all too good to be true.

I watch the back of her head fade away into the distance. Her hair, black with streaks of grey. Her white shirt blowing in the wind. Her legs taking excruciatingly slow steps. Her arms barely moving.

I start to think of what I would do if this didn't happen to me. I wonder where I would be if I just continued to produce failure after failure. And then I remember Samuel Tracker. And the car. And the exhaust-filled garage.

CH. 8

Sitting on my couch, puffing a cigarette, and drinking warm orange juice, I'm stuck on the meeting I had with Rick Ellsworth two days before. He called me up a week and a half ago and said that we needed to talk. I asked him what this was about, and he just told me to come to his office next Wednesday.

That day I open the door to his office and he tells me to have a seat. He asks me how things are going and I tell him some minor details. He's an old friend of mine. We met in high school and we both had our dreams when we went to college. I wanted to be an author expressing my passion through the written word, and he wanted to be a big-time publisher. Unlike me, he succeeded. Well pretty much. He's publishing some people that got big, none of the names that the majority of the public would know, but still he's one of the people in charge of this fairly well-known publishing company where he met his wife Samantha. Samantha and I, we had a little fling many years back after Lindsey broke up with me and before Rick told me that he fancied her. When we split up, it wasn't a harsh breakup. No shouting, no saying things we wished we could take back, no crying; none of that. One day she simply said, "I like you and all—you're a nice guy—but I just don't think this is working." I agreed with her, and we had one of those rare occasions where we remained friends—good friends in fact. And when Rick started dating her, there was no animosity between us. "Go for it," I said. And he did. And now he's happily married. And I'm not.

"Look Henry," he says, "I need to know how much progress you're making on your story."

I tell him I'm making progress but I still have a lot to go. Just give me a little more time and I'll have the story to him soon.

"Christ," he says. "That's what you said for the past four years. I need to see some substance."

"Look," I say, "I've just turned a new leaf. Something happened that I never thought would happen. Just give me a little more time. You won't believe what happened to me."

"I don't care what happened to you," he starts.

"No. Just listen. This is big. This is going to change the game," I tell him. "Just listen."

"No, you listen," he interrupts me—his face red with anger. "I've been helping you out for years. I can't keep forking up money for you to write a story that draws back a minor percentage of that loan. I already suffered from your last book. You're my friend. We've known each other since childhood. You and Samantha are on good terms too. That's why I'm still financing your ass even though I know the payback is shit. I know it'll be a loss, but if it's going to be a loss, I'd rather it not suck my wallet dry."

As he says those words, he feels slight remorse. But remorse or no, what he said is true. The only reason why he's helping me is because of our friendship. If it weren't for him, no one would ever publish any body of work that had my name on it. Even if it were a masterpiece, the greatest story ever told, something that will draw a bigger crowd than Gideon's Bible, they would see my name and throw it away. He's barely giving me enough money to survive, but it's still thousands times more than I deserve. If it weren't for our history, and the relationship I have with his wife—another head-honcho in the publishing firm—I wouldn't have any money whatsoever. None at all.

"Sorry," he says, running his hands through his hair and shaking his head, looking stressed out. "I didn't mean that. I just have some other things going on with my wife and the rest of my family. Don't take that to heart."

I'm completely understanding, "No need to apologize. What you've done for me is much more than I deserved. You've been more than generous. But you're not going to believe what happened to me just a few weeks ago." I then relay to him the story of how I ran into Coralline Thomson and she agreed to read over my work. "She said she would do it. I'm not kidding. She'll be calling me anytime. You understand what that means? She'll be my new mentor. She'll give me tips. For the first time in five years, I have hope for my career."

"You actually met her?" he asks.

"Yeah," I say. "Hand to God."

Not seeming that interested, he thinks to himself as if contemplating whether or not he should say what's really on his mind. Then he says, "You think, maybe, she was just being polite?"

I never thought of that, but it's been four weeks. And with those words my hope for my career is vanquished.

I lean back in my chair, still puffing my cigarette, still drinking my orange juice just remembering my conversation with Rick. One second I was filled with the hope I haven't felt since before The Devil's Redemption was published, and the next, all that hope gets tossed under the bus. Funny how things go from great to terrible.

I was burning with excitement talking to Jimmy about this. He couldn't believe it. There we were gossiping with unbridled delight, like schoolgirls about the hot football star they just got a date with. After that I planned on telling Frank and Mark and Carl and Hank.

Then I smile. Jimmy, Frank, Rick, Mark, Carl, Hank. I laugh to myself. No wonder the killer I created only attacks women. Everyone I socialize with is a man. Sure, I meet with Samantha every once in a while, but the only time it's not a business related visit is once in a blue moon. On top of that Rick is always with her. I haven't been with a woman in nine months, and I haven't had anything close to a relationship in over a year. Women must seem like fantasies to me—a myth that I'm pretty sure is real, but I don't have any evidence to prove it.

For these past couple of days, I'm in the process of realizing that sliver of hope I received from my brief encounter with Coralline Thomson was nothing. You know when you're crawling through the desert? You have no clue where the nearest trace of civilization is. You're so dehydrated that you're on your hands and knees because you don't have enough strength to stand. Sand flies in your eyes and dry panting mouth. Then when you think all hope is lost you see that water in the distance. You think to yourself, *I know I can survive if I just reach that water*. You start crawling faster and faster with that newfound hope. You find yourself edging closer and closer. And then, you know that moment just when you're about to reach it, it disappears. You realize that the water was just a mirage. A trick of the eyes. An illusion. That's what I've been going through. That illusion. That trick of the eyes.

I'm rubbing my head, still pounding from the damage it took these past two days, when I drank all that cope to wash down my ever-present self-pity.

Who was I kidding? Coralline Thomson giving *me* advice? I must have looked like a madman that day—all sweaty and shaking with my eyes bulging out of their sockets and my body trying to recover from seeing her in person. What a joke.

Well I guess it's back to writing failures. Where will I be in a few years? In a car in my garage like Samuel? Spending all my money on liquor getting drunk to nullify my self-loathing like Hank? Who knows? All that I can be sure of is that it won't be any place good.

My phone rings. I'm thinking of whether I want to pick it up or just sit back in this chair and ignore it. I really don't want to talk to anyone, not even Jimmy, my best friend. I just want to remain here on this couch, sipping on warm orange juice, puffing a cigarette, and wallowing in depression.

The phone rings again, and I decide to walk over to the table and pick it up. It's an unknown number. If it's a telemarketer I'm ready to tell them to fuck off.

"Hello," I say into the phone.

"Hi," a female voice says into my ear, "Is this Henry Riddick?"

God damn it, it's probably a telemarketer. "This is he."

"Hi. We met a couple of weeks ago. I'm Coralline Thomson," she says.

I stop. It can't be. I just found out she was a mirage. Plus the voice is so full of life, and she's saying more than one word a sentence. It can't be. But the only people I told were Rick and Jimmy, and neither of them would pull some kind of trick like this. It must be her. It must be. "Oh, yes. I didn't think you'd actually call."

"Well you gave me your number didn't you? And I did say I would call, didn't I?" she says.

I'm back in shock. "Well, yes. But-"

"And I'm a man of my word," she says, her voice so full of life and having regular social cues that I can't fully believe it's her. But I know it has to be. "Or rather a *woman* of my word, to be more accurate."

"I greatly appreciate this. Thank you so much for calling me back." I'm as full of excitement and fear and awe as the time I saw her outside the coffee shop. "So does this mean you'll read through my story and give me tips?" I'm once again sweating and shaking even though only her voice is present.

"Well that is what I said," she says.

She tells me to meet her next Saturday at noon and gives me directions to her house. You know that hope that just left me? It's back. You know that depression and utter despair? It's gone.

She really is going to help me out. She really is going to give me tips. Funny how things go from terrible to great.

CH. 9

At the bus stop, sitting uncomfortably on the bench, my nerves have already caused me to perspire. As much as I am excited about my soon-to-be encounter with Coralline Thomson, I also dread it with all my heart. I'm a nobody. She probably has never heard of me. Or worse, what if she *has* heard of me? What if she actually read my first book? That perversion of the English language. That excrement of the literature. What if she has? What would I say? How can I possibly expect her to help me? Oh God!

Well I guess I'll find out within the hour. This only petrifies me more, but I guess there is nothing I can do but wait.

The bus arrives and I find an open seat next to an old, tall, lanky man in raggedy clothing emitting a foul odor. Then again who am I to talk? My sweat-soaked body probably reeks worse than a man who just ran a marathon.

The man looks at me through his unfocussed eyes and says through clenched teeth, "Whatchu sweating so much for? No need to be nervous. I ain't gonna bite."

I feign laughter, "No. No. It's not you. I'm just a little nervous about something."

"Oh," he says, "What for?"

"Nothing much," I say, "just job related things."

He smiles and nods his head, "Nervousness for a job. I see. I remember many times sweatin' bullets 'fore an interview. You know what I do?" I shake my head He reaches in a bag he has to his right and pulls out a flask. "I find everything's better with good old nature's medicine. I tell you this works better than any pill them shrinks are shovin' down everyone's throats. Here," he brings the flask to me, "take a swig of good ol' Carl's medicine."

I shake my head, "No. But thanks for the offer."

"Suit yourself," he says, then takes a swig and puts it back in his bag. "So anyway, what's this job you're interviewing for?"

"It's not exactly an interview," I say. "It's more of a meeting I guess. An important meeting."

"Well you have fun with that I guess," he says and he gets up. "Anyway this is my stop. Nice meeting you. Just remember to not take this *too* seriously. I mean don't treat it like it's nothin' but just don't worry so much you end up creatin' an ocean of sweat."

I get up and let him pass, and he leaves the bus. Great. Now I can stay focused on my neurosis without interruption.

After a few more stops, I exit the bus. It seems that with each step closer to the house, my heart beats a few milliseconds faster. I know what will come. I know I will meet *her*. I know I will make a fool out of myself. I'll be the village idiot trying to impress a god. I'll be more out of place in her presence than a Mormon at a strip club.

I also can't help but wonder which Coralline Thomson will show up today, the life-filled person that spoke to me on the phone and was present during certain interviews, or the disengaged zombie that greeted me on our first encounter and was also present in the majority of her interviews. Who knows?

I realize that I passed the street I was supposed to turn left on because I was so flustered with fright and unworthiness. I turn around and start walking back.

After I turn right, I know that there's only one more street until I get to her house. My heart's beating faster. My arms are shaking like a diabetic with low blood sugar. My head is thumping hard. My insecurities and doubt are racing through my head. My worries are transmitted through my entire body. I'm having shortness of breath even though I've only walked a short distance on this cool breezy day.

I turn right. My mind races with warnings saying, "Don't do this to yourself. Turn back now. Turn Back!"

I find myself standing in front of her door, my finger hovering over the doorbell. The house is smaller than I expected, but it is her address. My mind screams, "Turn back! This is your last chance! Turn tail and run!" Finally I ring the doorbell almost praying that she's not there, or that this is the wrong house.

I hear shuffling in the house, someone walking down the stairs, and I'm praying, "Please don't be her. Please no. I'm not ready. I'm not worthy."

The door opens and sure enough it's her. Only she's not the same as when I met her the first time. Those endless bags under her eyes: they're vanished. That color in her face: it's back. Her pupil dilation: normal. But it *is* her. She looks at me a little puzzled and says, "Hello?"

I pause for a moment, taking everything in, and I say, "Oh hi, I'm Henry Riddick. You said a couple of days ago that I should come by and-"

"Oh yes. Of course, of course. Come in," she steps aside to let me in. "I was about to eat lunch. I have leftover pasta salad. Would you like some?"

"No, it's fine," I say walking inside.

"No please, I insist. We can talk about your story over lunch. Would you like something to drink?" she asks. "I have iced tea and lemonade."

"You're more than kind," I say. "Iced tea is fine."

She shows me the way to the family room and I sit down on a couch that is much more comfortable than anything that I own. I'm slightly more at ease by her calm temperament and the fact that she comes off as a regular person. The house is also comforting. In most houses of people that are wealthy, you see obscure paintings and random decorations strung through the house that only a lot of money can afford.

I'm fascinated by the blank walls and the lack of items to establish a person's wealth and clout. *How could someone this magnificent have such a plain house?* I wonder. *Why would someone so extraordinary own only things that are simply ordinary?*

Suddenly I hear a laugh to my right as Coralline brings in two iced teas. "I'm sorry but you have the same reaction that everyone who comes into my house has," she says. "You're looking not at what I have in my house, but rather what I *don't* have."

"I think the place is lovely," I say to save face.

"No it's fine," she says. "Many people say I should buy this vase or that rare sculpture. I personally don't care about having these worthless trinkets cluttering my living space just to prove to people that I am, in fact, rich. And don't even get me started on diamonds." She sets the two iced teas on the table and says she's going to get the pasta salad.

I'm sipping on my tea just running over in my head what I should say to her. My thoughts are racing too fast for me to isolate a single one. They're like bullets holding messages just whizzing through my brain.

She returns with the grub, and sets one plate down in front of me and one in front of her.

I take a bite, "This is very good. It's delicious."

She smiles, "No need to waste your compliments on me, I didn't make this." She now looks at me and wipes her lip with a napkin. "Now I had a chance to read your first story, The Devil's Redemption."

Oh god, she read it. This could mean that she won't even look over my new script. I laugh, "How unfortunate," I say.

"No need to be so down on yourself," she says, "Perhaps the critics were not fond of it, but it was written well. I do have some critiques about it, but the main problem was that you didn't focus that much on the characters. They were too one-dimensional. If it weren't for that, I believe that it would have been a much better book, and it would have done incredibly well commercially. And I can help you with that. So don't beat yourself up. There's no reason for self-deprecation."

She looked past that horrid failure. She still wants to help me out. Thank God. "Understand that I am more than grateful for your help. This means a lot to me. And to receive advice from you above all people. It means the world to me."

"Calm down on your flattery," she says. "I'm not as great as you think and I sure am tired of this bombardment of compliments."

"I'm so sorry," I say.

She laughs, "You realize that you just apologized for complimenting me? If there's one thing I hate more than being over complimented, it's unnecessary apologies."

"I'm sorry," I say out of impulse.

She laughs again, "You really are getting off to a bad start. Just calm down and think of me as an average person. Just your ordinary woman who happens to write. By the way, did you bring over the plot outline, summary, and what you have so far of the story?"

"Yes," I say a little nervously. "Yes, I did." And I pull it out and hand it to her.

She looks at it and reads the title, "<u>The Mind of a Madman</u>."

"It's just a working title," I say a little embarrassed.

"It's a good title. So do you want to give me the lowdown on what it's about?" she asks.

I try to make it as brief as possible because of my intimidation, "It's basically trying to capture the mind of an insane person. The two main characters that it jumps between are a psychotic serial killer who only attacks attractive blond haired women, and the investigator who's trying to catch him. The serial killer's mind gets more and more warped throughout the story as he picks off victim after victim, and the investigator tries to find out what's motivating the killer and the stress of his not solving the murders takes more and more of an emotional toll with every new victim."

She pauses and sits back, thinking to herself with her fingers strumming through her hair. "Interesting," she says.

"It's no good is it?" I ask.

"No, I like it," she says. "And besides, any plot can work if the story is written well enough."

"I hope so," I say.

"And by the way, relax," She says.

"What do you mean?" I ask.

She smiles at me, "You haven't taken more than one scoop of the pasta salad."

We continue to talk from noon all the way through the night. Every minute I feel more and more at ease. We laugh, we talk, and I ask many questions that I never thought I would have the opportunity to ask. Her calm disposition puts me at ease. She never seems to gloat over how much better a writer she is than me and treats me as if I were her equal, which is incredibly generous because, of course, I'm not. Before I leave she says to delay further writing until she gets back to me. I tell her I will and exit the door.

On the empty bus, no one is there to distract me from my extreme delight. My pessimism is gone, and has been replaced with hope.

I walk down the street strolling with a new spring in my step and see Hank Wiseman in the middle of the sidewalk, sitting with his legs straddling a plate and holding a fork in one hand and a bottle of Jack Daniels in the other. On his plate are tortilla chips with cold slices of Kraft singles on top. The edges of the plate are decorated with skittles.

"Hank," I say, "What are you doing?"

He smiles, "I'm dining alfresco!" He then flings back his head and laughs.

It's clear that his drunkenness has bloomed into full blown insanity. I smile contently and think to myself; *once again my future is uncertain.*

CH. 10

Jimmy Hansen, Carl Johnson, and I are sitting at our table in Henry's Bar, laughing and talking over a pitcher of beer in celebration of Coralline Thomson taking me on as a pupil. At the corner of the bar sits Hank with only his whiskey to keep him company. Still he's laughing to himself and muttering incoherent expletives-laden mumbles under his breath.

"I still can't believe it," Carl says, living his fantasies vicariously through me. "She's taking you under her wing. Just imagine, your next book will get assistance from arguably the greatest author of our time."

"I'd say *all* time," I butt in. "And I'm more than happy to make that argument."

"You know what's going to happen?" he says. "This book is going to be huge. You'll be on TV getting interviewed by all these people. You'll be big. I know it."

I laugh, "Let's not get ahead of ourselves. Just because I have Coralline Thomson's guidance does not mean I have her skill. Let's not automatically think that this is going to make me famous or anything."

"Are you kidding?" Carl exclaims. "This isn't some mediocre author helping you out. This is Coralline Thomson. *The* Coralline

Thomson. Author of <u>Our Nightmares are Our Desires</u>. Author of <u>Mental Requiem</u>. Three-time Pulitzer Prize winning author. *Three.* Trust me, big things are going to happen to you. I know it."

I smile, "That's nice, but let's not get our hopes up."

He excuses himself and heads to the restroom.

"I think he has to clean up his orgasm. He seems more excited about this than you," Jimmy says.

I laugh, "Yeah, he still hasn't learned that even when things look great, they can still take a downward dive. I'm almost resentful that she's doing this," I joke, "'cause now I'm going to have Carl harping on me every day as to what she taught me." I pause. "But on another subject, you still owe me seven dollars from that poker game."

Jimmy moans, "You're still on that? Jesus, it's seven dollars."

"Hey," I say, "I can make seven Ten-Ten-Two-Twenty calls with that kind of money."

He laughs, "Or you can buy a cellphone and be like everybody else in America." He pauses, "And how the hell do you even remember those commercials, those were like ten years ago."

"As for the cellphone, I'll be the one laughing when I'm the only one who doesn't have a brain tumor. And as for the Ten-Ten-Two-Twenty reference," I pause, "I'm actually not too sure myself. But anyway, pay up."

Jimmy shakes his head and then grins, "Alright." Then he pulls out a ball of change from his pocket—all nickels, pennies, and dimes. With it falls a bottle opener, three bottle caps, five crumpled up pieces of paper, and a broken lighter."

I smile, "Asshole."

We see Carl coming back from the restroom, his eyes sill in wonderment of what happened to me. He takes long strides with his lips creased ear to ear as if his girlfriend just accepted his proposal and he won the lottery, all in the same moment.

Jimmy looks at me, "Bet you seven dollars that he comes back still talking about you being mentored by her and continues the conversation as if there wasn't even a break."

"I have more faith in Carl," I say. "You're on."

Carl makes his way to the seat, still with that ever present optimism, and before he even sits down says, "You know you're going to be huge. She said that she would do it. You must feel incredible."

Jimmy and I smile as he grabs the change and scoops it back into his pocket. I shake my head a little bit and continue the conversation. We're all talking about the same thing we've been talking about for the last hour, thanks to Carl.

After another fifteen minutes or so, I go up to grab another pitcher. I stand at the bar to the right of Hank who doesn't even notice me. Two women come to sit at the seats to his left despite the odor. Hank looks worn out—gone. The disappointment of his life's dream accompanied by the copious amount of alcohol he has ingested over the span of his life has completely corroded his brain. After seeing him on the street with his plate of chips, cold cheese, and skittles, and bottle of Jack Daniels, I could tell that his mind has fully left him and there is no hope of him returning to sanity. As homage to his past failures and alcoholism, he drinks even more.

I catch the bartender's eye, "Another pitcher of Smithwicks."

He nods his head and starts filling up a pitcher.

To my incredible surprise Hank puts his hand on the woman to his left's shoulder and says, "Hey."

This is remarkable. Is Hank actually trying to pick up a woman? He hasn't made any advance on a woman that I can remember in seven years. The only way he got his last girlfriend was that she felt that she could save him and came over to talk to him. Who knows? Maybe this newfound insanity is just what he needed.

The woman looks a little disgusted and confused by the bizarre drunk that grabbed her shoulder. She is significantly younger, fairly sober, and semi-attractive, so I don't think this is going to go Hank's way.

She tries to be nice about the encounter but still inform him that she's not interested so she says, "Look, I just got out of a relationship, and I'm not quite ready-"

"I don't want to hit on you; I want *you* to hit *me*," he cuts her off.

"I'm sorry?" she responds.

"I want you to punch me in the face as hard as you can," he says.

The bartender returns with the pitcher and I start walking back to the table.

On my way over I hear Hank shout, "Hit me!" I turn around and the woman is staring at him in disbelief. "Hit me!" he shouts even louder. To appease his yelling, the woman taps him in the face. "As hard as you can!" he shouts again. The woman looks over at her friend and her friend shrugs. She then turns back to him and gives him a good whack. "Harder!" he shouts. She hits him a little harder. "Harder!" he shouts, and the woman cranks back her arm and clocks him right in the jaw. Hank nods his head and says, "Good. Good." Then turns to the bartender, raises up his hand and says, "Whiskey." After he gets his drink he slumps back over it with his head resting on the table. The two women look perplexed and decide to move to a different section of the bar.

Alright, I may have been wrong. Maybe he's not going to put himself out there again. Maybe this insanity just took something that we thought couldn't get any worse, and exponentially proved us wrong.

I return to the table with the pitcher, and the conversation shifts for a while to the topic of the decline of Hank's mental health. Granted this only lasts for a few minutes, thanks again to Carl. We express our concerns, and I can't help but hope that my future will change from Hank to anyone or anything else, through the help of my unbelievable new mentor.

After the pitcher is done we all decide to go our separate ways. Jimmy walks with me for a while. We laugh and joke about Carl's surging excitement of my luck, and Hank's bizarre antics with that woman. We're concerned too, but we can't help but laugh when something that peculiar happens. After all, funny is funny.

When I enter my house, I notice that I have a new message on the answering machine. While reaching for my cigarettes I hit play.

"Hi. This is Coralline Thomson. I have read your story and outline and found it quite interesting. I'd love to have you over sometime soon and discuss it. Please call me back when you get this message."

Immediately I grab the phone and dial her number. She answers, "Quite the insomniac, aren't you?"

I look at the clock and realize it's twelve past one in the morning. What if I annoyed her to the point where she doesn't want to speak to me or critique my book? My voice is filled with nervousness, "Oh my god, I'm sorry. I didn't realize what time it was."

She laughs, "Relax. I'm a little bit of the insomniac myself."

I'm overcome with relief. I didn't upset her. After what I saw at the bar today, she is my savior. My emancipator. The liberator of my future.

CH. 11

It is certainly noticeable, both internally and externally, that I am significantly more at ease in this future encounter with Coralline Thomson compared with the last one. I'm almost eager to arrive there. Sure there are still some butterflies in my stomach, but from the warmth she generated in the previous meeting, and the approval she gave my novel so far over the phone, I have a good feeling about this.

I ring the doorbell without even the slightest of worry in my head, nothing telling me that I'm unworthy. Nothing telling me to turn back. Just a healthy eagerness to converse with her and listen to her wisdom.

She opens the door once again with a large smile on her face and says, "Come in, come in."

I step inside and sit once again on her comfortable couch with her house's welcoming interior and nonthreatening ambience.

While walking to the kitchen she says, "Iced tea?" and I tell her yes and thank her.

She enters the room, holding two glasses of iced tea, a pen, papers—including the story, summary, and outline that I had given her—and a clipboard pressed against her chest so she can manage carrying everything.

"As for your story," she says, "it is well-written, engaging, gripping, an interesting concept, and at acceptable times humorous." She pauses and grabs the pages containing my story, "However, it runs into the same problem that you had in your previous novel; it lacks character development and the characters once again appear one-dimensional." I frown. "But that is a fallibility that can quite easily be rectified. I, in fact, suffered that same issue in some of my early work before I got published," she pauses, "but I've found some tricks to conquer that, and I'd be happy to teach you."

"And for that I am truly grateful," I say.

She looks at me thinking to herself and then pulls out her clipboard and clicks her pen. "I'm going to ask you a few questions."

I smile and let a single laugh escape my lips, "What are we doing now? Therapy?" I joke.

She stares at me for a couple of seconds just smiling, "Do you have any known allergies?"

"What?" I say caught off guard by the contrast of the need-to-know tone of her voice and the irrelevance of the question at hand.

"Do you have any known allergies?" she says again.

"No," I say a little confused. "Not that I know of. Why?"

She jots something down on her clipboard. "Have you ever suffered any hallucinations at any point in your life?"

What the hell? This really is therapy. "No. Never. What's the point of all this?"

She writes something else down onto her clipboard. "Have you ever been diagnosed with any sort of mental or emotional disorder?" she says still with that voice as if these were just generic questions you ask anybody.

"What? No. What is the relevance of all this?" I ask.

She writes once more on the clipboard. "All reasons will be

shown in time—I assure you. Just bear with me for a couple more questions. Are you on any medications, including over the counter, for any reason?" she says still with her eyes on the clipboard.

"No," I say perplexed beyond belief.

"Do you use any illegal drugs?" she asks still in that nonchalant tone.

"No," I say. "Don't you think these questions are getting a little personal?"

"Do you partake in alcohol?" she asks, pen in hand.

"Occasionally, yes I do," I say, wondering why I'm giving all these personal answers to someone I met only a few times. If it wasn't for who she was, I wouldn't answer any of these questions.

"How often?" she asks.

"I don't know, it varies," I say. "On average I'd say maybe thirty to forty a week."

"Have you suffered any traumatic experiences or any major tragedies in your life?" she says while jotting down information on the clipboard.

I ponder for a moment on that experience where Molly Idle's lifeless body entered the cabin door being carried by a frantic Jimmy Hansen as Lindsey and I stumble to our feet in fright. "No."

"Do you currently have any physical ailment bothering you?" she inquires.

"No," I say.

She sets down the pen and reads over the clipboard strumming her fingers through strands of hair. The entire time, she's contemplating what her next step will be.

It appears this bizarre physical and psychological analysis has concluded. I have no idea what relevant information she has attained through this process, but I remember something my dad used to tell me when I was a child, "If a person is better at something than you are, don't question their methods." And there is certainly no dispute that she is a much better writer than I am.

She leans back fingering her hair, thinking to herself.

I wish I had some idea as to what the hell is going on, but I am completely clueless. I don't know if I am right now witnessing the mind of a genius, or the mind of a nut-job. Either way it's better than my own mind. Following it sure hasn't worked for me thus far.

She puts her hand to her chin and pauses for a moment before removing it. "How badly do you want to expand your wings as an author?"

I look her square in the eye, "I would give anything—and I mean *anything*—to have a quarter of the literary clout that you possess. *Anything*."

She looks right back at me, as if she's seeing deeper into me—as if she can dissect my inner essence through those peering blue eyes. Her hand comes to comfort and rest a seemingly heavy chin. She's inside her mind once again, wondering what her next action should be. The entire time staring directly at me. This is getting really uncomfortable. First there was the bizarre verbal analysis, and now it appears as if she's sizing me up in some way that I can't comprehend.

"Alright," she says. "Alright." She reaches into her pocket and pulls out a small vial containing about a shot's worth of liquid. I stare at it knowing that this has something to do with me, but cannot pinpoint what or why. She holds the vial in her hand, her eyes glued to the glass container. "This," she says and holds up the small bottle for me to see, "This is something to help you write. It gets your mind going and allows you to draw parallels between reality and the absurd, while managing to keep you focused simultaneously. It is a creative stimulant and a mental relaxer all at the same time. It is the perfect assistant to an aspiring writer."

"What's in it?" I ask.

"I don't know exactly myself, but I do know that it is made up of mostly natural substances, as well as a few chemical additives," she says matter-of-factly.

I stare at the liquid and go through my head the strange conversation I just experienced. First it seemed like it was going to be much like last visit. Then the barrage of odd questions started, then the twenty minute pause while she looked over her notes and thought in silence to herself, and now she's holding this liquid and telling me it's a writer's helper. What the hell is going on?

"Now there are a few rules for when you take this," she says. "Make sure you take it tomorrow and not tonight. Do not drink any alcoholic beverage tonight, and be sure to go twelve waking hours tomorrow without eating or drinking anything. Then drink this, wait ten minutes, and start writing."

"Okay?" I say very confused.

"Do you have any questions?" She asks.

Do I have any questions? There is nothing occupying my brain besides questions. Like, 'What is this liquid that you just gave me?' or 'Why was I just analyzed like I was talking to a psychiatrist for the first time?' or maybe 'What in God's name is going on?' to name a few. But for some reason I say, "No."

I walk out of the door still trying to grasp the absurdity of that visit. That was a side of Coralline Thomson that I had never seen in either my visits, my conversations on the phone, or the interviews on television. What was that?

I turn and ask, "When do you want to meet again?"

"I'll call you," she says and closes the door.

I look at the vial trying to piece together what happened: what this is, why this meeting was so strange. Then I shrug my shoulders. If a person is better at something than you are, don't question their methods.

CH. 12

It's around four in the afternoon and I'm sitting in a chair at the computer doing the same thing I've been doing for the past thirty minutes that I have been doing for sporadic periods of time since I woke up: examining this vial of liquid that was handed to me last night. There is nothing significant about the container or the liquid that's inside. It is a glass vial without any designs or inscriptions and is screwed on by a tan colored top. Harbored inside is a clear liquid without any lumps or anything else that would make this significant. It looks as if someone took one of those airplane shots that you receive on a flight, tore off the label, emptied the contents, filled it with water, then screwed the cap back on. Yet for some reason, I'm drawn to it. A writer's assistant? What makes this so important?

The doorbell rings.

I pocket the vial. "Come in."

Jimmy opens the door and steps inside looking to kill some time with his old friend, "Really? You've finally stopped pretending that you might have any visitors that might not be me? I never thought you would accept it."

"I was just reading something on Yahoo News," I say, still

in my seat. "There's this three year old kid named Hunter who's deaf. Due to his deafness he's bound to speak in sign language. In order to say his name he has to go like this." I cross my middle and pointer finger on each hand, extend my thumb and move my hands up and down to make it look as if I was firing a weapon.

"Your point being?" he says.

"Now here's where it gets interesting," I say. "The school's weapons policy forbids any instrument that looks like a weapon. Because of this, they are asking the parents of Hunter to change his name."

"Well," Jimmy says, "that may have just been the most ridiculous thing I've heard all year."

I sigh, "As much as I give shit to the Republicans, the uber politically correct liberals are trying to prove that the conservatives haven't trademarked idiocy." I pause. "And it doesn't stop there. Each election, these politicians give middle school reading level speeches, and act as your every-day man, regardless of their intelligence. Because we don't want an intellectual—oh no, that would be terrible—we want someone we can have a beer with. That's who I certainly want leading this country." I say sarcastically. "A nincompoop with a beer hat." I sigh once again. "Every election it's a race to stupidity. To the moron go the spoils."

Jimmy smiles and looks at me for about ten seconds. "What's wrong?"

"What do you mean?" I ask.

"Don't play dumb," he says. "Every time you have something upsetting you, you go on a cynical rant about societal flaws in an uncharacteristically dramatic tone."

"Has it ever occurred to you," I say, "that what *is* upsetting me is the societal flaws."

"No," he says. "No it hasn't."

Why do I ever think that I can pull one over on him? We always seem to have that near telepathic connection. Close friends' understanding of each other is the closest thing to telepathy that we have on this earth. "I've spent most of today spending too much time inside my own head."

"That can be quite unhealthy," he says.

"Oh, don't I know it," I say. "I don't really want to talk about it. Luckily you came here to rescue me from my mind."

"If you don't want to talk about it, that's up to you, but in the meantime," he says looking around, "do you have anything to drink?"

"Scotch as always. I'll go grab it," I say.

Jimmy makes his way over to the couch as I pour out a glass of scotch and a glass of water and make my way over. I hand the scotch over to Jimmy and head back to my seat with my tall glass of iced water.

"Water?" Jimmy says. "Now I *know* something's wrong."

I laugh a little, "No, I'm just feeling a little sick." I lie for a reason that I'm not sure of.

Go twelve waking hours without eating or drinking anything. I hear Coralline Thomson's voice in my head. I pull out a smoke, light it, and take a large drag. When you haven't eaten all day, you try to curb your hunger with cigarettes. Cigarettes are appetite suppressants after all.

Jimmy asks, "So how did your meeting with Coralline Thomson go?"

"Bizarre," I say.

"How so?" he says.

I try to put this in words, "Well first she psychoanalyzed me, then there was a period of about thirty minutes where dead silence took place, and then," I put my hand in my pocket to grab the vial. For some reason I let it go inside my pocket and pull my empty hand out, "and then she said she would call me back and I left."

"Wait, what?" he says confused. "You're going to have to clarify this for me."

"I truly wish I could," I say and then give it a shot. "She pulled out a clipboard and started asking me all these questions. Like 'Have you ever hallucinated?' and 'Have you ever had any traumatic experiences?' and 'Do you use illegal drugs?' and 'Do you drink alcohol?' And then she stared at me in silence as if she was contemplating something in her head, but didn't tell me, and said she would call me back. After that I left the house just as confused as you probably are." I tell him this, once again omitting the part about the vial.

Jimmy laughs, "I don't know how that woman does what she does, but she sure is one odd person."

"Tell me about it," I laugh. Why didn't I tell him about the vial? What in my mind is restricting me?

"Well," he says, "I don't know her secret, but whatever it is, I'd definitely follow anything she says."

If a person is better at something than you are, don't question their methods.

"I guess I have no choice," I say. "At least if I want to get out of this rut of creating horrid novels."

"*Novel*," he says. "Singular. One. Uno."

I say, "Whatever. One is more than I need to know that I have to make a drastic change. When life gives you the gift of having Coralline Thomson be your mentor, you don't throw it away because of her idiosyncrasies. What is that saying again? Don't look a gift horse in the mouth."

"I guess you can take that approach," he says.

There's a pause for a while. He's drinking his Scotch, spilling occasionally on his shirt. He's always been a messy eater and drinker. For as long as I've known him he's been that way—always dropping crumbs on his shirt, spilling beer on his new clothes. At least back when he had the luxury of having new clothes. Now he's doing what we all seem to be doing; scraping by with the bare minimum. If life gives you lemons, make lemonade. Then ration that lemonade for the rest of your life, because that's all you get. You get handed shit, then you have to work with whatever shit life granted you until the day you die. That's the truth. Unless someone gives you the opportunity to have Coralline Thomson as your mentor. In that case, bear through the absurdities and bring that lemonade up for as many refills as you can drink.

I sip my water and take another drag of my smoke. My eyes gaze through my vast collection of literature—all my gods arranged in alphabetical order on each shelf. And I think to myself, 'How much would I give up to be an author—and I don't mean just having a book published, I mean a respected author—and not just a wannabe?' And I answer to myself, 'Anything and everything.'

I ask Jimmy, "What would you sacrifice to be remembered for your artwork? To be the next Da Vinci or Picasso or Michelangelo or Dali?"

"How many times have you asked me that question?" he says.

"Just one more time," I say. "Just answer it this one last time."

He moans, "Really? You're going to make me answer this question again? How many more times are you going to ask me?"

"This is the last time. I swear," I tell him.

"Anything," he says. I smile to myself content. That is exactly the answer I wanted to hear.

A few hours pass and Jimmy leaves. Our conversations dabbled on many subjects but the entire time I was debating on whether or not I should tell him about the vial that Coralline Thomson gave to me. Why would I not let myself tell him? I wondered. All she said is that it was a writer's aid. But for some reason I didn't want to mention it. As if it was something sacred and holy yet unspeakable. I couldn't figure out why I made that decision, and I still can't figure out why I'm so fixated on it. Is it the odd circumstances that led up to her giving me the vial? Is it the strangeness as to why she would give this to me? Is it the factor of the unknowing of what makes up the solution? Who knows? Maybe it's just the combination of all these factors as well as the disapproval of what he would think if I told him I was using a remedy to stimulate my writing capabilities. Like a cheap way to achieve literary improvement.

My fingers straddle the bottle, not sure if I really want to see what happens when I take this. A part of me filled with impatience to see what this does. And a part of me filled with dread of what this thing might do.

The little ampule of unknowing. The little vessel of uncertainty. The little potion of magic.

I shake it a little as if expecting something. As if it will explain anything. As if it will change colors. As if a genie will come out to grant me three wishes.

Looking over at the clock on the computer screen, I see that it's eight thirty. I woke up at eight fifteen. I guess it's been over twelve waking hours. I load up my story and open up the bottle.

I sniff it and immediately my stomach churns. The smell is so rank and god awful, I gag a little. It smells like Skol vodka, only astronomically more potent, mixed with vomit and urine. I have smelled some foul odors in my life but this definitely takes the cake. This is the most rancid thing I have ever taken a whiff of. From this odor appetizer, I can only imagine what the taste will be like.

This is my time to turn back. To say, 'No, I won't drink this shit.' Who knows what will happen once I drink it? Who knows what kind of mental catastrophe will occur after this single shot?

I shrug my shoulders. If a person is better at something than you are, don't question their methods. I open my mouth and down the hatch.

The liquid burns its way down my throat and I swear I can feel it go down my esophagus and enter my stomach. I immediately feel the need to vomit. I gag and cough hysterically.

You know when you're in third grade and you accidently

grab your dad's glass of swill whiskey. You take a couple of gigantic chugs from it because you think it's your soda. You don't know any better. You're young and you just want that high fructose corn syrup and caffeine rush. This is the first time you've ever tasted alcohol, and you start off with dad's cheap whiskey. You're about to throw up and you're coughing your lungs out so much that it's becoming hard to breathe. Take that and multiply it by one-hundred.

While coughing my brains out I manage to catch the time. Eight thirty-two. At eight forty-two I'll be ready to write, and—who knows?—maybe even eat.

My head's thumping and I'm getting a little dizzy. The entire time I'm coughing and coughing.

I stare back at the clock. Still eight thirty-two? I could have sworn it's been over a minute.

If someone were to ask me how I'm feeling, I wouldn't ever be able to relate it to the full extent. Not even the greatest writer could describe this feeling to a tee.

I'm exhausted, about to fall asleep where I sit. My eyes are growing tired. Yet somehow, even though I know it contradicts what I just said, I'm completely and utterly wide awake. Ready to run a marathon. Ready to read my entire bookshelf all over again.

Perspiration swims down my face and stings my eyes and drenches my shirt. I brush my hand across my hair and could swear that I felt my skin come off and stick to my hand. But when I look at it; nothing. Merely my arms cascading in sweat. However, my arm is beet red, and—can it be?—pulsing.

Time is no longer something I can track with instinct. Has it been a minute? Or has it been a millennium?

I look at the clock. Eight thirty-two. Wait, eight thirty-one? That can't be. Now it's back to eight thirty-two. Now eight thirty-three. What the hell is going on? Suddenly I begin laughing uncontrollably. As if some hilarity has taken place, but, for the life of me, I can't figure out what.

Now I can't stop laughing. There is no source of humor. There is nothing that seems in the least bit funny. I am in physical and emotional peril. At least I think I am. I'm not sure. Hell, I'm not sure of anything right now.

Suddenly I start to hear whispers. At first I can't make them out. Then it becomes more and more clear. It's my mom, my dad, Mark, Lindsey, Jimmy, Rick, Hank, Carl, my childhood dog, Samantha, Frank, my teachers, my pediatrician, the kid who used to bully me, Samuel, Megan, Coralline Thomson, my old boss—everyone I've ever met in my life. They're all whispering and shouting and growling and laughing and ordering and joking.

"Henry, walk the dog."

"Hahahaha!"

"Is this what you call clean?"

"You're going to have to take this delivery."

"Go twelve waking hours without eating or drinking."

"*Grrrrrr.*"

"Hey man you got any bud?"

"You really need to clean up your act."

"And all the faithful departed."

"Fuck you faggot!"

"Drink!"

"I'm going to prescribe an antibiotic."

"*Whoof!*"

"Hey Henry! Wait up!"

"Good one."

"Do you partake in alcohol?"

Jesus. What the hell is going on? I look at the clock. Eight thirty-three.

People begin to pop out of the walls. All with corkscrew faces and deep eye-sockets wearing plain clothing. They sink back into the wall. They walk around and exit through the walls as if they were apparitions. Maybe they are apparitions. Maybe I'm seeing ghosts. Maybe I don't know what the fuck is going on.

I look back at the clock, my computer fading away. Eight thirty-four.

Then the vomiting and tearing starts. I look down at my transparent desk and see a pile of clear liquid. Soon another pile comes to join it. Then another. And another.

I'm laughing, crying, sweating, vomiting, coughing, and hallucinating at the same time. What is going on? I start to stumble towards the door. I need fresh air. I *need* it. My vision goes black. Then it returns. It goes black again, and once again returns. I push the door open. Was there a door? I fall down. Struggle to get up only to fall down again. Then I black out.

CH. 13

My eyes peel open to see the sun brighter than it's ever been before. I turn my head to the left and right and see that I'm laying in-between two bushes with nothing as a pillow save a clump of dirt. I strain to sit up only to feel an aching in my body like I've never felt before. What was in that vial? I've had hangovers before, but this takes the cake.

After a couple of minutes of lying in the dirt, I gather enough strength to stand up and make my way out of the bushes.

"Rough night?" a man asks me with a toothless smile.

I shrug him off, ashamed to be seen in this situation and examine the area. I'm in the middle of some sort of park. Trees, flowers, vagrants, and families feeding ducks decorate my surroundings. My throat parched and stomach growling, I see a water fountain in the distance. Each step I take, I discover a new pain in a part of my body that I didn't know existed. When I see the water fountain all covered in green goo, slime, rust, and unidentifiable filth, I can't help but drink for a solid ten minutes.

Semi-relieved, I start walking so I can find some familiar territory. The acrid smell that infested my nose has now subsided and has been replaced by the fresh air, but my aching body, horrendous headache, mental fogginess, and the feeling of starvation are still incredibly prevalent.

When I'm in the area of stores and restaurants, I realize that I have no clue at all where I am. I can't recognize any of these stores at all. Jake's Eatery, Eggcellent Café, Hector's Smoke Shop; I don't recognize a single place. An old man is sitting by the curb smoking a cigarette and leaning his head back.

"Excuse me," I'm barely able to muster the strength to say, "What city is this?"

He looks up at me with a vacant expression, "What does it matter? We're all as good as dead no matter where we live."

Obviously this man has had a rough night too, or he's just crazy. "Do you have a cell phone?"

He looks up and lets out a laugh, "Do dead men carry cell phones?"

Alright, that's it. I'm going to be pickier with who I decide to talk to, because it seems that many people in this town have issues.

I continue to walk through the town trying to figure out where I am. It has a little bit of the feel of a medium-sized city, but still has some remnants of that folksy small town lifestyle. I see what looks like another vagabond sitting on the steps. He's got a cup filled with change on the ground in front of him as people pass by. A black man throws some quarters in the cup and as he passes I see the man sitting on the ground mutter the words, "Fucking nigger." I get closer and see the bottom half of a confederate flag tattooed on his left arm. The top is covered by a tee-shirt that is tattered and torn. He wears a hat that also has the confederate flag on it and reads underneath, "The South Will Rise Again."

Suddenly I think that I know the person somehow—at least some attributes about him. I'm almost positive I've never seen him before in my life, but somehow in some way, I know him. It's a strange feeling.

Then I look around at my foreign surroundings: Harvey's Bar and Grill, Half Priced CD's, Porktopia. I look up and down the street. All the people and the atmosphere. The pet shop up the road. The gas station down the street. And suddenly I feel a strange sense of deja-vu. I know this area somehow. This completely alien place is in some way familiar. I continue to walk down the street and this only reassures the feeling. How do I know this town? Have I been here before? If everything seems so familiar, why do I not have a clue where I am?

Lost in thought, I bump into a sane looking man, "Sorry."

"It's all right," he says and continues walking.

"Excuse me," I say and he continues walking as if he didn't hear me.

Who can blame him? I've met some of the people in this town, and with me all covered in dirt, what possibly separates me from the crazies?

I walk down the street and see a woman leaning against a restaurant listening to an iPod and smoking a cigarette.

"Excuse me," I say. Her eyes meet mine and she unplugs one headphone, "Do you happen to have a cellphone?"

"Sure," she says and pulls out her cellphone to give me.

"Thank you so much." In the middle of me saying this, she puts the headphone back into her ear.

I dial Jimmy's number. "Come on Jimmy pick up," I mutter to myself.

As soon as I put it to my ear I hear a woman's voice, "I'm sorry. This number is either out of service or disconnected. Please hang up and try again."

I guess I must have dialed the wrong number. I redial and hear once again, "I'm sorry. This number is either out of service or disconnected. Please hang up and try again."

Now I'm a little confused. Maybe he changed his number. How long was I out for?

I dial Carl's number. "I'm sorry. This number is either out of service or disconnected. Please hang up and try again."

Now I'm really confused and starting to worry.

I try Mark's phone. "I'm sorry. This number is either out of service or disconnected. Please hang up and try again."

I stare at the phone in disbelief. What's going on? Am I misremembering all their numbers? Is there some sort of problem with the phone lines?

As a last resort I try Hank's number, and once again hear, "I'm sorry. This number is either out of service or disconnected. Please hang up and try again."

I hang up the phone and give it back to the woman. "Excuse me."

She waves me off in irritation.

What the hell is going on? Did I die and go to Bizarro World?

It's clear I'm not going to figure all this out anytime soon. In the meantime I haven't eaten in a long time and my stomach's growling in agony. I look across the street and see a breakfast place called Sunny Side Up, and underneath the sign it reads, "Fresh Food Fast." I make my way over to it.

Before I enter, a slightly tall, trim man bumps into me.

"Oh, my apologies," he says. "I can be such a klutz sometimes." He laughs.

"No worries," I say.

I open my mouth to ask where I am but then something stops me. I feel a chill run down my spine, and I begin to feel slightly nauseous. I freeze. Something about this man. His blue eyes. His charming demeanor. Something just makes my blood go cold. I stand there with my mouth agape just staring at him with some irrational fear.

"Bye then." He smiles and then walks past me.

My eyes follow him, glued to his slender physique, wondering what happened. Why am I so suddenly frightened? What was it about that man that clicked some part of my brain into shutdown mode? I shake it off and walk back into the restaurant.

I see the hostess and ask for a table for one, when I see Coralline Thomson waving at me.

"Actually, I'll sit with her," I say and point in her general direction.

"Sounds good," the waitress says and walks with me to my table. The table is secluded. It's a booth in the corner with nobody in the booths in either direction and the adjacent table is also vacant.

"Can I start you off with anything to drink?" the waitress asks.

"A coffee," I say, "And two orders of biscuits and gravy." I pause for a second. "And fried eggs over-easy."

"And how would you like your coffee?" she asks.

"Surprise me," I say curtly in irritation and impatience to talk to Coralline Thomson.

The waitress is taken aback by my abrupt response but composes herself nicely, "I'll bring it out when it's ready."

I wait, watching the waitress fall out of earshot, and then turn quickly to Coralline Thomson, "What the hell did you give me?"

"No tears in the writer, no tears in the reader. No surprise in the writer, no surprise in the reader," she says.

"What?" I say.

"Robert Frost," she says.

"What are you talking about?" I say.

She sighs, "You'll soon be able to understand that expression better than almost anybody. Including him."

"Could you quit playing games and tell me what you're talking about?" I say in anger.

"You did say that you would give anything to achieve literary clout," she says.

Now I'm angry. "So tell me, what did vomiting, hallucinating, blacking out, and feeling some of the worst pain I've ever felt in my life help me with in my trip to literary stardom?"

"I'm guessing you don't know where you are," she says.

I raise my voice a little. "Not at all."

She puts her finger to her lips giving me the sign to keep quiet and I see that the waitress has returned with my coffee. I nod to her and say thank you and my eyes once again follow her till she's out of earshot.

"You're going to have some rough patches ahead," Coralline Thomson says, "but I assure you, you will receive the desired effect."

"Where am I?" I ask.

"If we can control the environment in which rapid cognition takes place, then we can control rapid cognition," she says.

"What?" I say.

"Malcolm Gladwell," she says.

My voice rises once again. "Why can you never make sense?"

"Tell me," she says, "I'm sure you don't know where you are, but don't you feel a strange sense of familiarity?"

"Yes," I say. "But why?"

"What if I were to tell you that we've found a way to breach our minds?" she says. "To tap into our subconscious in a very literal way."

"Jesus, could you spit it out," I growl.

"What if what we have always thought in our mind's eyes and mind's ears can, for a period of time, become our reality?" she says calmly.

I'm almost shouting, "Could you cut the bullshit?"

"This familiarity, this deja-vu, even though you know for a fact that you have never been here before," she says.

I've had enough, "What the fuck are you talking about?"

"Henry," she says, "you're inside your own story."

CH. 14

I'm taken back by what she just told me. The information seemed to have been too incredible—or even the word 'traumatic' seems to fit here—to be fully processed by my brain. I'm left at the dumbfounded state where it takes great strides to form syllables into words. Even more strain goes into turning those words into sentences.

"But...but," I say, "but that's impossible."

"Oh Henry," she says, "Why must you restrict yourself to only the realm of what is possible? It's the impossible that's where the fun is." She pauses. "Could you imagine where mankind would be if we never tried to reach the impossible? If we so easily quit when we found out something was merely not possible? We would be millennia behind where we are today. We would be back to only living 'till we're thirty, thinking that those that came down with strep or the flu were as good as dead. We would still be eating raw meat because we only saw fire as a source of destruction. There would be no such thing as medical science, modern language, or even literature, which we love so much, because we would be too preoccupied in an almost futile attempt to survive. So I ask you again, why limit yourself to the realm of possibilities?"

I'm almost speechless, "But...but, that's bullshit. There's no way. How could it? No. No way."

"Think about it Henry. Really *think*," she says, "Doesn't all of this seem a little familiar? All of this area, the people, doesn't it strike you as somehow familiar but you can't pinpoint how? But you know deep inside you that this really is the story?"

I think about it, because a part of me *knows* it. I think of the surroundings, the environment, the people that inhabit it.

Then I think about the man on the street with the confederate flag tattoo who called the man passing by a 'fucking nigger' under his breath. I did know him in some way. And then it hits me, Sam 'Bones' Logwood. His similarities are uncanny. It's exactly how I pictured him in my mind. He is a man who came from Arizona, raised from a racist dad and a fundamental Christian mom. He has four brothers, more crazy than he is, and two sisters who all went their separate ways after their parents were murdered. The murderers were never found, but for some reason Bones always thought it was done by African-Americans. He has no proof or even a good reason to back his hypothesis, but he got it into his head, and that's what he's thought since. He got his nickname, Bones, after one night he got into a drunken fight with two Mexicans and broke both arms, one leg, and a collarbone on one of them, and an arm and a leg on the other. The entire time he told his friends to back off; he wanted to 'teach these taco-fuckers a lesson without no fuckin help.' At the end the two Mexicans were on the ground screaming, 'Stop! You broke my bones!' Later it just was, 'My bones,' and then simply, 'Bones.' The name stuck.

Then I think about the other man I saw before him. The one who said, 'Do dead men carry cellphones?' John Harold, I realize. He was a little crazy, but mainly just depressed. He started spiraling after his wife died of cancer. If I truly am in my story, then he should be killing himself within the next couple days. But I can't be, can I? I mean, this is too much.

I'm starting to get a little calmer as this finally sinks in, and it's becoming much easier to talk, "But, how did you know I was going to be in this restaurant?" I say.

"It was a little bit of a guess, but a very well-conceived guess," she says. "In your story whenever there is a scene in a restaurant, it is this one. So I just guessed that you would be drawn here. After all this is where Richard Sweeney eats many mornings."

I think about the blue eyed slender man leaving the restaurant that had such a profound effect on me and shudder.

The waitress comes by with my food, reminding me that I ordered food, or even that I was in a restaurant, and says, "Here you go. Hope you enjoy." I nod dumbly and she walks away.

"But," I say to Coralline Thomson, "but how does this…how exactly…how?"

She sighs, "I'll try to explain it as best and as quick as I can. Have you ever heard of Isaac Thorn?"

"Of course," I say. "The famous science fiction author. Who hasn't?"

"Well," she says, "prior to his work as an author, he worked as a scientist. He was one of the most intelligent minds of the day. He worked in many fields, having studied many sciences: chemistry, biology, psychology, you name it. During the late fifties there was a resurgence in the interest of the mind. New drugs were being found to explore the vastness that makes up our subconscious and all and all the brain. An idea had been kicking around everyone's head, but nobody had successfully been able to break the initial stage: telepathy. It was an interesting concept—still is—but too many people thought of it as something that was simply impossible and not worth the time to even try. It was considered to be a waste of time, money, and resources.

"However, this seemed to fascinate Isaac, and he felt that this was somehow—with the right people working on it—possible. No one would finance him, so, after making a lot of money as a very notable scientist, he financed the entire thing himself. He went with his partner Phillip Arnold, hired a team of people and started to work on this project. He scratched the idea of getting telepathy on command, calling it 'absurd,' and instead thought that there could be some chemical compound that could lead to temporary telepathy. He knew they would not find long-term telepathy—if he succeeded with creating this—'till long after his death and another intelligent group of minds could isolate certain chemicals and expand upon his creation. They worked four full years until they created a compound that they thought might be possible. They had severe doubts, and even fears of what would happen, so they could not decide what to do next. Isaac, within those years, had become an animal rights activist in a way, and did not like the idea of animal testing. 'Animals' main desire in life is surviving; man's main desire in life is killing. If you're going to test a potentially harmful product, do it on the latter,' he was quoted saying. Thus, animal testing was out of the question. After about a year of procrastinating, and their funds depleting, Isaac and Phillip decided to drink the fluid themselves.

"As you can probably imagine, the onlookers were terrified by the effects and immediately called for an ambulance, but before the ambulance arrived, the two had blacked out. Unbeknownst to Phillip, Isaac was writing a story in his spare time. You know it as, 'Shattered Stars,' his first book, and only solo work. However, since Phillip didn't read the book or know a single thing about it, the reaction didn't turn out so well. Yes, Isaac ended up inside his own story, but Phillip was similar to an apparition fading in and out of the world in Isaac's mind. Phillip would show up occasionally asking Isaac, 'What in god's name is happening? Have I gone mad? Help me Isaac!' and then he would disappear only to show up in a new area sometime later.

"After a period of time though, Phillip stopped haunting his story. When Isaac finally came to, he found himself inside a low-security mental hospital standing over a pile of hundreds of papers, all of them written on in rushed, yet neat, handwriting. He asked someone what had happened, and they were surprised to see him acting so normal. They said he seemed like he was mentally comatose, just ferociously writing, eating, and barely sleeping. He asked where Phillip was, and they told him to go to bed for now, and they'd fill him in when he awoke. Later he found out that Phillip had killed himself after going insane and talking about this other world he would see with Isaac in it. He switched from the similar comatose state that Isaac was in to frantic screaming. After that he couldn't take it anymore and slit his throat with a sharpened knife.

"Isaac took this hard. When he came out of the hospital, he found out he was broke and with the feeling of guilt strong on his conscience. He gathered his things back from the hospital staff who held on to it for him. He also took the chemical compound that some of his coworkers had safeguarded ambivalently, and after deep consideration, he decided not to throw it away. After a while, he read his story. It was much better than anything that he had done in the past. He went to a publisher and was, within a short period of time, back out of poverty.

"Later he tried this experiment again with a close friend, Clive Smith," Coralline Thomson says and I nod in acknowledgement of the name. "Only this time, he informed him of his story that he started writing, and had him read the story, plot outline, and summary. The plan went superbly, and he, along with Clive, had another hit book on his hands. He enjoyed writing, but creating another world, and visiting it with a close friend was something completely unique and fascinating to him. They continued this for another fifteen years until Clive died of a heart attack. After that, Isaac, with plenty of money on his hands, retired. One day, many years later, I bumped into him on the street, similar to when you bumped into me, and told him I was an aspiring author and—way too cocky for my own good—asked if he could look over my work. He smiled and said yes. And that was when my career truly began."

CH. 15

I'm more taken back and confused than I was prior to her clearing things up. This whole situation is maddening. I am now starting to believe this whole thing, but can't figure out what to say. What do you say when someone just explains to you that you are right now in an experiment that nobody else knows, that was conceived back in the late fifties, that led to one person committing suicide and leads you inside your own story? What is there possibly to say? Your mind is full of questions but not a single logical sentence. How do you make a logical sentence when everything is so illogical?

"At first he thought he was on the astral plane when he saw the stars, illuminating lights of his story, and Phillip's specter. Who knows?" she says. "Maybe that is in fact where we are."

"So," I say slowly as if having to taste my words before I say them, "what is my body doing while I'm like this?"

"Your body is on autopilot," she says. "You're doing all that is mandatory to stay alive: eating food, drinking water, sleeping, but for the most part you're just writing. Writing like mad."

"How will I know what happened while I was under this..." I search around thinking of what 'this' is, "whatever you call it?"

"You'll have a place where you will write everything down. Every important encounter, anything that really matters; you'll write it down somewhere. My guess is that you'll have a file on your computer," she says.

I stroke my hair looking for something to say—wondering how I should take these absurd happenings—but nothing comes to mind.

"Also," she says, "it might be important to know that time will move slower here. I don't know the exact time ratio, but about one year spent in your story is equivalent to two and a half weeks in reality. That might be helpful to know."

A *year*? How long am I going to be in this insanity?

I struggle to say something. I *know* I should say something, but as far as my mind reaches, I'm coming up empty on words. There is an odd pause as each of us waits for the other to say something.

She reaches into her pocket and pulls out a driver's license and a credit card. "This is yours," she says. "You're now Jake Neilson, and I'm Jane Young."

I look at the license with my face and Jake Neilson's name and ask, "Why can't I be Henry Riddick, and you, Coralline Thomson?"

"It would be odd to have a character in your story named after you and me," she says. "It would turn off the reader, and give the critics something to gripe about. And since we both have produced novels, the characters in the story might know our real names. This is the best way for the sake of the story. So from now on call me Jane Young not Coralline Thomson; and I'll call you Jake Neilson, not Henry Riddick. Remember," she adds, "we are both minor characters in your story, so act the part."

"What am I supposed to do?" I ask wonderingly.

"What you're supposed to do is mainly fraternize with the other characters," she says. "You're biggest problem in your first book was that your main characters were one-dimensional and not deep enough. Learning more about them will help you dive deeper into them while your body is writing, and they will have much more depth. Trust me, this is very important. And, if you need to—but only if you need to—you can make alterations with the story."

"How do I do that?" I ask. "Do I just think it or something?" I say very seriously. After all this is my subconscious, why can't alchemy work in my own mind?

"No unfortunately; nothing like that," she says. "You actually have to physically alter it. It takes action. Imagine this is real life while you're here. You do not have any supernatural powers; you are simply you. Well an alter-ego of yourself. You are simply a man with nothing special. Nothing bends to your whim; you must change it physically." She pauses. "But I wouldn't do it that often for the sake of the story. Too many alterations could turn a good story into confusing garbage. Stick to the main story and only make changes when you think it is absolutely necessary and beneficial for the story."

I take all this in. So I just have to socialize with the other characters—talk to them to have them tell me everything. Seems easy enough. I scratch my head, once again a rush of too many questions blocking my mind from formulating actual words.

"Now it comes to an important matter that I need you to listen very carefully on. Can you do that?" she says.

"Sure," I say.

"Rules," she says.

"Rules?" I ask.

"Yes, rules," she says. "Are you ready to listen?"

Someone gives you a vial without explaining what's in it. They have you drink it, vomit violently, hallucinate, black out, then you wake up finding out you're inside your own story in which a serial killer is on the loose. And then they say that you have to follow their rules? What can you say? "Sure."

"First rule: Always remember that the only things that are real in this world are me and you," she says, "Everything and everyone else is a product of your imagination. They are illusions. Quirks of your subconscious that are alive *only* in this world of your imagination. This is incredibly important to remember for the sake your sanity. If you get delusional and start to believe that this is in fact reality—if you get any warning signs whatsoever—come and see me immediately. That can be terrible for the story, for you while you're inside the story, and for you when you finally return to reality. Do you understand?"

I nod my head.

"Good, now on to rule number two," she says. "Never become a main character. This is strictly for the sake of the story. When you become a main character, it will lead you to think that you can take over everything in the story and you will try to change everything inside the story, and when you are finished and are rereading the story, it will be a jumbled mess of mistakes and confusion."

"Got it," I say.

"Rule number three," she says. "Stay as close to the characters as needed, but never too close. It is important to stay close enough to gather information and dig deep into their lives so they can shape into three-dimensional characters. And also, when needed, change the paths of their lives if it is good for the story. But when you start to sympathize with them and develop friendships, you will make foolish decisions that alter the story negatively and you will be left depressed when you leave. Do you got that?"

"Yes," I say.

"Rule number four: Always remember that this will inevitably end," she says, "You may feel tempted to act foolish or to think that you are stuck here eternally after being here for a while, so what does it matter what you do? But get that notion out of your head. Inevitably you'll be back home with a great book on your hands. And the more you feel that this will not end, the more problematic your return will be. You won't be able to function properly. Everything will be confusing. Trust me, you don't want it."

"Alright," I say.

"Rule number five: Do not get attached to anybody," she says. "It may seem like a good way to deal with the very lonely homesickness of this whole experience, but it will only depress you when you leave. And that brings me to the sixth and final rule."

"And what's that?" I say.

She pulls me in so I'm listening closely. "Never *ever* fall in love." She pauses for a little to let that one sink in. "This is an expansion on rule number five, I guess in a way all of the rules are intertwined, but this is the most important rule. Love makes people impulsive and irrational and can lead to a train wreck of a story, and when you leave, it can lead you into a depressed sort of madness that will deteriorate your very soul. Do you understand all of this?"

"Yeah," I say.

"Good," She says. "Well in that case, I'll take my leave. I'll meet you here tomorrow at ten."

"Alright." I say, and she gets up and exits the door.

All of this strangeness is absolutely baffling. I don't know what to make of this. I had no idea what I was stepping into. How long will I be away from my life? How long in that reality and in this one? I sit alone processing everything that just happened. I still don't understand all of it. I probably never will. I wonder if she does. Hell, I even wonder if Isaac Thorn did. It's all a lot to process. Is this really going to be worth it? What kind of life is this for an author? To *live* in fantasy instead of writing it.

The waitress appears next to me, "Is everything alright? I see you haven't touched your food."

I shrug. If a person is better at something than you are, don't question their methods. And I dig in.

CH. 16

After your god informs you that you are inside a fantasy world that you have created, and then ditches you, telling you that she'll see you again tomorrow and does not give you any further instructions, what do you do? What do I know? Don't all deities mess with their faithful followers' heads a little? Just think about the Judeo-Christian's take on God. He told Abraham to slaughter his own son, then at the last minute said, "I'm just fucking with you," in so many words. Then again, didn't God kill all of Job's family, livestock, and everything short of his very livelihood, just to win a bet with Satan? Who knows what deities do or their reasons for doing it? Maybe they're just bored.

So without any further instructions or the slightest idea as to what to do next, I go for a walk.

On my walk, I see my subconscious' manifestation played out before my very eyes. There's a drunk losing his mind on every corner. A man whittling a bow and arrow with a fish gutting knife claims that this is for when the polar bears rise up after they land here when the icecaps melt. A woman offers her fellatio services for discount prices, but really gets you when the excise tax kicks in. At least a half a dozen people are insinuating that tonight they are going to commit suicide. And more people than I can count look like they're strung out on this drug or the other. *God*, I think, *my subconscious must be really fucked up.* I make a mental note to see a psychologist when I come back to reality.

Well I guess if my job is to fraternize with the morbidly insane people that inhabit my fictional world, then fraternize I shall.

I sit down next to what looks to be a man nursing a hangover, leaning his head back against the concrete wall with a hand rested on his stomach. His face is pale and he's holding a cup full of change with the hand that isn't on his stomach.

"Fuck off," he says. "This is my territory. It took me fifteen years to get this spot; nobody's going to steal it from me."

"What's so special about this spot?" I ask curiously.

He lifts up a finger and points to a twenty-four hour gym which has four attractive women running on treadmills facing our direction. I wince in a slight feeling of revulsion and sympathy that this is the pathetic state that life has led him to—getting hard from sweaty women thirty yards away through a glass window. Then I remember that none of this is real—not the guy, not the women, not even the twenty-four hour gym. I created it. And suddenly I feel even more guilty.

"Don't judge," he says. "When you haven't had anything for as long as me, you live with what you got."

"I'm not judging, and I'm not here to take your spot either. I'm new here, and I just wanted to have a chat with one of the locals," I say.

"You know that's not the only reason I sit here. I have other reasons. I'm not a total perve," he says, completely disregarding my friendly banter. He points to a cheap grocery store and then moves his hand to point to something behind him. "There's a food store there that sells foot-long subs packed with meat for three bucks, and a liquor store right around the corner."

I shrug, "Guess that makes shopping easy. Not a far commute."

"You bet your ass," he says. "So you're new here?" he says

as if what I said earlier just registered.

"Yep," I say. "Trying to find a hotel to stay in for now."

"Take this street up 'till when it ends and then turn left. Keep following that up, and then you'll see a bunch of hotels. You won't be able to miss it. I swear," he says.

"Thanks," I say.

"Don't mention it," he says, eyes still on the women's breasts bouncing in the gym as they run on the treadmills. "What's your name anyway?"

"Jake Neilson," I blurt out too excitedly. I should have said it slower. I guess I was over-focusing on it. I've been practicing in my head over and over. 'Jake Neilson. Jake Neilson. Jake Neilson. Jake Neilson.' Trying to get the pitch, tone, inflection, and speed right for once I get the opportunity to use it. And now that I finally say it, I say it with the same irrational enthusiasm as some child who just got the newest toy for Christmas and gloats about it to his friends in an attempt to entice envy. As if to say, 'My name is Jake Neilson and yours isn't. Nah nah nah nah nah.'

"Hey Jake," he says. "The name's Bill."

I extend my hand for a shake to secure that acquaintances have been met, even though formality says that he should initiate the hand-shaking-transaction.

He ignores my hand and says, "So what brings you out here?"

I freeze. What brings me out here? I don't know what. I've been told to talk with the locals, but I haven't been trained in what to say. Should I say a job transfer? Then he'll ask about my job. And what do I know about banking or real-estate or business management or any of the transferable jobs that are coming to my head right now. This wasn't supposed to happen. She should have given me some training, informing, explaining, or at least some run-throughs before she hung me up to dry. This is not my fault. This was her responsibility to make sure I can make it through this intact and not blow my cover. I'm like a puppy that's been stripped of his parents and litter mates right after birth, and placed not in the care of some people with a nice home, but instead been shipped across seas and dropped in the middle of the jungle. Awakening to some foreign area, helpless to the lions of inquiries, and the poisonous snakes of needed explanation. I am stranded in my subconscious, left with nothing but a copious amount of ignorance about what my next action should be. That's what I am right now. The ill-informed puppy in the jungle. That's me.

A tall black haired, clean shaven man with a strong build walks up and pauses in front of Bill and I. He's chewing a wad of gum, and has a gun in a holster. My nerves tense up.

"Bill, you make a friend or something?" the tall man says. "I've never seen you here before with anybody," he says, shifting the gum with his tongue so it's wedged in-between his cheek and gums.

What if I die? She never mentioned anything that happens if I were to get shot or stabbed or anything. I'm not immortal in this story, am I? Maybe. Nothing would surprise me after the barrage of insanity I've been hit with these past couple days. But I sincerely doubt that's the case. She would have mentioned immortality, wouldn't she? Come to think about it, shouldn't death have been one of the topics discussed? I mean, it's kind of a pretty big thing.

"Just someone decided to plop down and talk to me," Bill says. "He's new in town. Just wanted to converse. That's not illegal, is it? Unless you guys made a new law or something," he says with a semi-smartass tone.

"We're not the ones who implement the laws," the tall man says. "We only enforce them."

"So was there a new law that two people can't sit down and have a conversation on the sidewalk?" Bill asks.

"No. No there's not," the tall man says slightly disgruntled.

"A lot of nicotine gum today. Stress getting to you?" Bill says. "And by the way, did you catch that killer yet?" he says with a smile. There's a goading tone to his voice and a sinister look to his smile. The denotation: 'Did you catch that killer yet?' The implication: 'You'll never catch me.'

Then it hits me, 'enforce laws,' 'nicotine gum,' he's not going to kill me, he's detective Todd Reynolds, the protagonist of the story. The good counterpart of the serial killer. The yin to the killer's yang. At least for the story's sake, they need each other. And this man is a good guy. His job is to hunt down the villain as the investigation starts messing more and more with his mind. I have nothing to fear. But for some reason, this realization doesn't seem to put me at ease or calm me down in the least. On the contrary, it seems to make my heart beat faster, make my body perspire more, and instill in me a whole new form of anxiety. I'm not sure why, but this is what it does.

Furthermore, why's this Bill guy playing with the detective as if Bill were in fact the serial killer? I know it's not him. It's Richard Sweeney, the tall charming guy with polite manners I saw exiting the restaurant this morning. Not Bill Whatever-his-name-is.

"No, not yet," Todd says, "But don't you worry, we're getting closer." He adds a smile as if to say, 'I'll get you soon.'

"Glad to hear," Bill says.

Todd looks at me, "So you're new around here? What's your name?"

"Hen-" I stop myself. I was about to say 'Henry.' Come on Henry, get your game straight. "Jake Neilson," I say.

Detective Reynolds gives me a quizzical look for a few seconds, then shrugs his shoulders and says, "Where you staying?"

"I'm new here," I say, stating the obvious in an irritating conversational redundancy.

"That's not what I asked," he says, analyzing me—probably sizing me up for some crime. Probably wondering, 'Why is he so nervous? What's he got to hide?' He looks me up and down to put my face and physique in his memory to save for later.

"Oh sorry," I say maybe a tad too quickly, so I make an

attempt to speak slower which only sounds stranger, "I'm going to be staying at a hotel. Don't have one yet. I'll most likely find one today." I pause, then try to think of something that I can say that would draw suspicion off of me and make me seem more like a sane normal person that doesn't engage in criminal activity, "Do you have any recommendations?"

He's still eyeballing me—sizing me up. "Well as a member of this town I feel obliged to recommend the Douglas Inn. It may not be much to look at, but they try to compensate for that. The hospitality is great, and it's locally owned. It's not one of those big chain hotels like Holiday Inn or the Hilton. This is the only place you'll find it. So I'd recommend you give it a try." Then he adds in as if he forgot something, "And it's completely affordable. It has room service too. Check it out."

"Sounds like I will. Thanks a lot," I say, trying to sound like as much of an average, normal, sane, human being as possible.

"And you," Todd says pointing to Bill, "If I catch you jerking off in public again I'm gonna book your ass."

"It's been years-" pleads a smiling Bill, as if he's playing the detective, but this only makes him more of a suspect.

"And a shitload of arrests 'till you finally got the message," the detective cuts off Bill, then turns to me. "You might want to find some other people to sit down and have get-to-know-ya chats. Anyway, I'll see you around," He says that last part in a way that I can't tell if it was a friendly gesture or a threat.

My eyes follow the detective, still confused with why I was so nervous—more nervous when I found out that he was the protagonist detective in my story than I was when I thought he was bound to kill me.

"So what was all that animosity between you and the detective?" I ask.

"The cop's a prick," Bill says. "He keeps busting me about yanking my dick all the time. Fuck, it's not like I'm raping anybody. I just see the women in the gym and jerk off. I only do it at night, so no one can see. If I had a home I would do it at my house, but I don't, so what can I do? So one night, maybe five years ago, I'm spanking it to a woman in the gym. Her tits bouncing up and down. Her shirt wet and sticking to her breasts and making her nips easier to see. And there comes Officer Friendly catching me putting my parts away. He starts to book me, then sees who I've been jerking to. And just my fucking luck: it's his wife. So he starts smashing me against the wall and beating the piss out of me. He takes me in, and even with my lawyer seeing me all bruised up, I'm not able to sue or get out of shit. They just said I was like that when they booked me. Since then I always go in the alley and jerk it like a fucking animal. You see what these so called 'proponents of peace' that are supposed to 'serve and protect' degrade us to?"

I think about Todd Reynolds. Nobody knows him better than I do because after all, I am his creator. I know that he's almost always a by the books cop—doesn't rough up the suspects or plant evidence or anything of that nature—but then I also know that he was very protective of his late wife. I know his devastation at her loss, and how much it killed a part of him. I know this because I invented it. I know this because I invented *him*. So to hear that he lost his temper and roughed up some guy who was masturbating to the love of his life doesn't surprise me. What does surprise me is how this happened even though I didn't write it. Has my story gone rogue? Am I no longer in charge of this story? Has the absurdity slipped my grasp?

"Alright. But why did you act like that? Don't you want to avoid being mistaken for the killer? Instead you led him on to believe that you were. You're not the killer and this could bring a lot of horrible things to yourself by playing those mind games and insinuating that you are in fact responsible for those deaths," I say.

"How do you know?" he responds, looking straight at me.

"Know what?" I say.

He looks me dead in the eye with a futile attempt to

frighten me and says, "That I'm not the killer?"

I think for a second. If I was just an average person and not the equivalent to this world's God, then how would I know that he's not the killer? He could be, just as easily as I could be, just as easily as anyone could be. I know that he's not of course. But how could I explain that to him without ruining the story?

I decide to shrug my shoulders and casually say, "Intuition."

"Damn," he says. "Most people would be scared by that. By the way, if you're new in town, how do you know about the cross killer?"

"The news and other people talking," I say pleased with myself for coming up with something so quickly and for once sounding normal.

He gives me a suspicious look, then says, "Didn't think of that."

"So anyway, why do you pretend to be the cross killer when you're not?" I say, feeling a strange feeling, almost as if I reached a pinnacle moment in my assimilation into the story.

"I just like to fuck with that prick," he says.

"But it'll delay the killer from getting caught, causing more and more people to die while the police follow wrongful leads before they finally give this man justice," I say more out of curiosity than out of concern. After all, the more people that die, the better my story is.

He shrugs his shoulders, "Doesn't bother me. I'm not blond, attractive, or a female, so I'm definitely safe."

"But don't you feel any sense that this is wrong?" I ask.

He rolls his eyes, "What are you, a priest?"

"Alright," I say, "let's remove right and wrong from the situation. What about the effects it'll have on you?"

"What do you mean?" he says.

"I mean, being wrongfully accused, going to prison, going through the trials of being a suspect, and having your privacy violated. Doesn't that bother you?" I ask.

"Let me tell you about my typical day," he says with his eyes still glued on the women in the gym and their bouncing breasts. "I wake up; stare at these average-looking women, walk to get the same three dollar sub that I've had these past…I don't know how many years…, stare at these women some more, buy as many forties as the change in this cup permits, drink myself stupid, stare at the women some more, then go into a dark alley and rub one out while watching out for police." He looks down as if entranced in his own self-pity. "I'm bored. If whatever happens to me with those d-bags in blue changes something, the more the better. I need some excitement. And they won't hold me for long, since they won't be able to prove nothin'. I've got nothing to worry about."

"But there are cases of people being wrongfully arrested, and they stay there for tens of years," I say. "Which only adds up mathematically, that there are people who spend the rest of their lives in prison without ever getting out."

"I'm homeless," he says. "If I do end up going to prison, I'll end up having a home and food."

"What if you get the death penalty?" I reason.

"Death can't hold a candle to boredom," he says. "Death kills your body, but boredom kills your soul."

"Prison sodomy?" I'm grasping at straws. "Doesn't that bother you in the slightest?"

He laughs, "Hell, at least it's more action than I'm having right now."

I'm starting to get mad at how callous this man is about every subject whether it has to do with him or anybody else, "You do realize that you are insane."

"You're the one who sat down and talked with a complete stranger in a bad part of a town that you don't know." He smiles. "Suddenly I don't seem that crazy."

Yes, but I created you. I think. But for some reason saying this doesn't seem like such a good way to prove my sanity. Neither, I think, would it be wise to say that I created this town, every person in it, and that his whole world's existence is just a figment of my imagination, that everything he knows to be true is just my subconscious working in overdrive. No, that probably won't make me seem less crazy than he. I guess I'll have to find a different route. And I feel a little embarrassed that my imaginary friend is outsmartassing me. This is just too much. I decide to attack him in another way.

"You obviously have a disregard for authority. That much I can figure out immediately. You also don't care that people are getting killed because you have no fear of your own harm. So I'll chalk that up as lack of empathy. You feel that everyone else is worthless which could pertain to your disdain for police. Thus maybe a grandiose sense of self-worth. You mess with the police over and over again, and publicly masturbate despite the consequences as if they meant nothing, so I can say that there is some tendency to impulsivity. And my guess is that you have no qualms about consorting with criminals. All of those characteristics are traits linked with psychopathy. So I'd say that you are nothing but a sociopath who cares for no one else but yourself." I smile, content with my statement, figuring I had just managed to hit him where it hurts and arise some anger out of him.

He shrugs his shoulders, "So what made you come out here?"

I get up and walk away, dissatisfied that I didn't insult this figment of my imagination, so I give him the silent 'fuck off' treatment.

Are the rest of these encounters going to be equally as insane, or will I actually find a normal person out of this bunch of crazies? Because if I'm stuck in the nut farm, I don't know how long I can last and still maintain some resonance of sanity.

It was good that I was able to be pissed off at this guy and it seemed acceptable that I just walked away from him without answering his question, because if it weren't the case, I don't know what I would say. I've got to get to a hotel, and continue finding out about the characters tomorrow after I talk to Coralline Thomson. There are still so many questions I need answers to. What is my job? What do I say is the reason as to why I moved here? Am I married? Do I have any family? Why are there substories inside the story that I am unaware of and didn't write? And most importantly, what the hell happens if I die?

CH. 17

I've been sitting in Sunny Side Up alone since about 9:00 A.M. waiting for Coralline Thomson, or I guess Jane Young or whatever the hell I'm supposed to call her. I told the waitress that I'm holding off ordering food until my friend shows up. In the meantime I've been sipping on coffee neurotically for the past fifty some odd minutes with my mind racing at warp speed. I've been debating whether I should shrug off courtesy and simply order so I can focus on sustenance, as opposed to trying to run through a conversation that hasn't happened yet, since it's making me crazy and it seems futile due to Coralline Thomson's impossible-to-predict responses. Plus it's also making me uncomfortable because this is Richard Sweeney's diner of choice.

She left me so unprepared and left me helpless to this strange world. I have no idea of my background. Why did I move to this town? What is my backstory? What's my family situation? What's my job? And then the other questions: Why did things happen in my story that I did not write about in either my story so far or my plot outline? And most importantly; what if I die? These are questions that should have definitely been answered in our first meeting but were—for some reason beyond my knowledge—not.

I hear the quiet bell sound that tells me that someone either exited or entered the restaurant. I turn in my seat and see Coralline Thomson entering the door. She spots me, waves, mutters something to the waitress, and heads in my direction. My eyes are glued on her during her entire trip to her seat. The waitress follows her, and as she takes a seat she gives me a friendly greeting—as Jake instead of Henry—and I don't respond. I simply glare at her, staring a hole into her deceivingly innocent blue eyes. She orders a coffee and the waitress takes her leave.

Instead of watching the waitress fall out of hearing range, I continue glaring at her in silence until enough time has passed for the waitress to no longer hear our conversation. "You completely threw me into rough waters without a life vest." I have to admit I felt pretty good about that one. I had thoroughly rehearsed that line over and over in my head. After that, the conversation is pretty much a crapshoot.

"What do you mean?" she says.

"You told me to talk, but didn't give me enough preparation," I say.

"What did you need preparation for?" she asks.

"Everything," I say, anger clearly evident in my voice.

"Jake, what are you talking about?" she says. I'm even more angered that she called me 'Jake.'

I grunt in disbelief that she can't comprehend why I'm so aggravated. "Well, let's think," I say sarcastically. "For one, why did I move out here? Another good one would be, do I have any family? What's my job? Where did I move from? Am I married? Don't you think this could have been some good information to tell me before you hang me out to dry? How the hell am I supposed to talk with the characters in my story if I don't know what to tell them?"

"Make it up," she says.

"Make it up?" I say exasperated, "I could stumble over what I say, contradict myself, get myself into a hole that I can't get out of. Remember that Mark Twain quote? 'Tell the truth, you don't have to remember anything.' You should know that, with your always throwing out random quotes in lieu of actually conversing. I could get tripped up and get myself caught up in a web of lies that don't add up. Then what?"

"Jesus Christ," she says impatiently. "Aren't you an author? Is there any hint of creativity in that brain of yours? Make something up. That is your profession after all."

I'm taken back a little. This is the first time I've seen her flustered. Every time I talk to her she's always calm and level-headed, but now to see her with any remoteness of frustration brings me a mixture of satisfaction and uneasiness. I guess satisfaction because it slightly humanizes her, making her more relatable to us mortals, showing that she is not infallible and actually can experience those negative emotions. It also makes me uneasy because…well I guess because it humanizes her. Because if this story, me, and everything in it is not being watched by some all-powerful deity, then who the hell is it being watched by? Me? Now that really scares the shit out of me.

"So just make it up?" I think out loud.

"Now you're getting the hang of it," she says. "Just make it up and the story will morph around you." She pauses. "As long as you stay in the realm of probability."

"What do you mean?" I ask.

"Well if you say you're a banker that retired and came out here, the story will accept it," she says. "But if you say you're an international spy that is taking refuge here to avoid being detected by the government, it'll just chalk you up as another nut on the streets."

I take this in, thinking about it deeply. I'm starting to get less angry that I was thrown into this mess, and instead becoming fascinated by it.

She then adds, "Although I would recommend you stick to something that you know better. You know about literature and writing so I'd recommend you stay in that field so you don't get stumped. Also, as far as the family thing, I'd recommend you don't talk about them that much. Maybe say you're an only child whose parents passed away and don't have a wife, or come up with some reason why you don't have any family here. That would make things much simpler."

Interesting. Sure I can't wish it to rain and it will or cause earthquakes with my mind, but minor alterations with my character can take shape inside the story. I can't be an almighty god, but I do have minute divine powers. I am Jake Neilson: god of the monotonous.

The waitress returns with Coralline Thomson's—Jane Young's—coffee and asks us our orders. Jane orders an egg white omelet, and I order the Sunny Side Up special. It's three fried eggs (runny), crisp bacon, sausage links or patties (I chose links), cheesy hash browns, and toast with your choice of bread (I chose white). It may be a heart attack on a plate but it's a delicious heart attack on a plate.

The waitress leaves and I ask the main thing that's been on my mind these past two days, "What happens if I die?"

"I'm surprised I didn't tell you that yesterday," she says.

"So am I," I say a little impatiently.

"Well, that's where this gets interesting," she says. As if this whole situation wasn't 'interesting' enough. "Dying while in this story isn't only possible, it's essential."

I give her a perplexed look. My stomach is already feeling the preemptive sickness of fear.

"What happens when you die is you simply wake up," she says, and I feel temporarily relieved. "But you see, you will inevitably have to die sometime in this story."

"What do you mean?" That temporary calming is for the most part gone.

"You see," she says tentatively, "waking up when you die isn't just a pleasant side effect, it's a necessity." She pauses as I feel more uneasy. She's giving me the same tone that a doctor gives a patient when they're about to inform a patient that they have a terminal disease. "That's actually the only way *to* wake up." Her face looks as if she's preparing to receive a punch. "That's how you end this whole experience. You have to kill yourself."

CH. 18

My face turns grey, my stomach turns in a knot, and I'm starting to regret ordering such a large breakfast. Being sucked into a story seemed scary at first, but I was just recently becoming fascinated with it. Being able to live in a fantasy world—to literally live in it—seemed like an author's wet dream. But to actually commit suicide, to learn that death is your only salvation; that just took my fascination to a nasty turn. Everything completely turned upside down. Now instead of being filled with intrigue, I'm filled with terror. It's like when you find out the benign tumor on your elbow isn't at all benign. And now you find out that amputation is the one and only cure. That pure fear just sucks all the life out of you. Imagine that feeling. Now multiply it by a thousand.

"So... so... you've actually died?" I say in almost a whisper.

Realizing she's not going to be hit and not going to be the victim of a verbal lashing—at least for now—she unclenches her face, giving her facial muscles an unexpected respite. "Forty-three times," she says. "Forty-two have been published."

I shiver. Not only am I going to have to die, but my death is going to be published so everyone can read it without realizing they're reading someone's suicide printed on paper.

"How... how does it feel?" I ask still in that horrified whisper.

"It depends on how you do it," she says a little nervous. "I've done it so many times and in so many ways that it's hard to give an accurate description. I used to think that the bullet to the head was the best way. It was clean and quick, but that brief second where it enters your brain is incredibly painful. Now I've found that over-dosing on medication is the best way. It's best to get something that slows your heart down and lets you drift into nothingness. It's not that painful; but I won't lie, it's scary as hell. What's worse is when someone finds you or you don't take enough and you end up being stuck in some mental hospital in your story. Because this is your first time, and you might get too scared to take enough to do you in, I'd recommend you take a gun and bite the bullet." She pauses and realizes the accidental humor and the inappropriate time for it and adds, "No pun intended."

My body emits mild shaking, and I become more nauseous. Sure, occasionally suicide has crept into my head, and it's entertained my thoughts when I was in fits of depression, but never has it become something that I must inevitably do.

"Jesus," I mutter.

"If you want, I could help you when the time comes. Maybe shoot you in the back of the head the same way that George did to Lenny in <u>Of Mice and Men</u>. It's less painful and significantly less terrifying," she offers with genuine sincerity.

"Maybe," is all I can manage to say.

"Think about it this way; how many people have died and lived to tell about it?" she says with a smile trying to add some levity to this terrifying situation. Needless to say, this effort is futile.

"Right," I say with a feigned smile. At this point I want to desperately change the subject and deal with this only when I have to. I don't want to think about this, even though I know it's inevitable. I'd rather push it out of my mind for as long as I can. "I still have other questions."

"Alright," she says in less of that calming carefree nature that used to aggravate me so, that now I find myself missing.

"I've noticed some oddities while I was talking to some people," I begin, but that suicide is still on my mind. I make a conscious effort to sound as if it's not plaguing me constantly. "Things have happened in my story that I didn't write down. Characters that I didn't create. Past encounters that I am oblivious to. How can that happen?"

She sighs, and speaks less in that know-it-all voice that I have become so fond of. "Your subconscious is more powerful than your conscious mind. What you know or do in real life pales in comparison to what your inner mind can contain. Just as there are cases of someone with multiple personality disorder that have their alter-egos being more knowledgeable about different subjects or having a broader vocabulary than their regular personality; that too can happen in here. You can be talking to someone who uses a word accurately or states a fact that you don't know, but somewhere along your life you learned it, and while you may not know it, some part of your mind retains it. That's just an example on how impressive the subconscious can be. When you created the story, you only wrote certain characters and planned certain events, but deep inside your mind you've created an entire city with all the inhabitants and all of their backstories. The mind is so complex that even the most intelligent man that ever lived with the most advanced technology can't discern even a mere percent of its glory. That will never happen. With all our technological advances, and all our further exploration in the brain, we will never have a clue what is going on inside our own minds."

I'm starting to wish that I could just shoot the proverbial shit with the only person who actually knows who I am in this town, instead of every time a conversation comes up, it's about suicide or some psychological mumbo-jumbo about the subconscious. Whatever happened to talking about football?

"So," I say, "I have already created an entire story of every single thing in this town even though I'm completely unaware of it?"

"The mind is a magnificent thing," She says.

I decide to move onto a different subject to keep myself from thinking that I will have to eventually end my own life in order to retain sanity. "So if I'm only experiencing this world through my eyes, and I'm merely a minor character in this story, how does my body manage to write about all the happenings of the story told through the characters that I don't see at the time?"

"Yes," she says, "you in your physical form in the story may only be aware of a percentage of what is going on, but still the span of your mind is able to gather what is going on, including what you don't see, and your body in the real world writes all of that information down. You see, everything that happens in this story, regardless of whether or not you actually notice it, is a creation of your mind. The story is something that you have fathomed in your imagination, so everything that happens in it, your subconscious will capture. And since your body in real life is on autopilot and the only thing that is operating it *is* your subconscious, it will capture and be aware of all of it." She pauses as I stare, trying to comprehend this. "As I said, the mind is a magnificent thing."

I take in all of this. The fact that my mind can operate in a way that my conscious can't understand, how it can create things that I am unaware of, and how my actual body in real life can capture all of this insanity and write it into a story, I am bewildered by the complexities of the mind. I guess there's nothing much else you can do but shrug your shoulders and think *the mind is a magnificent thing.*

There was one thing that has been taking up brain space

that I figured I might as well ask because it's something to discuss and thus delay my mind from focusing on my inevitable suicide. "Something I've been wondering about. When Isaac Thorn created this... chemical compound, couldn't he have made a lot more money selling it to the government or something? I know he made a lot of money as an author, but couldn't he have made more just selling it?"

"Yes," she says. "Absolutely he could have. And he thought of that for quite a while. But then he was fearful of the reaction to someone who isn't brought into it under proper guidance, and of course how the government could pervert it."

"What do you mean?" I ask.

"Well," she says, "there are two components to that statement, so I will answer both of them separately. The first is if someone isn't under proper guidance." She pauses. "Are you familiar with lysergic acid diethylamide?"

"What?" I ask.

"LSD," she says.

"Oh," I say, feeling stupid for not knowing the acronym. "Well I've never taken it, but yes I know a little bit about it."

"Well," she says, "when it originated, it was initially used for therapeutic purposes. Scientists used it to try to treat psychopaths and schizophrenics—not the brightest idea in the scientific community might I add—as well as several other treatments. Through guided therapy, they successfully cured some people of alcoholism and several other forms of addiction. The problem with it was that it was hard to use the correct form of therapy. And in some cases it caused paranoia and people went into a state of terror. This still happens today when people use it illegally. Some have the most beautiful experiences that they'll ever feel in their lives, and others will feel nothing but an intense amount of horror." I think back to when I saw a couple of my friends on acid, and remember one of them suddenly became incredibly paranoid. As soon as his paranoia emerged, the other two—who were before that moment in pure bliss—immediately turned terror-stricken. "The ambience during that experience plays an enormous role. The music you listen to or the words that you hear or the actions you see can decide whether or not you will be in heaven or hell. It's a bit of a stretch because this chemical that we've taken is in no way like LSD, but it can be much more damaging if under the wrong management. Just take into consideration what happened to Phillip Arnold. Imagine if someone wasn't here to guide you through this experience. To give you warnings about what you should and shouldn't do, and help you out on your first endeavor. You would be in the purest form of confusion and fear, and that confusion and fear would lead to torment."

I'm getting more scared of this chemical all the time. Only five people in all of history have ever taken it, and what she's telling me isn't exactly putting me at ease.

"Next is the government's perversion of everything that is put out for the benefit of mankind," she says. "Isaac was most scared of that. He realized that once we were able to split and smash and mold atoms, we built the atomic bomb. And whenever we create new medications, they get tested out on innocent animals and then, when we find out that it's good enough on rats, we try it out on the poor. His science fiction mind pictured a world where his chemical could be used to create an alternate reality to help perfect soldiers into killing machines once they become desensitized to killing. All you have to do is tell the people that while they're under that state, the people that they kill aren't real. They perfect their warfare. They perfect their killing. And once they come out of the drug induced trance, they are used to killing. Real or not real doesn't seem to matter once you've killed enough people with real terror and real agony on their face. Desensitized killing. That's how to create super soldiers. It's cynical to think that that is what our government would do, but cynical or not, it's probably true. So that's why he decided to keep his creation a secret. He may not have had as much money, but at least he could sleep easier."

The waitress comes up and gives us our food and we remain silent except for our appreciation of the food. Still I'm thinking of suicide: that horrible ending to this mental exploration.

I think of something to say, "But don't you think it's cheating?"

"What?" she says.

"This whole chemical creating our novels," I say. "We're not doing the real work. Our body's typing away while we roam around just talking to people and literally living a fantasy."

"Either write something worth reading, or do something worth writing," she says.

"What?" I say.

"Benjamin Franklin," she says.

"Jesus Christ. Not this again," I say.

"But think about it. We are doing something worth writing. We're living in this world, experiencing things no one else experiences," she says. "And we are more active in directing our stories than most writers."

I don't say anything. I just roll my eyes.
We finish up our meals and head out. She says we'll meet again tomorrow at the same time. I'm left alone with my thoughts with two things going through my mind: my inevitable suicide, and desensitized killing. And I can't help but wonder if the two can be interchangeable.

CH. 19

Oh how far I've come. Just a week ago I spent my days in a dive bar getting drunk with my friends, and now here I am, in a fictional dive bar getting drunk with strangers that aren't even real. Also, I can't help but wonder if my brain in real life is suffering any of the damage from all the alcohol. I spent a lot of time wondering how different actions I take as alter-ego Jake Neilson influence real-world Henry Riddick recently. I know now that I've been liberated from the chains of reality, that I could be doing anything, and here I am sitting in a hole-in-the-wall bar drinking. But Coralline Thomson told me to socialize with this world's inhabitants, and I feel most myself with a drink in my hand.

I'm talking with this guy Howie. All I got of his last name was some drunken mumble that I couldn't comprehend and I felt it would be impolite to ask him again. He's a person that I believe could be quite bright if his brain wasn't so pickled. From the few coherent statements he makes, you can tell there's a hint of intelligence there.

From what I'm able to make out of Howie Mumbles, he's talking about how years back, Australia had to not allow the bars to be open on Election Day, because alcohol skews the voter's political preference. A study showed that drunk or slow minds had a tendency to lean right.

"Now there's some exceptions t' the rule," he garbles out. "I for instance, I am a flaming liberal *and* a staunch drunk. And nothin' really seems like (incoherent mumbles) change that." Then he mutters something and all I'm able to make out is "fuckin' AA."

He slips in and out of coherency for the rest of the conversation touching on gay marriage, abortion, racism, taxes, and many other policies. I'm someone that considers myself left of center, but Howie Mumbles is best described as left of liberal and a self-proclaimed staunch drunk. Still I remain polite in this conversation, agree (honestly) with most of what he talks about, and don't try to do anything to entice any severe emotions out of him. I'm well-rehearsed with dealing with the intoxicated.

I've found there are three main rules when talking to a drunken stranger. Rule number one: let the drunk do most the talking. Just nod your head and agree with him. Rule number two: laugh at his jokes and anytime he laughs. Rule number three: do not try to take away his alcohol. It's surprising how many people break this rule, and I've seen some catastrophes when people do. When you break one of these rules, you risk breaking your nose.

He pounds another three drinks and hits the road.

"S' ya round," he says, and without another word he's out the door. My eyes follow him out the door wondering what role he plays in the story. Maybe nothing. Maybe he's just an extra.

"You pick some interesting folks to start a conversation with." I hear a voice to my left. I turn around to see a familiar face chewing something.

"Detective Reynolds," I say surprised.

"In the flesh," he says. "Howie's a unique flavor of drunk."

I laugh, "Yeah it wasn't hard to pick out that he's an alcoholic-"

"Not an *alcoholic*," he cuts me off. "A *drunk*. Alcoholics either have done or are doing something about it. He's not. Last time he was in AA, he went into the corner, thinking it was the bathroom, and pissed right there. The only reason he went was because his wife gave him an ultimatum. Either get help, or she's taking off. So much good that effort did after that stunt."

"You know him?" I ask.

"Know him?" The detective lights up, "Hell, the cell is pretty much his second home. He's not there that long, he's pretty much a good guy and quite bright when he's not intoxicated, which is never, but he does quite a bit of stupid stuff when he's wasted."

"And from what I'm able to gather, 'when he's wasted' rivals 'when he's sober,'" I say.

"Rivals?" he says, "Ha! Surpasses it." He changes the subject, "So anyway, what brings you out here?"

"Well you know, I'm new, so I figured I'd hit a bar and try to meet people," I say.

He laughs. "I could have guessed that. I mean *this town*. What brings you to this town?"

"Oh." I laugh at my own stupidity. I then tell him my backstory, blurring fact and fiction as I go along. I tell him about how I was a high school English teacher (untrue) whose dad died when I was young of cirrhosis of the liver (true), and I just broke up with a woman who cheated on me (untrue). My dog Sparky had recently got run over by a car (untrue and completely unnecessary in retrospect), and my mom who had been fighting lung cancer (untrue) had finally died. She left me some inheritance money and with my life in shambles and nothing to look forward to (somewhat true), I decided to move from New York, New York, (state: true, city: untrue) and find somewhere else to start over. I felt that, if something didn't change, that suicide was a possibility (true).

"Well," he says, "Sorry to hear about... well I guess about everything."

"How about you?" I ask.

"What do you mean?" he says.

I say, "How did you end up becoming a detective?"

"The question you're looking for is *why*, not *how*." His gaze drops to his drink. "And it's an interesting but long story."

"I've got time," I say.

Originally he had no idea what he wanted to be when he was in high school, he tells me. He was friends with two of his classmates, Laura and Arty, but he wasn't as close to them as they were to each other. "I swear, those two were joined at the hip. Neither of them were so open with their problems. That's what I liked about them so much. Kids today, every time something mildly upsetting happens to them, they announce it to the world or bitch about it on Facebook. These two didn't say shit. And every day they'd have these big ol' smiles on their faces. I loved those smiles. Then one day Laura doesn't have that smile when she comes into school. I could sense then that something was wrong. I asked her if she was ok, and she said she was just tired. I let it go and didn't think much about it after that. But the next day she didn't have that smile and she looked terrible once again—not physically, but emotionally. And I tell you, either something happened or she suddenly came down with a horrid case of insomnia because that smile never returned. She smiled later, but not *that* smile."

He tilts back his beer, taking a hefty swallow, then places it back on the bar with a mild thud. He wipes off some spilled foam from his lips, looks down deep in thought, and then continues, "That innocent smile was gone. Now, I knew the only person she would ever tell if something big happened was Arty, her closest friend. So after a couple of months roll by, I ask him if one of her family members died and why she doesn't seem the same, and he said he didn't know anything. But I knew it was a lie. I could sense it. Then one day, a couple of years later, after we graduate, I'm talking to them, and I ask them if they ever read the book <u>The Hotel New Hampshire</u>. She says she started but she didn't finish. I ask, 'Why? It was a good book.' And she says that something came up. And Arty says to her, 'Yeah I should have known better.' I pause and think for a second. And the memory of her coming in the day the smile left her, pale, quiet, and red in the eyes hits me. I think of what The Hotel New Hampshire would have in it, and then it hits me: rape. And I think to myself, oh my god, she was raped. I have no way of proving it, and I may be way off, but that's what I thought. And that's when I realized that I needed to help people for a living. So on that day I decided I would be a psychologist."

"A psychologist?" I ask confused.

He lets out a laugh, but a sad laugh. One that's been poisoned by depressing memories. "Let me finish," he says. "On my second year of studying psychology, I had a life changing incident. It appears that I would have a number of them before I die." He mumbles that last sentence to himself, but I still manage to hear it and I think about the crash that happened to him that killed his wife and son. "Well, while I was in school, I made a new friend, and I was hoping soon to make a move. She was beautiful, smart, kind, funny, everything you could dream about in a woman. Sometimes it was hard to believe that she was even real." I had to restrain a laugh right there. "But even though I never had the chance to ask her out, we were still great friends. And then one day I read the news that she got in a car accident, hit and run. After ricocheting off the car, she smashed into tree. She didn't die on the spot though. She still had about an hour and change of agony before she kicked the bucket. And I realized that there was nothing I could do as a psychologist to help her at that point. And I realized that I wasn't depressed, that didn't come 'till later. I was pissed. At that moment I decided to drop out and sign up for the police academy. I wanted to catch the scum of this town. That motherfucker who raped Laura, and that coward who killed Sally and then fled the scene. I wanted them to fry!" He flails his arm in excitement, spraying a bit of beer on the bar, but doesn't seem to notice, "I realized that my perceptiveness on picking things up that others wouldn't notice, like <u>The Hotel New Hampshire</u> thing, would come in handy. After that I climbed up the ranks to detective and the rest is history."

We talk for a little longer. I can tell by his voice that he was surprised that he told all these things to a relative stranger, but we continued to talk until he left saying, "I gotta get to bed sometime. Gotta work early tomorrow." I nodded and reciprocated his farewell. I learned a lot about him. Hopefully that will help the story. While talking, I was observing him, to learn more about him, and I got the feeling that he was doing the same to me.

I look around, trying to find someone else to talk to. So far this has been a successful night I feel. Well, as successful as one can be getting drunk at a bar. I see someone sitting at the corner of the bar, resting his head on the counter, lifting it up only to drink large gulps of whiskey. Even when he calls the barkeep for more, his head doesn't leave the table. His beard is wild, his hair not combed, his belly protruding, and his face glistening with sweat.

He seems oddly familiar. That deja-vu feeling is strong again. I figure if that's the case, he must be someone of importance to the story. I walk over to him and extend my hand which I realize is futile because he can't see me with his head resting on the table like that and his face looking the other way.

In a friendly manner I say, "Hi. I'm-"

"Piss off," he mutters.

"I'm sorry?" I'm vexed at his less than kind introduction.

"I said 'piss off,'" he says not as much angrily as much as matter-of-factly.

Not sure how to respond, "I'm Jake Neilson."

He's now getting that drunken agitation. "And I'm Ron, and I want you to piss off." He slugs down his whiskey, turns to the bartender and shouts "Whiskey!" then drops his head against the table loud enough to make a thud.

Oh my god, I think and blurt out uncontrollably, "Hank!" I bring myself back and say, "I mean Ron."

He looks back at me, or at least in my general direction, and says, "What part of 'piss off' don't you understand?" Then he heads off to the bathroom muttering something about a "fuckin' dipshit." I presume he means me.

But in my head I can't believe it. That was Hank Wiseman—or at least an alter-ego of him. I'm laughing to myself. I was just conversing with my alternative future's alter-ego. This is rich.

How does this work? Why did that person seem so much like Hank? It couldn't have been coincidence. I'll have to talk to Coralline Thomson about that. Will there be more of these alter-egos. Will all my friends and everybody I know be in my story in some whacked out way. I go back to my seat laughing, probably looking strange, but I don't care. I'm stuck thinking about all of this. Maybe I won't miss my friends too much after all, if they're all here in some way or another.

Sitting at the bar smiling to myself, content in my own thoughts, I hear a woman's voice, "You're not from around here are you?"

I look to the source of this voice and see what I can only describe as beauty personified. Long legs, perfect breasts, not thin but not fat, blond hair, but what really gets me is the face: angular, but not too definitive to subvert her physical flawlessness; hazel eyes that look as if they can reach deep into your soul and see the good in the most wretched human being; and a full smile that stretches cheek to cheek.

I smile back, "What makes you think that?"

Still with that magnificent smile, Aphrodite says, "Well you came here by yourself; you seem friendly enough that you shouldn't have to do that. You're drinking, but not incredibly heavily so I'm going to knock off bad break-up and alcoholic from the list. The three people you talked to are not those that most people would normally start a conversation with, making you either a terrible decision maker or a foreigner. And those three people you talked to were all men, so you're not here to pick up women."

"I could always be gay," I say coyly.

"Yes," she says, "but there's a gay bar just down the street." She pauses and broadens her smile. "And you do not dress nearly well enough."

I laugh, "You caught me. Guilty as charged. I'm new here. You've got quite the detective skills you know."

"Not really," she says, "I just heard your conversation with detective Reynolds and bullshitted the rest." She laughs the sweetest laugh and I join her in my not-so-sweet laugh.

"Fair enough. Jake Neilson." I extend my hand.

She accepts it. "Adeline Stewart."

"So," I say, "What do you do Adeline?"

"I'm a professor," she states.

"What do you teach?" I ask.

"English," she says.

"As do I," I kind of lie.

"Well isn't that a granfalloon," she says.

"Kurt Vonnegut fan, eh?" I respond.

She puts her face in an O as if to say 'oh my god.' "No one ever gets that! They all look at me with that 'what the hell is she talking about?' look on their face."

I smile at being the one to have caused this much jubilation on her face. "One of the best author's ever, I'd say."

"*The* best, I'd say," she says, her smile getting wider. "Who's your author of choice?"

"Coralline Thomson, hands down," I say, so glad that I'm not lying for once.

"Excellent choice," she says. "So you're a professor too, what brings you out here. I don't think it would be a job transfer."

"High school teacher actually," I say and then relay to her the fictional tale of woe that brought me out here, this time leaving out the dog getting run over by the car. Adding it the first time wasn't necessary, and turned my story into less of a reason for leaving and more of a country song.

"Sorry to hear about all that," She says with what looks like sincerity. We talk for quite a bit more, and then she asks me what I like to do for leisure. I tell her pool, and she says, "Well, there's a pool table right over there." She uses her thumb to gesture to a section of the bar that has a vacant table. I tell her I'm willing, and she places a finger on my shoulder and blurts out, "But... If we play pool, I want to make it interesting."

"How so?" I say. And a part of me is thinking, *please be something sexual. Please be something sexual.*

"Thirty bucks?" she says.

"I'm in," I say.

I originally think I'm going to let her win in a way of politeness, but after she breaks and makes her fourth ball straight, with none of them being easy shots, I realize I don't have to. She beats me with me trying my hardest. Part of me is thinking in a misogynistic way, *I can't believe you got beat by a woman.* Then I rationalize, *well she is a fictional woman, so it's not like you really got beat.*

After some more friendly banter, she says she has to go. Her friend who wanted to go out and meet some guy after her boyfriend cheated on her has drank too much and is acting a fool.

"Sorry to leave you, but I've got a drunken friend to take care of," she says and then gives me an uninvited but not unwelcomed hug. "I hope to see you again." She starts to head to the door.

"So do I," I say.

And I really do (true).

CH. 20

It's interesting how much people open up to strangers when they're at someone's wake. I guess that overdose of pent-up emotion just needs to leak somehow. Maybe a stranger is the best person to open up to since the chances of them seeing you again are closer to nil than the chance of seeing a well-trusted friend. Then again, Coralline Thomson did say that people in this world are more willing to open up to me about things they normally would keep secret.

"Think about it this way," she said. "When people in the real world have some kind of issue they would like to keep secret, what do they do?" When time lapsed in my failure to respond she answered herself, "They pray. They talk to their ideal version of God. Do any of them really know what God's—if there is one—desire or thought process is? No, of course not. Granted, many think they have an idea, but deep down they know they are clueless of God's intentions. A part of them, whether they admit it or not, realizes that God is a complete stranger to them. But that belief that they are talking to God comforts them in some way that they don't feel with anyone else. And if you really think about it, you're the people of this world's God in a way. So maybe a part of them in their subconscious knows that you are their creator and they are willing to open up to you with ease. That's at least my theory." I was left wondering about the fact that my subconscious' manifestations also have a subconscious. *The mind is a magnificent thing*, I think to myself. But then again, maybe Coralline Thomson just likes to say 'subconscious' a lot.

Anyway, for whatever reason, these inhabitants feel the need to open up to me, which makes my job of extracting information from them so much easier. And with all these emotions flying around at this wake, I've hit the jackpot. But I suppose it's important to understand how I got to this wake in the first place.

About a week ago, after another one of my long and confusing morning conversations with Coralline Thomson, I had to ask her why the man at the bar, Ron, was so similar to Hank Wiseman. She explained that sometimes these stories create what she calls a 'Wizard of Oz effect.' Certain people that I know in the real world, for no particular rhyme or reason, will manifest into characters in my story. "Some will be easier to notice than others," she says, "while others will come to you over time. Some you may not even notice your entire time down here. Then again, it could be possible that he's the only one. The alter-egos don't even have to look or talk anything like their real life hosts, you'll just notice odd similarities that will make you realize that these are the people you know from the real world." God, how the hell can anyone get used to this way of life?

Later on that day I went to the bar, looking for Ron in hopes to start up a conversation with him, but he wasn't there. So I ask the bartender if he knows where he is, "Excuse me, do you know about a man named Ron? I can't remember his last name, but he was a bigger guy with quite a large beard and a little bit of a drinker. I was hoping to talk to him about something."

He stares at me for a little and says, "You haven't heard?" He then reaches under the bar, pulls out a newspaper and slaps it in front of me. "His last name's Madsen," he says. I look at the paper and see it open to the obituaries. Ah shit. There go my chances.

Well what the hell, I think. Might as well read it. A large section was written by his wife.

"Ron Madsen was found dead at ten in the morning of July 27th the way everyone would have suspected: choked to death on his own vomit. I wish I could say he was a good man, a loving father and so forth, but really he wasn't any of that. He was a selfish drunk that spent everyday drinking in his self-pity, complaining that no one loved him and people never gave him a chance and wah-wah-wah. His son and daughter will always know him as the guy with vomit on his clothes that read them to sleep a total of two times, in which he passed out mid-way through. He was horrible to everyone who was kind enough to give his sorry ass a chance and even worse to his family. If there is an after-life, he's probably burning in the deepest sewer of hell. If you feel the need to see the biggest collection of lowlifes and idiotic drunks, the dates and times for the services are listed below. I guess I'll be there too. He was a hated father, a despised husband, and will be missed by no one."

"Wow," I say, "They allowed her to print that?"

The bartender looks up after pouring a drink to some patron. "She's good friends with the publisher of the paper. There was a rumor that they're having an affair." He then mutters to himself, but loud enough for others to overhear, "But I guess the word affair isn't right anymore because her husband's dead."

"No," someone pipes up, "I'm pretty sure that it's still an affair if the widow had started sleeping with the person during the time of marriage."

"You're both wrong," another man says, "Affair just means that two people are sleeping together. The fact that either person has to be married is a common misconception."

"Are you kidding?" a third man joins the argument,

"Marriage and affair go hand in hand, at least linguistically. You have to be married in order for there to be an affair. The affair goes on as long as the two that are together have one that is cheating, and ends either when he or she stops cheating or the marriage comes to an end."

"Whatever," the bartender says. "Anyway, it's a dying paper anyhow. They can pretty much print anything they want now because they'll be out of business by the end of the year. No one reads the papers now with the internet and whatnot."

A thought manages to creep into my head. I didn't write anything about Ron Madsen. He was just a random person to inhabit this world. What if his death is because I found out that real life Hank Wiseman died, and my subconscious killed off his alter-ego in response?

"So tell me," one of the men says to another, "what about divorce? Is it still an affair if they are sleeping with someone after they get married?"

What if I'll never be able to go to Hank Wiseman's actual funeral because I'm in this state? And even if I do go, will I remember any of it?

"If they started the affair during marriage, then yes."

"It's an affair no matter when you have sex!"

"I've been overhearing this whole thing. Yes, it is a misconception that affairs can only happen in marriage, but the truth is marriage is the only time you can have sex with someone and have it not be an affair."

"What are you talking about?"

"If you're having sex with someone who you're wedded to, then that's not an affair. Every other case of sex is an affair."

"You're crazy."

I decide I need to go to Ron Madsen's wake.

So that leads me to about a week later back here at the funeral home at the wake. So far I've talked to several people, and because of the person who they're here to mourn, I've been able to see all flavors of insanity. Many of them with premature wrinkles caused by alcohol and drug abuse, making them look decades older than their actual age. Most of them are drunk or high currently. I've even seen a couple of them pull out flasks when they believe no one can see them in the corner. There's a couple of people from the bar including Howie Mumbles. He came up near-blubbering to me about how much he misses Ron. He's slightly more coherent than the first time I talked to him, but it's still hard to make out what he says. I did decipher him saying that it's so hard when all the memories you have with your friend are blacked-out. Out of the whole lot, I'd say the widow is the most kept-together. She doesn't look that depressed even. If I were to put any emotion to her, I'd say she looks pissed. She looks like the kind of person that is somewhere because it's her duty, but hates the fact that she has to be here at all. In fact, that's probably just the case.

    A fairly attractive woman bumps into me and scatters my train of thought. "Oops," she giggles, "my bad." Then she giggles some more. You don't need a canine unit to figure out that she's high as a kite and probably has some more on her.

    "It's ok," I say and we start to talk. At first she starts to string her words together slowly as if each word was a difficult task, and as she grows accustomed to her high, the words flow out more naturally—granted, accompanied by her fair share of giggles.

    "You know, he was actually my first you know," she says. "I haven't seen him in like—hehe—I don't know, fourteen…sixteen years. But there I was in high school and uh… but I still decided to come because I was—you know—hehe—a virgin before him. We—uh—he was uh, I was a freshman and he was a…junior? Or maybe he was a senior. I don't know, but we snuck out and we were in his car and uh I think Paint it Black was playing. Strange song to lose your virginity to, don't ya think? Well anyway, Paint it Black was playing, and well…you can guess the rest."

"Yeah," I say, "I think I got it-"

"We fucked," she says and then roars in laughter.

Then she looks up suddenly and wanders off without saying a word, constantly looking up at something behind me for split seconds and fidgeting with her dress. I turn around and see detective Todd Reynolds greeting someone near the entrance. I now feel weird in here too. He knows that I'm new here and don't know anyone, so if he sees me he'll wonder what the hell I'm doing here. And what am I going to tell him? I try to walk away and then see another familiar face. A slender, tall man with blue eyes, acting normal in comparison to the fellow occupants of this funeral home, enters. I know him. I've avoided talking to him, but I definitely know him. It's Richard Sweeney.

He smiles and chats with some people then maneuvers through the funeral home. Then his eyes fix on something. I follow his eyes and they're fixed on the stoned woman I was just talking to. I register everything. She's attractive, blond, and now in potential danger. And if I don't warn her or intervene, something will happen.

First Rule: Always remember that the only things that are real in this world are me and you.

I know this but she was so nice. She may have been stoned but she has an innocent heart. I can't let her die.

Everything and everyone else is a product of your imagination. They are illusions. Quirks of your subconscious that are alive only in this world of your imagination.

Yes, but she's innocent. She may not be real in the traditional sense of the word, but how do we know she doesn't feel some sort of pain?

This is incredibly important to remember for the sake of your sanity.

Alright, alright, I get it. I won't intervene.

I see the woman walking worriedly around, giving continuous glances up at detective Reynolds as she bumps into things neurotically. I give a glance at the detective and realize as soon as his eyes dart away from my glance, that he's been looking at me. My eyes settle back on Richard Sweeney, who's fantasizing sadistically with his eyes on the stoned woman who's making quick glances at detective Reynolds who's sizing me up, trying to figure out what I'm doing here. We continue this stare fest for quite a while until I bump into a man reeking of cigarettes and cheap booze.

"Sorry about that," I say automatically.

The grey haired man smiles, revealing a few missing teeth and says, "What do you get when you combine one Jew and four Germans."

Classy. Racist jokes at a wake. "I don't know," I say, trying to get away.

"A dead kike." He then erupts in laughter.

I back away as a black man puts his hand on this man's shoulder, and the guy brushes the man's hand away as if he was brushing off poison. "Look," the black man says, "This isn't the time to be a bigot. Somebody died, and there are people of all ages here. We don't want to hear your racist jokes right now. Have some respect for the dead."

The grey haired man says, "If apples hang from apple trees, and bananas hang from banana trees, what hangs from a maple tree?"

The black man turns away but the grey haired man grabs his shoulder so the man turns around and the grey haired man grins and says right in his face, "Niggers," and bursts into laughter again. The other man turns around and the semi-toothed man shouts, "Don't turn away from me you fucking jungle bunny," and punches him right in the face.

The black man socks the grey haired man back causing his nose to make a crunching sound. Blood drips down the man's face as others join the fight. Some are friends of one of the two originally fighting, but a lot of the people joining just appreciate a good brawl. I decide that this is my cue to leave. I walk out the door and light up a cigarette. I start walking down the street and make it to the curb when I see a familiar face walking. A much more sane face than anybody in that funeral home. And after today, sanity is just what the doctor ordered.

"Adeline!" I shout, and before she can turn I ditch my cigarette and pop a mint flavored tic tac in my mouth.

She walks over to me, "Last time I saw you, I was taking your money."

"You got lucky," I laugh. "And I was a little rusty."

"Sounds like you want a round two," she says.

"Double or nothing?" I say.

"You're on," she says. "But I can't talk now, I have to meet someone for lunch and I'm already late. How about Tuesday, at eight at the billiards hall?"

"Sure, but I'm not from around here. What's it called?" I ask.

She laughs once again with that angelic laugh. "It's called 'The Billiards Hall.' Do you need directions?"

"I'll find it. You look like you're in a hurry," I say.

"Alright," she says, "See ya then, and I'll be thirty dollars richer."

I laugh, "We'll see."

"Alright," she says, "Tuesday at eight. It's a date."

We say good bye and she walks away, and I'm left feeling a sense of serenity that I haven't felt in quite a long time. I can't pinpoint what exactly I'm feeling, but all I know is that I feel great. She hurries off to her friend and I smile in anticipation of Tuesday night. Then I hear a large thud behind me followed by several shrieks and someone in the funeral home shouting "Jesus Christ!" (I think it was the priest). Then other shouts accompany him with "Get him back in! Get him back in!" and "You dipshit, you broke the coffin!" It really isn't difficult to decipher what's happening in there. I can only imagine the trauma Ron's kids will have when they see their dad's corpse rolling on the floor of the funeral home. I then see the widow leaving the funeral home with a cigarette already lit in her mouth saying, "I didn't expect that, but I'm not surprised."

I wonder how Hank's wake was—that is if he died as well—in the real world. It can't be as crazy as this, but I imagine it would have its fair share of interesting characters.

I'm left thinking about this, my first time experiencing death in this created world, and I can't help but think that this won't be my last experience with death when I'm in here. And then I remember Coralline Thomson telling me about how I have to die to leave this world, and that one of the prominent characters in this whole thing is a serial killer, and I think to myself, *No shit Sherlock.*

CH. 21

There's no doubt in my mind: that last game of pool at the bar the first time we met was no fluke; Adeline is much better than me. To even the odds, her partner is her friend Alice who's worse than me, where my partner is Alice's boyfriend Steve, whose skill ranges somewhere in-between mine and Adeline's. Both of our partners are great people to be around, and significantly more normal than any of my friends in real life. The sane people in this town might be few and far between, but as crazy as my mind is, I can still create a few relics of normality.

"So to someone viewing this place as a likely possibility of living in, what can you tell me about it?" I say as I flub up a two ball streak, giving Adeline an easy shot.

"Well, I've grown accustomed to it. Yeah, there's quite a bit of wackos here," Adeline says, analyzing her next shot, "but it sure as hell beats where I come from."

"Oh," I say somewhat surprised, "so you're not from here originally?"

She circles the table to view the shot from another angle. It's an easy shot, but she's trying to see how she can gauge her shot so she's got another ball lined up after she sinks this one in. "Nope. I came from a small town in Missouri before this." She sinks the ball, setting herself up for another.

"Really?" I say, "If you don't mind me asking, what brought you out here?"

"Well," she says circling the table once again, "I met this guy, Randy, my freshman year of college."

"He was such a prick," Alice pipes in. "How were you not able to tell then is what I'm wondering."

"I was young and naïve to love. It happens. Anyway," Adeline returns to her original story with my peaked interest attentive, "we dated all the way through college and I found out he lived in the next town over, and with all that monotonous small-town lifestyle, and nothing really to do, we got a little stir crazy." She knocks another ball in, setting herself up for a significantly harder but still plausible shot. "So we decided to travel America, just going from place to place."

"Where'd you go?" I ask.

She laughs, "Where didn't we go? From California to Texas, to Wisconsin, to New York, we pretty much traveled the continental United States. Anyway, he was a little weird-"

"You can say that again," Alice interrupts.

Adeline laughs and circles the table once again. Now I'm wondering if she has incredible skill at this game, or if this table circling is some sort of obsessive compulsive ritual. "Well, he was a little weird," she says apparently obliging Alice, "and he would think that he would feel some kind of aura or calling once he reaches his destined place to live in. So we traveled and traveled, and sooner or later we came here. Finally he said he felt that calling. He knew that he would find something here. And he did," she says lining up her shot. "Her name was Jackie." She sinks the ball in.

"Sorry to hear about that. What made you stay here?" I ask

"Well, before he started seeing her—or at least before I found out—I had already lived here for over a year and a half, got a job as a professor, and made a lot of friends. Plus my sister,

Lucy, moved up here too." She laughs that sweet laugh. "She never really could stop following me, literally."

She finishes circling the table, and I see no way that she can make anything in. She analyzes it a little more. I say, "Looks like you're out of tricks here."

Punctuating each word, she says, "You are underestimating the capability of human ingenuity." She says that last word with great satisfaction as she hits the cue ball, bouncing off of three walls, clipping one of her solid balls, but still missing the shot. "Damn," she says. "That would have sounded a lot cooler if I made it in."

I hear what she told me about her college sweetheart dragging her across the states, settling her down in an unknown place, and running off with another woman. I feel genuine empathy for her and wish that I could help her in some way.

First Rule: Always remember that the only things that are real in this world are me and you.

Oh shut up, will you.

The game ends with Adeline carrying Alice's poor pool playing to victory. Granted they still won, but with Alice weighing Adeline down, and Steve boosting my playing up, the end result doesn't look as humiliating as the first time Adeline and I faced off mano y mano. We only have one ball left on the table, but I still feel emasculated in a way. Two men beat by two women in pool. Even I, who view myself as someone beyond sexism, can't help but let these thoughts creep in.

"Well," I say, "I guess, I'll get this pitcher."

"No, don't worry about it," Steve says. "I got it. You get the next one."

"Are you sure?" I say. "I could get this."

"I'm sure. Don't worry about it," Steve says.

Alice laughs, "Typical male chauvinism. Each one urging to pay for the next round in front of the women, as if we would swoon over the excess of money that they have that they can afford a whole pitcher. If it was just them around, they'd be trying to pawn off the responsibility to the other."

"Chauvinism?" I say.

"Sorry," Adeline says apologetically, "Alice here has never learned the art of saying thanks. She's too busy trying to be a feminist and saying that all things that men do are in some way sexist."

"Oh come on," Alice says. "'Feminist' as an insult? I thought better of you. Secondly, it has nothing to do with feminism. I'm just someone who's well-rehearsed in male psychology. I kind of have to be as a psychology professor."

"You really think you got us nailed down," I say.

"To a tee," she says. "The entire culture is based off of male's perpetuating their own ego in a manner that borders misogyny. Yes, there have been magnificent strides in eliminating that sexism with women getting the right to vote, and people over time accepting that women are equals, but that misogynistic society is still prevalent." I see Adeline rolling her eyes. "Men think that women are frail creatures that need the door opened for them, and need protecting because men are obsessed with the 'rescuing a damsel in distress' fantasy. Plus they feel that they can bed a woman with the simplicity of flaunting their wealth by showing they can do the simplest task of buying them a drink or a necklace or whatnot."

There's some silence and then I say, "If buying a woman a drink constitutes as misogyny, then I wouldn't mind a misandrist society."

Adeline and Steve erupt in laughter. Even Alice smiles.

"Alright," Steve says, "on that note, I'm going to go get the pitcher."

Alice pipes up, "Just remember that you're buying this because you lost and not to feed your pig-headed egotistical male brain."

"Oh, and *we're* the sexists," I say, and I get the opportunity to hear Adeline's wonderful laugh again.

Steve leaves to get the beer and I decide that, despite an undefinable urge to talk to and learn more about Adeline, I figure I'd dig into Alice's past. After all, that's my job in this story isn't it?

Alice has lived here since birth and has always had a deep fascination with psychology. Her younger brother has a slew of mental and emotional disorders which had only solidified her decision that she wanted to help people with similar ailments. She originally wanted to become a psychologist but decided along the way to teach it instead. "I don't know if I'm cut out to be a psychologist," she says. "I probably have the potential to be good at it, but I couldn't bear hearing all those issues, and I am the type of person that wouldn't be able to shake the feeling of guilt if one of my patients killed themselves. So I figured if I couldn't help them directly, then I could teach others the techniques for treating and dealing with people who need help." She then delved into some personal issues like past relationships that didn't work out and parental divorce, that she was hesitant to reveal, but with my divine digging (and I didn't have to dig much) I was able to uncover, and she opened up quite easily.

Later her story led to the inevitable tale of meeting Adeline at work, which was completely monotonous and should be bland and uninteresting, but for some unknown reason, excited me more than any other part of her life's tale. Nothing was too unusual about their meeting or their adventures together at work. It was just typical work-related humor, that I found myself laughing along with, and poking fun at coworkers that they didn't like. Nothing extreme, or crazy, or even that unusual was told in this segment, but this was my favorite part of what she said.

"So, how about you newbie?" Alice says, "Are you just passing through or are you going to settle down here."

"Haven't decided yet," I lie, trying to add a little mystique to myself for the sake of impressing Adeline. Why? I don't know.

And something tells me I shouldn't be, so I tone down the mystique a little. "Probably. I mean I hope to. It's just that I don't have a job. I'm leaning probably eighty-five percent I'll stay, fifteen percent I'll go. It all depends on me finding a job, I guess."

"I might be able to help you out," Adeline says and Alice looks at her confused.

"Really?" I say. "How?"

"You said you were an English teacher for high school, right?" she says.

"Right," I say, not following and a little worried.

She says, "Well, I've got a friend who's vice principal at a high school and-"

"Who?" Alice asks perplexedly.

"Shelly," Adeline says.

"Oh," Alice says looking a little embarrassed, "forgot about her. How's she doing?"

"She's doing well. Just had another kid, so I guess as good as someone can be doing with two kids running around." She laughs a little then gets back to what she was saying. "Anyway, I overheard her say a couple of weeks ago that they have a vacant position for a teacher—I think it was English—but I could set something up for you to meet her, and she might be able to help you out in filling that vacancy." She smiles at me, giving me a conflicting wave of emotions between joy of her offering to help me out, and nervousness of me actually having to teach English.

"You would actually do that for me?" I say.

"What do you mean?" she says.

"I mean, this is technically only the third time we met, and you're offering to help me find employment. I really appreciate it, but I just want to know why," I say with appreciation mixed with curiosity.

"I don't know," she says, thinking to herself. "You just appear a genuine good guy I guess. You give off an aura of trustworthiness. You remind me of... of.... of..." Yahweh? Allah?

Zeus? Odin? "of... well I can't put my finger on it, but just someone I can trust."

I smile with satisfaction and Steve returns and we play another round of pool, buy another pitcher, then another round, then another pitcher, and another and another. We play about eight rounds in total; Steve and I lose seven of them. As for the eighth: I'm pretty sure Adeline threw the match just to be nice.

After all of this, we split up and head our separate ways. When I'm sure Adeline is out of sight and I won't see her for the rest of the night I light a cigarette. *An English teacher, huh,* I think to myself, *that'll be interesting.*

I think of all this in my head, simultaneously worried and excited for this new job possibility. I know a lot about literature. I can't be that bad. After all if I screw up, I'm not even affecting real students. But for some reason, I can't shake the worry out of my head.

I'm in Adeline Stewart's bedroom fooling around. Initiating with some harmless touching as we caress each other, feeling a sweetness of harmony. My mouth rests on the nape of her neck. I don't know how I got here, nor do I care. It was as if there was no beginning to how this happened, as if I just happened to be here all along. She releases some soft moans as I take her shirt off revealing a pink lace bra. I slip her pants off showing matching pink panties. We kiss some more as we both lie down on the bed. Some people are shouting in the background. She probably left the window open, but neither of us are concerned about closing it. Not now. Not in this beautiful moment. Maybe not ever. My hands go around her back caressing with delicate fingers, finding their way to the bra strap. The shouting is getting louder and louder outside, but we pay no attention. I kiss her again and again and then unhook her bra.

My eyes open, staring at the near blackness of the ceiling of my hotel room, awakened by what sounds like two drunken idiots shouting outside. Damn it. I left the balcony door open. The dream begins to fade away. I fully realize that I was only having a sex dream about a fictional character that was created by my own mind, but I still feel cock-blocked.

I figure I should close the door and try to continue that dream even though I know it never works that way. I've had experience as a man without a relationship for a long time trying to find sex even if it's not real. Granted I know that no matter what I do when I'm in here, no form of sex is real, but I really don't want to entertain those thoughts right now. I get up and go to shut the door.

When I reach the door, I figure I might as well tell those two bastards who interrupted a very pleasant dream to shut the hell up. I lean over the balcony and open my mouth to shout as I hear a blast and see down below a man fire his gun as another man's brains decorate the hotel wall.

In an adrenaline shock haze I stumble backward and fall on the floor of my hotel bedroom with my head hitting the bed. You know that fight or flight response they say everyone gets under these situations? They should also add a 'shit yourself' response to it.

I crawl under the covers like a child with no idea how to protect myself—as if these blankets and sheets that provide warmth are made out of Kevlar, and will shield me in case that maniac breaks into my room because he needs someone else's brains to splatter.

You know that pleasant dream I mentioned earlier? It's gone. Hell, sleep in general is pretty much an option I can throw out the window. I lie in my bed, my knuckles turning white from gripping the blankets, and spend the whole night listening to the wind, footsteps, screams, and sirens from outside my hotel.

I need to protect myself somehow while I'm in here. Serial killers, strung-out junkies, overwhelming populace of nut jobs, and now people blowing someone's brains out for some reason I can't figure out, there's got to be something I can do. I need to keep myself safe.

But how? I wonder, *But how?*

CH. 22

Bill Hackley, known by his friends, acquaintances, and pretty much everyone, as Old Man Hackley, is rattling off different types of handguns and what their strengths and weaknesses are. I'm barely listening to Old Man Hackley's enthusiastic explanations. Listening to the reverence in his voice, you'd figure he was talking about rare religious artifacts. He reminds me of Jimmy talking about artists before he realized that I didn't care about paintings in the slightest. Old Man Hackley is the kind of guy that thinks the second amendment got the shaft when it had to settle for number two. He views it as the most important amendment, and pretty much the most important thing in the entirety of the constitution. I'm just grunting to give him the false pretense that I'm actually paying attention.

"Now with this work of art," he says, "you can pretty much guarantee you'll hit your target within forty feet. The recoil's a beaut too. It may not be the strongest, but don't you start believin' that it's weak. It doesn't take the keenest shot to make sure that you shoot your target dead."

I grunt once again with a semi-attuned ear, but I'm not thinking of how this gun will best protect me. Granted I probably should right now. I'm too focused on last night: the man's skull caving in in an instant, followed by grey matter splashing against the wall. I was too scared to go over to close the balcony door. So all night I lay in my bed, paralyzed in fear, with only the screams of horrified people passing by the scene to comfort me. This whole day has been completely surreal.

Finally after getting the courage to get out of bed from that night, I made my way down to the lobby. My eyes are bloodshot from lack of sleep, the skin under my eyes have bunched up in deep bags making my face look semi-skeletal. The hotel management and crew are all worried. That goes without question. But they're trying their hardest to remain calm, and encourage people to not fall into hysterics. A tragedy has occurred, but there's no reason to have unnecessary panic. Still, the management move in neurotic sleep-deprived jerks, and are excessively jumpy.

I make my way to exit. "Sir," I hear one of the hotel workers say. "Mr...."

"Neilson," I say. "Jake Neilson." The Douglass Inn prides itself on making its patrons feel as if they are at home, and one of their techniques to fulfill that is trying to memorize their residents' names. I find it an unreasonable task to ask of their staff, but they are surprisingly good at it. They made this mistake, but given the circumstances, I'm willing to forgive.

"Of course," he says, "Mr. Jack Nelson." I decide not to correct this. "Last night there was an unfortunate accident." Accident? Poor choice of words. But then again, given the circumstances... "And someone was shot outside. It may be a surprise as you leave, but the police are investigating the scene, so while you are allowed to go outside, I didn't want you to be shocked at an investigation going-"

"Don't worry," I say not wanting to continue this conversation, "I already heard from some people in the lobby."

"Of course, of course," he says, "naturally these things would get around quickly. I would like to apologize for the inconvenience, and as a gesture apologizing for any trauma," I realize from his face he regrets saying this last word, "or any inconvenience, we would like to offer-"

"Trust me I'm fine," I say. "This was because of some sicko. It's not the hotel's fault." I realize that he—or rather his superior—doesn't want word going around that the Douglass Inn is a place where people get shot. I'm not a business expert, but I can imagine that wouldn't be good for business.

"Yes, of course, of course," he says. "But if you feel inclined to order dinner for the next week, it's on us. Whatever you want, for how many times as you want for the week."

"Greatly appreciate it," I say as I leave the hotel.

The police investigation is near the front of the hotel doors. It's about thirty yards to the left, but I'm still able to make out the people working, and, sure enough, there's Detective Reynolds. He seems to be everywhere I go.

Accompanying him is his partner Lenny Johnson. *I killed you*, I think to myself with a strong presence of guilt. *You may not know it yet, and it may not have happened to you yet as far as you know, but you're already dead.*

Lenny's death is a crucial moment in the story. On a case unrelated to the serial killer, they chase down a fleeing criminal, and when the criminal finds himself out of places to run, he unloads his clip at the two detectives in pursuit. A bullet hits Lenny in the stomach, and as the man is reloading, Reynolds fires two shots in the man's chest. Lenny doesn't die immediately, and Todd does what he can to apply pressure to the wound; but before medical assistance can arrive for Lenny, he's already dead. That moment is when detective Reynolds really loses it. He feels responsible that he failed another person, and that guilt fuels into a rage-filled insanity.

But that's not until much later in the story. Still, I've never seen a dead man investigate a murder in person. That thought only entertains me for a little before I'm back in that wave of guilt. I get it. They're not real. But hasn't literature taught us that sympathy is not reserved strictly for the real. I know what Coralline Thomson—or I guess now Jane Young—would say to me, but killing someone isn't something you can just shrug off with ease.

Todd surveys the scene, looking at it from not just the angle of the shooter, but also of the victim and then generally scanning the whole area. He browses over me and the other two people exiting the hotel and goes back to the victim, then he looks back over his shoulder at me and gives me a hard glance. I drop my gaze and focus on the street in front of me.

I know that his eyes are still on me. When I was originally staring at him, and then awkwardly dropping my gaze, as if I was just caught in middle school checking out some girl, didn't help. I have a bad feeling about continuing to run into him. And each time I run into him, I feel that I'm coming off as suspicious. But as long as I don't do anything illegal, what's the worst that can happen?

I leave and figure I'd pick up a cell phone, the entire time thinking about the previous night. I have to admit I'm a little scared. Hell, who am I kidding? I'm downright terrified. After some more thought, I decide to make a beeline to Old Man Hackley's Smokes and Guns.

So that's how I ended up here. I talked to Old Man Hackley when I originally came in. He was someone that was actually designed in the novel, and not just one of the inhabitants that simply fill in blank space, so I figure I'd give extracting information out of him a go. I started with a generic question of how he started up his business.

"Well, when I was growing up I loved three things: guns, smokes, and liquor. Women were number four, but I figure you can't legally sell women." He laughs which transitions into a coughing frenzy. "But I figured, wouldn't it be great to open up a shop where you could pick up a twelve gauge, a pack of Winston, and a bottle of Jack. So I opened this shop here. I never got around to getting a liquor license, and decided I didn't have the time.

'Sides," he says, "I kind of like the name Old Man Hackley's Smokes and Guns. Adding Liquor in there would just be too wordy." I think about a shop that only sells guns, cigarettes, and liquor, and instead of thinking about the potential danger, I think that if someone was selling drugs outside the store, I just found Hunter S. Thompson's wet dream.

Although he's willing to talk more about himself and his personal views, I figure I'm too tired right now so I'll just get down to business. "I'm looking for a handgun," I say. "Something good for self-defense."

"Yeah, these streets sure aren't the safest. You'd be surprised how few people are buying nowadays," he says. "Sales aren't the greatest, but I can guarantee my product's the best quality." This part is a lie. Not the part about his stuff being the best quality—he's got a wide array of weapons that are all topnotch—but the part of the sales not being that great. I'm guessing he's probably trying to appeal to my sympathetic side so I'd be more inclined to buy, or maybe he's just trying to start up a conversation, because I know that with the serial killer on the loose, business is a boomin'.

He then goes into his description of the firearms, which borders on being sexual. I start to nod off with that lack of sleep really kicking in.

I've never been one for guns. In fact I'm politically opposed to it. Statistics show that those that own guns are more likely to be subject to gun-related violence. So, feeling conflicted about my own convictions and the danger that seems to be everywhere in this town, I point to the gun that he's holding and say that it's the one I want. *Come on,* I think to myself, *convictions only stand ground in reality.* Still I don't shake off that ambivalence.

He tells me to fill out a form, give him my number, and he'll call me with the results of the background check within the next seventy-two hours. Without another word, he sends me on my way. It can't be that easy to obtain a gun can it? No, of course not in the real world. I have to remember that I'm living fiction.

On leaving his shop, I bump into someone in my sleepless haze, and we both apologize at the same time. And once again I run into him. Blue eyes, black crew-cut, clean shaven, tall, and slender; it's Richard Sweeney.

I realize that bumping into him was no mere coincidence. I completely forgot about it, but most days he circles around this shop only letting enough time pass by for people not to notice him before he returns to check up on this shop. He has no desire to purchase a gun, doesn't have the slightest interest in guns, he much prefers knives for murder (he views it as more personal and even romantic), but he loves to see how many people run out to buy guns because of him. He feeds emotionally on their terror. The more scared people are, the stronger, in a manner of speaking, he becomes. He absorbs their terror, and views it as a personal victory for every person who would normally not buy a weapon in their entire life, get drawn to it by fear.

"I can be such a klutz sometimes," he says, echoing the response he gave the first time I met him. He doesn't remember me. He's very intelligent, don't get me wrong, but if you're not a blond attractive woman or someone connected to that woman, you're just a speck in his peripheral vision. Nothing of importance. Nothing of worth. Nothing of value. Just plain old nothing.

I remember what Coralline Thomson said about fraternizing with the characters of this story to extract information, and like it or not, he's one of the most important characters. So with some emotional difficulty, I manage to say, "I'm sorry, but you look somewhat familiar. Where do you work?" I figure that's a safe thing to say, considering that since his memory of people is so narrow—I know, I created him—he wouldn't have the slightest idea of whether he has ever seen me before in his life.

"Oh, nowhere of importance," he says. "Al's department store. I'm just a manager there."

"Yup," I say, "That's where I saw you."

He says, "I'm honored you remembered. I didn't figure that I make that much of a lasting impression on people." Oh, you'd be surprised.

"Anything new happening?" I say, not really sure what I mean, but I need to keep this conversation going and I'm too tired and uneasy to think properly.

"Just working and following this new Vince Randall case that's on the news," he says. I'm wondering how he can manage keeping up such a normal conversation while I know the kind of thoughts and images that are going on through his mind.

"What happened?" I say.

"Really? You haven't heard about it? It's pretty much on every time you flip on the television," he says.

It was a side story that I created that had no real impact on the main story, but I seemed to have forgotten about it. "Yeah, really," I say, "I actually haven't heard of it."

"Well," he says, "this man, Vince Randall, was a rich senate hopeful who was viewed as a bit of a philanthropist and was thought by everyone as a shoe-in for the nominee. He would donate heftily to charities and was liked by pretty much everyone. This was all fine and dandy until one of his political advisers, Paul Rankly, came home to find his wife hanging from a noose in his home." He tries to appear neutral, as if he's someone who knows how terrible this is but has heard it too many times to affect him, but it looks as if he's trying to restrain some joy while telling this.

"That's awful," I say.

"Agreed," he says. "Now this is where it gets weird." As if this wasn't already weird enough. "The police release an original statement saying that it is believed that the suicide could have actually been a homicide." I think I see him smile for a brief second. "That it looked as if she had died earlier and then been set up to make it look as if it was a suicide. Then out of nowhere the police retract their statement and say that it was a mistake. Now," he says, "here it gets even more interesting. A federal investigation is launched and there comes to light a large amount of money being transferred into several high ranking police officials' bank accounts from Vince Randall. So then Paul Rankly is charged with murder and Vince Randall is charged with whatever the charge is for bribing and trying to cover up a murder. So anyway, long story short, Vince Randall hires the best lawyers money can buy for him and Paul Rankly, and despite all evidence, those lawyers weasel their way into letting those two off the hook."

"Wow," I say, "I can't believe they got away with it."

"It's the justice system we live in buddy," he says with a smile. "The law isn't enforced equally by who's innocent and who's guilty, it's enforced by who's rich and who's poor."

"Yeah, I guess it's kind of sad but true," I say.

"I guess we really should take a note from Shakespeare," Richard says, "'the first thing we do, let's kill all the lawyers.'" He then laughs heartily.

I realize of course that this quote is from Shakespeare's Henry VI. It's a masterpiece of drama, and I do rather enjoy that quote, but coming from the mouth of a psychopathic serial killer with superficial charm, I feel a great sense of unease. Regardless of my unease, I accompany his laughter. Might as well make friends with these characters so they are more willing to open up to me.

We say goodbye and part ways. After I drift further away from him, that revulsion of being near someone who in every essence disgusts you begins to lift, and I'm able to think clearer.

I know that for the sake of the story I should talk to him, but I feel repulsed by his very presence. Talking to him for those few minutes made me feel physically ill and actually dirty. I felt as if I was bathing in grime.

But for some reason, I'm hit with something that I can't shake—a familiarity about him. Something about him reminds me of something or someone that I can't put my finger on. Could it be possible that he's another alter-ego of someone in real life? I think about this for quite a while. No, I decide there's no one that I could possibly hate that much that I would turn into a serial killer.

CH. 23

Adeline is forty-five minutes late. This really surprises me, because from what I was able to deduce, she appeared very punctual. Once again, I'm at The Billiards Hall meeting with Adeline for some rounds of pool and a fair amount of pitchers. Only this time, I arrived first and she's nowhere to be seen. I'm thinking of phoning her, but I decide against it. She'll arrive when she arrives, and if I call her for being tardy, I might appear too desperate. I guess I shouldn't care, but for some reason I do.

Luckily, Howie Mumbles shows up, drunk as usual, and gives me someone to play with until she arrives. I'm hoping that when she finally does arrive, he'll take the hint and leave.

When he came up to me, he was able to recognize me. He got my name wrong—"John" he called me—but then again, taking into consideration the condition he was in both times he saw me, I should be honored he remembered me at all. Plus, I still don't know his last name, so who am I to complain?

Add a couple of beers and my ability to extract information without even trying to with his already prevalent intoxication, and he starts jabbering away about his personal issues like he was simply relaying celebrity gossip.

"But my wife," he says, "when sh' left me. I never hurt like that in… in… in hell I don' know. Prob'ly ever." He's lining up his shot while stumbling a bit, with his eyes getting wetter. "But wha' could I do?" He bumps into the table, moving some of the balls, but I decide not to penalize him. "She was one of m' greates' loves. But she was tryin' to tear me from m' other. An'… an'… an' what would I be without it?" He takes his shot going nowhere near his intended target. He then looks up with a certain clarity and authority and says. "I am the alcohol and the alcohol is me."

"Maybe," I say venturing carefully, "have you ever thought about getting some help? I mean, you could try to sober up and get her back. Things don't always have to be-"

"Fuck AA," he says passionately. "I tried to ge' help. I *really* did." I remember what detective Reynolds told me about Howie showing up at a meeting so drunk that he urinated in the corner thinking it was the bathroom. "The prob'em is, the prob'em is, I know the way that things can go."

I line up my shot. "How do you mean?"

"My wife…" he starts, "my wife… she could still leave me y' know. Let me give y' an' e'sample. M' friend Dan," he says while pouring himself another drink from the pitcher, "my frien' Dan, his wife gave him an ultimatum: her or the bottle. An' unlike me, he go' better. Spent two years on the wagon. No' a single drop o' liquor. Clean as a whistle he was. And guess what?"

He's silent for a little until I realize that that question wasn't rhetorical and I'm supposed to answer, "What?"

"She lef' him jus' th' same. She couldn' stand him," he says. "You understan' what I'm saying?"

"I guess so," I say as I sink another ball in, making it three in a row.

"Let m' clarify," he says that last word as cla-ri-fy, as if struggling to make that word sound coherent. "M' wife could ha' easily jus' left me anyway. I don' know if sh'd stay or if sh'd leave. How the hell woul' I know that? Th' answer: I don't. Many of my friends lef'. Some by choice, some by work, some by marriage, an' many by death. But I'll tell you this inali'able truth: Alcohol is the only frien' that won' leave you."

"Yeah," I say, "but it might kill you."

He laughs. "True. I' give ya' that. It may kill you, but it will never leave you."

About an hour later I check my phone and realize that Adeline isn't coming. *Great,* I think, *I got stood up by my imagination. Is there anything more pathetic than that?* Yes, there might be: getting upset that you got stood up by your imagination.

Howie and I play three rounds of pool with the rule of loser buys the pitcher. So he bought three pitchers. Even though there's been three pitchers divided by two people, I'm still pretty sober. Probably because Howie drank over four fifths of those pitchers. But who am I to complain? I didn't have to pay a cent.

Howie and I talk for quite a bit more, but as he gets more and more drunk, I'm able to understand less and less of what he says. We delved into plenty of other subjects. I was able to uncover that he went to school for quite a lot of years and became an astronomer before he found his current position as a full time alcoholic. I knew he has some intelligence to him—or at least *had* before he drank it all away.

After he went on talking about what he remembers about planets, galaxies, solar systems, comets, and stars, I ask him what he thinks about the big question.

"God?" he ventures uncertainly.

"No I mean extraterrestrials. Are there any species on any other planets?" I ask.

He thinks for a second, "We may not b' alone in th' universe, b' we are certainly alone in this world."

He leaves me with that cryptic message as I decide to leave and meet some other people. I look at my phone, and it's 4:40 PM. I was supposed to meet with the most beautiful woman I've ever met. Instead, I spent the last two and a half hours with a depressed drunk. Still I realized that Howie was actually nice. Yeah, he's a raging alcoholic and bitter about pretty much everything, but in his heart I realize that he's genuinely good. He just has some demons to overcome. Even though I'm trying to look on the positive side, I still can't believe that Adeline stood me up.

I go for a bit of a walk to think quietly to myself. I figure I'd let my mind dwell on my minor misery even though I know that, even in real life, this is not a recommended way of coping.

There I was thinking that I'd be on a date with this beautiful woman. She seemed practically perfect in every way. Where did I get off thinking that this perfect woman would be interested in a guy like me? It's a humbling encounter that many men feel when a woman stands them up. I guess it's one of those snap back to reality moments. Maybe not the best phrase, because I know an actual snap back to reality moment would be much more violent. I have Coralline Thomson—Jane Young—to thank for that.

Walking with my ever-potent self-pity, I worked myself into a self-deprecating trance. Just making fun of myself in my head over and over again asking, 'What did you think would happen?' until there is nothing occupying my mind but internal insults and sadness.

My cellphone rings interrupting my thoughts. At first I think it's someone else's because I'm not used to having one, but then I realize that it's mine. And sure enough, it's Adeline Stewart. Some hope returns to me.

"Hello," I say tentatively.

"I am so sorry," she says as if she's out of breath. "I know I said I would meet you but something came up. There was an emergency. I'll tell you more about it. I really am so sorry. I didn't mean to-"

"No need to apologize," I say, lightening up. "Things come up. I completely understand. It's not your fault."

"But I mean it," she says. "I really, *really*, am sorry. This thing came up with my sister, and things got a little hectic and, given everything that was happening, I completely forgot everything. I'll make it up to you, I promise."

"Family emergencies," I say. "It happens all the time. We'll schedule it some other time. Don't worry about it."

"Tell you what; I'll take you out to dinner. Whatever place you like, I'll pay," she says.

"You don't have to pay," I say. "It really doesn't matter, but I'd be more than happy to go somewhere to eat sometime. I'll treat you," I say nicely.

"No I insist," she says. "It was my mess up, I should pay. It's only fair."

I see a little girl—seven maybe eight—walk out into the middle of the street to cross the road. She's singing along to something on her iPod. The pop music is blasting in her ears to the point where I can hear it from where I'm standing. I don't know why people have to blast the music so loud. When it's that loud it doesn't even sound that good. But oh well, kids will be kids.

"I'll explain all of this over dinner," Adeline says. "What day works best for you?"

The girl crouches down to pick up a stray twenty that happened to be there. Must be that kid's lucky day. As she goes to pick it up, the twenty flies away and she runs after it. I laugh to myself. This is just a precursor to adult life. No matter what you do, you'll always be chasing cash.

"Does next Saturday work?" I ask.

I hear the sounds of sirens to my left and look over.

"Next Saturday works fine," Adeline says, "What time would work for you?"

Suddenly a black sports car makes a screeching sound as it turns the corner and blazes down the street heading in my direction. I look down and see that the seven or eight year old girl has successfully stomped the twenty and is crouching down to pick it up.

Acting purely out of instinct, I drop the phone and run

toward the girl. She's facing the opposite direction and, with those headphones blasting, can't hear a thing.

I grab the girl and dodge the car, that's probably pushing eighty miles per hour, by a few inches. We dive out of the way and the girl scratches up her leg and starts crying, completely unaware that she almost got killed. As far as she knows, some crazy guy just picked her up and dove with her into another portion of the street. I then pick her up and bring her to the safety of the sidewalk as several police cars follow the black sports car in pursuit.

A man comes up to us and asks concerned, "Are you guys okay?"

"Yeah, we're fine," I say.

"I'm bleeding!" the girl screams as she points to a cut in her leg.

"You're a hero. You saved this girls life," the man says.

"Don't mention it," I say, really hoping he won't.

"He tackled me! He hurt me!" the girl wails.

A woman runs up to me in a business suit and says, "Do you mind if I ask a couple questions?"

"Um... sure," I say confused.

She starts asking me what went through my mind as I risked my life to save this girl, what my connection is to this girl, what my name is, how I found myself in this situation and several other questions.

Not sure what's happening, I answer all the questions truthfully. Or I guess as truthfully as the lie I created for this story.

Another man runs up holding his phone screaming, "I got it on video! That whole rescue, it's on my phone." Oh no.

Another man in his late forties runs up asking what happened, and hugs the girl assuring her that she's safe.

"He hurt me," the girl says in tears.

"No, uh-" I start.

"He saved her from a car," the first man that arrived says.

"I've got it on video," says the man holding his phone.

"Thank you so much," says the apparent father holding the girl. "If there's anything I could do to repay you."

"Don't mention it," I say, not out of an attempt of humility, but informing him that that is exactly what he can do to repay me.

The woman continues to ask questions about me, as the man hugs his daughter and more people come to observe the scene.

I find out later that the woman questioning me actually works for a local newspaper, but this is after I answered several of her questions without knowing. This is what makes local heroes. This is what makes temporary celebrities. As much as people eat up tragedies, that rare occasion of altruism really brightens their day. Soon I'll be in the papers, and, because of that video, on YouTube and possibly a local television news channel.

Rule number two: never become a main character.

CH. 24

"What the fuck is this?!" Coralline Thomson shouts as she slams down the local newspaper on the table in front of me in Sunny Side Up. She's red in the face and seething. There was no doubt in my mind that she was going to be mad, but this is a little over the top in my opinion. She never appeared to be one for a taste in theatrics, but she's piping mad and looks as though she's going to strike me.

"I can explain," I say, struggling to find an adequate explanation.

"Good," she says, "Because the question 'what the fuck is this?' normally calls for an explanation."

"It was purely instinctual," I say. "I wasn't thinking properly and saw this girl in the middle of the street unaware that she was going to get hit by a car and without thinking I-"

"Try thinking next time," she says bitterly. "And work on controlling your instincts while you're in here. When I told you the rules to follow when you're in the story, you were supposed to listen. So maybe you should work on either thinking, instincts, or listening. At least one of those needs improving."

"What was I supposed to do? Let her die?" I ask.

"Yes," she says. "That is exactly what you should do. Get

this through your head. No one in this story is real. If I stiff the waitress, I'm not stiffing anyone. I'm stiffing a fragment of your imagination. If I decide to be rude to someone, I'm not being rude to anyone. I'm being rude to your imagination. And if you let a girl die, *no one fucking dies*. Is this getting through to you?"

"Yes, I get it," I concede. "But it still just doesn't feel right. I mean, I know no one's real, but after you talk to enough people and learn about them—which you told me to do by the way—it's hard to not have some sympathy for them."

The waitress returns with our food. I had the ham and cheese omelet, and Jane Young—I guess I got to get used to calling her that—ordered the Egg White Delight. She refills our coffees and asks if we need anything else. We tell her 'no' and she goes off on her way.

"You know," I say, "if this is all in our imagination, you can eat the yolk. It's not going to kill you."

"I actually prefer it sometimes without the yolk. And quit changing the subject," she says. "The second rule I told you was to not become a main character. Now your goal for the near future is to diffuse your minor stardom before it blooms into the main character danger zone. If you ever reach that point, your story will become garbled nonsense. So proceed with caution."

"I'll do what I can," I say.

"By the way," she adds, "congratulations."

"For what?" I brighten.

"You made it to the local televised news," she says.

"I know." My recent brightness diminishes back into darkness.

I make my way to the dive bar with my head hung low. Adeline was elated on the phone saying things like, "Oh my God! I saw you on the news," and "I can't believe you risked your life for someone you didn't even know," and "You really are one in a million." The entire time I'm saying, "don't mention it," and "please don't mention it," and "I really mean it, please, *please,* don't mention it at all." This didn't have the desired effect at all. Instead of taking me seriously, she misjudged it for humility. And if there's one thing people love more than a hero, it's a humble hero. And that humility only makes people jabber more.

As I enter the bar, the bartender looks up and says, "Hey, it's you, the guy on the news who saved the girl." Everyone at the bar looks up and shouts in recognition and approval. Great. "First drink is on the house."

I sit at the bar and order a Tullamore Dew on the rocks. People come up from all over and ask what happened and what was going through my head, and I answer the same questions to thirty or so different people. Yes, this gives me an opportunity to listen to many different people's stories, but my goal for the time being is to diffuse the situation, not feed the fire of heroism. What I don't mind though is several people coming up to me and buying me drinks. Free drinks, even in fantasy, are not something I would turn down.

After a while I go to the bathroom and see engraved on the stall, "If God is good then he isn't God. If God is God then he isn't good." I realize that this is a bastardization of an Archibald MacLeish quote from the play "J.B." which states, 'If God is God He is not good. If God is good He is not God.' The occupant of the stall who wrote this may have written a bastardization of the original quote, but you have to give a vandal credit for going into a public stall and not carving a racial slur or saying that so-and-so loves cock. Plus he did spell everything correctly, which is, I realize, a rarity in the bathroom stall vandal community.

I stare at this carving for quite a while. "If God is good then he isn't God. If God is God then he isn't good." I mouth the words, repeating them to myself as if saying a mantra while using the restroom. I realize that this quote was used as philosophical satire to compare the belief that god is all powerful and all good with all the flaws that are in this world. But I instead take this as advice.

"I won't do it again," I promise.

I walk back to the bar and see that detective Reynolds is sitting a couple of seats down from me. He's eyeing me suspiciously and looks like he's been here for a while. Why can't I shake that guy? It's like he's everywhere at once. I find that he's one of the few people that hasn't come up to me to hear my tale of heroism. I wouldn't be surprised—given his nature—if he was watching with great interest how everything played out since I got here. He's probably just been viewing me in silence the entire time. And he must have been doing a good job at it, because I haven't noticed him until now.

After some people sitting in-between us leave, he breaks his silence. "Well I guess I ought to buy the hero a drink," he says in a tone that I can't tell if it's sarcasm or sincerity.

"No it's quite alright," I say, really hoping he'd just go away.

"Oh a humble hero," he says and smiles. "I insist. You are the hero after all. You did save that girl yesterday, didn't you?"

"Well yes, but it was all instinctual," I say.

He laughs a little. "What do you want?"

"I'll have a scotch," I say.

He calls over the barkeep and orders me a scotch, telling the bartender to charge the drink on his tab.

"So," he says, "tell me all about it. I've read it in the papers, but I'd like to hear the story firsthand if you don't mind." He stirs his drink with his pointer finger, the ice making a clinking sound against the glass, and looks at me as if we were about to start a game of chess.

"It's all in the papers," I say. "Anything I tell you will probably just appear repetitive." I look down, avoiding the game of chess.

"The papers lack that certain humanity." He smiles. "I'd like to hear it firsthand."

"Well alright," I say.

I relay to him the story of the rescue, giving several chances for him to change the topic or leave or simply stop the conversation. None of these chances does he take. Instead he bombards me with questions asking what was going through my mind. I tell him that it was all instinctual. Nothing really was going through my mind besides there's a girl on the street and she's about to get hit by a car. I had to do something.

"I know everyone in here has been making a big hype about it as if this was some kind of miraculous act of bravery, but if you took into consideration the circumstances, anyone would do it," I say, exasperated at the duration of the conversation.

"Trust me, in all my years working on the force, I can tell you for sure that not everyone would do it," he says and swigs his drink.

"Well most people anyway," I say, trying to brush his statement off.

"What about the guy with the video?" he says.

"What guy with the video?" I ask.

"The guy recording the whole situation on his phone," he says.

"What about him?" I ask confused.

"Why didn't he jump out and rescue her?" he asks.

"I-I don't know. I think he was recording something else and just got the video when he saw the car coming," I say.

"But he saw the car coming and just kept on recording," he says.

"I... well I guess so," I concede.

"I tell you, that's the thing that irks me the most," he says, getting a little red in the face and losing his cool which is a rarity for him. "Sons of bitch's just sitting there figuring they're going to get something recorded instead of actually helping. So many tragedies could have been avoided if those people simply dropped their phones and actually helped for a god damn change." He realizes he's going on a rant and quickly changes the subject, "But anyway, the point is, many people wouldn't help in that situation, so don't try to fake humility."

"I don't know," I say. "I think it's just having humanity."

"Let me tell you something," he says. "Having humanity has nothing to do with humans." Once again he stops himself from going on a rant. I can tell that this case with the cross killer is getting to him and leading him down a road to cynicism of the human race. "All I can say is that you did good. And nowadays, doing good is rare."

"Don't mention it," I say for the countless time today.

He leans back and smiles while stirring his drink. "You know, most the time I can get a person nailed down to a tee in the first ten minutes while talking to them. I can tell if someone has criminal tendencies, what kind of religion—if any—they practice, what they hold as their values, how much they drink on a given week, what kind of music they listen to, if they have any family, and if they have any mental or emotional disorders."

"Hmm." I nod, not sure of what he's getting at.

"And then there's you." He finishes the rest of his whiskey and turns back to me. "Anyway, it's been nice chatting with you. I'll see you some other time."

I say goodbye and watch as he cashes out and leaves the bar, giving a generous tip. I don't necessarily know what he meant by that, but I do have an idea. And that idea doesn't sound very good for my story's well-being. I'm not supposed to be a main character; I'm supposed to fall through the cracks. I'm supposed to be inconspicuous—incognito in a way. I'm not supposed to make a lasting impression. Now you see me, now you don't. That sort of thing. But instead, I've left a large impression on one of the main characters' mind.

I think back to the vandalism in the bathroom stall. "If God is good then he isn't God. If God is God then he isn't good." My mantra of remorse. My reminder that I can't do anything reckless like that again.

Several more people come in the bar, recognize me—or someone else tells them—and then make a beeline filled with questions and offerings of free drinks. Once again, I repeat the same story over and over again, continuing to say, "Don't mention it." Stardom is very overrated.

I know I have to make people forget somehow. Do I do something negative to counter their good impression of me? No, any news is bad news. Maybe I should just let the hype fizzle out on its own volition. Time terminates everything. No matter how big a story is, over time people will just not care anymore. They forget about it. Don't they?

CH. 25

This place is much fancier than what suits my comfort zone. Since I haven't been on a date in so long, being in a formal restaurant feels like I'm treading in unknown waters. Not to mention how the process of date etiquette eludes me. The closest thing to a formal date I have had in over a year is when Jimmy and I decide to go to a bar that has a dress code of long pants. Even that is incredibly rare.

She had asked where I wanted to go and I said, "You know this town better than I do. I wouldn't mind a good steak. I'll let you pick the place." And that's how I ended up at Sergio's Steakhouse, way underdressed and drinking wine that I can't pronounce. I thought I was dressing formal in a polo shirt and kakis, but everyone else's formal is a suit and tie. Adeline is wearing a stunning red dress that dances the line to be both sexy and tasteful. She's wearing a glamorous pearl necklace that she said was handed down from her mother who got it from her mother. I'm wearing a watch that was handed down from whoever owned it before they gave it to Goodwill. To add to my self-consciousness, it hasn't worked in over three months. And just my luck, someone asked me the time. After I reached down to get my phone, Adeline asked why I hadn't just looked at the watch. And, right in front of Adeline, the man asking the time, and the man's wife, I admitted that it was broken. Yeah, I'm really on a winning streak tonight.

"I'm still in awe that you saved that girl," Adeline says with excitement.

"It was nothing." I really have to change the subject.

She laughs, "Don't tell me 'it was nothing.' I saw the video on the news. You missed getting hit by the car by inches. With how fast that car was going, there's no question that girl would have died. And you almost died too." Well death is a relative term, but of course you wouldn't understand that. "So don't tell me it was nothing."

"Yeah, but you have to understand it was purely instinctual," I say, "So it really isn't like I actively saved her life knowing with full awareness that I was actually risking my life. So, given that part, it really isn't something to fuss about."

"Who cares about it only being instinctual?" she says with what appears to be irritation that I'm not accepting this grandiose complement. "That acting on instinct might say more about someone than if they had time to fully assess the situation. This instinctual action shows what you would do in a fight or flight situation regardless of the potential consequences. Most people are too overwhelmed by fear or shock to actually move. You acted in full heroism. When it comes down to crunch time, you're the man to be trusted."

I blush. I *actually* blush. "Maybe… I don't know… maybe you're right… who knows?" I have to diffuse the situation before this minor act of heroics explodes into the main character danger zone. "So anyway, with all this hype that we underwent, we never delved into why you couldn't make it to the plans we had at The Billiards Hall." I realize that I might be tapping on sensitive ground here, but if I don't put an end to everyone going gaga over that whole rescue scene, my story's in for some real trouble.

She looks up and brushes some hair away from her eyes to behind her ears and looks as though she's in deep thought. This look is familiar to me. It's the look someone has when they're unsure whether to tell someone something personal or not. Samuel Tracker had this look moments before he opened up to me about his sexuality, and asked me for advice. It's the look I had when I was debating on asking Coralline Thomson if she would read over my story (even if she was practically a zombie). It's the look Jimmy had before he told me "Never mind," and I caught him that night with a butcher's knife in his hand and talked him out of suicide. It's the look that Hank never has anymore at all. Or maybe, come to think about it, the look that Hank has all the time.

She looks down then meets my gaze again, looking as though she has made some kind of decision. Her face changes into a serious manner as her lips curl up a bit, but not making this subject look any less severe than it is. Despite this semi-stern look, she still radiates warmth.

"You know, despite what you may believe since you met me, I normally don't just open up and tell my deepest secrets to anyone," she says.

I give her an apologetic look. "I understand."

"But there's something about you," she says. "Some undefinable feature or characteristic that just gives me a feeling of safety and trust toward you." She pauses. "I really can't tell why, but something about you is just... is just... I don't know how to put it. It gives off a feeling of closure." It's similar to why people pray. "But I guess I can tell you even though this is a bit personal."

"I'm honored you would trust me," I say.

"My sister, you see, has been diagnosed a long time ago with severe depression," Adeline says tentatively. "Understand, she's one of the sweetest people alive, but she just can't shake the feeling of sadness off of her."

"Yes, I'm familiar with people diagnosed with that," I say.

She continues, "Well anyway, when I came to her apartment to visit, I went inside and saw that she had slit her wrists."

Oh my god. "I'm so sorry." And when I say I'm sorry, I

take a whole literal form of responsibility.

"She didn't die," she adds quickly when she sees my face. "But I was terrified. I phoned 911 as quickly as I could and applied pressure to the wounds."

"That's horrible. I can't imagine." My face is probably still white with guilt.

"She was probably doing it as a cry for help." She then adds quickly, "But don't think that I'm just incredibly callous. I mean this wasn't the first time." She gives a deep sigh. "When you live with somebody who has this illness, and you experience these kinds of things as often as I have, you become a little used to it." She pauses. "Don't get me wrong. I was terrified when it happened. Scared completely out of my wits, in fact. I just get used to the 'dealing with it' part. Coping with someone you love that has depression, to the point of being suicidal, isn't easy, but you always seem much more at ease when the shit hits the fan." She smiles, but not a wholehearted smile. "Sometimes it's surprising that that fan hasn't crapped out with all the shit thrown at it." Even though she's smiling her eyes are a little wet. Then she realizes something and gives a short chortle. "No pun intended." I smile a—what I hope to be—comforting smile, and her smile broadens.

The waiter comes by with our food. A large medium rare T-bone steak with a heaping pile of mashed potatoes and a side of asparagus is set down in front of me. Adeline gets the filet mignon with seasoned rice and mixed vegetables. I take a bite of what I can only describe as a taste bud orgasm. The steak is perfect, much better than anything I ever grilled, and possibly better than I've ever tasted in my life. I let out a pleasure-filled groan as if I was mid-coitus, and Adeline can't help but laugh.

"I told you this place was good," Adeline says.

"'Good' does not do this steak justice. 'Terrific' does not do this steak justice. 'Exquisite' doesn't even scratch the surface. Saying 'this steak will surpass the expectation of any food you could ever fathom and you would trade the rest of your life for one morsel of somebody's leftovers would still fall short. This is the food that defies all food. It is possibly the greatest thing to ever happen to this earth. This is proof that God exists," I say and Adeline gets herself stuck in a giggle fit.

"A little excessive there." She laughs. "I don't know what it is about men and steaks, but they seem to love them more than anything."

"I tell you, if it came down to a good steak or a woman, most men would have to make a difficult choice," I say.

"I really think that's only you," she says.

"Probably." I laugh.

Maybe I shouldn't have said that comment about a good steak or a woman. I think I might have drunk a little too much wine. But she's laughing with me just the same.

We chat away as we continue to eat our dinner. When we finish the waiter comes by to ask us about dessert. I say no, and at the same time she says she'll have the tiramisu. And then she says that I'll have the tiramisu as well.

When the waiter leaves Adeline says to me, "Trust me, you'll love it. Their tiramisu is to die for."

"I normally only eat desserts that I can spell," I say.

She laughs, "Are you telling me that you, an English teacher, can't spell tiramisu?"

"Fine." I laugh, "Let me rephrase that. I only eat desserts that I could spell going into high school."

"Spell tiramisu," she says smiling.

"What?" I say.

"Just spell it. I don't believe you," she says.

I pause for a second. "Well you have to understand I've had quite a bit of wine tonight. I'm not at my top-game."

"You can't spell it can you?" she says.

"No I can," I say. "I'm just laying out the circumstances in case any circumstances arise in which-"

"Now you're just stalling," she says.

"Alright," I say, "T, I, R, A, M, A-"

She erupts in laughter and says quickly through spurts of laughing, "T-I-R-A-M-I-S-U." and laughs even harder.

"My point is, it's a pretentious food," I say.

"What?" She's bawling her heart out.

"*Tiramisu. Tiramisu.* It just sounds like something that would be ordered by a man in a tuxedo as he's consumed by his own pomposity," I say. "Ice cream. Now that's a dessert that would be eaten by the common man. An everyday Joe would eat that. A Twinkie. That's a plumber's or a union man's desert. Fondue, tiramisu: these are deserts that would be dined on by the pompous crème de la crème of society."

"Who are you," she cries out in laughter, "Larry David?"

"Actually I learned most of my social cues through Seinfeld," I say, and we both have a nice long laugh.

We finish up our dessert and sit around a little longer having several pleasant conversations, and drinking more of the delicious wine that I still can't pronounce. I learn more about her, she learns more about me (or at least my in story façade), and we have several good laughs. Still she's trying to learn more about my heroic situation and still I'm evading it.

After we leave, we see the wonderful weather and decide to go for a bit of a walk before we part ways. I talk to her more about her friend Shelly, who's the vice principal for a high school, and if she can still get me a job. She says that she's more than willing to set up a meeting. I just need to send her my resume.

There's more of this pleasantry and then I stop suddenly with my eyes wide looking at the name of the restaurant in front of me. A memory comes back to me from long ago when I look at this sign. It reads, "Pantera Bread: Reinventing the Meal."

On my senior year of high school I was with a friend who had brought in a sandwich from Panera Bread. Another one of my friends, Adam Pines, misread it as "Pantera Bread." To which I responded immediately, "Reinventing the Meal." Then that started something that occupied a lot of excess time in our math class. We decided to come up with several different bread dishes that were all spoofs off of Pantera songs. A third person in our friend group, who was also creative and showed a fascination with heavy metal, joined us. After a while we extended these creations of Pantera Bread dishes to incorporate all heavy metal bands, and extended the restaurant from just a bakery and sandwich place to a full-on restaurant with entrees, salads, soups, sides, and drinks.

After we graduated, I went off to college and the whole Pantera Bread idea started to dissolve. Luckily, Jimmy, who was also a high school friend, went to the same college as I did, and we started it up again. We had a professor who would drone on and on in a tone of voice that actually put several of the students to sleep in the class. He was the most boring professor ever, so Jimmy and I decided to occupy our time making different dishes for Pantera Bread. After college was over, we decided to end our little fun. There seemed no point in doing it anymore, and I haven't even thought of it in at least five years.

"We have to go in here," I announce.

Adeline precariously ventures, "I don't know."

"Why not?" I ask.

"They barely get any customers. It's a wonder how they make enough to stay open," she says. "They blast heavy metal music so loud that it's hard to hear yourself think, much less other's talk. Plus the only people that ever go in there are pretty scary." She corrects herself, "Maybe not scary in the traditional way, but definitely weird."

"Come on," I say, "one drink."

"Well," she pauses, "I guess so."

I walk into the restaurant and go to the bar. "Excuse me!" I shout over the song Cemetery Gates which is on a decibel that could cause permanent hearing damage.

"What?!" the bartender shouts.

"Excuse me! Can I look at your menu?!" I shout again.

"What?!" he says again.

"Me!" I say pointing to myself. "Menu!" I say miming the hand motions for holding and reading a menu."

"Oh!" he says, handing me a menu, and then he says something I can't understand.

"What?!" I shout.

He shouts something else that I can't comprehend.

"Oh, of course!" I yell back.

"What?!" he shouts.

"Never mind!" I say.

"What?!" he bellows again.

I mouth the words 'never mind' very slowly and he turns away and goes elsewhere.

I look at the menu studying it, amused in this complete throwback to senior year of high school and early college days. There it is on the bread category, 'A Vulgar Display of Flower.' Under it reads that it is an unlimited amount of seven different types of bread and of course butter. Then there's 'Bagels From Hell,' which are toasted bagels with fiery chipotle cream cheese. Their special, 'Dimebagels,' which are day-old bagels sold for ten cents. You can order it to go if you like. Then it expands into other bands such as The Misfits with 'Night of the Unleavened Bread.' I browse the rest of the meals expanding beyond breads. There's 'Megabroth' and 'Enter Salmon' and 'Manwich Engaged' and 'Cabbage Bloody Cabbage' and 'Cream of Mushroomhead Soup' and 'Sweet Leaf Salad' and much more. I'm laughing in memory of the old days I had created all this and seeing it come to life.

I go to the drinks. There's a 'Gwartini.' If I remember correctly, that'll really knock you on your ass. So I browse over to the non-alcoholic drinks and know immediately that I have to order this. It may be utterly disgusting, but it is a necessity.

"Can I get the Pork Soda?!" I say. I realize that it's debatable of whether you can consider Primus heavy metal, but who cares? We were having fun.

"What?!" the bartender bellows.

"Pork Soda!" I shout.

"What?!" he shouts once again.

I bring the menu to him and point it out to him.

He looks at me questioningly, "Really?!"

I nod my head and he shrugs his shoulders and brings me the drink. I pay for it, take a swig, put it back down, and walk out of the restaurant.

"Pork soda?" Adeline says.

"Yup," I say.

"How was it?" she asks.

"Exactly as I imagined it," I say and laugh.

I walk her to her house, once again returning to that aura of pleasantry through the art of cleverly crafted conversation. We stand outside chatting away and simply talk about this and that and have ourselves some comforting laughter. Considering that I haven't been on a date for a year, I think this went nicely. I remind myself that I'm not really dating anyone, just a figment of my imagination, but still my imagination was very kind to me and a hell of a conversationalist.

"Well, I had a lot of fun tonight," she says.

"I as well," I say. "And thanks once again for taking me out."

"It was my pleasure," she says. She then pauses, "You really are such a great person." I blush. "No seriously, you saved that girl." Oh God, not this still. I thought we were done with that. "You have been understanding of everything that I did, even accidentally blowing you off."

"Well you had good reason to," I say. "It was a family emergency."

"But you didn't know that on the phone when I first called you," she says. "And there wasn't even a hint of anger in your voice."

"I guess," I say embarrassed. I'm not used to compliments.

Normally my friends and I don't spend the entire time complementing each other. Hell, we spend most the time talking about how terrible we are at our trade.

"Anyway, goodnight," she says and kisses me on the lips.

I pause for a second. My mind is racing. A part of me is thinking what happens if this relationship escalates to sex. If I'm really not having sex, then what am I doing in real life while I'm preforming the act in this world? Do I just start masturbating no matter where I am? Even if I'm in public? Or do I simply ejaculate on the spot? Maybe nothing happens. But what if it does? Also there's a part of me that can't shake the thought of Zeus coming down from Mount Olympus to court one of the humans.

"I'm sorry," she says. "I'm normally not that forward. Was that too soon?" She looks confused by my reaction.

"No-haha, no, it's just that you took me by surprise, that's all." I say, feeling like an immature kid, shocked that a girl kissed him. If she really knew what was going on inside my head, she'd think I was a neurotic nut job. "Trust me," I say, "there is no need for an attractive woman to apologize for kissing a single straight male."

"Hmm." She looks confused. "Well anyway, goodnight. I'll give you a call soon." And she's back in her house just like that.

I think that I wouldn't mind holding her, being with her, listening to what she has to say, and being as helpful as I can. She could lean on me, and, when I need it, I could lean on her. Wouldn't that be nice?

Rule number three: stay as close to the characters as needed, but never too close.

Alright I got it. But let me work on one rule at a time. I still need to diffuse that 'main character' bomb. I walk back to my place with a new spring in my step.

CH. 26

It's years ago. I'm not in my story, but in the comfort of my home with Jimmy, Lindsey, and Molly. It's a simpler time (if "simpler" is really the correct way to describe reality). The Incident obviously hasn't happened yet; after all, Molly is still with us alive and well. But we're not far away from The Incident. It's five days prior and we're all brimming with anticipation of the trip. We're drinking as we always did—still do, but then we were happy when we did—and we're having a good laugh at the expense of some grammatical slip that Jimmy said. What it was, I can't remember. It really doesn't matter. It wasn't really that funny. Happiness and intoxication always intensify hilarity.

"Anyway," Jimmy says, eluding the humiliation, "we're going to need to make sure we all pack everything that's needed."

"Don't worry," Molly says, "I've already packed the condoms."

We all roar into laughter. It wasn't really that funny, but once again, happiness and intoxication....

"So," Jimmy says chuckling, "for one thing, it's important that we all bring a week's worth of clothes—probably more in case something gets wet—towels and swimsuits-"

"Screw swimsuits," Molly says. "We should skinny-dip." We laugh at the not-humor. "Let our bodies flow free!"

Jimmy says with a mock stern tone, "I normally would be all for it, but I don't want this pervert," he points at me, "ogling my sweetie." He gives Molly an exaggerated hug and kiss on the cheek.

I laugh and say to Jimmy, "I'm more concerned at *you* eyeballing *me*."

We all give ourselves a hearty bawl of laughter, showing compassion through mockery, and appreciation through laughter. In my experience, healthy relationships can best be defined by how much you insult each other and how little you take offense.

"Well," I say, "I'm going to step outside for a smoke." Sure, I don't have a restriction for smoking in my house, but out of respect for Molly's asthma, I choose not to smoke indoors while she's around.

"Henry, I thought you were quitting," Lindsey says in a tone of disappointment that I can't decide if it's comical or sincere.

I decide to risk it and think it's comical. "Of course I'm quitting. If I had *quit*, then I wouldn't still be smoking. I'd be done with it. Quitting is easy; I've been doing it for years."

She laughs. "Well in that case… do you have a spare?"

"What?" I say. "You don't smoke."

"I used to, and I have a hankering suddenly," she says.

I pause for a second. "I feel a little guilty… but what the hell?"

"Alright," she says, "I'll meet you outside. Let me grab my coat."

"Whoa," Jimmy's voice rises with jocularity. "Someone's a corrupting influence." I laugh.

The teasing of "bad influence" and "peer pressure" follow me out the door.

Leaning back against the door, looking outside, waiting for

Lindsey, I whisper to myself, "Truly, this is the best of all possible worlds." I say this not in the satirical way of Voltaire's <u>Candide</u>, but more in the sincere way of Gottfried Leibniz, even though at that time I hadn't read any of his works. What could I say? My book was going to be published, I'm in love, and I'm about to venture on a week of shenanigans with my best friend, his girlfriend, and the love of my life. Being inebriated didn't hurt either. I was ecstatic and, believe it or not, optimistic.

Lindsey's increasing tardiness makes me wonder if she changed her mind and plays a little at my patience, so I reach for my cigarettes. Sure enough, I've left them inside. It probably fell out of my pockets and landed between the couch cushions. I turn around and open the door to go back to find them.

I'm immediately teleported to my bed with my head leaning against the wall in a drunken stupor. Lindsey is sitting in a chair in front of me. Jimmy and Molly are gone—Molly for good. Not only have I been teleported through the house, but time as well. It's a year later—well after The Incident that changed us all, and shortly after the critics had begun to lambast my story. This is also two days after I talked Jimmy out of killing himself. I was there for Jimmy, and for a long time had been there for Lindsey, but ever since the criticism I have pretty much only been there for myself—comforting myself through pity and alcohol.

Even though it's just recently after the first anniversary of her best friend's death, I'm being a self-centered asshole and not being there for the only girl who meant anything to me. She, on the other hand, is actually trying to comfort *me*. I wish I could have changed this whole time of my life. I was so concerned that the only important thing in my life was being crushed before my eyes, while the real important thing in my life was losing her patience with me.

"You're drifting right now," she says. "That's okay. Sometimes it's good to drift."

"Hmm," I say. The entire time she's baring her soul to me,

and I'm appeasing her with half-hearted, laconic responses.

"But I'm just warning you; while drifting can sometimes be healthy, sometimes you can drift too far," she says as her eyes get wet. "I don't want to lose you." A tear falls from her right eye and I give another emotionless grunt. "Because if you drift too far," she pauses choking on her words, "I don't know if I can get you back." She finally breaks down into a regular flow of tears. "Please come back to me."

My eyes flutter open and I'm back inside the Douglas Inn and, more importantly, in the present. I give a slight chortle. Living fiction, dreaming reality; one hell of a way to live. Yes, that's correct; both of those memories are real. Memories that I drowned out years ago breathe once again through the wonders of sleep. I haven't visited those memories in so long. The same way a person with a traumatic experience suppresses those memories of that horrible incident, so does the guilty party in a break-up suppress the happy times they shared and the reasons why they were at fault.

A vertiginous sensation overwhelms me. That's what most people don't realize: vertigo can also occur from being extremely low. Once again trying to suppress those memories, I look at the clock. In about three hours I have my interview for a job as a teacher. After getting dressed, I grab my complimentary breakfast and coffee, and head out. The entire time, Lindsey's lecture on "drifting" haunts me. As I said before, some people say they live a life free of regrets. Some people lie.

Once I finally get in, the principal and the department head greet me with warmth and what would appear to be admiration. It's almost as if, this is not as much a job interview as it is an honor for them to meet me. The principal, John Richards, surprises me that he's still breathing, much less managing a school. I'm not saying that he keeps himself in poor health. I'm guessing that he exercised every day and took care of himself in his youth. I'm just emphasizing 'in his youth.' It wouldn't surprise me in the least to hear that he is in his late nineties. And as for the department head, Ernest Winston, he is filled with more energy than I thought was possible in a human. He talks a mile a minute and is filled with an incredible intense enthusiasm at every word he says. If he weren't a department head, and didn't look so healthy, I would have presumed he made himself a speed/cocaine/coffee cocktail to help him through the interview. The vice principal, Shelly Lin, who helped set up this interview, is currently in a meeting and will be joining us shortly, or so the two men assure me.

Ernest's peppy rhapsodies begin the conversation. "We've heard all about you. Through Shelly, and of course your incredible act of heroism." I've got to deal with this still? I open my mouth to try and tell him to not mention it, but get no opportunity through Ernest's ability to talk continuously without breathing. "That recorded account was magnificent. I saw the video. Completely breathtaking. Breathtaking I tell you. It literally took my breath away. In a world where so many people are only concerned about their own wellbeing, it is refreshing to hear of a man who so selflessly risked his life. Absolutely refreshing, I tell you." I can think of so many ways how this man is going to get under my skin if I get this job.

I notice a rare pause for breath that gives me the chance to talk, but John takes my opportunity from me as he decides to pipe his crackling slow voice. "Yes, yes, it would certainly be refreshing to have a celebrity among our staff." *Celebrity?* Really? That's even worse than 'hero.'

"Absolutely!" Ernest chimes in emphatically. "Refreshing. Completely refreshing!"

"To be honest," I venture, "I believe most people would have done the same if they were in my shoes."

Ernest's face is stunned as if it had just been slapped. His lips mouth an enthusiastic O in disbelief.

"Hmm?" John smiles. "Humility: an excellent virtue."

Ernest takes the opportunity to once again parrot with enthusiasm, "Yes a great virtue. An excellent virtue."

This continues for some time until business must be gotten to, and we begin the actual interview.

"Well..." John begins "what do you believe... in your experience, is the most important aspect of teaching?"

"In my experience," I begin, wondering what the hell I'm going to say, because in reality I have no experience, "I find that the most important aspect would be to keep the students engaged and active." John closes his eyes and takes a deep breath, which I'm not able to decipher if that is a good or bad sign. "Many students, in my experience, tend to slack off. One thing to curtail this is to present the lessons in an interesting and engaging format." Still no response from John, but Ernest is nodding emphatically. But then again, he always is. "I've seen teachers give lackadaisical lessons, and they only succeed in boring the students to the point of drifting from their studies. Poor production in the teachers equals poor production in the students." I pause but John still has his eyes closed and has made no reaction whatsoever while Ernest just continues to bob his head up and down like a parakeet. "The other thing to keep in mind is that nowadays it's almost acceptable among their peers for students to not do the work and forgo the readings. My goal is to make the students who bypass the readings feel out of place, instead of accepted by and large by the student body."

Still no reaction from John who sits with his eyes closed and is utterly silent. Still Ernest nods his head frantically. Come to think of it, I'm not sure if John has breathed in the past minute. Initially, I thought that he fell asleep, but now I'm starting to think that the old man's heart finally gave way. This uneasiness is making me sweat and now even Ernest turns to look at John with what looks like alarm.

"Yes, quite so," the old man finally gives a sign that he is alive. Thank God. I've already seen enough dead bodies in my short time in this world. "That would be quite important. Keep the students engaged."

"Yes!" Ernest says in more excitement than usual, "Very important!"

Jesus, this is the weirdest job interview I've ever been to. One man on the brink of death, the other fresh from his coffee enema; I don't know how I'm going to make it through the rest of this.

With that, Shelly Lin, the vice principal who knows Adeline, walks in and introduces herself. She tells me that she "heard all about me," and mentions nothing of my 'heroism.' I like her already.

The rest of the interview is for the most part ordinary (at least question wise). General interview questions like naming three strengths and weaknesses, and very few questions that are actually related to the job at hand. It's much shorter than I imagined, at least if you subtract Ernest's long bouts of word expulsions. They say they'll get back to me in a few weeks and see me out the door. I have no idea if it went well or not, but I guess I'll find out soon.

I walk out, not sure of what to do, and I grab my phone and call Adeline.

"So how did it go?" she says immediately.

"What do you mean?" I ask.

"The interview," she says. "You didn't forget, did you?" She has some worry in her voice.

"Oh," I laugh, "that. I think it went well. I guess I'll find out soon. By the way, what is with the principal and the department head? For a minute I thought the principal died on me, and I'm pretty sure Ernest is on some high-grade stimulant."

She laughs, "Yeah, Shelly has told me about them."

"Anyway," I say, "You want to meet sometime soon?"

"Sure," she says, "How does coffee at 10:00 AM on Wednesday sound?"

"Hold on, let me check." I press the phone against my chest

and count to ten. "Works fine for me."

"Well then, it's a date," she says.

We say goodbye and hang up. Walking in the beautiful sunny day, I say to myself, "Truly, this is the best of all possible worlds."

CH. 27

She's running a little late again—not too late, not even ten minutes so far—but I'm a little worried considering what I know about her sister's suicidal tendencies. After all, that was the reason for her last no-show; every other time there had been no tardiness.

The coffee shop has an older feel to it. I don't think Wi-Fi is as much as a concern as having a welcoming throwback ambience. The lights are dim, the wood is stained to give a rustic vibe, and the windows seem intentionally fogged. Even though it's the summer, this seems like the place people would gather for warmth on a cold winter's day in the backwoods of some rural town.

Even the music is a throwback. The song nearing its conclusion right now is Mozart's Symphony Whatever-number-it-is. Don't blame me for not knowing the song; I'm not well-versed in Mozart's compilations. You could throw out any arbitrary number and I'd believe you. I don't know if this is a way to add a classier up-scale vibe to the place, or to just have people relaxed and engage more on conversation than singing along to the music. Neither would surprise me.

While waiting for Adeline, I figure I'd eavesdrop in other people's conversations. Some couple to my right is bickering over what punishment is suitable to one of their children who didn't do his assigned chores.

"He needs at least a week without being able to see his friends," the man says.

"A week seems too steep. A couple days at most," the woman retorts.

The man rejects this notion, "If we're too soft on him, he'll develop into a boy with no discipline. We need him to develop into a man. That is our job as parents."

"So what? He missed taking out the trash one day," the woman says. "This is the only time that I can actually think of that something like this happened. He's got a better track record than *you*. How long ago did you say you were going to fix the sink?"

There's another table to the left of me that also has a couple, but is not nearly as conventional. They are much younger; possibly still in high school, the latest I'll give them is late college. The man is thin, has a black shirt on and tight jeans with rips in it. I believe the jeans had been ripped prior to sale. The woman has abnormally long hair, dressed all in black, and is decorated with piercings in her ears, lips, and nose.

"Look babe, I would never cheat on you," the man says semi-attentive.

"I saw your phone. You're fucking her. She's your ex and you told me she was a whore. Why the fuck would you still be texting her?" she's saying with what looks like a mix of anger, a desire to be heard, and a fear of angering him.

The man rolls his eyes. "Jesus, calm down will ya? You're being a paranoid bitch. I didn't text her; she texted me. What was I supposed to do? Say nothing?"

A table adjacent to them has a family with two young children. They decide to discreetly move further away from the couple cursing at each other.

As Mozart ends, a new song begins. This one I know. I memorized it a long time ago when I decided to do choir for a year in high school. It's Beethoven's Ode to Joy. Granted, I don't remember the words now, but I still enjoy the tune.

Apparently I'm not the only one who enjoys this tune because some man behind me is singing along with it. "Freude shoener Gotterfunken, Touchter aus Elysium."

I turn to take a glance at who is singing, but before I do, Adeline places her hand on my shoulder and apologizes for being late.

Still the man is singing, "Wir betreten feuertunken Himmlesche dein Heiligtum."

I tell her there's no reason to apologize, and we go up to order our coffee. I order some coffee made with a Brazilian mix of beans, at Adeline's recommendation.

While waiting for the coffee we have some light conversation and, much to my relief, her tardiness had nothing to do with her sister. She had somebody calling her from work that had some problems that needed to be sorted out by the upcoming school year.

All the while the man continues to sing, "Seid umschlungen Millionen! Diesen Kuss der ganzen Welt!"

"So how was the interview?" she asks.

"Brueder ueber'm Sternenzelt Muss ein lieber Vater wohnen," the singing man continues.

"Odd." I laugh a little. "I mean despite John and Ernest's idiosyncrasies, I guess everything went well."

"Yeah, it did," she says.

"Wem der grosse Wurf gelungen Eines Freundes Freund zu sein," the man continues to sing.

"Why do you say that?" I ask her.

They hand us the coffee and we make our way to the table. I try to find the singing man, but it's too late. After the door closes, his sound is no more. He left, and the intentionally fogged windows make it impossible to identify him.

"I talked to Shelly." She smiles.

"Oh," I say, "she said it went well?"

"You got the job," she says.

"That quick? I thought-I mean these processes are normally longer in my experience," I say.

"The only thing you could have done was done something incredibly terrible to ruin your chance. You already had the job before the interview," she says.

"Your influence has that much clout?" I say, quite vexed.

"Of course not." She laughs. "They all knew you from the news. Being a hero gets you quite a bit of perks." I roll my eyes. Well at least I got a job. I guess saving a life can have some benefits. "Plus your resume, from what I heard, was, to say the very least, impressive."

I hear Coralline Thomson's voice, 'Just make it up and the story will morph around it.' I really am Jake Neilson: god of the monotonous.

I'm semi-relieved. "Well I guess this means I ought to rent an apartment."

Adeline smiles, and as the cause and effect principles always work with her, I smile too.

I think of the fact that I'm living here opens up a new realm of possibilities for our relationship. I could stay here; she could move in with me or vice versa. We could take our casual dates to another level. Both of us, with our secure jobs, could possibly settle down and get married. We could have children, raise them through good times and bad, deal with our children's teenage years together, teach them how to drive, be there at their graduation, smile as they grow into the fine young men and women they'll be, absorb each other's happiness as we see our children find a partner, get married, have children, and repeat the process that we did, become grandparents, grow old, and-

Rule number four: Always remember that this will inevitably end.

Alright, alright, I get it. Can't you let a man fantasize for a

little bit?

We go back to our conversation and somehow find ourselves on the subject of the nature of psychology.

"I've been trying to follow Alice in her conversations relating to psychology for quite a while," Adeline says. "I was hoping to start conversing with her and not seem like a complete dunce while talking to her, so I read some books and works on the topic. I was bored and read some newer views on psychology as well as some older ones by Sigmund Freud and Carl Jung. I even read the entire DSM V."

I laugh. "You read the DSM V? Boy you must have been *really* bored."

"You have no idea." She laughs with me. "But anyway, I came to the conclusion that there is a positive side to every mental illness."

"I don't believe it," I say.

"Try me," she says. "Name any illness."

"Alright," I say, "bipolar."

"Easiest one," she says. "People who are diagnosed with bipolar disorder are more likely to be creative people. Hemmingway: bipolar. Vonnegut: bipolar. Poe: bipolar. Woolf: bipolar."

"Alright. I guess that was too easy," I say. "How about OCD?"

"An obsession that includes cleanliness," she says. "Hygiene is always a good thing. Not to mention that being obsessed about a topic—while detrimental in some things—could lead to you solving something that everybody else gives up on."

"ADD," I say.

"Ever heard of stopping to enjoy the simple things in life?" she says. "Well, with ADD your always noticing what would be overlooked by most."

I think hard. What would be something that wouldn't have any benefit? "Multiple personality disorder."

She thinks to herself for a moment. Finally, I got her. Then she smiles and says, "Well you never have to worry about dying alone."

I laugh. "You know, you're quite the bullshitter. I wish I had as much talent in anything as you have in that aspect."

"I'm sure you do," she says. "What's some talent—no matter how trivial or odd—that you excel at?"

I think to myself. "Well, it may seem a little strange, but I can name the fourth song in any Beatles album."

She laughs, "That has to be the most obscure, specific, and weird area to have a talent in."

"You said 'no matter how trivial or odd,'" I say.

"Alright," she says, "let's test this." She thinks to herself then says, "Sergeant Pepper's."

"Oh please," I say. "Getting Better."

"Revolver," she says.

"Love You To," I say.

"Rubber Soul," she says.

"Nowhere Man," I say. "Come on, give me a challenge."

"Alright Past Masters," she says.

"Volume one or two?" I say.

"Two," she says.

"Rain," I say.

"Jesus," she says exasperated, "what are you an idiot savant?"

"Heavy on the idiot; light on the savant," I say, and we both start laughing. Her laugh; enhanced with divinity. Mine; tainted with normality. Normally in front of a person like her, I would feel inadequate or inferior in some way. But for some reason, something about her just doesn't make me feel that way. Instead I feel something that I just can't put my finger on. Comfort? Peace? Holiness? Content? Wholeness? I don't know.

We talk a little more and then she kisses my cheek and heads off. When she leaves I go up to order a piece of banana bread and then leave the coffee house, jolted from the cool comfort of the coffee house to the plain, hot, summery world that I enter.

I take a bite of the banana bread. The coffee was great, and the banana bread is delicious. Adeline sure has great taste in dining choices.

As I'm walking, what looks like a stray dog cautiously approaches me. His doleful eyes crave some sort of attention, while his bone-thin body is obviously craving nutrition of any kind. I break off a piece of the bread and hold it out to him. He gulfs it down, and gives me an accolade of hand licks. Maybe that's not as much an act of appreciation as it is the desire to get any other food that may have stuck to my hand, but I'm appreciative nonetheless.

As I walk away, the dog follows me. He found a deliverer of food. I have become his temporary god. He is the only one in this entire town to realize me for the god I am to them. When he follows me, some are a little wary of this starving dog, but I don't mind. All failures love the few acolytes they have, even if they're not human.

I continue walking with the dog beside me to see Coralline Thomson—Jane Young—before I continue my mission of talking to the characters in my story.

The meeting with Coralline Thomson was short and halfhearted on both of our parts. She came down with some kind of minor stomach virus, and I was trying to evade answering her on the progress of minimalizing my new stardom in this town.

"So how are you doing on fixing the damage you caused by breaking the second rule?" she asks.

"I think I've made a lot of progress. Actually, nobody really mentions it anymore," I tell her.

"You and I both know that's bullshit," she says. Apparently obscenities enhance when she's feeling ill. "I still hear people talk about it, so I know you, the person who actually caused the action, are still hearing it all the time."

"Alright fine. You're right. But listen Jane, I'm working on it, and in time the minor stardom will fizzle out on its own." I just realized that I said 'Jane,' and am surprised in how natural it flows off my tongue.

"I hope so," she says, "because if this escalates any further, then you're going to have a real mess of a story."

"If that happens couldn't we start over?" I ask.

"It doesn't work like that," she says.

"Why not?" I ask.

"Jake," she says, "this process is very complicated and explaining it would be very difficult, but I will tell you what I know in due time. Right now, I'm feeling quite ill, am very sleep deprived, and am having a difficult time thinking, much less talking. So I'll explain why at another time."

"In that case, do you just want to call it a day, and we'll meet up at a later date?" I ask, and she's more than willing to accept my offer. She left me with some advice to avoid conversations about saving the girl's life—which I've already been doing—and even recommended that I act a little irritated or even callous if that would lessen people's opinion of me. After that, I was roaming the streets again.

It's gotten dark. I've been on the streets going into certain places, talking with the locals, and then leaving. I decided to go to that coffee house and grab a decaf for the road. Adeline told me that this place was open late, so I figured I'd give it a try. Sure enough, I get there at 10:58, and the store closes at 11:00. I order some mix of Vietnamese coffee beans, and get it to go.

While walking back to my hotel, I wonder what the chances were of seeing that stray dog again. I figure I'd like to see him for some reason, even though I have no food to give him this time. I doubt a dog would like coffee. I take another sip and enjoy the exquisite flavor. The entire time I'm thinking of where to go from here.

Tomorrow, I should probably start looking for an apartment. I figure it would be more normal for someone to live in an apartment or house instead of staying in a hotel for such a long time. I should try to fit in. Normality would lead to inconspicuousness, and inconspicuousness would hopefully lead to people forgetting about me saving that girl. But I'm not going to lie; there are some perks to being a hero.

Yes I get it that I should not be a main character, but the way that Adeline's eyes light up when she talks about it, the way that in some way she adores me, hearing Adeline say something as simple as 'You really are such a great person' just warms a part of me. And what about 'When it comes down to crunch time, you're the man to be trusted'? I mean talk about an ego-stroke. Normally I try not to be vain. I'm the last person that someone would call a narcissist, but when someone like her says that, how can I not feel something? I'm not one to be vainglorious, but come on, cut me some slack.

As I'm passing an alley, there's a slight rustling. I move closer to inspect it. Maybe it's the dog. I wish I had some food for him; he's probably starving. Then it's less of a rustling and more of a dull thudding, then a banging against the dumpster. I feel some alarm, but figure maybe some drunks decided to have a little fun, and didn't want to wait until they get home.

Finally a woman falls down. It's hard to make out who she is, but she looks familiar. I take a step closer. I see blond hair, white skin. I take a couple steps to see if she's alright. She has some wet globs on her shirt. She coughs up blood and once again I freeze.

Now the panic kicks in. My thoughts aren't coherent enough to act. She's still alive, but only for a little longer. She's on her back trying to breathe, but choking, only getting a breath when she coughs up another shot of blood. Her head turns to face me, but I can't tell if she notices me at all. Her eyes are glazed over and her face is white with panic. A man crouches over her and delicately spreads her fingers and places his knife on the middle finger. Now I know what's happening. And I run.

I'm running as fast as I can. Even though my coffee has completely spilled out, I'm still clinging to the cup. Maybe I think it will act as a way to protect me. Maybe I find it to serve the same purpose that a teddy bear has to a frightened child. I don't know, but for whatever reason I'm clinging to it.

Panicking, I'm running faster than I think I've ever run in my life. I could break the mile in two minutes flat. Move out of the way Usain Bolt; you've got competition.

I have no clue where I'm going, nor do I care. I'm just running. Where am I going? Away; that's where.

I don't have an idea if Richard Sweeney saw me, but I don't want to find out. Yes, I know it's him. He went right for the fingers. He's beginning his process. I'm terrified.

I saw that woman's body, lying on the ground; the life trickling away from her eyes. Maybe there would have been a chance to save her, but I didn't take it.

When it comes down to crunch time, you're the man to be trusted.

Oh Adeline, if only you could see me now. But Coralline, oh Coralline, you would be so proud. I was faced with the possibility to potentially save someone, and instead of braving the situation, I turned tail and run.

You really are such a great person.

Oh fuck off! You're not real! None of you are real. You're just a product of my imagination. I am your god. I am everyone's god. And if I let one of you die, then nothing really happened. No one died. Just my imagination. *But that blood was real wasn't it? The woman coughing out her life and looking at you; that felt pretty real didn't it?*

I'm running away. I'm sure I'm far enough away, but I run anyway. I just keep running until there's no more energy left. I'm not even running in the direction of my hotel; I'm just running.

Finally I run out of energy and slump against the side of a building. I'm shaking, holding my empty cardboard coffee cup, trying to focus on stopping it from shaking.

The word 'coward' comes to mind. The word 'murderer' comes to mind. But those aren't the correct words. They can't be.

The words 'desensitized killing' comes to mind. But that's not right either.

The coffee cup is still shaking fast. I try to stabilize it by putting a second hand on it, but this doesn't work.

I just let someone die. I don't know who, but now she's dead. *It's not real!* But god damn it, it feels pretty fucking real to me.

I focus on my breathing, taking deep breaths. Inhale. Exhale. Inhale. Exhale. I feel my body shake less. I feel calmer, but still not complete.

So what do I do? Do I report this to the police?

Never become a main character.

Then what? Not say anything? Let some random person, maybe an innocent kid, find her? Let that stray mutt pick at her bones? Let him scavenge her leftovers?

But I already know Coralline Thomson's answer.

I give some deep breathing, clinging to my empty cup, and slowly relax.

Hours pass and I'm still in the same spot. Still focusing on my breathing; still clinging to my cup.

I see a man approach from a distance. He's whistling to himself, oblivious that someone just got murdered, just without a care in the world. He gets closer, still whistling to himself. The tune sounds familiar, but I'm too verklempt to decipher which tune.

He approaches and his face hints of familiarity. As he gets closer, I recognize who it is. My heart quickens a few beats per minute. My face gets paler. My already dry mouth gets the remaining moisture completely sucked out. It's Richard Sweeney.

I'm slumped against a building as he starts to walk by. I hold my breath as if this would somehow fool him. When he reaches me he stops. There are still some blood stains on his shirt. I try to swallow but there's no saliva there. My heart rate doubles; then triples. I thought I had sweated out all the moisture in my body. I thought I could perspire no more. I was wrong.

He slowly turns to face me. My breath quickens. *I'm dead!* I think. *There's no hope for me! He saw me!*

He looks at me. Analyzing me—possibly scrutinizing me—all with a pleasant smile. There are some dark stains on his clothes. You couldn't notice if you were just passing by—especially in the dark—but I notice. I notice everything. The way his blue eyes analyze me, as if processing or inspecting me. Seeing if I'm worthy. To what? To die? I don't know.

His eyes seem to glow because of the way the street lights are positioned. He wears a wool lightweight coat even though there's no need for it. It's hot, even hotter because of how fast my heart is going. He has a large grin. It goes from ear to ear. It's an indecipherable grin. I can't tell if it's an innocent grin, a lecherous grin, a sinister grin, or a charitable grin. That's his disguise, that indistinguishable face.

God if he's going to kill me, could he just do it already. If he doesn't kill me now, I'll die of a heart attack.

He reaches into his coat pocket. I can't even cry for help because my tongue's too dry to make a sound. He's going to grab the knife. I'm dead.

I close my eyes in a hope to satiate my fear. *Well this is it. It was a fun ride.*

I take a deep breath and hold it. There's a delay, and then I hear the sound of metal clinking around, then nothing. I open my eyes; see his face close to mine, his hand leaving my coffee cup, and now my panic has turned to puzzlement. I look in my cup and see about a dollar's worth of change, all in pennies, nickels, and dimes.

"God bless," he says.

He gives me a wink and starts walking away whistling a tune. I believe the tune was Ode to Joy.

CH. 28

Paranoia is a suitable word for my current state, but it doesn't encompass the entire feeling. Confusion works too, but once again doesn't sum it all up. Panic-stricken also works, but falls into the same problem. Terrified, baffled, immobilized, neurotic, crazed, unsure, perplexed, numb, enraged, depressed, drained, horrified, traumatized: all of these are good words, but wouldn't embody the whole feeling.

It's two days after I saw the woman coughing up her life, saw Richard Sweeney preparing his ritualistic slaughter, and saw him drop change in my cup and wink at me, and I haven't slept a minute. What I wouldn't give for the old forty winks to relieve me of this terror-shocked state, but sure enough I haven't had such luck. I tried though. I took a sick day from this story and just spent the whole day yesterday lying in my hotel room bed. I turned my phone off, put up a do not disturb sign—the whole nine yards—but sure enough it was to no avail.

Right now I'm sitting on the edge of my bed with the gun I bought from Old Man Hackley in my hands. I don't know what I'm doing with it. I have no idea what I'm going to do with it either. Yet for some reason it brings me comfort. I use my finger and stroke from the barrel to the hammer, and then guide my finger down to the grip handle. Finally my finger finds solace at the trigger.

This isn't me. I don't even like guns. My body, for the time being, is not controlled by my conscious mind. It's not me at all. My body has been hijacked by this sleep deprived man that lives inside of me and does things for reasons unknown to anyone, including himself.

How will I protect myself? Do I need protection? Is it even feasible for me to actually protect myself? Is the ability to keep myself safe an illusion? Is safety on its own an illusion? Is everything an illusion? I smile at that last question.

I hold the gun and point it at various objects in the room. Then I rest it against my temple. It's an interesting feeling. I put the gun in my mouth, barrel first. *It wouldn't be all that difficult*, I think to myself. *Tons of people do it every day.*

What am I thinking? I pull the gun out of my mouth and rest it on the bed. Why am I thinking this way? I guess too much alone time and too little sleep. I decide I need to go out. I put away the gun, grab my phone, and enter this crazy world once again.

I'm sitting in Sunny Side Up having quite a bit of coffee to wake me up. It succeeded in making me more awake, but not in making me more alert or coherent. Coralline Thomson called me a few times yesterday since I had apparently blown off our meeting, so I called her back and told her to meet me here.

She arrives riddled with agitation, "Where were you yesterday?"

"Jesus, Coralline," I say, "calm down will ya?"

"We're in your story, so call me Jane," she says.

"And you call me Ishmael," I say and laugh with no idea what's so funny.

"What are you talking about?" she says irritated.

"Honey," I say, "I was sort of hoping you would tell me, because I haven't the foggiest."

She gives a look of both confusion and concern, "Have you lost your mind?"

I smile, "That implies I had a mind to begin with."

"What's wrong with you?" she asks, starting to get nervous.

"Too much thinkin' and not enough drinkin'," I say. I kind of like that line. I decide that I'm going to use that again sometime.

"You're actually concerning me right now. Are you alright?" she says.

"I'm fine," I tell her, "I just haven't slept in two days and this coffee has just made me slaphappy."

"Two days?" she asks.

"Uh-huh," I say, "Two days."

The waitress comes by, causing a temporary pause in our conversation, and we order our food. Surprising myself when you consider all the events of the last couple of days, I'm not at all curt with her. On the contrary, I'm very pleasant. I am patient with her questions about how I want everything done and am even patient when she asked me to repeat myself. I should be understanding. After all, with my lack of sleep, my order was more confusing than normal. She takes her leave and Coralline starts questioning me again.

"You have to understand why I'm a little worried," she says. "Not sleeping for two days is unnatural. What caused this?"

My slap happiness dissipates, and I go back to the grave emotion I had previously. "I saw him."

"Who?" she asks.

"Richard Sweeney," I say, and I can feel the color run from my face as I remember the other night's events play once again through my memory.

"So what about him? I told you to talk to him after all. You should be seeing him, quite frequently in fact," she says.

"No you don't get it," I say. "I mean I saw him in action."

"You mean-?" I nod and her eyes light up with excitement. "That's incredible! I was hoping you would talk to him, but you actually saw him in mid-kill? That's great news!"

I honestly didn't know what her reaction would be, but I sure as hell didn't expect this. She's acting like a little school girl who just got asked out by her big crush. This isn't natural. I just told her that I witnessed somebody getting brutally murdered, and she's giddy with excitement. And just think, just a minute ago she was asking me if *I* lost *my* mind.

"Great news?" I ask.

"Yes," she says without hesitation, "great news. You witnessing key moments in your story, or something that really exposes the true nature of one of your characters, is a massive triumph for the sake of your story." Her smile fades briefly. "Wait, I just thought of something negative about this." Really? I told you that I saw someone getting brutally murdered by a psychopathic serial killer and then positioned so he can leave his calling card, and you managed to find something negative about that? Please, do tell. "He didn't see you, did he?"

I tell her no and then relay to her the whole story from the woman falling in the street to Richard confusing me with a vagabond and dumping change in my cup. She notices me giving off signs of remorse and empathy as I do, and this gets her unnerved. I guess not being as elated as she is over a witnessed homicide makes her feel a little uneasy.

"You seem upset by this?" she says.

I stare at her dumbly, baffled by her callousness. "Well yeah, I kind of just saw some woman get horribly murdered"

Now she's really concerned. "You do know that this isn't real? The woman that was murdered was only in your imagination. You do know that no one actually died?" she says these as if she's checking to see if I actually do know this.

I roll my eyes, "Yeah, I know, I know. But it's different

when you witness it as opposed to hearing it vicariously through me. It's just... it's just..." I'm scrounging around for a word, but can't find it because of insufficient sleep, "it's just different. Ya know?"

The waitress comes by, delivering our food. I can't remember what I ordered. When I see the plate, it's an omelet of some kind, but I'm not sure what's in it. Oh well, this won't be the first time I didn't know what I was getting into, so I take a bite.

As I start eating, the coffee wears off and my mind is slow and lethargic once again. Great, this will be another wasted day.

"So have you made any other progress recently?" Coralline asks.

"I guess," I say.

Trying to pry a little more she says, "Like what?"

I shrug my shoulders, "Stuff." I answer like a teenager trying to avoid a lecture from his parents.

She's gets a little red in the face, "You know you don't want to just shirk me off with laconic responses. Remember, I'm your only connection to reality while you're in this world." She annunciates 'reality' and 'this world' to make sure that I remember to distinguish the two from each other.

"I guess," I say, just wanting to go to bed.

She shakes her head a little bit. "You know you should really shake this whole apathetic bit. It doesn't suit you, and it can be quite counterproductive."

I give a half shrug of the shoulders and just grunt. We finish our food, say goodbye, and head our separate ways for the rest of the day.

When you've reached a point of sleep deprivation far beyond what anyone should endure, reality starts to blur. I fully realize the irony of me saying this, given the circumstances that I'm currently in, but it holds true nonetheless.

Time becomes irrelevant. If thirty minutes pass, it would

seem as if anywhere from ten minutes to three hours had lapsed. There's also quite a few other oddities to guide you. You sweat regardless of the temperature. The temperature itself is irrelevant. When it's hot you could feel cold, and when it's cold you could feel hot. On top of all of this, sometimes minor hallucinations can take place. For instance, at least ten times so far I've heard my phone ring faintly, and when I checked it, there was nobody calling. A couple of times I've heard my name called; both 'Henry' and 'Jake', but when I turn to look, nobody was waving me down.

So somewhere in-between one and ten hours after leaving the restaurant, it has gotten dark. The sun went down, which means that it is now socially acceptable to start drinking.

I weave my way into some dive bar. Even though I'm currently more sober than anyone in here, I feel more out of it than the rest of the occupants. I probably look drunker than anyone else too. I'm doing my insomniac stumble, my eyes have endless bags, the color is vanished from my face, my eyes stay on one area for prolonged periods of time and are unfocused, and on top of that I feel feverish.

As I sit at the bar, the bartender looks at me, wondering if I've had too much even though I've yet to begin. "You don't look so hot," he says. "Is everything alright?"

"Yep," I tell him, "just too much thinkin' and not enough drinkin'." I told you I was going to use that again. Although this time, entering a bar, it actually makes sense. But from the way I look, the bartender probably doesn't think it makes sense at all. I smile and look up at him. "Anyway, barkeep, could you hit me with a whiskey on the rocks."

"You sure?" he says.

"Haven't been surer about anything in my life since the last time I... the last time... I..." I forgot where I was going with this, "since I don't know. But I'm sure about this. Hit me, will ya?" I knock on the table.

He shrugs his shoulders and pours me a whiskey. I slug it

down and apparently forgot how much your tolerance drops when you haven't had sleep. Regardless, I slug down another, then another, and then another.

I try to start a conversation with one of the patrons of the bar. He's an older man with a grey beard and fairly long hair. "How's it going buddy of mine?" I slap him on the back. The alcohol and sleep deprivation have done their job to render me goofy.

He looks at me somewhat peeved and somewhat quizzical, "What are you doing?"

"What's a matter?" I say, "Can't a guy go out and get a couple of drinks on a Saturday night?"

He looks down and shakes his head. Then he looks back at me. "It's Friday."

"I can't keep track of all these days," I say. "Don't blame me. They all end in 'y'"

He curls his face into a frown, "You're not young enough or old enough to get wasted by yourself at a bar."

"Hey, that's age discrimination." I laugh.

"You need help," he says.

"Man," I say, "you have no idea." I pause. "I may need help one day, but I need something else right now." I then call over to the bartender and order another whiskey. I gulp it down and hit the road. "Nice chatting with ya." I hear him grunt and then I'm out the door.

I'm back inside the hotel room, not sure of how I got there. The walk was kind of a blur. That five minute to three hour walk just seems all fuzzy to me. Somehow I was leaving the bar, and now I'm lying on the bed in my boxers, holding a gun against my chest.

The gun makes me feel protected. But 'protected' doesn't tell the whole feeling. Secure works too, but doesn't sum it all up. Helpless also works, but once again fails to convey the whole emotion.

I lie there blinking, heavily believing that this might be the lucky night when I finally get some shut eye. My hands are resting on the gun; the adult teddy bear.
And right there, with my hand straddling the handle and my finger around the trigger; I fall asleep.

CH. 29

For a while I honestly thought I was on the path to going mad. I thought when I witnessed that horrific scene, I had finally breached the walls protecting my mind from insanity. I guess the jury could still be out on that, but at least I have gotten significantly better. It turns out one of the healthiest antidotes for losing your mind is sleep. Now that I have gotten some rest, I feel worlds better and am ready to take on this crazy story I'm living in.

Although I'm not going to lie, there's not much that's more terrifying than waking up to realize that you're holding a gun. In an even more reckless affront to gun safety, I fling the gun across the room in shock. It wasn't one of my brightest ideas, but luckily nothing bad happened. It just hit the wall and fell to the floor.

My phone rings shortly after I fling the gun, so I let it go to voicemail until my heart rate levels out. I take some deep breaths, gather my bearings and check the message. It's John Richards, the principal of the high school I applied for, telling me that I got the job, and to call back for details. He's stringing along his words slowly—after each word I'm wondering if it will be his last—speaking maybe ten words per minute, and gives me his congratulations. If any other person were to have left that same voicemail, with the same word count, it would have been a short one—maybe one and a half—minute message, but with him speaking it's at least ten minutes.

I go to the bathroom, splash some water on my face, brush my teeth, shower, change, then call him back.

The secretary picks up the phone and puts me through to the principal. I've had time to calm down so I'm feeling better at conversing, "Hi. So sorry I missed your call."

His crackling baritone voice greets me, "It's alright, it's alright." He pauses a long time for breath and then he thinks on how to concoct his next sentence. "I would just like to welcome you to our staff and congratulate you on the new position."

"I'm sure it will be a pleasure," I say.

"Indeed it will," he croaks. "We were very impressed by you. You've made... quite a name for yourself in our community," he pauses once again, slowly taking in air, "and I can only hope that you will live up to expectations." He pauses and then adds, "And I'm sure you will."

"Well I certainly hope to," I say.

After that it is mainly him relaying some information of when I will start and what subject matter I should cover. He tells me about different meetings and gives me the basic information. I thank him and then we hang up.

I make my way downstairs to get the complimentary breakfast, coffee and the newspaper. It occurs to me that I didn't look at the paper or any news channels for the past two days, so I didn't find any information about the 'cross-killer,' and I feel as if I should. In fact, I feel a sense of urgency that I can't understand. I find myself moving faster and faster as I make my way to the ground floor. I'm not sure why, but now I'm almost jogging.

I make my way from the elevator to the front desk, sweating for some reason I can't place. Sure, I was speed walking a little fast, but it wasn't that far. I ask them for the paper and go into the dining area. I grab some coffee and some eggs and bacon. I open up the paper and look at the picture of the latest victim and stop sweating. I met this woman before. She was the stoned woman that told me how she lost her virginity to Ron Madsen when I met her at Ron's wake. She was innocent, nice, goodhearted, and a genuine good person. But why do I for some reason feel relieved?

I remember that day I met her. We started chatting, the whole time she had the cannabis giggles. She was trying to tell her story—I'll admit it was inappropriate to bring up at a wake—about how she lost her virginity to Ron. The entire time she was taking pauses to let out some giggles until she looked up behind me and saw detective Reynolds and started to walk away paranoid. Then Richard Sweeney walked in.

I remember the way he was staring at her. He was looking at her as an object, but not in the way of physical attraction. It was a different way. Sure he had the look of wanting to do things to her, but not sexual. It was something even more evil. That sinister gaze that still haunts me. Then for some reason I remember him whistling Ode to Joy and I involuntarily shiver.

My phone rings, breaking the dark path my mind was going. It's Adeline, and my heart warms up.

I pick up the phone, "You have no idea how good it is to hear from you."

"Where were you these past three days?" she says with irritation, which is the first time I've heard her with a voice that wasn't pleasant.

"Scratch that previous sentence," I say

"I tried calling you the other day and you didn't pick up," she says. "I left a voicemail and you didn't call me yesterday either."

"Sorry," I say, "I came down with something and had my phone off. I didn't feel like talking to anyone. And..." I think to myself, "I don't remember getting your message. Maybe I overlooked it." I really have to get used to how these cell phones work. Besides my time in this story, it's been years since I've had one.

She sighs. "It's alright. Just try to be more punctual next time."

"Will do," I say. "So how is everything?"

"Alright," she says, "just a little stressful."

I'm a little concerned, "Why?"

"My sister is growing antsy in the hospital and started to blame me for putting her there," she says. "She even said to me, 'If I wanted to live, I wouldn't have slit my wrists.' Then she went off about how it was my fault she was in the hospital. I'm just... I'm just... I don't know. I could use someone to talk to. I just want to get my mind off of things."

I feel depressed that I caused this. Such a perfect woman, with such a genuinely good soul has to deal with this much on her plate. And just to think, I'm responsible for it. I remember being young when my father died. I was so angry that I cursed God. I think I owe him quite the apology. I'm sure as hell not doing a good job filling the position either.

"I'm sorry to hear," I say. "I could use someone to get my mind off of some things too."

"What's wrong?" she says with concern, and for some reason I feel honored.

"Just too much time alone lets the mind wander," I tell her the half-truth.

"Alright," she says, "does six sound like a good time to meet?"

"Sounds good to me," I say.

We decide that we'll meet at the bar we first met at and go from there. We hang up and I wonder what to do between now and then. I figure I'd look at potential cars and apartments so I can cement my station in this town. I put the paper down, and once more head out.

I walk around going from car dealership to car dealership

and check online for prospective places to live for a number of hours. My assimilation in this story needs to be complete. I need to appear the average everyday person, and just learn more about people through my secret private investigation.

I decide to go to the bar a little bit early. I grew tired of jumping from different car dealerships and staring at the computer screen.

It's about twenty minutes prior to when Adeline is supposed to show up, and I've started on a few drinks at the bar. I'm just minding my own business, trying to avoid replaying the other night's events in my head. As much as I try to focus on the bar atmosphere, I can't help but see those images in my head—her bleeding from multiple parts of her chest and stomach, her coughing up blood, her turning in my direction, her glazed eyes, her pale face.

"Well what are the chances?" I hear a voice to my right. He's once again chewing a wad of gum, sipping on his beer and sizing me up. It's detective Reynolds. "Running into you again? I don't get how we manage to bump into each other all the time," he says, placing the wad of gum behind his gums with his tongue and sipping on his beer. "Well, what do you know?"

"Well," I say, "it's a small world after all."

"Ain't that the truth," he says and then gulps down another generous helping of beer and goes back to chewing his gum like mad.

I know how this case is tormenting him. He's obsessed with it. He doesn't know who's behind it, and he's desperate to find out whom. Right now he's pissed off, and even though he's keeping his cool, his stress level is obviously rising. Anyone can tell.

I'm a little unnerved by the way he already knows me so well—the way he's always curious about my actions. He wonders where I am, and why I'm there. I can't stand it. I wish he'd just go away. I don't want to be a main character, and I sure as hell don't want to be a suspect. I hope that isn't where this is going. But I know him. To him everyone's a suspect. He doesn't put anyone past the capability to commit a crime. In his eyes, anyone could be a thief, murderer, or rapist. Anyone could even be the 'cross killer.'

"So what are you doing here, *new guy*?" He emphasizes the words, 'new guy.' I don't like it. It's the same way you would call someone a stranger. And strangers are capable of anything since nobody knows anything about them.

"Just meeting up with someone," I say.

"Ah," he says and slugs down some more of his drink and chews greedily on his gum. "So you've made some friends here already?"

"Yeah," I say. Why can't this guy just leave me alone? I'm not the guy you're looking for, and all you're doing is getting sidetracked and screwing up my story in the process.

He slumps back and faces the wall. "This town is fucking crazy. It has a thin veneer of peace and order, but if you break through that—and it doesn't take much—you see that it is inhabited by filth. The slime of this city oozes through the cracks and goes unidentified. The bastards linger like cockroaches after a nuclear assault. The innocents die and the motherfuckers live on." He slugs down the rest of his drink. "That, my friend, is this great city. That, my friend, is where we live."

He looks around and orders another drink. He's already pretty lit, and it has caused his normally fairly calm demeanor to fade away. That calm façade has dissolved and has given way to what he is truly feeling: pure unbridled anger.

"But it won't be like that for long," he says. "I'll find that fucker. I'll bring him to justice. You can only hide so long." He downs the rest of his beer, which was almost completely full. "Well it was nice chatting with ya." He gets up and walks away.

I start to shake uncontrollably for some reason. I'm paranoid. I remember that night. I don't want to witness another scenario like that, and I sure as hell don't want to end up in some prison.

I start with some deep breathing. It helped me the other night—when I was in a much more traumatic situation—so why shouldn't it work now?

Inhale. I hear the woman gurgling, trying to catch her breath. Exhale. She falls to the ground, her life fading away. Inhale. She coughs up blood, and Richard Sweeney crouches over her, preparing with the knife. Exhale. I run, flee the scene like a coward.

"Jake." I hear a voice behind me. Her voice tears me out of my disturbed trance.

I turn around and embrace her. I hug her tight and kiss her hungrily. Upon the locking of our lips, I feel calm. I feel at ease. My problems dissipate in the wind. She is my antidote. I hold that kiss for a long time. The entire time I'm wondering how I managed to be with someone so wonderful, so majestic. I feel protected in her embrace, and more importantly I feel that she is protected in mine.

Rule number five: Do not get attached to anybody.

It doesn't matter, I go on kissing. When I let go I look at her, and she has a perplexed look on her face. I quickly look to my left and, standing out the door, Todd Reynolds is staring at me. I don't know why. I don't exactly care. I look back at her.

"Is everything alright?" I ask her.

"It's… fine. I was just going to ask you the same question," she says.

"It's fine. I just needed that," I say.

We walk to the bar and she says, "Are you sure you're okay? You look a little pale, and while that was flattering, it was kind of intense and we're in the middle of a group of people."

"Sorry," I say, "I'm not much of a fan of PDA either, but this was different. I've just been thinking a lot, and spent the last couple days alone. Too much alone time isn't always a good thing."

"I understand," she says. "I've been there before."

We have a drink, talk a little bit about her sister's experience in the hospital, which is painful for her to discuss, but she feels willing to confide in me. Her sister hasn't really been taking hospital life that well. She blames Adeline for putting her there and is still showing suicidal tendencies. After the drink we decide to go for a walk.

"I don't know," Adeline says. "It just doesn't seem fair that so many of us are blessed and find meaning in the world, yet others find the world so bitter that they don't even want to keep breathing. Someone once told me that life is a rollercoaster." She smiles gloomily. "But it just seems that some people's rides just continue to go down, and never up."

We're walking aimlessly. It's a beautiful day, and we have no idea as to where we're headed; we just decide to let our feet guide us.

"I don't know," I say. "As I see it, we all have ups and downs—granted some of us more downs than others—but what we really must do is appreciate the moments when we do elevate, no matter how minor the up is." I put my arm around her shoulder in an attempt to comfort her. "But I know depression, and it's hard for people to realize the good times. I'm not saying it's easy; I'm just saying it's possible that she'll get better. With the right medication, the right support, she can make it. I know she'll make it. After all, one of her support pillars is you." I pause. "I wish I were that lucky."

She smiles, "You are."

We look at each other for a while, just smiling in the serenity of being in each other's presence. Just in that sublime feeling we walk in silence.

The area is starting to look familiar, yet the familiarity is haunting. Even with my arm around her, I still feel uneasy. I remove my arm because I feel something terrifying coming on. I look around and recognize this place fully. This is where I witnessed that murder.

The involuntary shakes begin. My heart starts pounding. I start to sweat. The shaking just continues to get worse. My breath shortens.

"Hold on one second," I'm able to muster the words out. I lean against the side of a building and crouch down.

"Are you alright?" The worry is obvious to see in her.

"I'm fine. I'm fine." No I'm not.

"What's happening?" she says. "What's going on?"

My mind is firing rapidly. What did I make up for my story? There has to be some reason for doing this. What can I tell her?

"Should I call an ambulance?" She's panicking.

"No. No, I'm fine." Is this a panic attack? I never have those. It can't be.

"Look at me," she says and I do. "Breathe slowly. In through your nose. Out through your mouth."

I do as she says, but I'm starting to feel lightheaded. My chest tightens. This isn't a heart attack, is it? No.

The woman was right there. Richard was right there. He was killing her and I saw it. And what did I do? Nothing. I just ran.

Inhale. Exhale. Inhale. Exhale.

I start talking, "It's just my mother," inhale, "she died, you know." Exhale. "And her," inhale, "one year anniversary," exhale, "was yesterday." Inhale. "I didn't think," exhale, "it would affect me like this," inhale, "but I guess," exhale, "it did."

It's all a lie, but I have to come up with something. Even though it's a weak explanation, it's all my brain can muster at this moment.

"Look at me," she says.

She places her hands around me and straightens me out. From what I know about panic attacks, you're supposed to seclude yourself from other people to calm down, but her presence actually helps. Feeling the warmth of her hands heals me in a way. She then plants a kiss on my lips and leaves it there for a long time. When she removes it, I've already started feeling better. She really is my antidote.

I take a couple deep breaths, and tell her I'll be okay. I calm down, or rather, she has calmed me down.

When I'm finally able to function properly she says, "Do you want to talk about it?"

"No," I say, "but thanks. Maybe some other time."

She holds me for a little bit and then I put my arm around her and walk her home, both of us in the comfort of each other's embrace.

CH. 30

Memory is such a boggling area of the mind. A memory can be spurred by the oddest, most mundane or trivial actions. A song on the radio can remind you of a girl that you once loved, or a close friend who is now deceased, or some odd and seemingly irrelevant experience that you two shared. Oddly enough, the sense of smell has a large association with memory; for instance, a whiff from a baseball mitt can bring you back to a game-saving catch you made in little league, followed by the post-game celebration and comradery with your teammates in the dugout, that had gone dormant in your mind for so long. Memories can be distorted, you can have entirely false memories, or you may only have fragments of memories that you have to piece together. Regardless of what the reason for having this memory, how it relates to my current situation, or the instigation for the recollection of this memory, I experienced a flashback to one of the earliest memories I can recall.

I am sitting with my father (where at? I can't be sure, perhaps it was not a necessary factor). I just asked him a question that I can't remember what it was about. Perhaps it was about marriage or family or the future—I truly can't recall. But I can recall the intense stench of whiskey fresh on his breath. I have hardly any memories of my father when he was sober. He died from cirrhosis by the time I was nine, so this must have been early in my life and I wasn't able to comprehend fully what he was saying.

He lights a cigarette and talks as if he were not only talking to me, but a crowd of people. He speaks as if it was a parable, as if he were Jesus holding a smoke and a whiskey on the rocks, talking to the only disciple he was ever able to attain: me.

"There is a man standing at the edge of a dock. The dock stretches deep, deep into the ocean." He stirs his whiskey and takes another drag from his smoke. "Out about forty yards further lies his only son. He adores his son and would do anything for him, for there is nothing and no one that he cherishes more than his only offspring." He ashes his cigarette and takes another large swallow of his cheap whiskey. "Surrounding his child is a large group of sharks circling the child; closing in on their prey."

I twinge with discomfort, imagining the terrifying scenario. My dad notices this but continues without hesitation, "The child has not been attacked yet, but in less than a minute the father is sure that his son will be devoured." He takes another long drag from his smoke; the cigarette almost down to the filter. "The father also knows that his instinctual desire to jump into the ocean and save his child is completely futile. The only thing he will accomplish by jumping into the ocean is that the sharks will have two people to eat instead of one. He is standing on the edge of the dock contemplating this for just a second; just mulling the death or two death situation over in his head for mere moments. He ponders this for less than two seconds, but this is the most painful moment of his life. He then decides to jump into the ocean and swim for his boy in the useless attempt to save his life. Before he reaches the child, a shark grabs him by the waist and drags him under. After a few moments of intense pain, he finally dies not having even reached the boy and realizes that he accomplished nothing."

I sit there patiently, hoping that my father will tell me something to redeem the depressing aspect of the story. I'm hoping that I will find some moral or reason for him telling me this horrible story. My eyes have started watering and grow red. I have that dry feeling in my throat that always precedes a waterfall of tears. My father looks at me with a mild vacancy in his eyes, stubs out his cigarette, and says, "Think about that, Henry." Then he downs the rest of his whiskey and stumbles into the family room to enter an alcohol induced coma.

I wonder why he told me that story. Such pointlessness, such depression. There is no moral. There is no purpose. And that is when I felt the first tears start to fall.

This memory appeared to me early in the morning. I was simply drinking my coffee and then came this unwanted haunting. A ghost of irrelevance. A shadow of meaningless despair. I can't think of any rational reason why I would remember this. It would be a memory best left buried. It wasn't traumatic in the traditional sense, but it was definitely unsettling. I knew I was to meet with Adeline once again at the same bar where we first met much later in the day, so I decided to shake this irrelevant nightmare of a memory from my head.

I arrived at the bar a few minutes early as always. This is great for giving me a chance to converse with the locals—that is what I'm supposed to do after all—and learn more about the people who inhabit this world. Many times I find a mindless drunk or a bore, or many times I find people who are too guarded to let people know anything about them; but not this time. Granted the man I'm talking to cannot be considered by any means as friendly or personable, but he definitely is interesting.

"I initiated my adult life attempting to enrich my mind by what modern society deems the social norm: enrolling in college," he says, telling his life story as my odd powers seem to allow people to do. "I haphazardly transitioned from class to class, not seemingly following any identifiable pattern. Many are undecided in their major, but I was undecided and found each class irritating by its very essence."

"How so?" I ask in the usual polite way to show a person who's speaking that I am engaged in what they are saying.

He gives me a look to show frustration that I interrupted him. "Every subject and every class was told through the lens of a certain bias or, in many ways, contrived out of nothing but the imagination." I am about to ask what he means by this, but then decide to not interrupt him again. As if knowing what I was about to ask, he answers for me. "For example, English featured vast collections of supposed *engaging* literature." He emphasizes 'engaging' in a tone to imply mockery. "Most of the stories are fiction and are created solely for the point of entertainment or to relay themes through untruths. Mostly I find the stories themselves lacking in pertinent information or hard fact. If we live in an illusionary world, then we no longer allow ourselves to be grounded by concrete fact."

The man's bitterness is incredibly prevalent. I can see a rant of the irrelevance of everything building up and, while I am so tired of hearing pessimism concealed as realism, for some reason I am interested to hear this man continue.

"The majority of these stories—especially the current ones—are successful merely because our society is attracted to the brutal and vulgar," he continues. "Most of the bestselling novels are filled with horrific and graphic acts of brutality. The ones that aren't are either erotic—pandering to the part of us that loves to fantasize about what we would do in an ideal situation but are too cowardly to do—or are littered with obscenities to keep the imbecilic reader's attention by each expletive; training the reader to finish the story the same way an owner guides a dog to obedience with treats."

"You have an aversion to curse words?" I ask him.

"If your desire is to attract the focus of your listener to the stinging expletives you use and have them ignore the message that you're trying to relay, then by all means, swear away," he says,

"But as for me, I prefer to have the person hear what I say, at least to a point."

"What do you mean 'to a point'?" I ask.

He once again gives me that look of irritation. "What I mean is if someone is such a dolt that his imbecilic mind can't comprehend the type of language that you use, then it is a waste to even talk to that person. In much simpler terms I mean: don't dumb yourself down in order to have others understand you. If they don't understand, then they are not worth your clarification."

I nod and take all this in. "Not all literature is fiction. What about nonfiction?"

"Nonfiction is fiction in disguise," he says.

"What do you mean?" I ask.

He says, "Every nonfiction story—whether biographies, autobiographies, interviews, or memoirs—are told through the lens of bias. Every story that you hear recollected from someone has been warped, whether from intent or accidentally, and shaped into a new not entirely nonfiction recap. Whether it's a faulty memory or with the conscious intent to harm someone's reputation, the end result is the same: the truth is not pure. And pure truth is the only thing that interests me."

"Weren't there other subjects that you could find more fitting?" I ask.

"I tried," he says, "but to no avail. Philosophy was one I tried and, as you could probably tell, I was not satisfied. So much of it seemed to rely on the value we place in a selected group of minds that our history deemed worthy of recognition. Also the grey area—which is very obvious—was very irritating. I figured I would go a more technical route and try science. But even this required too much speculation. Even something with as much evidence as evolution—which I wholeheartedly believe in—does not have enough information to be declared a concrete fact. We still have to consider it a 'theory.' The big bang theory is another obvious idea that requires a stretch of the imagination. What is the cause that initiated the big bang? Questions without solid answers that cannot be argued at all were something that I tried to avoid."

I stifle a laugh. If the reason he didn't enter the field of science was because he found it to not be fact oriented enough, then I doubted he would ever find a solution.

"Then I found math," he says. "That entertained me for quite a while. Unfortunately, you have to take other classes besides math to get a degree in math, and after a while I found the problems too formulaic to hold my interest so I dropped out and set my eyes on another idea." I begin to say something but then stop because I realize this will only irritate him. "I decided to write a book."

"But I thought you didn't like books," I say, then realize that this interruption would anger him and feel a tinge of guilt.

"But it wasn't the *book* aspect of the book that I had an issue with," he says. "I have no aversion to paper, ink or any of the physical attributes of a book. My issue was the bias. I decided to write a book that was impossible to contain a bias." I luckily stop myself from saying 'how so?' thus avoiding the dirty look. "It would be a book about the origins of each word. I meticulously looked up thousands of words and wrote an origin to each word. This took me three years to complete, and I actually got a publishing deal."

"Great. So what happened?" I ask.

He gives me that dirty look again. "It was not a success to say the least. If the book were to be in normal font, then it would be the size of one of those old unabridged Merriam-Webster dictionaries, so we had to minimize the font which led to dire consequences. It turns out that a book describing word origins is virtually useless in a world where everything is just a Google search away. The only crowd that this would appeal to are the people at the age where they have an aversion to technology, and the majority of those people are elderly and many have poor eyesight. And that, is where the small font size became detrimental to the sale of the book."

I sit back empathetic to his troubles. After all I know what it's like to write a failed book, so I can relate. We failures are a breed that stick together. However, I am interested in a book solely about word origins.

"What's your favorite origin for a word?" I ask.

He puts his head back and thinks for a second, scratching his head. Then he says, "I'd probably have to go for 'spoonerism.'"

"I don't even know what that means," I admit.

"It is in simplistic terms, a slip of the tongue," he says, "An example of this, as said by the person who this word originated from himself, is saying 'our queer old dean' instead of 'our dear old queen.' It was named after William Archibald Spooner from Oxford who was famous for saying these tongue-tied statements. It was established in... I think 1921?"

"Spoonerism," I say, testing the word on my tongue. "I think that might be my favorite word now too."

"I never said that was my favorite word," he says. "I only said it was my favorite origin for a word, primarily because it reminds me of all the slip-ups he was known to say as well as all the others I've heard people say over the years."

"So what is your favorite word?" I say.

"Hippopotomonstrosesquipedaliophobia," he says with a smile.

"What does that mean?" I ask.

"The fear of big words," he says and I laugh. With how bitter and technical this person seemed, this rare glimpse of humor caught me off-guard. "Granted the more common word is **sesquipedalophobia** and was merely extended for the sake of humor and exaggeration. But it still makes me laugh. And **sesquipedalophobia** isn't really all that short a word either."

"What are you guys talking about?" I hear a voice behind me and see Adeline.

"Words," I say.

"You're having a conversation about words?" she asks.

"Actually, yes," I say and laugh.

"That's like someone baking flour," she says, "or someone writing a book about words for Christ's sake."

The man I was talking to gives her a dirty look. Adeline looks at me as if to ask, 'What I say?'

I tell her, "I'll tell you later." I turn back to the man I was chatting with. "Anyway it was nice getting to know you." We say goodbye and I walk to a vacant table to talk to Adeline.

When we get to the table, she asks why he gave her that look, and I relay to her the info that he actually wrote a book about words and it was an utter failure.

"I feel so bad," she says. "I didn't mean to offend him. Do you think I should go over and apologize?"

"To be honest," I say, "from what I was able to gather from his personality, I think he would be irritated if you bothered him. He's not a really social person, and he's got a tough hide."

She feels remorse even though her crime was not that great. But what attracts me is that this remorse is not a façade. It is not a veneer of kindness and empathy she has, but true kindness and empathy. So far I have not found a single characteristic that is not endearing. Normally when I'm only able to see virtues and no flaws, I am uneasy. Yet for some reason, I do not have this feeling. I have full trust in her. No part of me believes that she is trying to hide something or has an ulterior motive for her altruism. It is just who she is.

I'm overcome with a strange feeling for her. Of course there is sexual desire, but there is also an inner deterrent as if by following through with the act I would desecrate a holy relic.

We talk for a while about life; how her sister is doing, how her friends are doing, if I've found any potential places to live in yet. We talk about the upcoming school year and my new job.

We talk, we laugh, we shoot the shit, we drink, and no

matter how monotonous the subject matter is that we are talking about, there is never a dull moment or an awkward silence.

The night winds to its conclusion and I walk her to her house. We chat about this and that and laugh all the way there. When we arrive at the house she pauses at the door contemplating whether or not to invite me inside. I decide that if she offers I'll accept her request—but only if she offers. She jingles her keys a bit as if waiting for me to ask if we wanted to move this inside. Her eyes tell me 'the ball's in your court.' We stare at each other a little, seeing who will make the next move. After the time elapses she kisses me and says goodbye.

I walk away as I always do after one of our dates: with the ancient inner optimism that I buried a long time ago reborn. I am in complete blissful serenity.

Yet for some unknown reason, the memory of my father telling me the parable of the sharks comes back. And for some reason that I can't figure out, I feel like the father on the edge of the dock.

CH. 31

The last few weeks have been a busy time. I've had to review my teaching syllabus. I've had several dates with Adeline. I've had a couple of my morning scorns from Coralline Thomson. I've had several discussions with the man who doesn't know he's dead yet: John Richards, the man who doesn't know the definition of too much coffee: Ernest Winston, and several other conversations with the only normal staff member of the school: Shelly Lin. All the while I've had occasional flashbacks to the night I fled Richard Sweeney's ritualistic murder. Even with all this, I've still made time to orchestrate the schedule for my upcoming school year.

Finally the day has come to start my job. I was completely confident in how the first day would turn out. It would be a simple day of orientation and discussing the syllabus. My first class of the day was for sophomores. One thing I've learned from my first day: sophomores live up to their name.

I've arrived in my classroom early to start the day. My desk is filled with several sheets of paper to hand out to the kids and, I guess to fulfill the stereotype, I even put an apple on my desk. On the wall rests pictures of animals doing different tasks with bold lettered words like '**Discipline**,' '**Achieve**,' '**Respect**,' and

'**Determination.**' Underneath reads some quote describing the virtuous attribute.

I wasn't too concerned with how the class was going to go over. The first day shouldn't be that crazy. Kids are tired from waking up early after they've slept in all summer. They're too shy to make a scene or act a fool. They want to give off a good impression. It'll be difficult to get them to actually talk, and it'll take a lot of prying to get them to contribute their ideas. No need to worry about any trouble. The biggest difficulty that I'll have is to try to get the students to say anything and not fall asleep. Then the first class happened. Shows what I know.

The students enter and it finally hits me how difficult it is going to be to memorize everybody's name. There are thirty children in this class and four subsequent classes, so I'm going to need to think of a technique.

I start by taking roll call. I announce everybody's name and try to remember everyone by categorizing them with alliteration. There's Black Billy, Asian Annie, Zit-faced Zack, Four-eyed Fiona, In-the-closet Chris, Out-of-the-closet Collin, and Stuttering Steven. My new mental names for them are akin to what would come out of a bully's mouth. There's a little bit of guilt, but I have to find some method to remember. If it seems a bit racist or prejudice or mean-spirited, that is not my intent.

I walk slowly in front of the class, pace back and forth a little bit, pause for the effect of grabbing their attention and then say, "There is nothing to writing. All you do is sit down at a typewriter and bleed." I pause and wait for the class to look at me with interest in what I have to say next. Nobody is impressed. One boy's eyes are half closed. Another girl looks stoned. Zit-faced Zack is trying to pick his nose without anyone seeing. Well, I walked into this, so I might as well finish it. "Ernest Hemingway."

A girl raises her hand. I'm not sure who it is. If I were a betting man, I'd give four to one odds her name is Barbara.

I point to her. "Yes, Barbara."

She looks to her left and right and then behind her and says, "It's Rachel." Not even close.

"Sorry," I say. "Go on."

"What's a typewriter?" she asks.

Jesus, how old am I? Or maybe there's just no hope for this generation. "Prior to computers, writers would type on a typewriter which is similar to a keyboard. There would be a sheet of paper that would come up as you write and if you messed it up severely you had to scrap the whole sheet and type anew."

Some boy with a tie-dye hoodie on and a mild case of acne raises his hand.

"Yes, Phil," I say.

"Sean," he says. Alright, oh for two. "Why would anybody still write if you had to like completely start over if you like screwed up?"

"You wouldn't have to start over; you only had to retype a page," I say.

But like Sean has like more questions to like ask, "But like still, it'll be like, like really hard to still like write anyway. Why would like anyone like want to even do that much work?"

"It is hard work, and they deserve our respect for many reasons," I say. "In fact, if they needed to look up information to research for their story they had to look them up in books since they couldn't use the internet to just search for the answer for something." Sean's jaw drops a little and I imagine him thinking, 'like wow.' "But these great writers, who wrote beautiful works of literature in a time when it was much more difficult than today, have shaped our modern society in a large way. As for why they wrote it, well for one thing, a job's a job. Many others just wrote because it was something they absolutely loved doing. So many of these authors that we will read died penniless. Oscar Wilde and Edgar Allen Poe are just two of the many who died in poverty. Yet their works live on."

I decide to switch it up and attempt something that a

teacher of mine did back in high school, "I give you this opportunity to ask me any question about my life in a way to get to know me. It can be anything and I'll answer it truthfully. If it's too personal I'll simply tell you so and we'll move on to the next question. So fire away." I wait for a minute and no one volunteers. "Anyone?" A boy in the front row raises his hand. He's black, and since there are only two black guys in the class I figure I've got a fifty percent chance that he's Black Billy. "Yes, Billy," I say.

He looks a little confused. "It's Rick."

"I'm Billy," a girl in the back right corner says. Damn it. Billy can double as a girl's name and there are three black people in the room; two males, one female.

"I'm sorry," I say. "Rick, go on with your question."

"What's your favorite football team?" he asks.

"The Giants," I say, too embarrassed to admit it's actually the Bills.

Another boy raises his hand. I point to him, "Yes, Don."

"It's Ron," he says. I decide I'm no longer going to try to guess people's names.

"Sorry," I say, "What was your question?"

"Who is your favorite baseball team?" he asks.

"The Yankees," I say, feeling much more confident about my answer.

A girl raises her hand. "Yes," I say pointing to her.

"Are you married?" she asks.

"No, unfortunately," I say.

Another girl raises her hand and I point to her, "Yes."

"Do you have a girlfriend?" she timidly asks.

"Yes," I say.

A boy raises his hand and I point to him saying "yes" again.

"Have you ever smoked pot?" he asks.

"Yes," I say, "I mean no." The class giggles.

"Yes," I say pointing to another person.

"Were you ever arrested?" he asks.

"No," I say. And then somehow a silent deal is made throughout the students to stop raising their hands and just start firing questions.

"What's your drug of choice?" some kid asks.

"I have none," I say.

"Does that mean you like them all equally?" another kid asks.

"No, I haven't done any," I lie.

"Have you ever boned a dude?" some guy spouts out.

"What? No!" I say. The class is really getting out of hand and I can no longer tell who's asking the questions. Just random question after random question.

"How many times have you been arrested?"

"Never," I say.

"What age did you lose your virginity?"

"That's too personal," I say.

"To a dude?" the same kid finishes up his sentence.

"Alright!" I yell. "Everyone knock it off!" The questions cease and there's a moment of silence save the giggles dying down. "Everyone pick a partner and ask them ten *appropriate* questions about themselves. You have five minutes. After that, each pair will talk about their answers." This settled them down for some time but the rowdiness didn't fully die; it was just rowdy light. I still have thirty minutes left of this class. And those thirty minutes were much longer than any half-hour interval I've ever experienced in my life. And just to think, I've got four more of these classes.

After experiencing all of my other classes, I've concluded that not only do sophomores live up to their name, but every other grade should likewise be named sophomore. Even the seniors act like children. I'm going to hate this job, but I guess I have to have some job and this one's as good as any.

Adeline should be joining me soon. We decided to meet once again at The Pool Hall, one of our signature places to go. Like always, I came here early and once again I'm greeted by Howie Mumbles stringing random words together in a barely coherent fashion. He showed up here obviously intoxicated, but even if he weren't drunk at all when he got here, solely from the amount I've seen him drink sitting next to him, I'm impressed he can still manage to sit on the barstool without falling over.

He may be a rambling drunken fool, but there's something redeeming about him. His insanity and alcoholism are somehow endearing. He's a genuinely nice guy who doesn't try to harm anyone intentionally, and tries to not be as reckless as possible while fueling his addiction. Never once have I seen him drive a car, which is good because I wouldn't be surprised if, since I've been in this story, he's ever been below the legal limit.

"Ya' see, ya' see, the problem wi' people is that they're so fuckin' stupid," he says. "There's all this so many people," he stretches his hands out and does a semicircle to show all the encompassing people around us, "but I can ha' a mo' intel'gent convuhsation wi' a brick of wood."

"A brick of wood?" I say smiling.

"Um... I mean... a piece o' brick?" he says.

"You mean a brick wall?" I offer.

"Yup, that's it." He finishes another half a glass of whiskey and orders another one.

"Jesus Howie," I say.

He looks at me with a look of hurt in his eyes—if it's possible to see anything in those glassy eyeballs—and says, "Ya' shouldn' throw stones i' ya can' see da thorn in ya' own side."

"Wha-huh-what?" I say flabbergasted. "I don't know if I should be baffled by the level of stupidity in that sentence or impressed that you can still expel words considering the amount of alcohol you've imbibed."

He nods his head as if in an attempt to not pass out and

shifts the gaze of his half-closed vacant eyes to me. "Don' complain ta' me (incoherent mumbling) ya' can' unduhstan' ma' way of speakin'."

"That's the thing Howie," I say. "You don't speak. You just ejaculate words and see where that takes you."

He looks down as if depressed and I feel guilty. I was only hoping to relieve some of this morning's stress at work by joking with him, but I think I managed to actually hurt his feelings. To make up for this I buy him a drink.

He smiles, "Yo' a gentleman an' a schola'."

I see Adeline in the distance walking towards me. I turn to Howie, "Sorry but I've got to go. My friend's here. I'll catch you some other time."

He jerks his arms wide and to the sky, spilling a little of his drink. Looking up he says, "Fly free little birdie."

"Whatever that means," I say and I take my leave.

I greet Adeline with a hug. She's wearing a different perfume than usual; it is very alluring. It has the scent of a lilac mixed with berries, and a very potent fruity wine. Her lips are parted in the magnificent smile that seems like her standby facial expression.

"Two questions: why does everyone seem to naturally like you and why do you have a tendency to talk to the crazies?" she says.

"Well I find normality so mundane." I laugh. "Sane people convey basically the same few topics every time they speak. But with the wackos, you never know what to expect."

"But I swear, everyone just opens up and talks to you and will tell you practically anything," she says, "even if you just met them. Hell, even people who don't trust anyone innately trust you. You're like the George to everyone's Lenny."

"Well luckily I'm not going to shoot anyone in the back of the head while telling them how we're companions," I say and she laughs.

We make our way to the pool tables and I set up the game. Something about her seems more appealing than usual. She's always been a monument of beauty, but something about her enhances my attraction to her which I did not believe was possible. She has that new perfume, but I don't think that's entirely it. Her attire is elegant, but then again, it always is. But something is different about her. She seems slightly more seductive, but just slightly.

"You want to break?" I ask.

"No, you break this time," she says.

"Are you sure? I'm a firm believer in ladies go first," I say.

"Now we are at an impasse," she says. "Two people both insisting the other go first. The only way to move forward is for someone to make the first move." She smiles coyly.

I smile back and go to the table to take the first shot.

I talk a lot about my first day at work and she laughs and says several times that she's heard even crazier things from Shelly. "Just remember," she says, "it'll only get crazier. But then again, by assessing who you start conversations with, I bet you can handle crazy pretty well."

We go through a pitcher and about half of a second before we decide to leave. Neither of us are interested in finishing the pitcher, and I see Howie weaving on the barstool, somehow managing to still cling to his seat. I have no idea why he's been here that long or—knowing how quickly he finishes his alcohol—how much he must have drank. The other question I have is how he can possibly afford all the liquor he buys at bars. If I were an alcoholic, I'd at least be an economic alcoholic and buy from a liquor store. I hand him the rest of the pitcher.

"Go' bless ya' ma' frien'," he says. "Nex' time I'm buyin'."

"Sure you are Howie," I say and proceed to walk Adeline home.

We talk for a while; just the usual mundane subject matter

of how our days went, how our mutual acquaintances are doing. The laughter is rich, and the jokes are in high supply. And then finally we arrive at her house.

We walk up to her door slowly, and once again she jingles her keys. We find ourselves wondering what to do next. Both of us contemplating our next action. Both of us having the same desire, but too timid to propose the question. She smiles at me and I smile back. There's a silence and for once I can consider it awkward. It's just a stalemate that we're in. Both of us are experiencing an odd vulnerability that we're not used to. She's still fidgeting with her keys, I'm smiling dumbly back at her like an imbecile. There's a similarity to this feeling from a couple of weeks ago when we were in the same position and, after time elapsed, she kissed me good night and we headed our separate ways. But this vulnerability is much more intense and the period of silence seems much longer. We both know what we want to do, but neither of us is brave enough to suggest it.

Then I remember her words at The Pool Hall. *Now we are at an impasse. Two people both insisting the other go first. The only way to move forward is for someone to make the first move.* So I take her into my arms and kiss her deeply.

We're on her front stoop locked in each other's embrace, our lips pressed together; not worrying about any onlookers.

"Let's take this inside," she whispers in my ear.

We go inside, bumping into furniture as we make our way to the bedroom, all the while caressing each other.

She already has her shirt off revealing a black silk bra. I grab her thigh and lift her onto the bed. I caress her smooth milky white skin. My hands wrap around her body as my lips attend to her chest. I unhook her bra and—I'm going to cut myself off right there. I'm not one to kiss and tell.

But I will say this. Granted I've had quite a long dry spell. It's been almost a year since I've been with a woman; and even before that I was no Don Juan. But I have had sex with a number of women over the last few years. I'm not *that* sex-deprived. I would consider myself only slightly less than average when it comes to frequency. But this was the first time in at least five years that I've made love.

Afterward we lie on the bed under the covers. I am in pure bliss. For a period of time we have become one. There are no troubles occupying my mind. I am free to live; free of guilt and sorrow.

I simply lie there without even the faintest desire for a post-coital smoke. I am completely satisfied physically, emotionally, mentally, and even spiritually. She rests her head on my chest; her head copying my breathing, going up and down and up and down. I stroke her blond hair and look down at her. Up and down, up and down. I smile, entirely serene. Truly this is the best of all possible worlds. I lean my head forward and kiss the top of her head, taking in her scent. She turns her head and kisses me a few more times, then lays her head back on my chest. Once again I stroke her hair and her head goes up and down, up and down. Until this moment, I have never truly known the definition of serenity. Finally I am at peace.

The sixth and final rule: never ever fall in love.

CH. 32

Even at the table, waiting for Coralline Thomson to meet me for a late lunch, the night with Adeline is not completely over. I've had five classes today, and some work to look over, but I'm still in that night. When you are truly in love with a person, you are never actually away from that person no matter the physical distance between the two of you—at least not entirely. It's that pure emotion that is rare between people where you don't have the faintest proclivity to look at another person or fantasize about another person no matter how attractive they are either physically or emotionally. You are solely faithful to that person, both mentally and physically, experiencing that phrase that is overused but you have actually attained: true love. Sublimity becomes your standby. Unfaithfulness becomes a foreign concept.

Coralline Thomson sits in the seat across from me, "Hi Jake."

I take a moment of delay, as if I were a computer glitching due to an overload of euphoric data, "Hi Jane."

She looks at me quizzically for a moment with a sense of unease. "Are you okay?"

I stare back at her, still with that sublime smile on my face,

"Yes, of course. Why do you ask?"

"I don't know," she says tentatively, "you seem a little… different I guess."

"Can't see why that would be," I say.

She looks at me—not unlike the time she analyzed me before giving me the serum to enter this world—and says, "Alright. Well I just was wondering how you were doing with-" she cuts herself off. "Are you sure you're alright?"

I laugh and shake my head, "Jeez, how many times do I have to tell you? I'm doing fine."

She cocks her head a little to the right. "Alright." Then she continues, "I just was wondering how you were doing with talking to everyone in the story. Are you getting enough detail about them? Do you find them easy to open up or are they too guarded?"

"They are divulging information without much effort," I say with my mind half-focused on the conversation, and half on the previous night. I still remember Adeline's head on top of my chest radiating warmth during a post-coital cuddle. The scent of lilac/berry/fruity wine perfume still fresh in my nose. "It seems that whenever I have a chat with someone, they immediately go into deep secrets and tell their life story. You know, it's the 'prayer concept' that you mentioned earlier." In my mind, mine and Adeline's bodies are still intertwined.

"That's good to hear," she says. "That's the case most of the time. However, sometimes—depending on the world that your mind has created—it can be quite a strain getting characters to divulge information. But luckily-" she cuts herself off again and stares at me for a little with her eyebrows furrowed and her eyes narrowed, "What's with the smile? Are you sure you're okay?"

I laugh. "I already told you I'm fine. I'm great in fact. Haven't been better."

"Why such a positive attitude?" she asks.

I laugh heartily, "Oh my god, can't a guy be positive without being subjected to suspicion?"

"I'm just curious," she says.

"I had a good day at work—some of the kids made me laugh—and all and all my job is treating me well," I say. "It's not a crime to be happy, is it?"

"No it's not a crime," she says, "but it also isn't the end goal. Be happy all you want, but don't let the euphoria interfere with what you came here to do."

The waitress comes by. This one has a southern accent and a down-to-earth sense of humor. I laugh heavily at her humor, and we exchange a handful of jokes. The entire time I laugh with her, Coralline Thomson scrutinizes me more and more with each laugh. It's almost as if, with each individual spurt of laughter, Coralline Thomson's eyes narrow just a little bit more. I order a half a Reuben and she orders a generic cheeseburger.

When the waitress walks away, Coralline Thomson asks me accusingly, "Are you high?"

I roar with laughter. "Trust me, if I was high, I'd have ordered a lot more than a half a sandwich."

"Why did you only order half a sandwich? You normally have more," she asks.

The truth behind why I ordered only half is that I have a date later with Adeline for Chinese food. But I really don't think telling her this would go over all that well. "I had a bit of a snack on my lunch break. I knew we were meeting today for lunch but I was really hungry. Must have eaten too much I guess."

She analyzes me for a little bit longer. I'm not sure if she bought it, but she decides to let it go. "How about the other topic that we discussed? How has your act of heroics panned out? Has it died down as you anticipated?"

"To be honest, no one has mentioned it to me since the last time I talked to you." To be honest, I'm full of shit. A little less than two hours ago a senior asked me if I was that 'one dude on the news who saved that chick from getting squashed by a car.' But on the whole it is dying down, and I just want Coralline Thomson to cut out the lectures of how much I screwed up. Telling me how much I fucked up isn't going to rectify the situation.

"That's good to hear," she says. "Keep up the good work. Remember, you're like an undercover spy in this world, meant to obtain information from the surrounding people. But the first rule of being a spy: it only works if you travel incognito. If you make more than a fading impression on people, then you are in for some serious trouble."

We finish our meal. I eat less than half of my half a sandwich and we depart. Coralline Thomson may not have asked any more times if something is wrong or if I'm sure I'm okay, but her eyes did it for her. I leave the restaurant, not only pleased that I'm leaving Coralline Thomson, but also ecstatic that I'm going to see Adeline Stewart again.

I'm at the restaurant—early as always—ordering a whiskey sour while I wait for Adeline. There's a Breaking News segment on the TV about some senator and presidential hopeful who had just been arrested for spending campaign money on a high-class prostitute who he claims that he loves. They're talking about how he was favored among the Republican base for the next election, but now most of the community no longer likes him. I smile to myself. *A whore, my kingdom for a whore.*

Todd Reynolds is sitting by the bar, finishing his food. Every once in a while he takes breaks to write something on a sheet of paper. He seems intense about it. He didn't have much food, just some appetizers to tide him over, but luckily he hasn't taken his time to irritate me. At first I was a little nervous that he would come over to give me grief as usual, but he has merely been watching the news, writing on that sheet of paper, and eating his meal without bothering anyone. He pays his bill, folds up the piece of paper, puts it in his pocket, and heads to the bathroom.

The place is not all that fancy—apparently Adeline realized from our date at the steakhouse that upscale is not where I fit in best. This is just a regular restaurant that Adeline said was really good. "I haven't tasted a better eggroll anywhere, and I would consider myself an eggroll connoisseur," she said. Which is good, because I believe that an eggroll really makes or breaks a Chinese restaurant.

But the atmosphere isn't intimidating in the least. There's everything from families in polos and jeans, to teenagers in shorts and a T-shirt. To my right are two men in their early twenties who are talking to each other that are an odd pair. They're not odd in how they look, but in their mannerisms. One is timid and speaks in a quiet hushed voice, seemingly wary about everything he says and what it will come out like, while the other is loud and vulgar and hasn't a care in the world if people overhear him or what they think.

"Look... I have to tell you something, but I need you to keep this between us. You can't tell anyone else," the timid man says, which is an odd request, considering the level of volume in the other man's voice. Whether the other guy keeps his mouth shut or not, the entire restaurant is going to hear their conversation.

"What is it? You can trust me." the loud man says.

"You know Samantha?" the timid man says and the loud man nods his head. "Well... she's kind of pregnant."

The boisterous man fills his face with disbelief and a little bit of agitation. "Jesus Christ!" he says, "You have to stop cumming in her; she's not a sock!"

"Keep it down man," the timid man says looking around.

"Fuck man," the vulgar man says a little quieter, but still loud enough for anyone who's paying attention to hear.

"She wants to keep it," the timid man says. "What should I do?"

The loud man takes a deep breath and says, assessing the situation, "Look, she's head over heels for you. You give her an ultimatum: either she gives the child the boot, or you're kicking her to the curb."

"I can't do that," the quiet man says exasperated. "It's her choice. She either has the operation, or she keeps it. But whatever she decides; I'm not influencing it. I wouldn't be able to live with myself if I forced her either way."

"How's it going Jake?" A voice interrupts my eavesdropping. Who was I kidding when I thought detective Reynolds wasn't going to harass me?

"I can't complain. How are things with you detective?" I ask, looking at that big old grin—that act as if we were best buddies. No, not even *he's* going to ruin my day.

"Same old, same old," he says.

"What were you so focused on writing over there?" I ask in a futile attempt to keep this a friendly conversation without any negative insinuations about me.

"Oh that." He laughs. "I was just doodling. When I was young, my first dream was to be an artist actually. Surprised I never told you that."

"Nope," I say. "You never mentioned it."

"So anyway, what are you doing here?" he asks.

"I'm meeting someone," I say.

He gnaws on that huge wad of nicotine gum. "Same girl that you practically made out with as a greeting in front of the bar about a month ago?"

Why does he still remember that? "Yup. Same one."

"Beautiful girl," he says. "Blond hair, very feminine, quite a looker." He moves the wad behind his gums, and you can actually see the Nicorette's bulge against his lower lip.

"I guess she is," I say dismissively. For god sake, won't you just leave me alone?

"Well glad to hear that," he says truculently. He slaps my shoulder gently and points to the TV with the Senator caught in the scandal. "One hell of a story right there huh?"

"Yup," I say. "I guess so."

"You see, the thing is, if he only fucked her once, he

wouldn't have gotten caught," he says, starting a tangent that, although I'm not sure where it's going to lead, I'm not looking forward to it. "Most criminals get away with it—even murderers. If he were to say, 'I want something different than my wife, and my hand's not working,' and just did it once, he probably would have gotten away with it. But these... vermin—these swine—these degenerates—these... creatures; they aren't satisfied with just once. There's something innate about these specific subset of criminals where they just can't stop, no matter what. And sooner or later they get sloppy, and sooner or later these creatures—these rejects of society—sooner or later they get caught." He slaps me on the back and winks at me. "Anyway see ya' 'round." He walks out the door leaving me with only my uneasiness to accompany me.

That speech must have been prepared—at least the general idea of it. He must have been just sitting there doodling and rehearsing that speech to give me as he occasionally lifted his eyes to look at the news.

And then the doodling sticks in my head and I remember him saying, 'when I was young, my first dream was to be an artist actually.' And it hits me. The artistic history, the death of his wife, the quitting cigarettes; could he be Jimmy Hansen's alter-ego?

No. No way. But, could he be? Todd wanted to be an artist when he was young; Jimmy is an artist. Todd is trying to quit cigarettes and is chowing down on nicotine gum; Jimmy has always been quitting cigarettes. Todd feels responsible for the death of his wife and child; Jimmy feels responsible for the death of his girlfriend who was the woman he loved. The similarities are too much. I really think he is. The fucking 'Wizard of Oz' effect.

Maybe if our first few meetings were different, we could have actually developed the kind of friendship that Jimmy and I share. Maybe if he didn't see me leave the hotel where a murder was committed the night before. Maybe if he didn't see me at a wake chatting it up with the next serial murder victim after I had told him that I just got in to town. Maybe if I didn't flub-up my own fucking name when we first met. Maybe things could have been different if I didn't make those few simple mistakes. Could we have been friends? Could we have had that near-telepathic connection?

He has to be Jimmy's alter-ego. He showed up to Ron Madsen's wake who was Hank Wiseman's alter-ego. They had to have some sort of connection. Could they have been friends? Or could he have had the same relationship with Ron that Jimmy and I have with Hank? This is crazy. My best friend thinks I'm a suspect, at least in a sense.

Adeline shows up to greet me in a rose colored shirt and khaki pants. Once again she's wearing that attractive perfume, and once again she approaches the conversation with that hint of seduction. Later that night we make love and once again it was majestic.

Afterward I'm lying on the bed in that beautiful trance; my nose filled with that lilac/berry/fruity wine wonderful concoction. For a second I think of Pavlov's dogs and conditioning and wonder if every time I walk past lilacs or berries or drink an especially fruity wine, I'll become aroused. But that thought only passes for a moment until I'm grounded back in the situation I'm in; lying in bed in pure bliss with the woman I love.

She's got her head on my chest once again, listening to me breathing, feeling the heart that she owns beat intensely. When I inhale, she rises. When I exhale, she falls. But that fall only lasts for so long because I always inhale again. We are connected; we are one. Catholics believe that when two are joined in matrimony, they no longer are two individual people, but a singular being. That concept always eluded me when I was younger, but now I believe I can finally understand.

I take a moment to think of Todd Reynolds. If he really is Jimmy's alter-ego—which I now am almost positive he is—maybe I can fix the relationship we have and develop a sort of friendly one.

But then I'm back in the moment with Adeline's head resting on my chest as I stroke her hair compassionately. Inhale: rise. Exhale: fall.

CH. 33

It's been six weeks since I first started my job teaching—also six weeks since I had first made love to Adeline Stewart. The weeks have been a blur even though I have been mostly sober throughout them. I am intoxicated in something stronger than alcohol: bliss. Meanwhile I've just been spending time with Adeline, running into Howie Mumbles for some of his drunken rants, avoiding Todd Reynolds who seems to have a gravitational pull on me, and constantly hitting 'ignore' to every one of Coralline Thomson's phone calls. The fact that I haven't spoken to Coralline Thomson in about six weeks really amplifies my bliss. At the age of thirty, I think I should have outgrown daily lectures.

Just a few weeks ago I rented an apartment. It's one of those rentals that are on the second floor of a single family home, but it's surprisingly spacious. I don't require that much space anyway, but having extra room is always good. Now I can finally stop living in a hotel and actually have a place that I can call home. On top of that, I also bought a car to get to and from work and maybe go somewhere special if I ever choose to. Pretty productive six weeks if I do say so myself.

I'm walking to the coffee shop Adeline introduced me to in order to meet her on a beautiful Saturday afternoon. It's sunny—not a cloud in the sky—and the temperature is a cool sixty-eight degrees with a light refreshing breeze. Perfect day to go for a walk. Fall is in its early stages, and you can see the leaves begin to change.

There really isn't any better season than fall. You don't have to worry about the blazing sun and immense heat practically causing you to faint on those horrible summer days, and you don't have to worry about trudging through a foot of snow in frigid weather like those cold winter nights. The temperature is perfect. All of the vegetation begins to change color. Sure the plants sprouting to life in spring is a welcoming feeling, but the majestic death of all of the trees give a season-long lasting spectacle of wonder. Sometimes death can be more impactful than life. Hell, just ask Jesus.

I walk past an alley and see Detective Reynolds walking. Luckily he doesn't see me so I just quicken my pace and alter my route a little so I can avoid him. I know he's my best friend's alter-ego, but it's not the same in this story. If things were different in real life—if the first few times Jimmy and I met were different—would we have the same relationship? He hates me and I want nothing to do with him? It's a troubling thought, and it interferes with my utopic state of mind, so I shake it out of my head.

I see Old Man Hackley standing outside his store puffing on a long cigar clenched between his teeth, taking long drags and just enjoying the beautiful day. I start to pass him.

"Hey!" he says with a large smile on his withered face. I nod in acknowledgment and he continues, "Don't tell me…Phillip. Phillip Deangelo."

"Nope," I say. "Nice try. Jake Neilson."

"Ah shoot," he says, looking slightly embarrassed. "I normally am good at names. But I know I sold to you. How ya' been? Been to the range at all?"

"No," I tell him. "I'm just using it in those just-in-case scenarios."

He laughs loudly and shakes his head. "How the hell ya' think of hittin' your target if you never practiced. You should make time to go up at the bare minimum twice a week. Get your hands used to it. Get the feeling of the gun's grip right in your hands. Feel the recoil and learn to adjust to it. You learn how to operate with that kickback. Let me tell you something." Jesus, not now. "Many—I tell you *many*—people buy a gun and think 'oh great now I'm safe'. But then crunch time comes. Some guy breaks into their house and they fire and don't know how to operate it. And you know what happens?"

I know what he wants me to say. Might as well fuel his ranting. "What happens?"

"They fire and miss and next thing you know the wrong man dies," he says with a passion. "Let me ask you another question. How many guns do you own?"

"Just that one," I say.

"Ha!" he shouts. "What do you think you're doing with just one? Who do you think you're fooling? That's not protection. You need one to carry on you, and at least one at home. Come on in buddy, I got special prices."

"Maybe some other time," I say.

"Come on," he says. "Let me ask you something. You have a wife? A kid?"

"No sir," I say.

"Well at least tell me this. You got someone special right? Someone you love?" he asks.

"Well, yes," I say, getting annoyed with him trying to sell me.

"Now, let me ask you something," he says. "What would you do if something happened to that someone special? What if your home was raided and she was attacked, and you could have saved her but the gun was too far away? What if you're walking down the street and some crazy pops out of nowhere, and you failed to protect her?"

"I don't know, I guess," I say.

He says, "Well I can answer that question for you." Please

don't. "You would feel like shit. You wouldn't be able to live with yourself. Now don't you want as much safety as possible?"

"I might come by some other time," I say, really wanting to avoid talking to this guy.

"Well let me tell you something," he uses his catch phrase again. "Every minute you're not as safe as you can be is another minute where something terrible could happen to that lovely lady."

"Maybe some other time," I say, starting to walk away.

"Suit yourself," he says. "Hope to see you soon John."

Well at least he's closer to my name than the first time he tried it. "See you around," I say and keep walking.

I keep walking to that coffee shop. That line Old Man Hackley said plays in my head: *Every minute you're not as safe as you can be, is another minute where something terrible could happen to that lovely lady.* What would I do if something happened to her? I sure as hell know that this town is far from the safest city. And while I don't think that the solution to that problem is more guns—one should suffice—I can't help but wonder how horrible it would be if she suffered by the hands of all the wretched criminals in this town. Some people are just evil, and I can't be with her every second of the day.

I see Adeline and greet her with a hug. I may not be able to be with you all the time, but I promise to do my job to keep you safe. I'm probably being too neurotic, but that's just my nature.

We go in and get our drinks and we decide to go for a walk and make the most of this wonderful day. She orders an iced coffee and I follow suit and order the same.

"Let me ask you something," I parrot Old Man Hackley's repetitious way of speaking. "Have you ever frolfed?"

"What?" she asks.

"Frisbee golfed," I clarify.

She laughs. "Not since I was in college. Why do you ask?"

"I don't know. It's been such a long time since I've done that and I guess it just popped into my head," I say. "Is there a course nearby?"

"Actually yeah there is," she says. "Wait, you're not actually thinking of going?"

"Well to be honest," I say, "I was wondering if you wanted to go sometime." Immediately she bursts out laughing. "What?" I ask.

"You're not serious are you?" She laughs.

"Why not? It was a fun time then; it should be a fun time now," I retort.

"Sure *dude*," she says. "I'll bring the bud if you bring the bowl."

"Oh come on." I laugh. "It's not *just* a stoner sport. Many people just play it to have some fun and enjoy a beautiful day."

"Wow," she says, "you really are the Thomas Edison of inventing ideas for dates."

"I thought it was a good idea," I say. "But if you don't want to, we can do something else."

"I never said I didn't want to," she says.

"Well you made a pretty good implication though," I say.

She says, "Who knows? Maybe it would actually be fun."

"Thanks for your incredible enthusiasm," I say and she laughs.

We make our way to the bench of a park, I put my arm around her, and we watch the ducks and swans swimming in the pond. Luckily today's park's inhabitants are heavy on plants and animals, and light on vagabonds.

I rest my head on her neck and nuzzle in her warmth, delighted by her scent. The perfume is different this time. It's a lighter scent and I feel wonderful in her embrace. I feel safe, protected, at home, and at peace.

"Jake?! Jake Neilson?!" I hear a voice of feigned surprise and immediately feel the life drained out of me. I know that voice. I look up and see Coralline Thomson in obvious fake jubilation. The blood rushes out of my face and I turn pale.

"Co-Co-Ja-Ja" I try to speak, but the words won't escape me.

"It's Jane Young. Remember?" She looks ecstatic. She's a much better actor than a writer considering that all her writings have been tainted by cheating.

I don't know what to say so I nod dumbly with my mouth agape.

"How do you know her?" Adeline asks.

I start to think of what to say. "I uh… she was uh… she was uh…." How do I know her? What do I say?

"Don't be embarrassed Jake," Coralline says without missing a beat. "I used to baby sit Jake when he was little," she says to Adeline then turns to me. "So how have you been?" she asks, giving me a big hug like old pals who haven't seen each other in years.

I'm sitting on the bench and limply return her hug with one arm and say, "Um… alright I guess."

"What brought you out here of all places?" she says in that bullshit delighted voice.

"I don't know," I say, trying to find the words. "Change of scene I guess. I don't know. It's a long story."

"Well, I'd love to hear it sometime," she says, then turns to Adeline, "And what's your name?"

"Adeline," Adeline says, extending her hand. "Adeline Stewart." I see something in Coralline's face when she hears Adeline's name, as if the voice hit her like a bee sting and caused her to wince.

"And how do you two know each other?" Coralline says, not leaving at all and showing no signs to do so anytime soon.

"Well… uh…" I start.

Adeline interjects, "We've been going out for a few months now."

Coralline smiles, but under that smile, I can see anger brewing. She's thinking, *God damn it Jake, you fucked up again.* "That's wonderful to hear," she says.

You know that guy who's been avoiding his wife, claiming

that he has to work late when really he's banging his mistress? He's been building up excuse after excuse and lie after lie and his wife has started to grow suspicious. He knew that he would have to end something, or it would all blow up in his face in one big shit-storm. He no longer has feelings for his wife and has fallen in love with this other woman, but is too chicken-shit to end the relationship so he just keeps delaying and delaying. And then one day, the wife finds him with his affair and all hell breaks loose. That's what I am right now. That lying adulterer who avoided the confrontation for too long and now the shit-storm is blowing up in his face. That's me.

"We really, *really*, should meet up soon and catch up," She emphasizes that second 'really' with a sense of urgency.

"Yes, we definitely should," I say slowly.

"How about tomorrow at ten in the morning at Sunny Side Up?" she says.

"I... uh... I have work that day," I say, and Adeline looks at me quizzically.

"That's Sunday," Coralline fakes puzzlement. "Last I remember, you were a teacher. You didn't change careers, did you?" Damn it she's using the information I gave her as artillery.

"Uh... no," I say thinking. "But I have a lot of um... paperwork to do."

"You don't even have a half an hour to spare?" Coralline asks. "I just want to chat."

Adeline adds in here, "Come on Jake, you can make some time for her."

"Um... sure, I guess." I'm trapped. "Why not?"

"Great," Coralline says, "I'll see you then. Remember, ten o'clock at Sunny Side Up."

We say goodbye and we part ways. This is great; tomorrow I'm going to get another tongue lashing from Coralline Thomson. Well, I guess this was inevitable.

I take Adeline's hand and walk her home.

CH. 34

I haven't had a cigarette in a couple months now. Not going to lie; Adeline was pretty much the main reason for that improvement. Most women are not attracted to a man that smokes and, either consciously or unconsciously, I was definitely trying to be attractive to her. Also, before I entered this world, I was drinking to a point where—even though I wouldn't consider it alcoholism—someone could easily make the case that it was problematic. But for the last month and a half or so, that too has decreased significantly. But right now I could definitely go for a breakfast of Marlboro Reds and some scotch to wash it down.

I've been walking to Sunny Side Up with my head running over possible excuses to explain what Coralline saw, but coming up weak. There's really not much I can say. She caught me with my arm around Adeline's shoulder and my face nuzzled in her neck. She saw the guilt of an unfaithful man when I turned to look at her. She saw me trying to speak as someone who's obviously going to spout bullshit to try to cover their ass—only letting syllables escape because they know there's no way of coming out innocent. To top it all off, she heard Adeline's words, 'We've been going out for a few months now'.

I'm Humbert Humbert exposed. I'm Oedipus just realizing the extent of his crimes. I'm Romeo realizing his mistake. I'm... I'm... I'm out of metaphors. I'm fucked.

I walk into the restaurant and see Coralline Thomson glaring at me as soon as I enter the door. There's disappointment, worry, and a distinct unbridled rage subdued in that uncomfortable stare. The hostess greets me and I tell her I'm with Coralline and smile and wave to her. She just keeps on glaring.

I sit opposite of Coralline and the waitress asks me what I want to drink; I tell her a coffee and she leaves. Long after the waitress leaves, Coralline doesn't say anything and just continues that death glare in this uncomfortable awkward silence.

"Look Ja-" I start.

"When I told you about the rules, you were supposed to listen," she says. "Were you listening?"

"Well, yes-" I start to speak again.

"Then what the fuck was that?" she interrupts me again. "What the fuck did I see yesterday?"

I start to say, "Look, that can be explained. You see-"

She stops my explanation again, "Listen Henry, when I told you those rules, I didn't just do it for shits and giggles. There are potential dire consequences for breaking them. And you broke the most important rule." I notice that she's using 'Henry' instead of 'Jake' and I'm left feeling a little uneasy.

"What you saw yesterday wasn't what you think you saw. You see-" I say.

Once again she cuts me off. "Don't bullshit me Henry. I know what I saw, and I can tell what love looks like better than anybody."

"Jane-" I say.

"Don't fucking call me that!" she says a little too loudly, then calms herself down. "I think you've been too involved in your story. Call me Coralline for now. I think you need a little dose of reality."

"Okay, Coralline, did I develop a relationship? Yes. Is it pleasant? Yes. Am I in love? Far from it," I say

"Do you even know who she is?" she asks.

I laugh. "I think I have a good idea."

"I really doubt it," she says and I look at her confused. "Answer something Henry. Have you fucked her?" I wince at her making such a crude statement.

"Well, yes I've slept with her, but it wasn't love," I say. "It was just fooling around." I say, feeling horrible. I am a liar and a bad one at that. And the immense guilt I feel is probably completely evident on my face.

"I said don't bullshit me Henry," she says.

I say a little too loudly. "I'm not bullshitting you! Yeah we had sex, but I don't love her!"

And Peter denies three times before the cock crows.

"Listen Henry, there always will be some person of your dreams in these stories. The story takes everything that you desire in a partner, and puts them into a fictional person. Sometimes it's loosely based off of a person you could never get but were infatuated with and then it perfects them, and many times it's simply the collective characteristics of your dream girl come to life. She seems too good to be true. There's a reason for that. She's not true. She's a fucking lie. I didn't think of telling you this because the chances of you running into her were so minimal that it didn't cross my mind. It's hard to resist but you absolutely must. Listen to me Henry, this is for your own safety," she says.

"Jane-" I start.

"Coralline!" she says, getting red.

"Sorry, Coralline," I say, "you can choose to believe me or you can choose not to, but I don't love her," I lie adamantly.

"For Christ sake Henry," she says. "You can try to bullshit me, but you'll be unsuccessful. But one thing's for sure, you can't bullshit yourself."

I'm getting angry. "Fine," I say. "You know what? I do love her. Woop-de-fucking-doo. But you know what? I've loved other women before. And guess what? I've gotten over them. This world is shitty, and if I find solace in a beautiful, caring, funny, smart, woman—big deal. When I snap back to the real world, you know what I'll do? I'll cope. I'll cope like the rest of the world when they break up with someone, or when someone dies, or when they have any fucking negative impact that happens to them. My dad died when I was nine years old. I learned to cope. I saw a friend die right before my eyes when her boyfriend—my best friend—was futilely trying to revive her. You know what I did? I coped. I made the biggest mistake of my life and drove the love of my life away from me. Can you guess what I did?" I look at her, egging her on.

"You just don't get it," she says to herself.

"What don't I get?" I say; my anger obvious.

"She's not real," she says. "You are dating fantasy. You're going out with your imagination. You're trying to make a good impression on your subconscious."

"Jane-" I say.

"You're *fucking* an illusion!" she shouts and grinds her teeth.

The waitress comes by slightly alarmed by the obvious fight that we seem to be in, and she looks at both our faces flushed with anger.

"Hi," she says. "Can I get you two anything to eat?"

Despite my discontent, I try my hardest to be polite. I succeed for the most part. Obviously I can't feign delight and shrug off my anger entirely, but I do a good job not taking it out on the waitress. I order steak and eggs and Coralline orders an egg white omelet. The waitress smiles and leaves quickly, noticing the obvious tension.

The waitress falls out of earshot and Coralline speaks once again. "You really don't get it, do you?"

"Maybe," I say. "Could you at least inform me of what I don't get?"

"Do you know who Adeline Stewart is?" she asks.

"I am the one who's sleeping with her. I've been dating her for a few months," I say. "Yeah, I think I have a good idea."

"No-" she starts.

"Yeah, I get it," I say. "She's an illusion, right?"

"That's not what I'm talking about," she says gravely. "The name. Just think of the name. Adeline Stewart. Does that ring any bells?"

"Yeah," I say. "The girl I'm dating. What's your point?"

"Jesus Henry," she says. "You can be really fucking dense sometimes. Just think of the name."

"Nothing's coming to mind," I say. "It might help if you inform me."

"Think Henry," she says. "Think really hard."

I fake smile irritated and shake my head. "Still coming up blank."

"Henry," she says. "She's going to die." I look at her confused. "She's a victim of Richard Sweeney."

My smile drops and I turn pale. This is when Romeo kills himself.

CH. 35

I'm a ghost. White as a ghost, cold as a ghost, brainless as a ghost, emotionless as a ghost, and dead as a ghost. There is nothing in me. I have left, checked out. My body is vacant.

It's been a long time that I've been staring at Coralline, my mouth open slightly, my eyes not blinking, my eyebrows raised in shock, and my palms clammy. No words are spoken. None need be. Maybe they do, I don't know. But right now I don't know what to say. I'm still just trying to process what she just told me. The inevitability. The horror. The severity. There's no doubting it; I've fallen head over heels for Adeline, and now I'm hearing that she's going to die? No. No way. It can't be. I won't let it.

"I know this is difficult to take in," Coralline says. "But it's essential you remember what she really is. She's not real Henry. She's an illusion. She's make-believe. She's your imagi-"

"Bullshit," I barely say over a whisper, my strength drained. "You're full of shit." I shake my head limply. "It's all lies. It's not true." I'm still shaking my head. Then my voice rises. "You're fucking full of shit!"

"Henry, calm down," she says.

"No," I say. "You're a liar. There's no way. I would have known that. She's not going to die. You're a fucking liar. You...

you... you... you lying bitch."

"Listen Henry," she says soothingly, "it's true. I was hoping this wasn't the case, but it's true. She has to die, Henry. But she doesn't really die. She's not really real. She's *fiction* Henry. You have to come to terms with that." I just sit there shaking my head.

The waitress comes by with our food. She says, "Here you go" softly, then puts the food in front of us, looks at both our faces, and walks away fast.

The world is becoming undone. The sky is falling. The sky is falling and there's nothing I can do.

"Henry, she dies and you can't interfere," Coralline says.

"Why... why not?" I say.

"Because her death is essential," she says. "She's the one where Richard slips up. She puts up a fight and stabs him in the leg. She then starts to wrestle with him and she manages to tear off one of his gloves. Richard tries to clean up after he's done but they get his DNA and fingerprints and are able to track him down. She's Richard's last kill. After that, Detective Reynolds finds him, chases him down and kills him."

It all comes flooding back to me. I knew how it would end, but I forgot the name. She didn't have that big of a role—at least in the amount of time she was in the book—but her role was incredibly important for the sake of the story. Without her, there is no end. Who knows how long this book would extend for? All the time, it would get more and more unraveled until I'm only left with a confusing combination of words that are meaningless.

I don't know how I forgot. Maybe it was the fact that—at least for my story's sake—she's more important for an action than for character development. She was intended to be in only two chapters—just a couple of paragraphs in each. Maybe I was so intrigued with this fictional world that, when I met her the first time, the name didn't register. Maybe it was being wrapped up in love that I purposely made myself forget her name. Maybe it was a combination of all three of these. Maybe it doesn't matter. I don't know; I just forgot.

"There's got to be some way," I say, "some way that I can change this. It doesn't have to be her that this happens to. It could happen to somebody else. He could get caught some other way. He could...." I drift off, thinking of any possible way that it could play out differently.

"No, Henry," she says gravely. "It has to be this way."

I can't take this. She can't die. She can't! There has to be another way.

"What if...?" I start searching once again and come up empty.

"I'm sorry," she says. "There's really no other way." She pauses. "That's not the only reason you should distance yourself. Even the story's sake pales in comparison to the real potential damage: your sanity." She pauses again, trying to be as calm and considerate as she can. "Horrible things can happen if you get too attached. If you fall too much in love with her, you will be more in love with her than any other relationship you've had. Your mind has created her as everything you've ever desired in a woman. It's an unfortunate side effect of the story. And if you do fall in love, horrible things can happen, and probably will. You will be ripped apart when you return to the real world. You'll be more crushed by this than anything you've ever experienced before. It's inevitable. And in extreme cases, it can cause suicide." For the first time since I believe I've known her, I see her eyes start to get wet. "Trust me," she says. "This is not a path you want to go down, as hard as it is to avoid it. You may be torn up inside by leaving her and letting her die, but the alternative is worse."

I can't imagine it being any worse than this. I'm in love, and haven't experienced anything close to this in years. I don't believe I have ever felt a similarity to the depth of this love ever in my life, even though I've had much longer relationships. That includes Lindsey: the only other woman I can honestly say that I truly loved. Even she didn't evoke as much passion or wholeness as I feel when I'm with Adeline.

"Please Henry," she says, "save yourself. Don't go down this path. In this world, love is the most dangerous thing you can experience. You have to promise me you'll let her go. You won't try to stop this. You can't get involved deeper."

I try to say something, but instead just let out some air that barely qualifies as grunt status.

"Promise," she says more forcefully.

"Yeah..." I say. "Sure."

"Promise," she says. "I need to hear you say it."

"I... I... I promise," I say.

"To do what?" she says.

I'm a little agitated and definitely distraught. "I promise to not stop Richard Sweeney. To distance myself from her," I say, not sure if I'm lying.

"Good," she says, then looks at me for a while. After a long look searching for something, she decides to eat her food.

I stare back at her chowing away at her egg white omelet, blowing on her coffee and sipping on it; the irritating sips and noise of silverware on plate sting my ears. I look at her, wondering if that concern she displayed was sincere or feigned. It looked real. It sounded real. It seemed real. But now she's scarfing down her breakfast as if nothing is happening. As if my world isn't crashing down around me. As if I hadn't just landed into the ninth and final circle of Hell. The ninth circle: Treachery. As I just agreed to betray the woman I love and let her die. Hell isn't punishment enough.

She finishes her meal and looks up at me with my untouched plate. I can't eat. Not only am I no longer hungry and feeling nauseous, but I don't deserve to eat. I am not worthy of food.

I'm analyzing Coralline, trying to figure out what kind of person she is. She seemed so compassionate and sincere about my troubles and my well-being, but now moments after telling me I have to let someone who she knows I'm close to die—in a sense murdering her—she was able to polish off a whole meal without the slightest delay.

"You should go now," I say. "I need some time alone."

"Alright," she says. "I'll give you some time, but we should definitely meet sometime soon. How does Wednesday at four after you're off work sound?"

"Sure," I say, and she gets up and leaves.

I sit alone wondering what my next action should be. Do I really go through with this? Let Adeline die? Walk away from her now? Never see her again and know that I'm the one responsible for her death?

"Is everything alright?" the waitress asks, surprising me.

"Yes," I say. "It's just... it's just... well it's just complicated."

She looks at me somewhat confused. "Okay," She says and walks away.

It's not until she's halfway across the restaurant that I realize that she was talking about my food. I've got to get out of here. I slap down two twenties—way more than it costs, but I don't care—and walk out of the restaurant; my food untouched.

When I get outside, I see a man smoking a cigarette. He's leaning against the side of the store in a semi-squat just puffing away.

"Is there any way I can bum a smoke?" I ask.

He nods his head, fishes one out of the pack, and hands it to me. I reach into my pockets instinctually for my lighter, forgetting I don't carry one anymore.

"Sorry," I say. "Do you happen to have a light?"

He laughs. "You want me to light it for you, too?"

"Sorry," I say. "I've been quitting but just had a rough day."

"No worries," he says.

I hold the lighter up to the end of the smoke. Well, two and a half months down the drain. I light the cigarette, inhale deeply, and hand the lighter back to him.

I know I should really go home and think about everything with a clear mind. I should really contemplate everything Coralline

LIAM MORAN

Thomson said and analyze carefully what my next move should be. So without missing a beat, I head to the nearest liquor store.

CH. 36

Monday morning I'm teaching grammar to a bunch of uninterested kids. Monday night I'm pondering my next maneuver with Adeline—my brain marinating on a twelve pack of Budweiser. Tuesday morning I'm discussing the poems of Emily Dickenson to a classroom of semi-attentive students. Tuesday night I'm stirring over the possibilities of what to do about my dilemma, puffing away on a cigarette and stirring my scotch. Wednesday after work I'm telling Coralline my final decision to let Adeline die and to not interfere in any way. Less than an hour later, I bump into Adeline and now I choose that I want to prevent her death. Later, I'm alone at night with my troubles and whiskey, once again unsure. I have that Rush lyric playing through my head: "If you choose not to decide, you still have made a choice."

The old catch-22. Damned if you do; fucked if you don't. Do I sacrifice my story and sanity, or do I sacrifice my love? I've always been a bit of a romantic at heart, but then again, I always did kind of value my sanity. No matter how much I try to decide, I can't make up my mind. There is no clear-cut answer. She's an illusion, a figment of my imagination; I get it. But then again, I've never loved someone so passionately in my life. Even if the person isn't real, the love is definitely real. That can't be questioned. Can it?

Thursday at lunch break I'm looking over tests—grading and making corrections. Thursday night I'm stewing over an abundance of whiskey and self-loathing, deciding my course of action and making corrections. Friday morning I'm trying to quiet one of my students talking about some new hit TV show while I'm telling them about the importance of the narrator's loss of Lenore in Poe's "The Raven." Friday night I'm at a dive bar while someone's telling me that Nirvana's original band name was almost called "Fecal Matter." Is this my subconscious telling me something I had forgotten or just some wacko spouting bullshit? I don't know. I don't exactly care either. I'm too concerned thinking about the potential loss of my own Lenore. All the while, that old "Free Will" lyric plays in my head, "If you choose not to decide…"

On Saturday morning I go to a Starbucks, grab a coffee and sit outside, reading the paper and puffing a cigarette. And that's when I see the big news—huge news for my story—when I see that Detective Lenny Johnson got shot. This is the part of the story where Todd Reynolds really starts to lose it.

There was a murderer that they tracked down. They weren't completely sure if he had done it. They had a good idea, but he was still just a suspect. But as soon as he took flight when he saw the detectives, their doubt had been removed. The man had robbed a convenient store a couple of weeks back, and had blown a hole in the clerks head, killed a male bystander with two shots to the chest, and put a hole in a woman's abdomen. The woman had cracked her head against the floor hard and was knocked out. The robber thought they were all dead, but miraculously the woman was able to make it. She described what she had witnessed to the detectives, and they managed to track down the perpetrator.

When he fled from the detectives, they chased him, and got him caught with nowhere to run. Out of options, the man turned around and fired at them wildly. He wasn't a good shot to say the least. He just closed his eyes and fired haphazardly, praying that he made contact. Luckily for him—or unluckily depending on how you look at it—he got Lenny in the gut. He fumbled with his clip, trying to reload, and Todd put two in his chest to take him down for the count. Todd made sure that the man was no longer a threat and then went back to check on his partner. He did all he could do. He called for assistance shouting, "Man down! Man down!" into the radio. He applied pressure, praying to God that his friend will make it out alright. But it was all in vain. Help was on the way, but help was already too late. Lenny Johnson had left this world by the time assistance arrived. And now Todd Reynolds is at wit's end. The "scumbags", as he calls them, that corrupt the streets are going to pay, no matter what the cost. And he'll find that cross-killer if it's the last thing he does. And considering that this is all a novel that ends when he shoots down the serial killer, that will be the last thing he does.

The article discusses all of the accomplishments he had achieved in both his career and personal life. It discusses the hours of voluntary community service. It mentions the family he has that are in deep mourning that will immortalize him in their memory, and relate stories to their children, and their children's children. Giving your life to uphold justice is a big deal. And it definitely will be something that will be passed through generations.

The wake will be this Friday at the same funeral home that held the lifeless body of Ron Madsen. Only I'm guessing this wake will be a little more orthodox and a little less violent. The funeral will be on the following day, complete with Amazing Grace played on bag pipes and a six gun salute—the whole nine yards for police officers.

I was one time at a funeral for a policeman. He wasn't a detective, just a regular trooper. He was my Uncle Ricky. He wasn't my real uncle; just a close friend of my dad's. I was young at the time—couldn't have been more than eight. My dad had already shown the first signs of his cirrhosis. His skin was all yellow, he was tired by even the minutest movement, and he was scratching away at some uncontrollable itch throughout the entire service. I had to go to this service even though I didn't know him well. At the beginning, I was more in distress watching my dad regress further and further in his sickness than by the person being mourned. But I remember, even though I didn't know him that well, the memorial hit me emotionally. When everyone saluted as the guns were fired, and the bagpipes played while they lowered his body in the grave, even the meticulous folding of the flag, it just hit me in a spot that I can't explain. My eyes welled with tears. I didn't know the man that well, but it was quite a spectacle.

As the day turns into night, I find myself in another dive bar putting down my fourth beer as Tucker Smith yammers away at my ear. He normally doesn't talk to anyone. He's highly sensitive and extremely insecure about himself. That's a fortunate thing for most people, because he's socially awkward; and when he speaks, there's hardly anything that rivals the level of irritation he can provoke in anyone. Unfortunately for me, that whole 'prayer concept' comes back to bite me in the ass.

"So I just-I sometimes don't seem that comfortable talking aloud," he says just above a murmur—hardly enough to make himself audible. "But I know-I know that if I can just be comfortable—you know—comfortable with talking in front of people, I could be big. I could be anything I want. I could be a movie star. Or a businessman. Or a policeman. Or a rock star. Or a teacher..."

"Uh-huh," I say, tuning him out.

He's one of the most awkward and suspicious people I've ever met. His mousy voice is just above a whisper. His face is all scrunched up as if he's constantly stricken with a foul odor. He jerks his hands and neck awkwardly when he talks. He's always so jumpy. Hell, even his name sounds suspicious. His first name: an obscure name that is hardly used. One of those rare names that everyone perks up to with interest. Only to be followed by the most generic last name that everyone would think of when the question is asked, "What is the first last name that comes to your head?"

All the while I'm knocking back my fourth beer wondering what to do with Adeline. Do I let her die? Do I let the biggest love of my life die? Does that make me a murderer? What does that make me?

Tucker, he's still nursing his first beer that he got a little more than an hour ago. And he continues his constant irritating babble. "Or a lawyer. Or a news anchor. Or an astronaut. Or a banker. Or a doctor. Or a soldier. Or any of the other respectable members of society. But instead I'm a barista. And I was barely able to get that that job to begin with. And the customers; they can be so uppity. They can be so horribly mean. One time—just last week—a man came in cursing at me because I didn't get his order right. I said that I was sorry and would correct it, but he just went on shouting and making fun of me. And then another guy one time threw a fit because he wasn't allowed to bring his dog in the shop. He made a scene, and it was so embarrassing. And then the kids. Oh my god, the kids are terrible. They're all-"

"Look," I say cutting him off with irritation clear in my voice. "Because somehow you're not able to tell, I'll just blatantly inform you. I don't give a shit. I've got some issues I have to sort out, and I just want to be alone with my thoughts. You get it?"

He looks at me stunned. I know how sensitive his character is, and that if he has someone rude to him at work or something bad happens to him like that, he'll stay inside for close to a week, just feeling depressed and turn himself into a hermit. He's the most sensitive person in this world, and I just threw his opening up to me back in his face, and I feel terrible. But, god damn it, he was getting on my nerves.

"I'm sorry," he says timidly. "I didn't mean to irritate you. It's my fault. It's just that-"

"No," I say. "It's *my* fault, not yours. I'm sorry. I've just got some issues going on right now, and I kind of lashed out inappropriately. It was wrong of me and I apologize." His eyes start to well up, and I can't take it anymore. "Ah, fuck it. I'm outta here." I slug down the rest of my beer and head out the door.

I know he'll take this hard. He's so sensitive. Even the slightest attack on him can leave him emotionally paralyzed for days. There he was opening up to me and telling me his deepest secrets, and I just shoved it back in his face. If I remember my story correctly, in just a little while he's going to get the shit kicked out of him. I wonder how long that will leave him emotionally paralyzed. This is not going to shape up to be a good month for Tucker Smith.

I go back to my apartment and pour myself a good sized scotch on the rocks, and mull over the dilemma I've been trying to process this past week. I light a cigarette and take another sip of the scotch. Nicotine to stimulate my mind; alcohol to numb it.

What do I do? The question of the century. Sanity or love? Sanity or love? What's more important: my mind or my heart? This wasn't the first time the question was asked in the history of man, and it won't be the last. But I really doubt if the circumstances have ever been even remotely close to this.

I figure I'd do a pros and cons list. I pull out a pen and paper and start to jot down the list.

If I let her live:
> Pro: I'll be able to be more deeply in love with her than I have been with any other woman.
> Con: My story will be ruined.
> Pro: There will never be a relationship that comes close to the one I will have with her, and I will have that love for a longer period of time.
> Con: My sanity would be jeopardized.

The scotch didn't help me much so I pour myself a second hefty portion in a glass and light a second cigarette.

If I let her die:

Pro: I'll have a successful story on my hands with the potential of attaining fame.

Con: I'll indirectly kill the love of my life.

Pro: I'll have money and no longer have to scrounge by on the bare minimum.

Con: I'll fucking kill the love of my life.

Pro: I'll still have my sanity.

Con: Will I really?

I'm not going to lie; either way looks shitty. The old catch-22. Damned if I do; fucked if I don't. I pour myself a third scotch and once again light another cigarette looking at the list over and over.

My phone rings and, just my luck, it's Adeline. The woman of my dreams. The woman I would die for. And the woman I'm pondering to let die.

I wonder if I should answer it; just staring at the phone, contemplating my next action. Damned if I do; fucked if I don't.

I pick up. "Hello?" I say wearily.

"Hi Jake," she says, filled with positive energy. She sounds so delighted to talk with me that I can't help but feel that horrible guilt.

"Hi Adeline," I say shakily, trying not to slur my words. Most people wouldn't be able to pull off sounding somewhat with it after they've imbibed this much liquor, but me—I'm a veteran.

"I was wondering what you were doing tomorrow. I was seeing if you wanted to go out," she says. "Personally, I've been aching to get out and do something, maybe go for a walk. I'd like to enjoy the day outside. I'd even be willing to go Frisbee golfing like you so suavely proposed last time," she jokes. "What do you say?"

I know I should delay my response. I shouldn't see her until I have a clear understanding of a game plan. Most people with this much alcohol and in the middle of a difficult decision would pause too long and appear suspicious. But I come up with an excuse right away. I tell her I've got a nasty cold and don't want her to catch it. Like I said, I'm a veteran.

"Sounds terrible," she says. "I can tell that your voice sounds different." No shit, I'm completely wasted. "Well, you get back to health as soon as you can. Do you think you'll be healthy enough by Wednesday?"

I know I shouldn't. I should come up with some other excuse to fend her off for the time being. I need to regroup when I've developed a game plan. There's no need to go in when I don't have a plan of action. It would be ill-advised.

I hear Coralline Thomson advising me against it. *You will be ripped apart when you return to the real world.* I hear her warning me. *You'll be more crushed by this than anything you've ever experienced before.* Her words haunt me. *In extreme cases, it can cause suicide.* I take all of this in. The decision needs to be made some time, but I can't make it now, despite all of Coralline's warnings. But then I also shouldn't meet with her on Wednesday because I know I shouldn't see her until I've made a final decision. Seeing her will only make it harder. No way will I see her.

"Sure," I say. "Wednesday should be fine."

"Alright Jake, I'll see you then," she says. And then she adds those three wonderful, terrible, gut-wrenching, powerful, horrible, glorious, abysmal, words. "I love you."

Here I am. Trapped. Those words hit me like kryptonite. I'm crumbled, lost my power, unable to move or think. I pause a little too long, but can probably blame it on my cold if she ever brings it up. "I love you too," I say. And it's completely true.

We hang up and I'm back in my misery. The decision has just become more difficult, but I have to decide on something soon. I'm shaking and starting to well up around the eyes. Why did she have to say those words? Why did she have to say it now?

I pour myself a fourth scotch and light a cigarette, once again playing over what I should do in my mind, but the scotch makes it more difficult to think coherently.

Once again that old tune starts to play in my head, "If you choose not to decide, you still have made a choice."

CH. 37

Almost a week later, and still no closer to making a decision. I'm jumping back and forth between choices. I'm like one of those kids picking petals off a flower: I kill her. I kill her not. Only this oxeye daisy has limitless petals. The more I pick, the more petals return to the flower. The eternal question: I kill her. I kill her not.

Meanwhile, in an attempt to get the dreadful dilemma off my mind, I swing by a dive bar called The Midas Touch, where an essential moment in the story is about to happen. I figured I'd be here for this, because witnessing it in person might enhance my story. Plus it kills time and delays me making that fatal decision.

Detective Reynolds has just finished his fourth whiskey and has now switched to beer which he is drinking in a hurry. It's Friday night, and he's in a suit after coming straight from Lenny Johnson's wake. He'll be hung over for the funeral tomorrow, but currently that's not on his mind. He's depressed, bitter, in a rage, and he wants something to calm him down. Like many men, unfortunately, alcohol is his number one coping mechanism.

In a little bit, Tucker Smith is going to walk in this bar and sit by himself nursing his beer as a baby would sip from a bottle. Detective Reynolds will see him and eventually lose it. With

Tucker's mousy way of speaking and the fact that—just by chance—he has a bad case of being in the wrong place at the wrong time, Todd Reynolds has for a long time suspected him of being the cross-killer—one of his many suspects. Just looking at Tucker, you would expect him to be a creep in some way. He looks and acts like your text-book serial killer: quiet, without any friends, nobody's ever seen him with a woman, slithers in and out hardly uttering a word. He's inconspicuous. Only he's too inconspicuous and that always creates suspicion. They always say the same thing after each mass shooting or a serial killer is caught. "He was always so quiet." They say you should always watch out for the quiet ones.

Todd chugs his beer with a passion, only taking breaks to chew vigorously on his gum. Tucker hasn't arrived yet—he won't until the detective is much drunker. Once he does, and orders his Budweiser, sipping on it like a baby, Todd Reynolds is going to let loose like a rabid dog. I pity Tucker Smith. He doesn't know what he's in for, and the fight is going to be horribly one-sided. It'll be painful to watch as Todd's fist hits Tucker's face repeatedly. That horrible *thud* sound as fist connects to jaw. That awful crunching sound as his nose squashes and his blood sticks to Todd's knuckles. I probably shouldn't have come today, but this is a pinnacle moment for my story, and I am still trying to make the most out of it.

There's a group of kids barely old enough—if even old enough—to get in a bar, that are completely stoned. Their eyes are as red as the side of a fire truck, and they're laughing at nothing all that particularly funny. One of them is completely silent and is just sitting there dumb, chowing away at two plates of onion rings and a burger. The ketchup falls from his mouth landing on his chest and stomach, and his chin is coated in that red smear. The other three—two boys and one girl—turn and see him struggling to get the food in his mouth and laugh harder.

"Fuckin' armatures," the man sitting next to me scoffs. He

looks like he's in his mid-fifties with peppered hair that could use a trim and a greying beard. He's got a bit of a potbelly on him and has put away quite a number of beers since I've seen him. He turns in my general direction and says in a way that I can't tell if it's to me or to himself, "You can smell the dope from here, you don't need to fucking advertise it."

"You don't approve?" I ask.

"Listen," he says, "I don't give two shits if they get high or not, but if you're old enough to get into a bar, you should be old enough to hold your pot."

"I guess you're right." I shrug.

"I know I'm right," he says. "Kids acting like dipshits like that are the reason it's not legal. Nobody's gonna take you seriously if you're giggling like a moron all the time."

I think of when I've seen young people drink excessively and remember all the ways they acted like complete idiots. Vehemently claiming they're not drunk while wanting everyone to realize how drunk they are. Swearing to the contrary but exaggerating their level of intoxication. I remember people pissing themselves, vomiting on themselves, and stumbling around and knocking things over; breaking valuables accidentally. But I decide not to argue. It's not a huge concern of mine, and I don't want to argue with him.

"They look pretty young," I say. "If I were to guess, I wouldn't say they were over nineteen."

"They probably got a fake," he says with disgust.

"Maybe," I say.

"And I tell you what," he says. "You know who paid for their bullshit IDs, right?"

I shrug, "Who?"

"Mommy and daddy," he says.

"I doubt that," I say.

"Don't be an idiot," he says. "I'm not talking directly. But kids these days don't work. They sit on their ass and have their parents pay for their drugs and alcohol. 'Hey I need to buy a gram. Mommy, daddy, I need twenty dollars.' 'What for?' 'Oh just a new video game.' 'Sure honey.' Later that night they come home all chink-eyed and stupid and their parents are baffled why their kids look so strange. The next day, they repeat the process anew." He slugs down some more of his beer. "This generation is the worst. The fuckin' worst."

"Maybe there's some hope for them," I say. "Who knows? Maybe they'll learn from their ways and do something different. Really make a change."

"Well, I fuckin' doubt it," he says. "But keep dreamin' buddy. In the meantime, I'm gonna hit the shitter." He gets up and heads to the bathroom.

I look back at detective Reynolds. He's pounding away on whatever-number beer he's on. He's starting to look pretty loaded. And he's seething. The deep breaths in and out quick; his thoughts ranging between bursting into tears and committing brutal arbitrary murder. His heart rate is jacked and he doesn't know what to do. This is when something bad happens, and, in a matter of minutes, will happen. On the speaker Ozzy Osbourne is singing "Crazy Train". At the same time, Detective Reynolds is derailing.

Where the hell is Tucker Smith? He should be here by now. Or maybe it's just a little bit longer. But Reynolds is hammered and ready for a fight and Tucker is nowhere to be seen. That wormy man should be ready to take his pounding. I feel bad for him, but it is essential. Todd's relentless beating of Tucker illustrates him losing control. It's the case getting to him to a point where it blurs the lines of his sanity. I wish I could stop it, but I can't. I can't for the sake of my story.

I scan the bar looking for Tucker. Where is he? Why isn't he here yet? I look at the entrance wondering when he'll pop in. Should only be a matter of minutes. If he doesn't get here soon then-

Crash! My train of thought is broken by a bottle shattering upon my head. The broken bottle careens against my cheek, forming a large gash. I can feel the blood pouring out of my skull. I'm grabbed by the front of my shirt and see the face of Todd Reynolds as he drives me back. My feet are moving backward, trying to gain traction but failing. I'm barely able to place my feet on the ground—only succeeding in quickening my collision to the wall. I hear men scurry away as screams encompass the bar.

Ozzy's still bellowing away, "I'm going off the rails on a crazy train!"

We topple over a barstool and it crushes under our combined weight as my head hits the wall with a loud thud.

I start to shout, "What the fuck are you-"

He silences me with quick right to the jaw, then accompanies that with both fists repeatedly. *Thwack! Thwack! Thwack!* The sound of my face being pummeled and my head bouncing against the wall again and again and again.

He's much stronger than I am. There's no chance of me winning this. Even if I do pull off a punch, I'll probably end up getting arrested. So I put my hands up to cover my face and take the punishment. *Thwack! Thwack! Thwack!* That dull thud of fist to flesh to bone to wall. That sickening thudding of head to wall as my ears begin to ring.

"You motherfucker!" he shouts. "I'll get you, you sick motherfucker!"

My arms over my face in a poor boxer position. Left, right, left, right, right. Then the power punches come. He curls his right arm back, grabbing my collar with his left and lets loose a haymaker. Then he lets loose another. And another. I'm able to block some. But even the ones I block just delay the impact. Instead of his fist hitting my face directly, it first travels through my arm.

Someone tries to grab him, he pushes him away with one arm, and my attempted savior trips over a barstool and falls down with a crash.

All of a sudden, Todd seems to become more aware, as if he's sobered up a little. I guess letting out that much of a beating can have you sweat out the alcohol.

He backs up wide-eyed, realizing what he's done: the brutality of it, and how it can affect his job. He walks backward, stunned at what he did, as I lay in my pool of blood. He slaps down a handful of cash on the bar—apparently paying for his tab, or the damage, or maybe both—and walks out of the bar without saying a word. Everyone steps aside terrified as he makes his way to the exit.

Only after he leaves do people come and help me. One person attends to the man sprawled out on the floor who attempted to save me.

My tongue licking up the sweet taste of blood from inside my mouth. I use my tongue to count my teeth and some of them are loose. Luckily, they're all still there. My nose hurts like hell. I wonder if I got a deviated septum, because it's a little hard to breathe. I reach towards the back of my head and remove a piece of glass—broken off from the bottle—that had embedded its way into my scalp. It's all coated in blood—smeared in that awful blurry redness. My head is throbbing; each side of my temples pounding, *thump, thump, thump.* My ears are still ringing loudly and over the speakers and thumping and ringing I hear Ozzy screaming, "Mental wounds not healing. Who and what's to blame? I'm goin' off the rails on a crazy train! I'm goin' off the rails on a crazy train!"

"You alright?" a man asks me, who I can barely see through squinting eyes.

"I doubt it," I say.

"Jesus, you sure took a beating," he says. "What was that all about?"

"Fuck if I know," I say.

He asks, "You need some help?" and offers me his hand.

"No," I tell him. "I think I got it."

I push myself up with weak arms and hear the barstool cracking some more as I do so. I stand up and lean against the wall—my hand draped over my pounding forehead.

"You want me to call an ambulance," he says. "I'm not gonna lie; you look like shit."

"No, I got it. I'll just walk over there," I say. "The hospital's not that far."

"You want me to accompany you?" he offers.

"No, but thanks," I say.

I walk over to the bar and look at the bartender, "Can I get a shot of whiskey for the road."

"Take two," he says. "It's on the house." He then pours me two shots of whiskey and I down them quickly. Yeah, it may not be the brightest idea to drink after possibly getting a concussion, but whoever said I was the brightest guy?

I reach for my wallet. The bartender tells me not to bother and I head out the door.

I'm staggering toward the hospital clutching my head, wrapped up once again in my dilemma. What do I do? The question of the ages. The aching in my head only makes the decision harder.

The delirium and drunkenness are the limitless petals on my oxeye daisy. I kill her. I kill her not. I kill her. I kill her not.

CH. 38

When a grown man walks by in public with his eye swollen to the size of an orange and black as coal, everyone has to gawk. They see the stitches in the back of my head, the fresh scar on my cheek, and that defeatist look that every loser in a fight wears, and they just stare. People my age shouldn't be getting into fights. Yeah, sure, if a teenager walks around all bloodied up, that's just a stupid kid being reckless, but a grown man should be beyond fighting. But me: I just keep on strutting.

Some sixteen year old kid looks at me and says, "Jesus, man, what happened to you."

"You should see the other guy," I tell him. "He's probably still soaking his fists in ice-water." And I just keep on walking.

I decided not to press charges or file a suit. I don't want to be a main character, so the less activity I do that increases my depth in this story, the better.

But it's probably still going to get around. Somebody's bound to tell one of their buddies, "Hey, you remember that guy who saved that girl from getting hit by a car? Well he just got his ass handed to him by a detective." And then they'll tell two friends. And they'll tell two friends. And they'll tell two friends. You know the drill.

Sooner or later, the gawking faces will have suspicion and uneasiness accompanying their shock and revulsion. But for the time being, I'm going to just keep on strutting in broad daylight. If people want to stare, let them.

It wasn't as bad as I thought it would be. My septum wasn't deviated. There were no broken bones. I only have a mild concussion after the lopsided onslaught I endured. Plus they had to do some stitching on the back of my head. That bottle got me pretty good. On the whole, I look worse than I am.

Monday morning I walk into my work, still not looking that well, but much better than before. I wonder if I can manage to go with this unnoticed. Ernest Winston—as hyper as ever—is the first to greet me and his mouth is contorted in a large circular O as his eyeballs seem to be bursting out of their sockets. Well, I guess that answers that question.

"Are you okay? What happened? You must tell me what happened," Ernest says in what appears to be his panic-mode.

"Oh," I say, "It was nothing. Just some drunk in a bar attacked me."

"That's horrible. Simply horrible," the words charge out of his mouth. "I can't imagine what you went through. I simply can't imagine."

"I don't know," I say, still trying to shrug it off. "I guess these things happen. He probably had some issues going on and decided to take it out on whoever was nearest to him." Well it is *kind of* the truth.

"This town is run by hooligans. *Hooligans*, I tell you!" he says.

"Well, there certainly are some rough people in this town. But the good people do outweigh the bad," I say. "At least I hope."

"An optimist as always," he says. "That's what I like about you Jake. Well, if you need anything, feel free to ask for it. I'm always here. Always."

"I'll be sure to remember that," I tell him, and head to my

first class.

The students look at my bludgeoned face, and they all stare, some of them with open jaws. For once I have their undivided attention. Maybe I should bloody my face before every class. I may have just unlocked the eternity-long secret for teachers.

The questions start flying.

"What happened to you?" a sophomore asks.

"Well, somebody attacked me," I tell them.

"Did you get a few licks in?" another student asks.

"I'm more of a pacifist." Especially when the other guy is on the force. But I don't add that last part.

"Where was it at?" a girl asks.

I wonder if it's appropriate to say that it was at a bar, but I admit it anyway. Some of the students look surprised that I was at a bar. I guess they don't imagine their teachers having any social lives. Then again I wasn't with anybody. I was just at a dive bar alone. But I figure that's one of those things I shouldn't mention.

"Your eye looks huge," one of the students says. "And that's a sick gash on your face." He adds, "Can I touch it?"

"No, you cannot touch it," I say ridiculously. Why the hell would anybody want to touch a gash or a black eye anyway?

"So you didn't fight back at all?" another kid says.

"No," I say. "Like I said, I'm a pacifist."

"Pussy," A short scrawny student who wouldn't win a fight against a cripple half his age mutters under his breath.

"Hey! Another word from you and I'm sending you to the principal's office," I warn him. It's quite a warning; especially since Principal Richards might croak while talking to him. Taking that into consideration, it's quite a traumatic threat.

The scrawny student grunts in irritation and slinks deeper into his chair. The ultimate weapon of a teacher: the principal threat.

Each class is the same. Sure, I finally have their attention—even the ones whose brain is still marinating from this morning's blunt—but all they want to do is ask me more and more questions about my beating. Now I have their peaked interest, but I can't do anything with it.

The next day after work, Adeline gives me a ring. I pick up saying hello and she's filled with energy and concern, and wants to inquire more about how it happened.

"I heard from Shelly," she says a little too loudly into the phone. "Are you okay? How bad is it?"

I assure her I'm fine. "It's not really that bad. Just some drunk at a bar misplaced his rage. It's really nothing to worry about. Although the concern is quite flattering."

"We should really get together sometime soon," she says. "I want to see you. What's your availability like?"

"Well..." I say, "I think Friday I'm free."

"Alright, I'll see you then," she says. "Friday at five. Swing by my place."

"Will do," I say, and realize the mistake I just made.

She says goodbye and we hang up. For a split second, I forgot that I shouldn't see her. I have to make that dreadful decision uninfluenced. How could I forget that? That horrific problem I've been mulling over constantly had somehow slipped my mind. I guess Detective Reynolds must have really screwed up my wiring. But I guess the decision's made. I'll have to see her Friday. I just have to keep on reminding myself not to be influenced.

I ring the doorbell to Adeline's house, and she greets me with her mouth dropping a bit and some color fleeing her face. I didn't think I looked *that* bad. I had a week to recover. If this was her response after a week of healing, I can't imagine what her face would be like if she saw me fresh from the beating.

"Stunned by my beauty?" I smile.

"Jesus, Jake," she utters breathlessly.

"You should see the other guy," I say. "He's probably still

soaking his fists in ice-water." I smile at the line. It was a pretty good line. But why does it somehow sound familiar? Did I unknowingly jack it from somebody?

"How-how did this happen?" Her mouth is still agape.

"Well," I say. "It began with a fist colliding with my face. There was a wall involved, and a beer bottle if you can believe it. But the actual way it happened is that someone brought back their arm and pushed the escalated speed of his fist directly into my-"

"Enough with the jokes," she cuts me off harshly. "You could have gotten seriously hurt. Did you file a report at least?" I'm flattered at her concern.

"No," I say. "I figured it would only-"

She cuts me off again. "You didn't file a report? Jake, this man could be a nut. If he did this to you, who knows what he's capable of? Or worse, he could have a personal vendetta against you for some reason." Now you're getting warmer. "You shouldn't be so callous about this stuff. There are some deeply disturbed people in this city, and if something happened to you-if you-if somebody..." Her eyes start to get wet.

"Calm down," I say soothingly and take her in my arms. Now I feel the guilt coming in. She cares about me. I know she does. And maybe there are certain things I shouldn't joke about. Maybe I use humor as a coping mechanism too much and other people don't enjoy the joke as much as I do.

I hold her tightly and she kisses me dryly on the lips. Now I feel even more guilt. I wonder if she can taste the betrayal on my lips.

I've been debating on whether or not I should let you die, and here you are worrying about me with the deepest concern in your heart. Not a shred of cruelty. You're wondering if you could still live your life if I were to die, and I'm wondering if I should bump you off. What kind of person am I?

Always remember that the only things that are real in this world are me and you.

Yeah, I get it Coralline. But sometimes it's just not that easy. Sometimes when you experience *real* compassion and *real* love, it's hard to separate fact from fiction.

The rest of the day is fairly mundane. It's mainly a lot of lounging. I relay to her the story of the fight I got into, if you can call such a brutal ass-whooping a fight, but I omit the part about it being Detective Reynolds who was doing the beating. It may eventually get around to her—news like that travels fast—but I don't worry about it for now. I'll deal with that when the time comes. Hopefully it never will, but that's thinking wishfully.

After that we watch some TV, and she offers to cook me dinner. It's pot roast, and it's hard to resist even though I really should. I guess it's a meal for the wounded warrior kind of thing. And of course, even though I really shouldn't, I tell her I would love to stay for dinner.

We drink quite a bit of wine, which is probably a terrible idea for me, considering that I'm a week into my concussion. The doctor said I shouldn't drink for a month and I only lasted a week. I guess never listening to people's warnings is a common theme of mine, and nine times out of ten, it comes back to bite me in the ass.

We're both a little loopy from the wine and mine is enhanced with my brain injury, and although I know it's a terrible idea, and I know I really, *really*, shouldn't, we end up making love.

We lay in bed after the deed is finished with her head resting on my chest and me stroking her hair; my mind half in and half out. That guilt is more powerful than ever.

I haven't even decided if I'm going to let her die. I'm still contemplating if I'm going to kill her in a manner of speaking. And here I am having sex with her? Where do I get the gall?

She notices me drifting into my mind and waves her hand in front of my face. "Hello? Earth to Jake. Earth to Jake." I laugh. "What? Did that beating really scatter your brains that much?"

"I think that blame rests mainly on the wine," I say. "Plus there wasn't that much brain there to rattle anyway," I joke.

What am I doing? Am I flirting? This is someone who you've been seriously contemplating if you should let some psychopath off, slaughtered like a ritualistic sacrifice. Jesus Henry, you've really hit a new low.

She says, "You know, you're unlike anybody I've ever met." Story of my fucking life.

"That's probably a good thing," I joke once again. For Christ's sake Henry, do you even have a conscience? Is there even a fragment of morality in that twisted brain of yours?

"Always with the jokes," she says. "It's just that once I think I have you pinpointed—I think I've got you all figured out—you throw a curveball at me."

"What do you mean?" I ask.

"Well... it's like this," she says. "You're always such a pleasant person. You're concerned for other people. You're understanding of others' shortcomings. And then here you are, all bloodied up from a bar fight."

"Well," I say, "to be fair, I wasn't the one who instigated the fight. I didn't even throw a punch. You're knight in shining armor just got pummeled and accepted it."

"Well I just don't know what to expect from you," she says. "Another thing is you're so guarded."

"Guarded?" I laugh. "I don't remember anyone ever claiming that I was guarded."

"It's just that we've been in a relationship for a good amount of time," she says, "and you've barely shared anything personal. Sure, we've had moments of intimacy—I'm not downplaying the relationship we have—but you've barely shared any secrets with me. You haven't really opened up and told me anything deep. You know what I think?" Her hand starts stroking my stomach.

"What's that?" I say.

"I think you're afraid to tell anything intimate to anybody because you're afraid that you'll somehow get hurt," she says, her hands still stroking my stomach. I'm feeling uneasy now. I look down in her beautiful hazel eyes and long blond hair, and I feel some strange unsettling sense of déjà vu.

Have I been here before? Why does this all sound familiar? Meanwhile I'm still stroking her hair as her head lies on my chest; the ends of her blond hair tickle my stomach.

I open my mouth and the words flow out automatically as if I were a robot just meant to say these words. They're automatic—part of my programing. You decode the system and these are the words: "If there's anything you want to know, just ask. I'm an open book. All you have to do is open to a page and start reading."

Why do those words sound so familiar? That déjà vu feeling strong once again. Her blond hair. Her stroking my stomach as I stroke her hair. Her laying her head on my chest. Her keen hazel eyes piercing my soul.

And then she utters those peculiar words in that odd sentence structure. "Forget some question that I have to ask. Tell me some genuine intimate detail of your life. Or even something inside your mind. I'm too tired to dig for your soul, just reveal a little bit of it to me. Just a piece."

And then it hits me: she's Lindsey McClain.

CH. 39

I walk directionless and hurriedly, my mouth puffing away on a cigarette neurotically. I cash the smoke and immediately fish out another one. It's probably the fourth one I've had in the last ten minutes. If I keep up this pace, I'll die of lung cancer before I come to a conclusion on the haunting decision. Probably just as well.

I think you're afraid to tell anything intimate to anybody because you're afraid that you'll somehow get hurt.

Last night's words and that memory from so long ago hit me.

Forget some question that I have to ask. Tell me some genuine intimate detail of your life. Or even something inside your mind. I'm too tired to dig for your soul, just reveal a little bit of it to me. Just a piece.

The same words from two different women play simultaneously in my head. But they're not two different women, are they? Not really. That 'Wizard of Oz' effect. That god damn, motherfucking, disastrous, 'Wizard of Oz' effect.

I'm cranking away at my cigarette, working the cancer faster and faster into my lungs. That looming decision on my mind. I've been putting it off, but now it's time to decide. To kill or not to kill? That is the question.

This would have been easier—yeah, still hard—but significantly easier if this new factor didn't come into play. She's Lindsey McClain's alter-ego. Adeline Stewart and Lindsey McClain are one, in a manner of speaking. Not only is Adeline the woman who currently holds my affection; she's also the one that I tossed aside with self-pity and regretted ever since. The one that got away. The one I threw away. And now, it could all be reset. She's my second chance. Press the reset button and roll the dice.

Not only is she Lindsey's alter ego, she's the perfected form of Lindsey. She's Lindsey 2.0. All of Lindsey's shortcomings—the few that there were—are rectified. That damn catch-22 back again and stronger than ever. Damned if I do; fucked if I don't.

My eyes drift to the right and I see Old Man Hackley with a big brown stogie in his hands, tucked secure between two fingers. Smoke rises upward from the end of the cigar and the butt is all gnawed and nasty. He's wearing an old ratty light-weight jacket, patched up crudely, and decorated with permanent stains and the occasional hole the size of a cigar. I make the mistake of making eye-contact and I see a flash of recognition in his eyes.

He points one of his stubby fingers holding the cigar at me. "Don't tell me," he says. "Howard. Howard Ramsey."

"No," I say, hoping this will be short. "Jake Neilson."

"Damn it," he says, shaking his head. "I really am good with names usually. But I know a former customer when I see one. I sold to you didn't I?"

"Yes," I say. "Yes you did."

"Still have only one gun?" he asks, putting the half-smoked cigar back in his mouth and taking a drag.

"Still have only one," I tell him.

He lets out a large laugh accompanied by a mouthful of smoke. "How in the hell do you expect to do anything with that?"

I tell him, "I'll make do." Why can my conversations with

him never just be a short concise chat? I don't want to talk to him. I don't want to talk to anyone. I have much bigger concerns flowing through my mind, predominantly my life unraveling.

He taps his stogie and a chunk of ash falls to the ground. "Let me ask you something." Please don't. "I remember you saying you had a special someone in your life, am I right?" I nod irritated. "Well you ever thinkin' of puttin' a ring on it?"

"Well..." I say, "well, it's kind of complicated." Understatement of the century.

"What?" he asks. "You a queer or somethin'?"

"Huh?" The bafflement is clear in my voice.

"Hey, I'm not judging," he says. "Sure I'm no fan of the Dems—they call 'em jackasses for a reason after all—but the only thing that makes me red as hell is the ability to protect myself and my loved ones. The second amendment, buddy. But when it comes to queers and gay marriage, I've got no problem. I ain't no bigot. If faggots gonna marry, faggots gonna marry. No skin off my ass."

"No," I say adamantly. "She's a woman. I'm not gay." I'm a little too loud and angry for my liking. I don't know where this guy learned his selling techniques, but I don't think that using words like 'faggots,' and implying that your customers are gay are the desired sales tactics. But then again, like I said, I'm not in sales. What do I know?

"Hey-hey-hey, easy," he says, trying to soothe me. "I didn't mean to say that you were a homo or anything, and I didn't mean to offend your politics. If you don't agree with homo-marriage, that's your business. But I got a right to free speech too. It's what makes America great."

"I don't have anything against that!" I say angrily again. "I, in fact, support marriage equality."

"Then why you gettin' so uppity when I mistook you for a queer?" he asks.

"I wasn't. I mean, it was for another reason. It's just-fuck it. I'll see you another time," I say and walk away with a purpose.

What's the purpose? I don't know. But there's definitely a purpose in my strut.

"Alright," he says. "You take care Henry."

I freeze. What did he call me? He called me Henry. I know what I heard. But then I remember the other names he called me in the past. Philip Deangelo, Howard Ramsey, John; he may claim to be good at names but he sure as hell isn't. Even still it did rattle me a little.

"It's Jake," I call over my shoulder. "Jake Neilson." And I keep on walking.

Old Man Hackley saying 'Henry' really shook me up. It was a snap back to reality moment. A wake-up call for a long—*very long*—dream. I'm not Jake Neilson; I only want to be Jake Neilson. I'm Henry Riddick. I'd love to be the high school teacher who's in a relationship with the perfect woman; but these are only desires. In real life, I'm Henry Riddick: the failed author wishing for greatness. I have a brother, Mark, who's going to get married soon. I have friends: Jimmy, Carl, and Frank. I have a former mentor: Hank. I have acquaintances/publishers that are keeping me from homelessness: Rick and Samantha. I have a new association with Coralline Thomson. I have a life. A shitty one, but at least it's real.

This alter-ego of mine—Jake Neilson—he's what I never had and *can* never have. He's fantasy—a character in a fictional world that I made up. I must always remember that. Sure I've been living his life. Feeling with his hands. Seeing with his eyes. Tasting with his tongue. Smelling with his nose. I've been reading his books, eating his food, shaving his face, working his job, and fucking his girlfriend; but it isn't me. I'm not in this world. I'm mentally catatonic, just sleeping and eating and drinking and writing furiously. My body is in another world; giving laconic responses to people who don't know what is going on with me. To be or to pretend to be? That is the question.

A little bit in the distance I see a man with his wife and

children walking by. There's a boy who's probably about four or five and a girl who's maybe ten at most. He and his wife look to be about in their mid-thirties. They're a little bit on the rougher side. They look like they've been through their fair share of troubles, and the man looks like someone who's bruised his knuckles multiple times.

As they are about to walk by, Howie Mumbles comes from out of sight and pisses on the side of a building. The four look in disgust as the man tells his family to walk ahead, and clenches his fists heading toward Howie. I quicken my pace.

When Howie finishes draining his long stream, the tough-looking man spins him around and slams Howie against the wall before he can zip up his pants.

Howie's pecker is swaying in the wind as he screams, "Poli' bru'ality! Poli' bru'ality!" I turn my pace into a light jog.

"I'm not a cop!" the tough man screams. "Which is bad news for you. What the fuck is wrong with you?" He shakes Howie violently.

Howie's dick flops to and fro with each shake, and he keeps on shouting, "Poli' bru'ality!" The horrid attempt to form words but creating barely anything more than a series of syllables.

"I was with my family." The man shakes Howie harder and smashes him against the wall. "My kids don't need to see that. My wife doesn't need to see that."

Howie's pecker does a clockwise swirl; still he's shouting, "Poli' bru'ality! Poli' bru'ality!"

"I told you I'm not a cop! Want me to show you?" Some of his spit flies on Howie's face.

Still Howie is shouting his drunken, borderline-gibberish mantra, "Poli' bru'ality! Poli' bru'ality!" Now I start sprinting.

The tough guy's voice rises louder. "How about I knock all your fucking teeth out?! Huh?! How about that?! Will that shut you up?!"

I reach them, breathing heavily, "Hey man," I say

breathlessly and motion my eyes to his drawn fist, "You don't want to do that." I pant again. "This guy's got some issues. He's one of the biggest drunks I've ever seen, and things haven't been good for him."

"Who gives a rat's ass?" he says through clenched teeth. "Life's been tough for all of us. You think I don't have issues? But someone's gotta teach these shitheads a lesson."

"Think about it," I say. "Do you really want to get arrested for beating him up? Is he worth it?"

He nods his head over at Howie, "You don't think fuck-face over here will get arrested too? Maybe it's worth it."

"The penalty is much worse for battery than public intoxication or urinating in public. Trust me, you'd get the shitty end of the stick," I tell him. "Plus, look at what you have to lose. You've got a family to look after; he's got nothing." I can see that I'm starting to calm him down, if only slightly. "Look, I'll walk him home. I'll make sure he doesn't bother anybody else and that he sleeps off his drunkenness."

He stares at me for quite some time, contemplating what to do. Then he gives Howie one last shove against the wall and lets go. "Fine. You want him; you got him. He's your responsibility now. But if I see him again, I can't promise I'll be so forgiving." He walks back to his family, angry and unsatisfied.

"My Kni' in shinin' armo'," Howie says, looking at me.

"Shut up Howie," I say to him. "And zip up your fly for Christ's sake." Howie fumbles with his zipper and ends up succeeding after a long struggle in putting his parts away.

I wanted to be by myself to think about my decision. This plague on my mind. The catch-22. I need to make a decision; and I need to make one now. But I did promise to walk Howie home, and I'm a man of my word.

"So anyway," I say, not sure if what I'm going to say is polite or not but I say it anyway, "do you have a home or do you live in a shelter or what?"

"I ha' a home," he utters. "I's a frien' of mine's."

"You know how to get there?" I ask.

"Cour' I kno' how ta' ge' there. I be' livin' there fo' months," he says with what may be agitation.

"Alright," I say. "Show me the way."

I wonder what kind of arrangement he worked out with his 'friend' that allowed him to have a roof over his head. Drugs? Prostitution? Unethical favors? I don't know. It's got to be something illegal. Knowing his personality, it's not likely that someone offered shelter to him just for his company.

We make our way into a pretty bad part of town and I start to get uneasy. I guess poor shelter beats no shelter any day, but this area is pretty scary. The houses are falling down, the streets are dissolving, the sidewalk is littered with cracks; this place is far from ideal. In order to calm down my uneasiness I decide to have a conversation with him.

I wonder what to talk to him about, but all I can think of is the issue I'm facing. Sanity or love? No matter what I try to think of, it always comes back to that. Do I let her live—sacrificing my story and sanity—or do I let her die and sacrifice my love?

After thinking about it hard, I decide that if I were to confide in anyone about what I'm facing—or even just mildly hint at it—it would preferably be with someone who's so drunk that they'll forget everything I said in a matter of minutes. And even if they didn't, nobody would believe them. Sure it would be ill-advised to say *everything*, but maybe if I just say a little, I could feel a little bit better. Watch out. The fourth wall is about to be cracked.

"Howie," I say, "do you mind if I ask you a question?"

"Sho'," he lets the syllable out.

"If you were to—let's say—have to choose between love and sanity what would you choose?" I say. "If one decision made you lose the person you love, and one would make you lose your sanity, what would you do?"

He bursts into laughter and I become angry. I know he doesn't know the level of seriousness regarding this question—how could he?—but his laughter to my difficult decision makes me mad nonetheless.

He's still laughing, "Yo' askin' the wrong perso'. I los' ma' sanity ages ago," and he laughs some more. But then something changes in him. He becomes a little more sullen and becomes more serious as if this sobered him up, if only slightly. "Bu' then again, maybe if I ha' ma' sanity, I woul' still ha' ma' love." He looks at the ground. "Bu' to be hones', if I ha' ma' sanity—ha' it all—if hypothe'lly I had ever'thing in the worl', I woul' trade it all in fo' jus' one mo' night wi' the woman I love." He's sulking a bit. "An' tha's the truth. You can quo' me on tha'."

Those words, coming from an unexpected source stick with me. I'm marinating in the insightful ramblings of a drunkard. We've all heard some variation of that statement somewhere in our life. Whether it's a friend mourning over a lost love, a widow or widower, or even from some cheesy movie; everyone's heard it somewhere. But hearing it come from a down-on-his-luck, depressed, drunk, who can barely speak because his blood alcohol content is probably point three something, has so much more emotion to it.

He stops walking and says, "An'way, this is ma' place. Thank ya' once again. An' may ya' ha' a blessed day." He hiccups, fights back some vomit, and marches into his home.

I think about my dilemma. To be or to pretend to be? To kill or not to kill? Those are the questions. My second chance is in this world, caring deeply for me—but it's not real. It may not be real, but the love is real. That's for sure. And this is Lindsey McClain; the girl I made the biggest mistake of casting aside, born anew; reincarnated into a perfected version.

I think of what Howie said—or rather, tried to say: *If I had everything in the world, I would trade it in for just one more night with the woman I love*. That cliché hits me deeply. I'm one of those teenage girls bawling her eyes out at the over-used one-liner in some cheesy chick-flick. Even though I physically shed no tears, I'm internally weeping. Was I about to let her die? Was I really about to let my second chance—my new and updated Lindsey—fall victim to a psychopathic killer?

The decision is made. Fuck sanity. Fuck my story. And fuck Coralline Thomson. Adeline lives.

CH. 40

These last five weeks have been fairly mundane externally, but internally it's been pure chaos. Sure, now I know what I'm going to do. The decision is made to save Adeline, to remain in the story, and rekindle my second chance. But now that the 'what' is answered, I'm on to the 'how'.

Do I tell the police? Tell Detective Reynolds—the same man that beat me senseless and views me as a suspect—that I know that the killer is Richard Sweeney? And what evidence do I have? Do I just go in there and say 'So anyway, I'm kind of like your god and invented this whole world, so I know who the killer is'? Yeah, I really doubt that's going to work. Then again, I did see Richard in action, preparing the ritualistic slaughter. Do I tell them what I saw? And then I have to answer why I didn't come by sooner. What will I say then? 'By the way, this whole world is actually a story come to life in my subconscious, and for a long time I wanted to preserve the story so I didn't say anything. But now I changed my mind, so if you could lock up Richard Sweeney, that would be great.' Great idea Henry. Have fun living the rest of your days in the looney bin.

Alright, so what's my other option? Kill him? Well I do have a gun. But do I have it in me? Can I gun-down a person viewed innocent in the eyes of the law unprovoked—see the light go out in his eyes—and still maintain some fragment of what makes me me? Can I live with myself after that? Is murder in my potential repertoire? I remember Coralline telling me about Isaac Thorn's fear of people using this elixir to create perfect soldiers. I remember her saying 'desensitized killing' and I shiver a bit. Plus what happens if I get caught? I could go to jail. What will be my excuse? Do I tell them that I knew he was the 'cross-killer' because this is all a story that I wrote? Then it's back to the funny farm for you, Henry.

The entire time I'm in mental turmoil, life continues around me. I go to a movie with Adeline. I ignore a phone call from Coralline. I go to work discussing Hemingway's <u>A Farewell to Arms</u> while a kid in the back is knuckle deep searching for a booger. I ignore a phone call from Coralline. Adeline and I go to some posh restaurant dining on smoked salmon and creamed spinach. Coralline calls me. Can you guess what I did?

I'm sure Coralline's probably been fuming. Who cares? Let her fume. She's probably been trying to track me down. But I haven't told her where I moved to, and she hasn't tried to interrupt me at work. Thank God. But all the while, I'm keeping a keen eye out for Coralline so I could duck out of sight if she were to appear. No way is she going to catch me with my face buried in Adeline's neck like last time. No way in hell.

But for the time being I'm on another date with Adeline viewing different paintings and sculptures, trying to appear worldly. It's times like these that I really wish I listened to Jimmy when he would go on and on about his idols.

"Very Da Vinci," I say, looking at some abstract painting.

Adeline looks at me quizzically and says with what would appear to be disagreement, "You think?"

"Well, kind of," I say, trying to save face. "I mean, sure, it's not exactly his style, but you can see the influence if you look hard enough."

She turns toward the painting once again and furrows her eyes, really looking hard. "Hmm," she says, and then walks to the next painting.

Very Da Vince? Who am I kidding? I really should stop pretending like I know anything about art. The only Da Vinci painting that I can list off the top of my head is the Mona Lisa. What the hell do I know about Da Vinci or art in general for that matter? Quit trying to impress her, and come clean. It will be a lot easier to be honest and just let her laugh at your lack of culture than delaying the humiliation with this façade, but then again I never really did listen to sound advice. Even my own.

"Hmm," I say, pretending to take in the new painting to its fullest value. What would someone who knows something about art say? Whatever you do Henry, don't say 'very' and then list some artist who you know nothing about. "Very Monet," I say. God damn it, Henry. Do you *ever* listen?

She turns to look at me with that confused expression once again on her face. "It *is* Monet," she says in a deadpan tone.

"Well," I say, trying to think of some way to get out of this one, "then that certainly does explain it."

She's got that half-perplexed, half-disbelief, look on her face once again, then shakes her head and moves on to the next painting.

Well, that wasn't so bad. I may have made a fool out of myself, but I did do it with accuracy. What are the chances of that? I name some painter that I come up with off the top of my head, and it turns out to be correct? There's definitely a positive spin you could put on that.

Now I'm staring at some wavy looking windmill on a farm with a sun setting. Learn from your mistakes Henry. You don't have to say anything. Most people just enjoy the art and look around. Look at Adeline; she's soundless, just taking in awe of the paintings and your stupidity. Don't say anything. Just close your lips like a dummy and nod.

"You can see that the painter was influenced heavily by Michelangelo." God damn it Henry. This is your brain talking to you—the very little bit of it that you have. Listen. You're making an idiot of yourself.

Adeline turns and smiles at me. "You really don't know anything about art, do you?"

"Honestly," I admit, "most of the artists I know double as ninja turtles."

She lets out her delightful laugh at my expense.

"If you were to offer to give me a free Rubens, I'd probably bring a plate," I continue and her laughter doubles.

We walk from painting to painting and just enjoy the artistry without talking about it. Now that she knows that I have no sense of taste when it comes to art, I don't have to pretend and feel like such a fake. Plus, she stops talking about the history of each painting and the artists and all that other babble about artwork. Sure, I respect art. I know the blood, sweat, and tears that the artists pour into their paintings. I know a lot of artists are mad and have killed themselves in fits of depression. I know that it's a lot of hard work, and they have to deal with all the people who dislike it and the critics who simplify their self-proclaimed masterpiece. I respect art and the artists who make them—I really do—it's just not my cup of tea is all.

We're next to some sculpture of a man fighting a lion. I've never seen this before, but it's definitely interesting. The lion is baring his teeth—really viciously—preparing to pounce on his prey and turn this chiseled hero into dinner. The man is clad only in a loin cloth, holding a spear trying to either ward off the lion or plunge it into his neck—I can't tell which—while baring his teeth, mimicking the ferocious lion. A scar in the shape of a paw is dug into his chest. Even if he succeeds in offing the lion, he'll probably die from infection due to his nasty scar. But he's hell-bent on defeating the lion nonetheless.

"Don't you think he'll die from infection anyway?" I ask

Adeline. "I mean that cut looks pretty nasty and, given the limited clothing and crudely formed weaponry, he's probably either in cave-man times or in a third-world country. Wouldn't this victory be in vain? I mean, what's the purpose to continue fighting?"

"Yeah," she says, "he'll probably die. Even if he wasn't wounded, the lion would probably still win. The spear isn't that sharp and the man doesn't look strong enough to make a fatal wound with the weapon. But that's not the point."

She drifts off and I say, "So, what's the point?"

"The point is the fight." I give her a questioning look. "I think it was William James who taught the forced option. When you are—let's say—on a mountain that will avalanche anytime and the only possible option you have is to make the jump to another ledge but you know—you *absolutely* know for one-hundred percent certainty—that you will not make the jump, what do you do? That's when you have the 'leap of faith.' The point isn't that this man doesn't have a chance to live; it's that he continues to fight in spite of it. It's a vain attempt, but the other option is to just lie down and die. Accept his fate. Become lion-food. But he continues to fight, even though it's futile. He continues to fight because it's human nature to survive. Even if you're only delaying your death for a little bit, you always must go down with a fight."

I nod my head respectfully. "Powerful stuff."

"Then again," she laughs, "I could always be interpreting it wrong. Who knows? Maybe he just sculpted this because he thought it would look cool. But for some reason, I don't think I'm wrong."

I smile and let my eyes drift through the museum. Suddenly I feel cold. The blood drains from my face. There he is standing about thirty feet away. There he is staring that repulsive gaze, his mouth contorted in a slight grin. There he is, staring that hard glare, eyes glued on Adeline. It's Richard Sweeney.

That sick grin that you can't decipher. Is it lecherous? Is it charitable? Is it joyful? Is it sinister? You can't tell. Who knows?

But I know. I know the truth that lies beneath the grin. I know the inner-workings of his twisted, disturbed mind. I know his fantasies. I know his repulsive desires. I know his hallucinations. I know everything. I know it all. I created him. I created that scumbag and now his eyes are locked on Adeline. That lion circling the almost-defenseless villager; baring his jagged teeth through that perpetual grin.

Stay calm, Henry. You need to leave now. You need to think of an excuse, but you need to act natural.

"Come on, let's leave this place," I say to Adeline. "Too many pretentious farts anyway."

"But we've been here only a short time. And the artwork is beautiful," Adeline pleads. All the while, Richard Sweeney's lips are curled—oh so slightly—as his eyes continue to dig holes in Adeline. The lion is licking his chops.

"Yes, but what does it matter when I have the most beautiful piece of artwork ever, right here," I say and kiss her cheek. "Plus the artwork only effects my eyes; not my other organs," I joke, as Richard moves a little to the left to get a better view.

"You pig," she says, slapping me playfully on the shoulder.

"What?" I say. "I was talking about my heart."

"Yeah," she says sarcastically. "Uh-huh. Sure you were." She doesn't want to, but she agrees to leave nonetheless.

We make our way to the exit—our arms intertwined—and I'm sure Richard is still staring. I give a look over my shoulder and see that I'm right. He's further away, but just as terrifying. His look is less of that of someone viewing a stranger—or even someone gawking at an attractive woman—and more of a man at a chessboard contemplating his move.

It's set. He's made his inevitable decision. She's on his list. It may be weeks, it may be months, it may be close to a year; but he's going to try sometime. He's positioning himself to take out my queen. So now it's the big question: what's my next move?

CH. 41

"Yes, I'm an atheist, but my road to atheism wasn't the typical path. I didn't decide that my life was filled with so much turmoil that there could be no God; nor did I decide that God's existence couldn't be, because of the horror that inhabits this world. In my opinion people who choose atheism through this route shouldn't have concluded that there is no God. They should have instead concluded that there is a God, and they just hate him," the goateed man sitting next to me continues to babble.

No, I didn't ask him if he was an atheist or anything close to inquiring his religious views. Nor did I even remotely broach the topic. He just figured I would like to know. There are always these types of atheists. I'm an atheist myself, but I don't go around telling strangers, 'Hey, guess what? I'm an atheist.' Similar to Christians who are hell-bent on saving your soul from your assured damnation, there are also atheists who think the only possible conversation is why they're an atheist and how stupid religion is. They're both equally annoying.

I came to this bar earlier than usual with the hopes that nobody would be here. I needed the liquid courage for today. Today is going to be a big day if things end up going to plan. There's a reason that I wore my longest shirt and have avoided sitting slouched over; I'm trying to avoid revealing my concealed firearm.

It's odd carrying such a powerful weapon. I know it's not allowed in bars, but I figured I'd just stop by for a quick drink to settle my nerves. But that drink ended up turning into another, then another, then another, and so on. There's that clammy feeling on my hands. My mind is racing with questions. What if someone sees? What if I get arrested? What's the punishment for bringing a firearm into a bar? Could I serve jail time? Am I actually going to follow through with this?

The goateed atheist continues, "No. That wasn't the reason I found godlessness. I figured—similar to Descartes first meditation—that God could always exist and be evil instead of good." Congratulations, you've successfully proved that you've taken Intro to Philosophy. "God could be cruel, or negligent, or similar to a father that disappears for long periods of time and then shows up occasionally to check on his kids. Maybe God just created our existence and simply watches with curiosity without interfering. Maybe he's just bored. I couldn't leave that possibility out."

"Uh-huh," I say and take a large swallow of my whiskey. The alcohol burns away at my esophagus as the guy next to me burns away at my patience.

Much to my dismay, the goateed man keeps on informing me of his story of how he found nothingness, "No, I had to really think—dig deep—you know. Like Descartes and his meditations." Come on. If you're going to use basic philosophy, at least add some variety. Try using Socrates' 'The unexamined life is not worth living.' I'm sure you can fit it into your spiel somehow. "And after I thought long and hard about it, I came to the conclusion that-"

"Sorry," I interrupt, tired of hearing him spew his mental masturbation. "But I really have to go." I swig down the rest of my whiskey. There was a good portion left, but there's no way I can stand listening to this man stroke his own ego any longer. "It's been nice chatting with you. I'm sure we'll meet again sometime soon."

He's a little hurt by my abrupt departure, "Oh you're leaving so soon?" Yes, and you made sure of that.

I tell him, "Sorry, I have a date." Well, in the very, *very*, loose sense of the word.

"Well," he says, "I hope to see you again sometime." Yes he does.

"Sure," I say, "I would love that." No. No I wouldn't. I make my way out of the bar. This is going to be quite the interesting night.

I'm at Old Man Hackley's Smokes and Guns—or rather—I'm *outside* of Old Man Hackley's Smokes and Guns. I'm in the shadows just chain-smoking like mad. I've been here for hours and it's already gotten pretty late. I'm hoping that Hackley won't step outside and spot me for one of his long irritating chats. He's not the one I'm looking for. Not today. I'm looking for that tall, slender, polite, manager at Al's department store who doubles as a psychotic serial killer in his spare time. I'm looking for that deranged psychopath that barely qualifies for a human being. I'm looking for Richard Sweeney.

Why hasn't he showed up here yet? He always circles this area when he's bored. That sicko feeds off of the fear of innocents. He loves those people who would never in their life think of buying a gun—scared out of their wits—now attempting to find some sort of safety. He feeds off that negative energy. Sucking in that terror as a baby suckles milk from their mother's teat.

Is this one of those rare days that he chooses not to check up on them? Or did I miss him? What if he's not here because he's at his job today? Or what if he's busy doing his other 'job'? What if-? Oh God. What about Adeline?

I fumble to get my phone out of my pocket and look up

when I hear someone. It's Old Man Hackley locking up his store and preparing to head home. And right when I'm about to go back to calling Adeline, I see *him*. Richard Sweeney's walking slowly, taking a gander at the gun shop as he paces by. His face is complete with that disgusting grin. I can't wait to see that grin gone forever. Only to grin again when the skin decays from his face and his skull grins in death. But he'll be six feet under by then, and infested with worms and maggots. I step out of the shadows.

"Sam?" Old Man Hackley lights up when seeing me. "Sam Johnson."

"Not now Bill," I say curtly.

"Hey-hey-hey," he says, grabbing my shoulder in a friendly manner but with the need for correction. "'Bill' is on my birth certificate and birth certificate alone." I'm pretty sure it's actually 'William' that's on his birth certificate, but whatever. "The name for you—and everyone else to call me—is 'Old Man Hackley'."

"Sorry," I say. The annoyance is clear in my voice. "Old Man Hackley." He smiles. "But I *really* do need to go. I'll chat with you some other time. But there's something important. *Really* important that I have to do *now*." I turn around and scout for where Richard Sweeney ducked off to. Damn it! Where the hell did he go?

"Don't let me keep you," he says. "But let me ask you something. Have tested out your gun yet?"

"No," I say spotting Richard turning the corner, "But I will soon." And I start to jog in the direction of Richard Sweeney.

I find him a bit of a distance ahead of me once I round the corner and follow. The entire time I'm keeping space between us. I can't jeopardize the situation and get too close causing him to become suspicious. I have to be safe and ready for my kill. But at the same time I can't be too far away when I fire. I've never shot a gun before in my life, and I'm bound to miss if it's even remotely difficult.

I think that maybe if I follow him long enough, I'll end up in some remote place. But even if the immediate location is vacant, there could always be people close enough to hear a gunshot go off. It's late but it's not *that* late.

Maybe I can sneak up on him. When I'm in that remote location I could gradually quicken my pace, then come up behind him and bring the butt of the gun down hard against his temple. Boom! KO'd. If he's still alive after that, I could drag him behind a dumpster and finish the job with my hands. Asphyxiate the motherfucker. Feel his pulse drain beneath my fingers and watch his body struggle for breath unconscious. But that's so barbaric. Am I capable of that? Also, I don't have gloves. They'll get my finger prints. Well, I guess they created shoes and the butts of guns for a reason. Maybe I could just beat him to death. Watch the blood crust against my shoes and gun-handle. But once again; so barbaric.

I think briefly of removing my socks and putting them over my hands to block out the fingerprints. Then I could choke him once he's unconscious. But couldn't they get my DNA somehow from that? I don't know how these things work. In the TV shows and movies they always catch the murderer. I'm fucked. But then again, Richard's gotten away with so many murders. Yeah, but he's a professional; I'm an amateur.

Damn it. I've never even thought about killing. Even if I shoot him and get away, couldn't they match the bullet up to my gun? They do that in the movies, don't they? But what's my other option? Not follow through with this? Every day that he's still living is another day that Adeline's in mortal danger. That catch-22. Damned if I do; fucked if I don't.

Maybe I should just give up. I mean, maybe I should try again another day. Wait for my moment. Wait until I can get him when I know I won't get caught. What's the point of me saving her life if I end up behind bars unable to see her, and without the desire to be seen? Who wants to date a known murderer? What's the point? The point is Adeline will still be alive. Even if you can't see her, your love still lives. And that's what really matters, isn't it?

I have to go through with this. I say under my breath, "For Lindsey." Wait what did I just say? "I mean, for Adeline," I mutter the correction.

This isn't Lindsey. I mean, yeah, she kind of is. But this is her perfected. If this is the life you choose to live in, you have to cast aside the old one. No more Freudian slips.

Richard turns again behind a building. I jog lightly to catch up to him—but not too fast to draw suspicion. I realize I've been staggering a bit—probably still a little drunk from the bar—and wonder if maybe I haven't been as stealthy as I've thought. I feel a rash of fear that I'm going to round the corner and see Richard waiting for me—that perpetual grin plastered on his face—knife in hand; readying it for my exposed belly. But this fear turns out to be misplaced. He's about thirty feet in front of me, walking slowly without a clue that he's being tailed. His mind is probably too occupied with those images dancing through his head—those disgusting hallucinations of corpses and grotesque murder.

Finally, I've got him where I want him. He's in a dark secluded alleyway, with nobody in sight. I start walking a little faster. I've still got some time. There's no exit from this alley for another thirty yards. Maybe if I get lucky he won't take that exit, giving me more time.

I'm stifling my heavy breathing from the jog. It's not that loud and I'm not that out of breath, but when you're trying to sneak up on someone with murderous intent, every sound is amplified in your mind.

I take the gun from out of the back of my pants and turn off the safety. All the while I'm creeping slowly along; a lion stalking his prey.

For once you're the prey, Richard. How does that feel? Huh? How does that fucking feel? For once, it's going to be you who's the victim. It'll be no more killing for you. Justice will be served. No one will know about it, but justice will be served nonetheless.

There's a dumpster about ten or fifteen feet from me. Maybe if I get to that dumpster, I can rest my gun on it to steady my shot. Maybe I can shoot with more accuracy. The guy who blew a hole in the other guy's head right outside my hotel way back got away scot-free. Maybe there's hope for me.

There's all this glass and junk laying around the dumpster haphazardly—really messy. People should really try to throw things out. Just like I'm about to throw out this piece of trash. I'm bringing Richard Sweeney to the junkyard in the sky.

I make my way over to the dumpster, eyes still focused on Richard. I'm all blurry-eyed from my semi-drunkenness. It may mess up my shot, but if I didn't drink, I wouldn't have the balls to do this.

He starts to slow down. Maybe I can pull this off after all. Calculating by the time I get to the dumpster and his positioning, I'll have a pretty clear shot regardless of the inebriation.

I stagger a little more, preparing for the kill. The lion prepares to pounce.

Suddenly my foot catches on something and I fall over. Right before my head hits the corner of the dumpster I hear my weapon discharge. Then it all goes black. Boom! KO'd.

CH. 42

"As you probably figured, I've had to pull some strings to keep you in here this long. I'm normally by-the-books, but for you, well for you I made an exception." Detective Reynolds smiles, talking in a calm, collected tone. Finally he's got me where he wants me, and he's going to milk this opportunity for as long as he can. "Don't think you can sue us or anything like that. Yeah, what we're doing may not be exactly ethical—and we may be dancing on the line of what's legal—but that's all we're doing. We're just dancing—not crossing over."

I awoke a couple of days ago handcuffed to a hospital bed with doctors doing a neuro-test. Another concussion. Another month of recommended sobriety. My brain's been doing hard time these last couple months. I hope none of it's permanent.

After finding out my blood alcohol level, they shipped me off to the police station where I was charged with handling a firearm while intoxicated and discharging a firearm in public. Sure it was accidental, but I still have to pay a fine. Neither of these crimes are enough to qualify for jail time, but they are allowed to hold me for a period of time. They can't hold me much longer; they're pushing the legal limitations as it is.

Detective Reynolds, despite his suspicion of me and that he

despises me to the core, has not broken any laws in his treatment of me. He hasn't beaten me at all. The case is digging at his mind—making him lose it more and more everyday—but he's still by the books. Sure there have been some passive aggressive attacks. The handcuffs are way too tight—tighter than what's necessary to restrain me, and way tighter than what is normally used to restrain someone—but there was nothing worse than that.

But I know that every day that I'm in holding is another day that Adeline remains in danger—in peril, and entirely ignorant about it. It's crossed my mind to just tell them that the killer is Richard Sweeney. But then they'll ask for proof. And what do I do then? I either tell them about the crime I witnessed so long ago and refused to tell them about, claim that I just have a hunch, or confess that everything here is a product of my imagination. The first option will draw suspicion, the second will just make me look like an imbecile, and the third will be a one-way ticket to the looney bin. Shitty options. So, despite my desire to get out of here and my fear for Adeline's safety, I don't utter a word about Richard. When it comes to the truth about the cross-killer, I keep my lips sealed.

"So now," Detective Reynolds continues, chewing steadily on his Nicorette, "I'd be interested in hearing what happened once again. Why did the gun fire? How did you find yourself in this situation?"

"Are we going to do this again?" I ask. The metal handcuffs are digging into my wrists hard, making it more difficult to think with each extra second of discomfort. "I've told you how many times now?"

"Well I'd like to hear it again." He smiles. "I'm bored. You must be bored. You haven't had much social interaction these past couple days. So what do ya' say? Let's kill some time. Tell me the story once again."

The handcuffs dig deeper into my skin and as much as I want to think of something else, or concentrate on the conversation at hand, my mind keeps going back to the discomfort in my wrists.

"I have the right to remain silent, don't I?" I ask.

"Yeah," he says. "Yeah, you do. But are you sure you want to exercise that right? In my experience, folks who don't want to talk are trying to hide something. They're scared they won't stay true to their lie. They're scared they'll slip up. And that always draws suspicion. And you wouldn't want to draw suspicion to yourself, do ya'?"

"Fine," I say. If he wants to play it his way, let's play it his way. I haven't done anything wrong. I've got nothing to hide. Well, then again, in a way, I've got *everything* to hide. "I was out, my gun concealed in my pants—which is my right by the way." Reynolds nods and I continue. That damn digging in my wrists making it so hard to think. "And then I swung by a bar." Oh shit. I really fucked up now. I just admitted to entering a bar with a firearm, and I can see Reynolds' face light up like a kid on Christmas morning. Great job, Henry. You just keep on digging that hole. When you think you've hit rock bottom, you prove everyone wrong by picking up that shovel and digging deeper. Sure it's not a felony or anything, but it's another fine he can tack on me. It's not a kill shot to put me away, but it's a slap to the face—and these slaps are getting annoying. I figure I'd continue. "I drank a little there."

"How much? I don't remember you saying you entered a bar," he says with that 'gotcha' grin on his face.

"I don't remember," I say. "That hit to the head I took really messed up my memory."

"Well, it was apparently enough to make you stagger to the point of falling over." He sees me grimace and his smile widens. "But this is the first of me hearing of you entering a bar. Why'd ya' leave out that tidbit of information? I told ya' I would like to hear everything."

"I don't know," I say once again. "I guess it's that hit to the head again. It really shook me up."

"Well go on," he says. "Continue."

"So anyway, it was late at night," I tell him. "And I was walking home—a little drunk I admit—and suddenly I felt uneasy. I don't know if I heard something. I can't fully remember—that head thing again—but I started getting nervous, like, like somebody was following me or something." Wow Henry, you just flipped what you were doing to someone else. Someone was stalking *you*? You were just about to put a bullet in Richard Sweeney. You lying bastard. But I'm impressed. You may be lying, but for once you're good at it. "This town's not safe you know." He nods his head. "So I took out my gun, afraid that I might be subject to murder or something else horrible. And I looked over my shoulder—gun in hand, worrying about my safety—and I tripped. While I was falling, I must have accidently fired my gun. It wasn't on purpose. It was just a mix of panic and reflexes."

He just stares at me with that 'gotcha' smile still on his face; his teeth chomping away at the gum, sucking the nicotine out of it like a leach sucking blood.

"You know when I first met you, I got a little suspicious," he says, still casually chewing on his gum. "You were nervous; stuttering and fidgeting like a man with something to hide. I also wondered why someone—even someone new in town—would sit down and have a chat with a scumbag such as Bill Walker." I guess that's the full name of the homeless guy I met who was gawking at women exercising in a gym while hinting to the detective that he was the cross-killer just to fuck with him. "Even if you didn't know who that was, why start a conversation with a bum on the street in a bad part of town? Sure you could be a naïve, incredibly over-nice guy who always sees the best in everyone, but I didn't think that was the case. But even still, those aren't the things that make me feel the most uneasy. What makes me feel uneasy is how I'm able to read most people. Tell what kind of music they listen to. Know what religion they are. Know their relationship status. All that shit. Yeah, I make mistakes sometimes, but for the most part I'm pretty accurate. And then with you... with you I wasn't able to read shit. I didn't know what religion you were, if you had any mental illnesses, your family situation; none of that. And that was what really made me anxious."

He chews more on his gum and looks at me with examining eyes. He's trying to read me; but admits I'm a wordless book. What's the point? What do you expect to find? I'm not guilty and you can't hold me forever.

"You have to let me go," I say angrily. The handcuffs cut deeper and deeper into my skin.

"Eventually," he says with that big smile on his face.

"No," I say. "You have to let me go *now*."

He chews away at his gum; his smile as broad as ever. "And what would incline me to do that?"

For once I return his smile. I have to get out of here as soon as I can. Not for my sake—for Adeline's sake. "Well, there's been this rumor going around about a certain detective who went apeshit on someone in a bar. He hit him with a beer bottle, broke a barstool, and beat his face bloody. Maybe the victim went to the hospital after that and found out he was concussed by this raging detective. That's some damaging rumor." My smile is getting broader with each word. "And all that man who took the beating has to do is confirm it. All he has to do is contact a lawyer. I wonder what harm that could do to that certain detective."

Reynolds gives a big hearty laugh. "Jake, you got hit with discharging a firearm in public, handling a firearm intoxicated, and you just admitted to bringing a firearm into a bar. Are you sure you want to add blackmailing to your resume?"

My smile fades a bit. "Yeah, but you'll still get injured in this process. Are you willing to risk it?"

He's still got that broad smile plastered on his face as he lets out a few more chuckles. "Sure, I might get suspended from duty for a period of time. If you get lucky, I might even get kicked off the force for good. But that's blackmail you're talking about, Jake. That's up to a year in prison. And the fact that you screwed over a detective may not sit well with the guards. Not to mention, you're quite a pretty man, Jake. You'll probably be *really* popular in prison. Oh, yeah, you'll make a lot of *friends*."

My smile drops and I feel a little nauseous. I didn't think this threat through. The worst part about this is a *year*. A whole year in prison. A year where I'm not there to protect Adeline. A year where that maniac is still on the loose. Alright, I need to think of a new tactic. Even if the only remaining option is hoping for the best.

"So," Reynolds says, continuing that repetitive chewing, "now that we got some free time to just shoot the shit, I'd like you to settle my curiosity." He's still got that grin going cheek to cheek on his face. "When I first met you, you said you were new in town. And nobody seems to have known you before that—at least the ones that I've talked to. But just a couple weeks after, I see you at Ron Madsen's—the least likeable man ever to exist—wake. Now tell me: why would that be?"

"You do realize that he choked to death on his own vomit," I tell him, somewhat anxious. "It said so in the papers. Are you honestly insinuating that I killed him?"

"I ain't insinuating shit," he says. "I'm just curious is all. You're new here—nobody knows you, you know nobody—and yet I find you at the wake of the most despised and bitter man I've ever known. Can't you see why I'm curious? So tell me why?"

"If he was so despicable, why were you there?" Good job. Great comeback, Henry.

"I ain't answerin' that," he says.

"Why not?" I ask.

"'Cause I'm not the one in cuffs," he says, still mashing up that nicotine gum between his cheeks.

Alright, think of an excuse Henry. You can do it. "I met him in those couple of weeks. Yeah, he wasn't the most social person, but I still talked to him a little. And considering he was as close a friend as anyone in this town at that point, I decided to go." That was an answer. Not a good one, but an answer nonetheless.

"You see," Detective Reynolds says, "that answer just doesn't sit well with me. You couldn't have developed *that* much of a friendship in such a short time—especially with a man like Ron Madsen. Then there's that time I saw you coming out of that hotel—the very hotel that someone was murdered outside the night before—and that—well that doesn't sit well either. And when you shifted your eyes quickly when we made eye contact while you were walking out; that *really* didn't sit well. Then I think about the fact that the woman you were chatting with at Ron's wake ended up dead a few months later, and, well, that sure-as-shit didn't sit well with me. And I think of the nervousness you had in our first encounter, you being at a wake of someone I can't imagine you knew that well, you talking to a woman at that wake who ended up getting murdered a few months later, you walking out of the hotel where that murder took place, and you shifting your gaze too quickly from me; and none of that sits well with me. Now, I fully realize that this could all be coincidence. This could all be a series of suspicious occurrences that just so happened to play out; but I don't think so. I may not have proof, but I'm narrowing my suspects. And after each interaction I have with you, there's always a 'why'? *Why* did you go to the wake? *Why* were you so nervous? *Why* did you drop your gaze? *Why* were you at the hotel where the murder took place? *Why* did the woman that you picked to have a conversation with end up getting murdered? You see what I mean, Jake? And I guess when I really think about it-"

The door opens and another detective enters with urgency. He's black, about six foot two, and pushing two-hundred—mostly muscle.

He looks at Reynolds, "Reynolds, you need to come here."

"Give me a little bit, Richards. I've still got some questions to ask Jake over here," Detective Reynolds says with mild irritation.

"It's the cross-killer again," Richards says.

Oh my god. What if it's Adeline? But he never strikes so soon after making his pick. He puts them on his list and offs them after a good amount of time goes by. He'll never strike within the first week. It's not his style. He's a complete psychopath—there's no denying that—but he's a psychopath with a pattern. Every action he takes is subject to ritualism.

Reynolds turns to look at me, but still talks to Richards, "When do they believe it happened?"

"They predict last night, but the autopsy will show it with more accuracy," Richards says.

I can see the look of confusion on Todd Reynolds' face. That smile is gone. I've been in here for the past few days, so I couldn't have committed the crime, if the autopsy shows this estimate to be correct. Maybe I'll finally be cleared from his list of suspects. After that I can just focus on keeping Adeline safe. I'll keep her safe by whatever means necessary.

"But there's something different about this one," Richards says.

Detective Reynolds turns back to face Richards, "Well, what is it?"

"The fingers," Richards says. "The killer uses the thumb and middle finger of each hand to make the cross over their eyes." Reynolds nods at him giving him the signal to keep going. "With this one, it was the middle and pointer fingers. Everything else was the same. Knife wounds, precision, the ritual, the attractive blond victim; it's all the same."

"Fuck," Reynolds looks down and mutters. Then he looks back up to Richards. "Do you think this could be a copycat?"

"Fuck if I know, sir," Richards says. "But if this psycho develops a cult following, and more of these guys start popping up, we're in for some real trouble."

"No shit," Reynolds says. The pace of his chewing picks

up. "I've been near having a stroke from just trying to find this one prick. I don't know what'll happen if more of them start popping up."

They continue to talk as if I weren't even there. It's unprofessional, but I guess this case is getting to them. They're no longer playing it tight-knit anymore. They're slipping up, talking about the case in public, and in front of someone Detective Reynolds views as a suspect.

As for this murder, it's not a copycat. It's the same guy. There was an obvious difference in the victim that they're so easily overlooking. I remember this part of the story well. Because of this woman's slight difference that Richard Sweeney overlooked until after she was dead, he decided he needed to alter the ritual a bit. She didn't fit the characteristics perfectly of who he kills, so he switched it up oh so slightly. And for right now, I'm getting tired of them arguing and speculating of the possible causes and being so off base. It's really getting irritating.

"Do you think maybe...?" I say tentatively. "Maybe, did she dye her hair?"

The two cops look at me in silence for a moment. Reynolds has that confused look on his face, and Richards is filled with suspicion.

"How did you know that?" Richards asks, furrowing his eyes.

I shrug my shoulders, "Just a guess."

The two of them stare at me; trying to piece all this together. Their eyes are narrowed and their mouths are slightly open as if they want to say something, but can't find anything suitable to say. I start to feel uneasy under their hard glance.

Here I am, picking up the shovel and digging deeper, searching for rock bottom. But in the meantime, I'm just making a bigger and bigger hole.

CH. 43

 They could only hold me for so long, so after enough time had passed, they had to let me go. That murder could have helped draw suspicion off me if I just kept my mouth shut. It happened when I wasn't able to commit it, but I just had to say something. I just had to open my mouth like an idiot. Now I'm back to being a suspect—or at least suspicious. How would I—if I were any regular Joe Schmoe—know that the victim's hair was dyed without even being informed who the victim was? They can't pin anything on me, but they're still going to keep a close eye on me.

 I got off with just a few fines. They're hefty fines—I'm not denying that—but they're only fines, nothing more. The real problem is the revival of my semi-fame. Now people recognize me from the newspapers, and they wonder why I shot off that gun. Why was I in that situation? So much suspicion and so little explanation.

 Sure, most people will overlook that section. It was news, but not huge news. Still it wasn't that small a matter either. If people know me in the slightest, they would have read that article. My coworkers will have read that. The people who I bump into frequently will know what I've done. And Adeline, she'll know what I did. And what excuse can I give? I was nervous? It doesn't help that it mentions that I was intoxicated in the papers. I'm really not looking forward to that conversation.

On top of all this, they had to confiscate my gun. I don't know if it was standard procedure or if Todd Reynolds pulled some strings to make it happen, but it's confiscated nonetheless.

Adeline left many messages on my phone; each one increasing in anger. She knows full well what I've done, and she is not happy to say the least. The decibel escalates each time I switch to a new message.

"Are you kidding me Jake?! You got arrested?!"

Next message:

"What the hell is wrong with you?! Firing a gun intoxicated?! Are you out of your fucking mind?!"

Next message:

"Jesus, Jake, why the fuck would you carry a gun around anyway?! And don't you think this is something you should have told me?! You think maybe this is something I would have liked to know?! I expected better of you!"

She's pissed, and this is not an interaction I'm looking forward to. But I thank God she hasn't said the two words that I was scared of hearing the most: 'it's over.' That was the biggest fear I had when I went to check my messages. The relationship is still salvageable; I just need to do some damage control.

Well, I guess I'll have to talk to her sooner or later. I figure I'd give her a call after work and man up.

When you're walking through a place where everyone knows you got arrested, nobody actually stares at you—at least when you're looking. Every time you look at someone, their eyes are elsewhere. They intentionally *don't* look at you. They avoid looking at you. But you know the second you turn around, their eyes are back on you. You turn back to look at them, and their eyes are occupied on something else. But you know, yeah, they looked. That's how I am with my coworkers at the school.

You know that woman who fell for the wrong guy? She's normally a majestic beauty—her looks cannot be matched. But now she walks around; her eyes all swollen and blackened. Bruises decorate her body from head to toe—product of a boyfriend who all her friends are too polite to tell her to break it off. Nobody says a word. They just pretend that everything's fine. And when she walks by—all busted up because some guy looked at her the wrong way—everybody makes a point to not stare. But as soon as they can't be seen; their eyes are glued on her mashed up face. That's what I am right now. The woman with the abusive boyfriend who everyone intentionally tries to not look at. That's me.

Unfortunately, it's only the staff that doesn't look. As for the student's: well, this is one of the few times that all of them are attentive.

I'm talking about Mark Twain's <u>Adventures of Huckleberry Finn</u> with my class, and all my students are attentive. Even Zit-faced Zack is eager to hear my next word. But this silent attentiveness is only temporary.

"Did you shoot a gun off?" one of the students asks.

"I'm sorry," I say, annoyed at the inevitable break in silence. "I don't see what that has to do with Huckleberry Finn."

"I heard that you were wasted," another kid pipes up.

"Ya-yeah," Stuttering Steven manages to spit out. "I hu-hu-heard that t-t-too."

"Could we please get back to the topic at hand?" I say. "Last time I checked, none of this has anything to do with Huck Finn."

"He really fired a gun? Where?" Black Billy asks.

"Yeah," some student, who never volunteers to answer any questions, jumps on this opportunity. "It was in some Alley in the middle of night. He got arrested and everything. It was crazy. It's in the papers."

"He got arrested?" a couple of kids ask each other unaware—or at least unconcerned—that I can hear.

"You got arrested?" someone asks me timidly.

I start getting really irritated. "Look," I say curtly. "If Mark Twain did not write it, we are not discussing it. Is that clear?"

"Fuck man, that's crazy," one of the students says and the children start talking to each other, blatantly ignoring me.

"Did you shoot someone?" a semi-inebriated student asks.

"No, he didn't shoot anyone, you idiot," a student corrects him. "He just shot at nothing and got arrested."

"Hey!" I shout. "Next person that talks earns himself a ticket to the principal's office. Do I make myself clear?"

"Why would he shoot at nothing?" one of the kids asks.

"Beats me," a tall lanky kid says.

"Hey!" I shout. "Both of you to the principal's office, *now*!"

They completely ignore me along with the rest of the class. They just keep on talking and ignore the lesson and my punishments. The comments just keep on coming to the point where I can't keep track of which kid is talking.

"Well why the hell did he fire?"

"I don't know."

"I didn't even know he had a gun."

"Well, what? Did you think he would just tell us he had a gun?"

"I don't know. I guess it's just unexpected, you know?"

"Like, this is, like, pretty crazy. Our teacher, like, got arrested."

"Yeah, and he was hammered."

"No he wasn't."

"That's what the paper said."

"Yeah, that's what my mom told me too."

"Drunk off his ass."

"That's it!" I shout. "Yes, I fired a fucking gun! I was fucking drunk. I tripped and shot the gun on accident. If you immature fucking idiots are going to act like children and not listen in class like a bunch of fucking retards, then I'll just get it out there. I fired a gun, and was drunk. Any other questions?"

I can't believe I just said that, and from the look of the students, neither can they. They're all wide-eyed and open mouthed, stunned that a teacher would curse and call them all a bunch of 'retards.' I'm going to be in some deep shit for this one. I could possibly get fired for this. Nowadays, using a word like that is almost viewed as the same degree of severity as a racial slur. I'm screwed.

"Alright," I say. "Now back to Huckleberry Finn." The bell rings, signifying the end of the class period. "Ah-fuck me." I slump back on my desk. "Well go. Get the fuck out of here."

Stunned, the students file out silently until they're far down the hall. This is going to spread like wild fire. Each one of those students will tell two people. Then they'll tell two people. Then they'll tell two people. Well, you know the drill. Sooner or later, I'll have to explain myself, possibly hearing the words, 'you're fired' uttered slowly from principal John Richards as I expect him to die. Oh well. I guess the only thing to do is wait.

John Richards calls me in on my lunch break, disappointment clear on his face. His eyes are barely open. Who can blame him? If he puts in the effort to open his eyes all the way, his old heart might give out from strain. Meanwhile, he's just been sitting in silence, scrutinizing me with his half-closed eyes.

Finally, he begins his slow lecture. "Bar fights... blow-ups... run-ins with the police.... You know Jake... in some ways you remind me as a younger version of myself." And you remind me of an older version of death. "Granted...this was all before I started working... at least a real job. By that time I put most of that... behind me." He scratches the few remains of his grey hair desperately clinging to his scalp. "You know, I was arrested once." He pauses. "Did I ever tell you that?"

"No sir," I answer respectfully.

"It was a long... long time ago, when I was very young." He tells me through that terribly slow, crackling, voice. Each word I wonder if it will be his last. "I got into... quite the nasty fight with my brother." Two questions: Did you go by a different name back then? And did it result in the death of Abel? "But that was... long... long ago," he continues that horrible crackly voice. "Bar fights happened too.... I wasn't an angel." No, but you're as old as one. "And... yes... while this may have... tethered off by the time I started working... I still had some experiences I'm not proud of."

"I understand sir," I say.

"But my point is," he brushes his fingers through his few clinging grey hairs, "I kept my home problems separate from my work." He takes in a deep breath, holds it for a period of time, then lets it out. "Do you understand what I'm getting at?"

"Yes sir," I say. "I do understand. It will never happen again."

"Good," he says, nodding his head. "Good. Well, tomorrow you will give a formal apology to the class... you will have to deal with whatever the parents say... and you will have to... diffuse the situation." He rubs his bald head with his wrinkled right hand. I'm guessing this is to keep him awake. "Do you understand?"

"Yes sir," I tell him.

"Good," he says. "Well... consider this... a warning. If this were to happen again... I would not be so generous.... So let's make this never happens again."

"Absolutely, sir," I say, and head out of his office.

Thank God. I came out of this basically unscathed. All I have to do is make it through the rest of the day, and then I have to face the hardest situation: Adeline Stewart. God help me.

I'm on my way to Adeline's house; dreading every step I take in her direction. I called her up and she gave me one of those short, curt, concise, conversations that women give when they are beyond angry. She was biting her tongue on the phone the entire time, waiting to blow up at me. She wants to blow up at me—she really does—but she's waiting for the right time. If the lion chases the elk too soon, the elk can get away unscathed—or at least without feeling the full extent of the pounce. Adeline's waiting for her right opportunity to pounce. I'm guessing that'll be when I get to her door.

I'm outside her house—pausing for a second before I ring the doorbell—just preparing myself for the onslaught. This will be a tongue-lashing like none other, and if I'm going to receive some shots, I want to at least prepare myself. Finally, I ring the doorbell.

Adeline answers the door with a stern, scornful, look on her face. She glares at me for a little bit in silence, and then begrudgingly invites me in. Still, she hasn't pounced yet.

She makes her way to the table, and although she doesn't say anything, it's obvious she wants me to sit across from her. She stares at me, her eyes burning mine, making it hard for me to maintain eye-contact and then she starts to pounce.

"You know," she says, "there are some times I like a surprise in a relationship." I open my mouth but she cuts me off. "Like a surprise gift, or vacation, or any romantic gesture." She shakes her head and raises her voice. "But there are times I like a certain predictability. Like—I don't know—I'd like to predict that you won't get into a bar fight, or won't carry a gun, or get arrested for shooting a gun off in public while shit-faced."

"Adeline-" I start.

"Don't 'Adeline' me!" she yells. "What the hell am I supposed to expect? One moment you're risking your life to save some girl, and the next you're getting arrested for being an imbecile!"

I try to calm her down. "Listen, it's just-"

"And then I hear from Shelly that you cursed out your classroom today and called a whole bunch of high school students 'retards?'" she interrupts me. "What the hell is wrong with you?"

"There are just some things going on that-" I start again.

"And when did you get a gun?!" she yells. "I would have liked to know that! Why don't you tell me these things? Why are there so many god damn surprises?" She's bordering on tears. "I want to know who I'm dating. I want to know who you are. I don't want you to keep things from me. And I sure as hell don't want to find out in the fucking morning paper!"

"Listen, I want to be honest with you," I say, lightly touching her arm. "No more secrets. I promise." Henry, you liar.

There's a moment of silence, and we talk through some of our issues. I tell her to ask me anything, and I tell her the truth—well, kind of. Let's just say I tell her the truth up to the point where she wouldn't think I was totally bat-shit. That includes lying about not trying to kill Richard Sweeney. So I guess I'm actually telling more lies than truths.

After a while I convince her to go for a walk. We've calmed down for a bit, and decide to talk about it outside. Luckily I'm safe from extreme blow-ups by being surrounded by people. The elk finds safety in the herd.

She asks me my history, and I tell her the truth—or rather the lies I created for this story. I assure her that she won't have any more surprises. I promise her.

As we walk, talking to each other, we bump into a man. And then I'm face to face with that motherfucker again. That vermin bumps into me and utters those words he always says.

"Sorry, I can be such a klutz sometimes," Richard Sweeney says those same words he said to me the first time we met. He truly is a pupil of repetition.

On his face is that perpetual semi-smile. That smile. So indistinguishable. So sickening. So horrifying. So... familiar. Why do I know that smile? Where have I seen it before?

"It's okay," Adeline says, placing her delicate hand compassionately on his tainted shoulder. "We should have been paying attention."

"Oh please," he says, "you two had each other to talk to.

What's my excuse? I'm walking solo." He laughs, with that smile still stuck on his face. He just butchered a woman a few days ago, and still that wretched smile remains. How can you do that? How can you fake it that well? How can you kill someone and have that pleasant smile as if nothing happened. You fucking psychopath.

"Well, I assure you it's no big deal," Adeline says, laughing with him.

That *smile*. That god damn smile. I want that smile gone—I want it gone *forever*. And I want to be the one who makes it go away.

"Well, I ought to be heading off now," Richard says through his slight smile. "You two have a good one." And without another word, he's off.

I watch him leave. Some woman goes to put her phone in her back pocket and accidentally drops it in the process. Richard quickens his pace, picks up the phone and calls, "Ma'am, you dropped your phone." How can he act so normal after doing such an atrocious act?

"You see that?" Adeline says, and I realize then that she has been watching him as well. "He's a nice, charming, kind, person. But most importantly, *predictable*. He bumps into someone; what does he do? He apologizes. Someone drops their phone, so he picks it up and gives it back to them. Just what you would expect someone to do. Why can't you be more like him? Just a little more predictable."

That smile on his face digs at me. The slight curl of the lips. The indescribable expression. It prevailing even though he just did something horrible. The whole familiarity of it.

And then it hits me.

CH. 44

I'm back in my junior year of high school, at the age of sixteen, and I'm lonely. But being lonely doesn't necessarily mean being alone. No, I had plenty of people that I associated with. I called them friends at the time, but that wasn't what they were. They were just people to kill time with. I had physical relationships with women, but nothing romantic and no one I would now qualify as a girlfriend. Once again they were just people to kill time with. The only people that stood the test of time were Jimmy Hansen and Rick Ellsworth, but I wasn't even that close to Rick at the time. I had plenty of people to talk to, but barely any who would listen.

I was still suffering from the loss of my father; wondering why he would leave me. The answer was simple: he loved his liquor more than he loved my mom or me. Sure I had seven years to recover from that loss, but every time I saw somebody's father come in to pick them up, my eyes couldn't help but wet, if only a little.

But last year I found salvation. Last year my messiah arose to drag me from my melancholy and give me a whole new world to live in. Because last year was the first time I picked up a book by Coralline Thomson. I picked up that book and immediately I was an addict. She was still fairly new, but I read everything she wrote.

From <u>Rock the Boat</u> to <u>Close Your Eyes</u>, I read them all. Now I found a new escape. Now I found a way to leave this depressing world and find solace in fantasy.

Before her, I didn't read much of anything. Sure I picked up a couple of comic books when I was younger and I begrudgingly read my assigned readings, but that was pretty much the extent of my reading. But after her, I was hooked on literature. Then I was opened up to Poe, Dickenson, Vonnegut, Dickens, Woolf, Hemingway; you name it.

At the current moment, I'm putting my textbooks away in my locker so I have a lighter load in my backpack for lunch. We were allowed to leave the school for the duration of our lunch period if we wanted to get food elsewhere. There was a McDonald's just a little bit away—maybe five minutes walking distance—and Jimmy and I were craving some McNuggets.

I leave the book <u>Salute to Death</u>—Coralline Thomson's newest novel—in my book bag. I always leave my personal books there because I'm afraid someone might steal them. Also, I never know when I'll be hit by the inclination to read during some free time. I just got the book yesterday and I'm already a hundred pages into it. It's shaping up pretty nicely. For the past few books, Coralline Thomson took a turn for political themes in her novels. First it was <u>The Night of The Wolves</u> which showed our country's lust for war. Then there was <u>Dreams of the Donkey and the Elephant</u> which showed the potential horror of a two-party system. Now <u>Salute to Death</u> is the tale of a full-blown patriot who volunteers for the army and sees atrocities being done to both the good and the wicked. The novel shows both the physical death of soldiers and civilians and the symbolic death of normally good people's morality. She is truly a master at her craft.

Jimmy leans against the locker and says, "You know St. Peter has been telling everyone he's gonna kick your ass."

Old St. Peter. His actual name is Peter Lindbergh. I take great pride in the fact that I concocted his fun nickname. Peter believes that it's because he's religious and we're all making fun of him for being so gung-ho about Jesus all the time. He embraces this with a smile with that mindset of, 'I'll be laughing when all you heathens are burning in hell.' But the truth is, that's only part of the reason why we call him 'St Peter.' The main reason is that there's a passage in the bible where Jesus calls Peter a 'rock', saying 'upon this rock I will build my church.' You see, Peter Lindbergh was never the most intelligent person to say the least, and everyone used to say he was 'as dumb as a rock.' So combine his inclination to religion and his stupidity with the rock metaphor and the fact that he's so aptly named Peter, and you've got a great combination for a nickname to make fun of him without him knowing it. It's a good thing he doesn't know the extent of why we call him St. Peter, because he is one big, strong, guy. When he starts spouting out some biblical nonsense, we egg him on shouting, "Preach it St. Peter" and just giggle to our hearts content. As for why he wants to kick my ass, well that's another story entirely.

    We were playing basketball in gym and were both going for the ball. We end up colliding with an immense force. My hundred-something body hits his three-hundred-something mass hard, our legs get intertwined, and somehow he's the one who gets injured. Either when he hit the ground or when our legs got further intertwined trying to separate, he ended up breaking his kneecap. He was on the floor bawling his eyes out like a baby straight out of the mother's womb. There's always an uneasy feeling seeing a fat man cry. Because of his broken kneecap, he couldn't play offensive line on the football team, so he has to sit on the sideline. And who does he blame for all this? You guessed it.

    "Well, I don't think that gimp can kick the shit out of anyone for a long time," I tell Jimmy.

    "Oh look at you," Jimmy says sarcastically. "Mister tough guy." He laughs. "You may be all macho on the outside, but I bet on the inside, you're already pissing yourself."

"Don't get me wrong," I say, "when he finally recovers I'm gonna be terrified. But until then, why worry? I still have quite a bit of time until I have to fear anything. He can barely walk, much less kick my ass."

"Whatever," Jimmy says. "You ready?"

"I'm ready." I close my locker, and we head off to McDonald's.

As I'm walking in the direction toward McDonald's I see St. Peter, and he apparently sees me because he's calling, "Hey! Hey Henry! Get your ass over here!"

Jimmy looks at me warily, "Come on man, just keep walking."

I look around and see that there's no one in sight. If Peter really wanted to kick the shit out of me, this would be an ideal opportunity. But then again, him being on crutches and in a cast, I doubt that's going to happen.

Ignoring my friend's advice, and taking Peter's, I decide to make my way to him.

"How you doing St. Peter?" I smile at him and he's furious.

"I'm going to fucking kill you, you fuck!" Peter shouts, shooting saliva in my general direction.

"Wow," I say, still smiling. "Using 'fuck' as both an adverb and noun in the same sentence. Looks like somebody learned a new word today. You know you can also use it as a verb." I pause. "Although, looking at you, you probably won't have that opportunity often."

"God damn you, Henry!" Peter shouts again.

I shake my head overemphasizing that 'tsk, tsk, tsk' sound, "Breaking the third commandment. You shouldn't have taken the Lord, Thy God's name in vain, St. Peter. Now you just bought yourself a one-way ticket to hell. Looks like all that praying and preaching was for nothing."

Jimmy butts in, "Henry, I think we should go."

"Once I get out of this cast and I'm better, I'm gonna kick

the shit out of you, Henry. I'll wipe the fucking floor with you." St. Peter's still seething.

"You know wrath is one of the deadly sins, St. Peter," I say, egging him on.

"I'm gonna fucking murder you!" Peter shouts.

I know I shouldn't aggravate him more. The more I piss him off, the more he's going to take it out on me once he's healthy. I'd have to be *really* lucky to stand even the slightest chance against him in a fight. But on the other hand, I'm having way too much fun.

"Peter," I say, "that's the sixth commandment. You've already assured your trip to hell. Now do you want to make sure there's no redemption for you? Satan punishes those based on the severity of their crimes. What's next? Adultery? Masturbating? Skipping Sabbath?"

Peter starts, "Once I get out of this cast, I swear-"

"But you're in that cast," I say. "You can't do shit. You can't hurt me for a long, *long*, time. You're an asshole, Peter. You're a self-righteous asshole to everyone. And right now, I'm having a little revenge. And I tell you, it sure is fun."

His face becomes serious all of a sudden. "I heard you were at Sally's party the other night and you were drinking."

"I was," I say. "Oh, how much I drank. I drank, I smoked pot, I made out with two chicks, and I almost fucked one of them. I was engaging in all the hedonistic pleasures and I was loving it. I tell you, I absolutely *loved* it." I love how pissed he gets at everyone drinking and doing drugs and engaging in pleasures of the flesh. He thinks it's all a sin. And since he's not doing it, he thinks nobody should. But I'm having so much fun just saying it right to his face.

"You shouldn't do that," Peter says.

"Oh, but I *did*," I say. "And you know what? I'm gonna do it again, and again, and again. It's *so* much fun."

There's something inside St. Peter that's stirring, as if the few brain cells he has are formulating a comeback that will hurt. But try as he might, he'll never come up with anything strong enough. He's tried many times to shame or hurt me emotionally, but he's failed every time. I've got a strong hide, and he's too stupid to formulate anything powerful enough.

"What about your mom?" Peter says.

"What about her?" I ask.

He looks at me hard, "Do you really want her burying another body from alcohol?"

A flip switches in my brain. Rationality and reason goes off; rage and hate goes on. I would have to be really lucky to win a fight against Peter Lindbergh. For instance; he would have to have a broken kneecap and be on crutches for me to beat him. And luckily for me, today's that day. I swing my right leg hard into the cast covering his kneecap.

The cast can only protect so much. But the force from my foot colliding into his knee makes him shout a horrific squeal. His hands instinctually go for his kneecap, and he drops his crutches and falls down on his back hard. His head thumps on the pavement.

I give another six kicks to his kneecap—*Wham! Wham! Wham!*—and he shouts and screams and cries. Then I stomp hard; raising my foot high and stomping hard right on that tender knee. Jimmy's shouting something, but for all I care, it could be gibberish.

I jump on top of him, with him in too much pain to put up a defense, and bloody his face with my fists. I swing wildly like an animal in hysterics, focusing more on the force of the punches than where they land. I blacken his eye and break his nose, but none of this registers. All that matters now is the thudding of my fists against his skull. My fists feel a slight pain, but it doesn't concern me. He screams loudly and Jimmy shouts, but that doesn't concern me. Blood oozes from his nose and sticks to my fists, but that doesn't concern me. All that concerns me is how much pain I can inflict and that rhythmic *thud, thud, thud,* of my closed fists colliding with his face.

Jimmy finally succeeds in tearing me off of him and I accidentally step on Peter's balls in the process.

"Henry!" Jimmy shouts. "Henry! Calm down!"

Peter's wailing away and sobbing in agony. Blubbering and streaking tears down his double chin. There's always an uneasy feeling seeing a fat man cry.

Finally I'm starting to come to. My blackout rage has finally started to die down. "We-we-we-we have to get out of here."

"Where the fuck do we go?" Jimmy asks hysterically.

"Where we were planning on going," I say. "McDonald's."

"We can't leave him here like this!" Jimmy shouts.

"Fuck him!" I shout back and start running to McDonald's.

I don't know how long it took Jimmy to struggle with his decision, but ultimately he ended up joining me. The whole way there, we could hear Peter wailing.

Later, I'm in the bathroom of McDonald's washing the blood from my knuckles. Everything starts to dawn on me of what's going to happen. With Peter bawling at the top of his lungs, someone's bound to find him. Once that happens, the principal will be notified, my mom will find out, and a whole shit-storm will go down. I don't want to deal with that right now. Sure, I feel guilty about what I did—yeah he did push my buttons, but my response was excessive—but I just don't want all hell to break loose. And what if the cops get involved? Then I'm really fucked.

So I look in the mirror, and practice. I contort my face in different ways, trying to find the perfect expression. I need to appear innocent.

I manage a strange smile. It's oh so slight. It may not be innocent, but it's definitely not guilty. It's something... indescribable. I find it mesmerizing. The slight curl of the lips. The vacant—almost imbecilic—look in the eyes. The indescribable expression. The smile prevailing even though I just did something horrible.

I used that smile when I was called down to the principal's office, hiding my bruised knuckles behind his desk. I used it when I talked to my mom that day. And in both incidents, I was decreed innocent.

After that day, that smile was gone—never to be used again. After I constructed that slight smile in the mirror, washing the blood away from my hands, I never saw it again—until I saw it on the face of the psychopath in my story. He is me. He may be a warped, perverted, snapshot of me; but in some loose way, he's me. That fucking 'Wizard of Oz' effect.

CH. 45

I'm working that tobacco into my lungs; draining the nicotine like Dracula drains blood. I'm sucking at that cancer as if it was the only thing to sustain me. I'm like a starved infant inseparable from his mother's tit. All the while I hear Adeline's oddly ironic question played repeatedly throughout my head:

Why can't you be more like him? Why can't you be more like him? Why can't you be more like him? Why can't you be-

"Shut up!" I surprise myself by shouting aloud. Some people passing me on the sidewalk look at me strangely. So what? I don't care. Let them look. Let them think I'm a nut-job. I've got more important things to worry about.

I am Jake Neilson—no, scratch that. I am Henry Riddick. Jake Neilson is my alter-ego. But I am also Richard Sweeney. He's my other alter-ego. How can that be? How can I have two alter-egos? Simple, Henry, Richard Sweeney was you before you breeched the story, and as soon as you breeched it, you created a second alter-ego, Jake Neilson, who is your conscious self come to life in the story. Fuck. I wish I had Coralline to figure all this out with. But I can't see her. I really can't. I've got to figure all this out by myself. My only help will be nicotine to stimulate my mind and alcohol to slow it down and moderate it.

But if I'm Richard Sweeney, am I actually a psychopath? Am I actually capable of the barbaric acts that he does without batting an eye? No. Of course not. He just sprang to life off of a single moment of my worst period in life. Mix that with my natural self-loathing, and boom, you've got a concoction that has some tie to you in real life.

But he still is you, isn't he Henry? In some way, he's still you. You can fight that feeling all you like, but it doesn't shake the truth. And he wants to kill Adeline Stewart who is the incarnation of Lindsey McClain. Does that mean that you secretly want to kill Lindsey? Is that what all this actually means?

"Shut the fuck up!" I shout at my mind and everyone near me looks at me nervously. "Sorry," I mutter and quicken my pace to the liquor store. I've had enough stimulating my brain; now it's time to numb it.

This whole workday was a mess. I had to do damage control for my blowup at my students yesterday. I gave a formal apology to the class, and the students took advantage of the fact that I couldn't penalize them so harshly because of my situation. They talked out of turn, made crude and vulgar comments, completely ignored the lesson. Next it was the complaining parents I had to talk to over the phone. All the while, this whole clusterfuck was going on in my head. I could barely focus on teaching my lesson or what the parents were saying because my head was going in light speed trying to figure out why Richard Sweeney and I share this connection.

I enter the liquor store and see Howie Mumbles stumbling around. I hope to God he doesn't see me. I should just turn back now and go to another place to buy booze.

"Hey!" the clerk shouts at me, looking angry. "You're not allowed to smoke in here."

I realize that I still have a cigarette in my hand. I've never done that before. How the hell could I have possibly forgotten that I was carrying that? I never do that. "Sorry," I say, and flick the cigarette out the door.

I turn back and see Howie's slit eyes open up a little in recognition, "Jay'! Jay' Nelson!"

Ah fuck. Howie's like that tumor that you keep removing but somehow it always finds its way back into your life. "Hey Howie," I say.

"Jay' I nee' a favo'." Howie stumbles over to me.

I roll my eyes, "What is it Howie?"

"Loo'," he says, "I' a lil broke." He pauses with his eyes looking upward as if trying to figure out what he was trying to ask for. I'm pretty sure that if I was close enough I could hear the hamsters drunkenly staggering through wheels in his brain. "Uh... is there any way I coul' ge' a lil money?" He looks eagerly. "I promise I'll pay ya' ba'."

I just want to avoid him so I can get back to thinking about my situation. Whatever will do that quickest, I'll do. Well, I guess I'm funding his alcoholism. "Sure Howie."

"Go' bless ya'," he says, hiccups, sways a bit, then steadies himself.

"What do you want?" I ask.

"Whiskey. Jus' a fifth," he says. "I' on a diet."

I don't understand the logic—I doubt there is any—but I pick up a fifth of Jack Daniels anyway. I'm not sure if that's the type of whiskey he wants but I just want to get done with this as fast as I can.

"Acshley..." he says, "coul' I change tha' to a handle?"

I sigh and put back the fifth and pick up the handle. Then I grab a second handle for me. I'm not going to drink all of it tonight—I'm trying to calm down; not commit suicide—but I have a feeling I'm going to be plagued with this inner dilemma for quite some time. So I pay for the two handles, hand one of them to Howie, head out the door, and fish out a cigarette.

While I'm outside lighting my cigarette I hear Howie shouting at me, "Jay'! Jay'! Hol' up!"

God damn it. What could he want from me now? I'm sleep-deprived, on edge, and in mental and emotional turmoil. Can't you just leave me alone? I can't think clearly, much less deal with your craziness.

"What is it?" I say, making the irritation clear in my voice.

"Le's jus' walk together," he says. "Le's jus' walk."

"Not now, Howie," I tell him. "I don't want to talk."

He sounds truly distraught and lonely, "We' don' ha' to talk. Le's jus' walk. Jus' walk."

"Fine," I concede. "But as soon as you start talking I'm ditching you to the curb."

"Deal," he says, and we start making our way in the direction of my apartment.

I thought it would be okay to be followed around by this moron in silence, but it's getting kind of awkward. He's holding his end of the bargain by not talking, but it's odd just walking with someone in silence. I figure I'd break the silence myself. But what is there to talk about? What's the only thing to talk about? But you can't, Henry. You can't have anyone hearing the insanity that is the truth. And you'll ruin your story if you mention it to anyone. Well, yeah, but I've already made the conscious decision to dismiss the story and embrace this world. There's no one else around. Who cares if you tell a drunken lunatic the truth?

"There's something I have to tell you Howie," I say. "Maybe you could help me with this." After all his words did help me with my last big decision.

"Alrigh'," Howie blurts out.

"You see, this is all a story," I tell him. "Everything is made up. Everything is fiction. You are not real. Nobody that you know is actually real. This whole town is fantasy."

"I kno'," Howie says.

"You know?" I ask him surprised.

"Yeah, it's li', ever'one here is a phony," he says. "No one really matters. We're all jus' specs in the gran' scheme o' things.

It's li', if you were lookin' from a tall buil'ing, we'd all be ants. Insi'nifican'. You, me, the whole worl'. None of us matter."

Great, this conversation just turned into one of the conversations I had when I just started smoking pot with pseudo-intellectuals.

"No," I say. "I mean this is all a story that I *wrote*. Everything in my subconscious came to life in this world. I'm real, but none of you are. You're just characters that I invented in my head."

"Yeah," he says, nodding in drunken agreement. "Ever'one writes their ow' book. That's their life. And we all ha' to direc' our own stories ourselves."

Here I am, bringing a bulldozer to the fourth wall, but the bricks are too strong to break because they're laced with alcohol and stupidity.

"No. I don't think you're getting me," I say. "There is a second person in this world who is also me. He's someone I created in my mind, and he's evil. We have a connection, but he is a psychopath."

"Yeah," he says. "It's li' duali'y. One side o' ya' is good, the othuh' side o' ya' is evil. The thing is we ha' to... we ha' to figh' back the evil instincts, an' lear' to accept the par' o' us tha' is tha' way."

I have to stop this conversation. I feel like I'm back in college getting stoned with some kid in my philosophy class. The entire time we're trying to talk about something deep, but really we're just being imbeciles. He doesn't understand me—how can he?—and nothing he's going to say to me will help me out in the least.

"Jesus, if you weren't perpetually wasted, you would think I was crazy. Anybody would who wasn't intoxicated," I say.

"Don' be so hard on ya'self," He tells me with deep compassion clear in his voice. "I still think ya' crazy."

"Thanks Howie," I say. "That means a lot. Now if you

don't mind, I'd like to be alone, so if you can just go somewhere else, I would really appreciate it."

He heads off and once again I'm free to plague myself in silent self-scrutiny. Now it's just me, my vices, and the insanity going on in my head to accompany me. But then again, I always did prefer insanity to stupidity.

When I get back to my apartment I figure I'd hit the weights for a little—just some curls with the dumbbells to exercise the craziness out of my system. Exorcizing my demons by exercising my body. After that I pour myself a glass of Jack Daniels on the rocks and drink heartily.

So here I am. I am Henry Riddick, Jake Neilson, and Richard Sweeney. The perverted trinity. But what does this all mean?

Does it mean that I'm actually a psychopath? Does it mean that I'm capable of all the cruel actions that Richard does so easily? Of course not. It probably means that I concocted the worst possible character for myself out of self-loathing or that the 'Wizard of Oz' effect has no other bearing than just coincidence. Are Detective Reynolds and Jimmy Hansen exactly the same? Of course not. In fact, they share more differences than similarities. Ron Madsen and Hank Wiseman were much closer to being similar, but still had their differences. Even Adeline Stewart and Lindsey McClain aren't matched up completely. Sure, they share the most in common out of all the pairs I've spotted, but they still have their differences. Thank God for alcohol; I'm finally starting to think clearly.

The question is what to do. The answer is simple: kill Richard Sweeney. I'll have to plan this out. I have to find a way to get another gun or find some other way to kill him while ensuring that I won't get caught.

The 'what' is easy; I just have to focus on the 'how.' In the meantime, the most important thing is to keep Adeline safe and out of harm's way.

So now I have to kill Richard Sweeney, even though in some way, he's me. Funny, I never thought suicide would be so difficult.

CH. 46

Once again I'm at Sergio's Steakhouse enjoying my alcohol-induced bliss with Adeline; finishing off my medium-rare steak and polishing off another bottle of fancy wine. All my problems are the farthest thing from my mind. The only things occupying my mind are joy and love. The whole shit-storm of my newly discovered alter-ego does not enter my mind. For the first time since I discovered it, I've gone an entire meal without thinking about it. Now I'm just drinking the wine I can't pronounce, enjoying an exquisite mouthful of meat, and laughing and talking and joking with Adeline.

That beautiful smile stretches cheek to cheek and her chest rises with every spurt of laughter. Her long blond hair bounces to follow suit.

"You know I'm still mad at you," she says those words in contradiction to her body language. When someone tells you that they're mad at you after they just burst into laughter and still have that cheerful smile on their face, it's hard to take them seriously.

"Come on," I say. "How can you stay mad at this face?"

She laughs some more and sips daintily on her wine. "It's hard," she says. "And you're wearing me down, but you haven't quite left the doghouse yet."

"What could I do to make it up to you?" I ask.

"Hmm." She strokes her hair thoughtfully. "Well you could start by being a little more honest."

"I've been honest," I lie. "What do you think I haven't been honest about?"

She says, "You've been hiding the fact that you're a smoker from me."

Oh shit. "What makes you think tha-"

"I could smell the tobacco on your clothes," she says. "I wouldn't have minded if you told me. But we've been dating a long time and you've never lit up or mentioned anything. You've been hiding it from me."

"I was around some people who were smoking and it must have stuck to my clothes," I tell her. "Believe me-"

"Jake," she cuts me off, "this isn't the first time I've smelt it on your clothes."

"Alright," I confess, "I've been quitting smoking for a long time, but I do occasionally smoke still. It's really hard to quit, but I'm really trying. I actually lasted a couple of months while we were dating."

"That's all I wanted to hear," she says.

"But I'll tell you what," I say. "I'm not going to smoke anymore. I'll throw out this pack and be done with it. Starting tomorrow-"

"Don't give me that empty promise bullshit," she says. "You don't have to quit for me, and I'll bet that you're going to continue for some time, but you should do it for your own health. Have you tried the patch?" I shake my head. "And if worse comes to worse you can always switch to those electronic cigarettes. They're still probably not good for you, but they're probably better than all the crap they stuff into cigarettes."

I smile. "If they actually put 'crap' in the cigarettes instead of all that rat poison and urinal cake material, it might actually be healthier." She laughs at that and I join her. "But I will say, I may not quit right away, but I'm going to try. I'm going to try a lot harder."

"That's good," she says and takes another sip of her wine.

My eyes scan the area, just taking in the ambience. The windows are faded and the lights are dimmed. The floors are finished nicely and there's a marble countertop where the hostess greets everyone. Sometimes it's important just to really look at your atmosphere. So much of our life, we merely go from point A to point B without noticing our environment. When you take some time to look, you can find it quite enjoyable.

Then my eyes focus on him. Richard Sweeney's in a booth about twenty or thirty feet away from us, and his eyes are glued on Adeline. That perverted version of me is staring at my girl and having the most grotesque fantasies run through his mind. His visions play like a million snuff movies; and in each one of them, Adeline's the star.

How long has he been here? I don't know. How long has he been visualizing those millions of alternatives of what to do with Adeline? Probably since he's gotten here.

"I think we should pay our check," I say. "I feel that we should probably leave."

"Dessert first," Adeline says. "You remember their tiramisu."

"Yeah, but I'm stuffed," I say. "We should really go."

"The night is young," she protests.

"Yes," I say. "But we can continue the night elsewhere."

She's still adamant about not leaving. "But this is such a wonderful place, and I can go for another bottle of wine." Methinks the lady doth protest too much.

I look back at Richard Sweeney sitting alone; gnawing away at that red meat with his eyes in a hard glare on Adeline. The revulsion of it all. Imagining what he's imagining. I can't help but wince.

I turn back to Adeline. "It's different," I say. "You look simply ravishing in that black dress. As for me; I look like a schmuck."

She laughs a little and says, "Come on. You don't look *that* bad."

"That may have been the nicest thing anyone's ever said to me," I say and she laughs some more.

My eyes dart quickly over to Richard and I feel my stomach curl. Then I call over the waiter and ask for the check. When the waiter leaves, Adeline gives me a passive aggressive, "Really?" and I tell her I'll make it up to her.

"You better," she says and I play a little jumping game with my eyes between Adeline and Richard.

It seems like an eternity until the waiter comes back. I'm sickened by Richard's cool vacant eyes and expressionless face.

Luckily I have cash, so when the waiter returns, I'm able to pay quicker. I stare at the bill for a long time, too distraught to do the math, so I tip well over twenty percent. Through some difficulty I'm able to coax Adeline into leaving, and next thing you know, I'm out in the cold weather. The entire time I'm leaving, I'm wondering if Richard will attack us while we're not looking. It's an irrational thought—he never strikes in public—but I think it nonetheless. I've never been so grateful for the cold breeze outside in my life.

"Were you trying to impress me?" Adeline asks.

"Hmm?" I say.

"You were waving around all that cash and tipped way too much," she says. "What was the deal with that?"

"Oh," I say. "It's just that…" I try to think of an excuse, "sometimes I have panic attacks. You saw me that one time months ago. I felt one coming on so I wanted to get out of there as quickly as possible." It's a lie, but a pretty good one. "Sorry for leaving so early. I just didn't want to make a scene or anything."

"Oh," she says. "I didn't know that. Sorry for trying to stay so adamantly. I hope I didn't stress you out."

"Please," I say. "You have nothing to apologize for. It's just my own craziness. Nothing you have to concern yourself about."

"Alright," she says, leaning up against me and grabbing ahold of my arm. "But—I guess I shouldn't say this but whatever—you don't seem like a person who would have panic attacks. You seem pretty much together."

I try to think of what to say. What would explain this? How could I wrap this into the character I invented? I remember that Mark Twain quote: 'If you tell the truth, you don't have to remember anything.' How true.

"Sometimes the people who have panic attacks can surprise you," I say. "It doesn't happen to me often but when I'm in public places—or sometimes at random—these attacks just hit me. I don't know what causes them."

"I guess," she says, and we walk in silence for some period of time.

While we walk, we pass a bar blasting Barry McGuire singing "Eve of Destruction." I love that song. Such a catchy tune and such a gritty voice. Barry's bellowing, "But you tell me over and over and over again my friend. Ah, you don't believe we're on the eve of destruction." I can't help but sing along.

As I pass, I see another familiar face. And once again, this is not a face that I want to see. It's Detective Todd Reynolds sitting outside the bar puffing away on a cigarette. I didn't remember envisioning him cracking and going back to smoking. But then again, I guess this story now has taken on a life of its own. I guess I'm no longer in control.

Still, his eyes glare at me accusatorily. He exhales a cloud of smoke and his expression reads, 'Come on. Push my buttons. Just do something so I can finish the job I started at that bar so long ago. Come on, try me.' Knowing what's good for me, I'm not going to do anything to irritate him. I may not always listen to good advice, but I'm also not an idiot.

I quicken my pace and keep on walking. The entire time, his eyes follow me with that menacing gaze.

I put my arm around Adeline who's pretty cold in this weather. She looks at me and asks, "Where do you want to go?"

"My place?" I suggest.

"Ah, I don't know," she says. "Your place is pretty far and it's cold out here. How about my place?"

"Sounds good to me," I say, and finally we have a destination.

A couple blocks away from her house, I see another familiar but not friendly face. They seem to always come in threes. Coralline Thomson sees me from a distance and I meet her glance. I wonder if she'll say something. It would definitely be like her to piss on my parade.

The next thought I have is whether Adeline will see her and remember her from the only time she met Coralline. I need to do something to distract her. So, doing the first thing that comes to mind, I grab Adeline and kiss her hard and long. I make a point to stare right at Coralline as if I'm doing this intentionally to piss her off. And that kind of is what I'm doing. I can see Coralline putting on a slightly disappointed scowl.

When I remove my lips from Adeline's, she looks surprised and says with mild anger, "You know I don't like PDA."

"Sorry," I say. "I guess the moment just hit me."

I guide her so she doesn't see Coralline. We make our way out of her sight and I give a slight glare over my shoulder, giving her the, 'go on, I dare you' look. She doesn't say anything or move in my direction and just continues to look at me with that slightly disappointed look.

Later, as I'm lying in Adeline's bed with Adeline sound asleep, I think of the three apparitions that haunted me today. First it was Richard Sweeney, then Todd Reynolds, and to close it all off, Coralline Thomson.

The three people that I wanted to see least, I had the unfortunate pleasure of seeing all of them. I wonder if this is an omen of some kind. In the bible, everything happens in threes. Noah had three sons. Job had three daughters. Peter denied knowing Christ three times before the cock crowed. It's always a three.

One thing that crosses my mind after I saw these three people today is a slight uncertainty. I know the order in which they *should* frighten me the most, but for some reason I can't figure out which one made me feel the most uneasy. I really hope this isn't an omen.

CH. 47

"Murderers! Cowards! Baby killers! You will all burn with the scum of the earth! You will roast with the pedophiles, lechers, and sodomites in the fiery pit of hell!" an old man shouts with his eyes crazed and limbs flailing to and fro. In one arm he holds a sign of the aftermath of an abortion with a heading that reads 'Abortion Is Murder'. He continues to shout while motioning frantically with his arms, "The Lord shall smite thee! He will punish all of you! You cannot hide through your false idols and deals with Satan! For He is all-knowing, and He will find you!"

While walking to meet Adeline I seem to have found myself passing a protest rally outside of Planned Parenthood. I'm pro-choice but I've always been able to see both sides. Yet this particular radical is causing other protesters unease. Many are trying to distance themselves from this long-bearded man shouting with vehement anger. I guess when people start out for what they believe is a good cause, there's always bound to be some crazies who tag along. It happened with Vietnam War protests, it happened with Occupy Wall Street, it seems to always happen. And the worst part is, it's always the crazies who hang around the longest.

This lunatic is still loud and strong, "Innocent blood is on *your* hands, you heathens! You can hide from us behind the walls of your hospitals and government and atheist orgies, but you cannot hide from the Lord!" Atheist orgies? Whatever. Don't let sense stop this guy. He's on a roll. "Cast the sin out and seek the truth! You are murderers! All of you: murderers! And this stain is one that you cannot wash out!"

The rest of the protesters shuffle uncomfortably from the preaching of this zealot. I'm not saying that the pro-life argument doesn't have any merit; but as always, it's the craziest who are the loudest.

"You! You there!" Please don't be me. I look up and sure enough his finger is pointed at me. "Are you a murder accomplice? Do you stand with the evil that is abortion? Do you agree with the murder of unborn babies?"

Whatever you do, Henry, don't answer this. Just keep on walking. "Actually I am pro-choice," I mutter, half-hoping not to be heard. "But I do see both-"

"Murderer! Heathen! Baby killer!" he shouts accusatorily. "You will rot in the darkest pit of hell! You will be skewered in the lake of fire! Murderer! Baby killer!"

"Hey if you're in heaven," I say, "then I'm content just being as far away from you as possible."

I leave and the crazed man shouts behind me, "Murderer! Heathen! Murderer!" while the more rational members sing a prayer or try to concoct a catchy chant. But for blocks down the road I hear his scorn, "Murderer! Heathen! Murderer!"

I meet Adeline at the movie theatre and greet her with a hug. She's happy to see me but is a little peeved with my tardiness.

"What took you so long?" she asks.

"Sorry," I say, "I had a late start and then I got caught up in the middle of this protest rally outside of Planned Parenthood. I got into a little argument with one of the people. It was nothing really."

She laughs, "Yeah I saw that group of people. Did you see

the old guy with that long beard flailing around and shouting his biblical mumbo-jumbo?"

"Yup," I say. "In fact, he's the one that I got into the argument with."

"Really?" she asks and I nod. "I would have expected better from you. That guy was wacko. The trick is to not sink down to their level."

"I tried," I tell her. "But I was crossing them and he singled me out asking my views in his *oh so subtle way*, and I couldn't help but respond."

She laughs some more. "When you see a crowd like that, you always cross the street. No matter who wins the argument, you never actually *win* talking to a guy like that."

"Yeah, he did get under my skin," I tell her.

"You should have taken heed to that old saying, 'Never argue with an idiot because they will drag you down to their level and beat you with experience,'" she says.

"Yeah, I guess so," I say. "There's also that Mark Twain quote, 'Never argue with a fool, onlookers may not be able to tell the difference.'" She laughs at that and we buy our tickets.

We end up seeing some romantic comedy. Luckily it's not too mushy and is a tad on the raunchy side. The premise is pretty typical; boy meets girl, girl is out of his league, at first they hate each other, later they fall in love, some tension happens to separate them once they're in love, and finally there's a big eureka moment for them when they put aside their petty differences and realize that they're the ones meant for each other. It's completely predictable; just the same as every other romantic comedy, only with different jokes. But then again sometimes predictability can be good. Sometimes it's relaxing to know exactly what's going to happen and then watch what you know is going to happen, actually happen. I guess that's why it's fiction.

As practical as the movie was, it was still amusing. Many scenes had me laughing hard. I'm not saying it was bad at all, but it's not going to win any Oscars. That's for sure. Just a typical movie about typical love with typical characters doing typical things in a typical plot. Nothing to write home about, but enjoyable nonetheless.

Afterward, Adeline and I go to a Mexican restaurant to talk for a while. We talk about the movie for a little bit; what parts made us laugh, what parts we liked, what we didn't like, you know the deal. Then we start to talk about work.

"So how are you enjoying your new job?" she asks.

"Well," I say, "I'm still doing some damage control from that blowup I had a while back."

"Still?" she says.

I tell her, "Yeah, I can't discipline the students as harshly, and the students know that. So they take advantage. Plus the angry parent calls have escalated since then. They're not just calling about that one incident, but it seems that ever since I shouted at their kids, they've targeted me as the prime teacher to bitch at." I sigh. "So it goes."

She grabs my hand affectionately, "Don't worry. It'll pass." She pauses. "I'm not saying it's going to be soon, but over time, it'll pass."

"I guess," I say and smile gratefully at her.

There are some people who feign compassion but have an ulterior motive. Others merely go through the motions; they show empathy merely because that is what is expected of them. Then you've got people like Adeline Stewart who are purely and truly altruistic just because that is their nature. Bless them.

We finish our dinner, and I'm feeling fine off of a couple of large margaritas. I walk her to her house, kiss her goodbye, and head towards my apartment.

The alcohol isn't enough to make me stagger, but it's just enough to make me feel blissful. Not a care in the world. Euphoric we stand; sober we fall.

I open my door and walk up the stairs holding the railing

for balance. I misstep and almost take a tumble down the stairs. Geez, maybe I'm drunker than I thought.

When I get inside I look to my left and see Coralline Thomson sitting in a chair.

"What are you doing here?" I ask. "How did you find me?"

She turns to face me and I realize she's holding a gun in her lap. Nothing quite sobers you up like walking into your own home to find someone holding a firearm. Immediately I'm alert and beyond frightened.

"Coralline, what are you doing?" I ask cautiously. "Why do you have a gun?"

"Henry, we need to talk," she says calmly and serious.

"We can talk just as fine if you put down that gun," I say.

She stands up and walks toward me, "You've been getting too sucked into this story now. I'm afraid if you don't wake up soon, you'll be beyond repair."

"Listen Coralline, I'm fine," I say. "Just put down the gun."

She continues heading toward me—gun in hand and in that cool collected voice, "You're not fine. You've been becoming more and more a part of this story. You're losing it. You've fallen in love with an illusion, and pretty soon you won't be able to separate fact from fiction. You'll go insane. I've seen it before."

"I know what is reality," I assure her while talking frantically. "I know this is fiction. But this is the world I've accepted. I'm going to live here as long as I can, but I'll always remember what's real. I won't lose it. I promise."

"Henry, this can be easy if you let it," she says. "It's not that painful. Just turn the other direction. It'll be like the ending of <u>Of Mice and Men</u>. Just accept the inevitability. Turn around and you'll wake up. It'll be hard to cope with at first, but it's easier now than later." She seems like she's holding back tears. "Trust me."

She continues moving toward me—her gun swaying back and forth rhythmically with her steps. I'm close to pissing myself.

It can't end now. Yes, I know what reality is, but this is the reality I've accepted. This story is the truth that I want. I'm no longer Henry Riddick; I'm Jake Neilson. I have become the story. She can't take that away from me. She can't!

"Coralline, calm down. I'm fine," I say. "Let me just let the story finish. I'll leave Adeline alone. I'll step out of the whole thing. I'm not doing this for the sake of Adeline; I'm doing this for the sake of the story. Let the story finish, then you can kill me. I swear."

It's all a lie, but I have to say something. I'm in love. Even if I'm in love with a figment of my imagination, it's love nonetheless. And she can't take that away from me.

She lifts up her gun, pointing it at my face. Her eyes are empathetic but slightly afraid. She's a little worried. She doesn't want to kill. This is probably her first time killing someone; at least someone other than herself. Her eyes are wet and her hand is shaking a bit. "Please turn around," she says. "I'll do it either way, but please turn-"

I quickly grab the hand holding the gun with my left hand and jerk it out of the direction of my face. Luckily I got her while she was nervous, or else I wouldn't have had this opportunity. She struggles and puts both hands on the gun trying to move it toward me. I grab her and we start to bang into walls. She's got her grip tight on the firearm, and she's started hitting me in the face as if that would weaken my grip on her wrist.

She shouts, "God damn it, Henry! I'm doing this for your own good!"

I slam her hand against the wall; right on the corner where it would deal the most pain. Still her grip is tight and she refuses to let go of the pistol.

We're thudding from wall to wall; bouncing around like a pinball, all the while knocking things down. She's still hell-bent on killing me, and I'm fighting for my life.

Finally we trip up and go tumbling down the stairs. We're

summersaulting and spinning around as we continue our fight down the stairs. Sometime along the fall, she must have let go of her gun because I can hear it go, *thud, thud, thud,* following us.

We reach the bottom and our combined weight crashes hard against the door. Next thing I know, I'm scrambling on all fours trying to find the gun before she does.

Finally I find it and point it at Coralline shouting, "Don't move! You move one fucking muscle and I shoot!"

Then I look at her laying there: her neck completely twisted, a couple teeth knocked out, some dried blood running down her nose, her mouth slightly open, her chest still, and her body as stiff as a board. And that's when I realize that I'm pointing a gun at a corpse.

CH. 48

I'm pulled over on the side of a bridge overlooking a large river. In the back is a duffle bag stuffed with the body that once was Coralline Thomson. Looped around the straps is a rope tied in a knot connected to the dumbbells I have. I don't know if this is how it's done. I've never been a member of the Mafia. Never have I disposed of a body into the East River. I was a shitty writer, then a shitty teacher, and now, finally, a shitty murderer.

In the dead of night, with the cracked windows letting in the cool breeze, I hear that crazy, old, bearded, man shouting in my head. "Murderer! Heathen! Murderer!" How true those words ring now.

It was the other night when I dragged Coralline's lifeless body up the stairs and set it upright in a chair. I sat across from the corpse; disgusted with myself and left with the question: *what to do now?*

My heart was still thumping in my chest, racing from adrenaline and fear. I fish out a cigarette and stare at her. Oh the thoughts that run through your mind when you look at a dead body that you—inadvertently or not—killed.

Murderer! Heathen! Murderer!

She almost looks like she's staring at me, asking, "Why?

Why did you do this to me?" Her vacant stare looking just to my right shouts disbelief and betrayal.

I remind myself that this was not murder. She merely woke up back in the real world. If anything, I brought her back to life—revived her—no way is this murder. But it doesn't feel that way. Oh no, it doesn't.

Desensitized killing.

I wonder if someone will call the cops. Did we make too much noise? And then what will I do? Hide her? Where?

That scene from <u>A Tell-Tale Heart</u> plays in my head. The man lies to the police, being completely hospitable, leaving no sign that he's guilty of anything. All the while, he hears the *thump, thump, thump,* of the old man's beating heart.

You cannot hide from the Lord!

But my 'Lord' is dead. My deity from the age of fifteen onward has been her, Coralline Thomson. And I have killed her. I think of Nietzsche. God is dead, and I killed her.

I look at her some more, wondering what to do with her. The dried blood running down her right cheek; the smeared blood of her nose, her neck contorted in a horrific position, her eyes cool and vacant.

Murderer! Heathen! Murderer!

But I didn't mean to! It was an accident! And even if I did mean to—which I surely didn't—it was her or me! I am no murderer! I am no heathen! I am just a man fighting for his life! It was just do or die, and I didn't want to die!

No matter what I say to myself, I cannot quiet that old, bearded, man shouting in my head. No matter what, he haunts me.

I have to leave the room. There's no way I can stay here and retain sanity, so I go off to bed. All the while, the lifeless body that was Coralline Thomson sits on the couch, just as she did when I entered and she wanted to kill me.

I lay in bed for quite some time; tossing and turning in that vain attempt to sleep. People don't sleep after a night like that.

There's no way. It's impossible. I watch the clock: 1:00 AM, 1:30 AM, 2:00 AM, 2:30 AM, 3:00 AM, and so on. Finally, at what I would guess to be around five thirty in the morning, I fall asleep—well maybe.

I had a dream—but maybe it wasn't a dream. Sometimes when you close your eyes, your imagination takes off to a dreamlike state that isn't quite a dream. But it sure as hell felt like one.

Whatever it was, I wasn't in a body. I was a soul floating above two bodies. There was no substance to what I was. I was merely part of the air. A specter, unseen and unable to affect anything. I was looking down at two bodies lying still. Neither was breathing or showed any life. The area may have been a morgue, but it seemed more sinister than that. Both bodies were sprawled out on tables.

On one table laid my body. It was the body of Henry Riddick—or Jake Neilson—or whoever the fuck you want to call me. On the other table was Richard Sweeney. Both bodies were close together lying in the sweet silence of death.

It was like that for quite some time; both bodies peacefully ignoring each other in their death.

Then there was a flash and with it came the image of me holding a gun at Coralline Thomson just realizing that she was dead. I felt my stomach curl.

All of a sudden, there was a chanting; like some ancient ritual. But the chanting was in English. It was: "Murderer! Heathen! Murderer! Heathen! Murderer! Heathen! Murderer! Heathen!" over and over again. It continued to get progressively louder. It was agonizing and physically pained my hovering soul. With each chant, the pain would double. First a dull sting; and later an excruciating burning.

That's when it started to change. I watched the bodies: Henry Riddick/Jake Neilson and Richard Sweeney start to morph; as if the chanting was pulling the bodies together, making them one. Each of their body parts would dissolve and regroup in the center where a third bed was now separating them.

Finally, they had completed their fusion and were one being. One disgusting, filthy, ugly, being. And right before I woke up, the new morphed body opened its eyes and came alive.

Upon waking, I feel my stomach doing spins. The contents are going to make a reappearance no matter what, so I rush to the bathroom. I vomit a long and powerful stream. I hope this purges the evil out of me. Then I vomit again. And again. And again.

My esophagus burns with agony. If I did sleep it was for only about fifteen minutes, but the dream felt much longer than that. The dream felt like a century. A century of just an essence in agony watching the horror transpire.

I decide to take a shower; hoping this will wash the guilt and murder off of my body. After the shower I feel no better than before. Still as shameful. Still as dirty. Still with ungodly filth.

I walk outside and head into my car. I buy a large duffle bag at one store, and a long sturdy rope at another. Isn't that how they do it? Don't the murderous scum buy their objects to dispose of bodies at different stores so they won't get caught? I don't know. I didn't spend any time in the criminal underworld. I never thought I'd be in this situation. I feel horrible. I feel slimy; gifted with a stink that will never wear off. I feel like a... like a...

Murderer! Heathen! Murderer!

Shut up! Leave me alone! I have enough baggage to deal with without your scorn. I did not kill her. If anything I gave her life. I awakened her to the real world. She's now in reality, free to associate with whomever she pleases.

I drink some coffee—unsure of what to do—and then head back to my apartment, waiting for the time to pass. If I'm going to dispose of the body, it's better to do it at night.

I start stuffing the body into the duffle bag, gagging the entire time as I touch the cold sickening body. I manage to vomit only twice in the process.

I feel a little like Patrick Bateman. Is that what I am now?

A fucking psychopath? But I can't help the feeling. The entire time I remember the dream of my body and Richard Sweeney's morphing into one.

I tie the duffle bag to the dumbbells and wait for night to fall. At around one in the morning I get the courage to dispose of this body. I put it in my car and drive to the bridge over the river. And that's how I get back to where I started.

I'm sitting in my car, windows cracked despite the cold, so I can ward off that stink. How much of it is real and how much of it is manifested in my mind, I don't know. All I know is that it smells horrible.

It's been about twenty or so minutes since the last car has passed and no cars appear close in either direction. I make my move.

I step out of the car, grab the body, and drag along the dead weight of the body in the bag as well as the dumbbells attached to it and bring it to the edge.

I lift it over the railing—feeling sick once again—and watch it go tumbling down into the water making a large splash.

I can't help it. I vomit another two times and then start dry-heaving. The clumps of my puke fall down over the edge to accompany her body in the water. The whole thought of it makes me sick, but I have nothing left in my stomach to expel.

I start my car up, turn around, and head back to my apartment, hoping to get some sleep. My hopes are futile, because sleep doesn't come to rescue me from my thoughts at all. I'm just stuck in guilt and shame and self-disgust. Over and over in my head, the words play as an unholy mantra: "Murderer! Heathen! Murderer!"

I look at the clock and watch it tick by: 2:30 AM, 3:00 AM, 3:30 AM, 4:00 AM, 4:30 AM. But no matter what, the salvation of sleep never comes to rescue my weary mind.

At close to six thirty, I decide I can't wait any longer. I hop in the shower and realize that no matter how distraught I am, what

I must do cannot wait. I must protect Adeline at all costs. After showering, I jump in my car and head—well over the speeding limit—toward Adeline's house.

I'm outside her house, way too sleep-deprived, and I ring her doorbell. I hear the thud of her feet stagger tiredly toward the front door.

She opens the door and sees me coated in sweat—despite the cold—my eyes with giant bags and looking crazed, and in a mixture of slow reaction because of sleep-deprivation and over fidgety with nervousness.

"Jake?" she says, surprised.

"Move in with me," I blurt out.

"What-where-where did this come from?" she asks.

"Does it matter? I'm in love with you; you're in love with me. Move in with me," I say, wiping some sweat off of my forehead with my arm.

"This is kind of sudden, and I like my place..." she starts.

"Then I'll move in with you," I say adamantly. "It's as simple as that."

"Jake, no offense, but you look like shit. What happened to you?" she asks.

"I've been sick. It doesn't matter," I say. "Move in with me. Or I'll move in with you. Whatever you want."

"Jesus, Jake," she says. "This is kind of sudden, and I'm tired, and, fuck, I need some coffee."

She invites me in and we discuss this some more. I'm still sweating bullets and she's pretty confused how all this came about. She makes me some eggs and, even though I feel sick to my stomach, I choke it down.

"I'll get my stuff tomorrow and move in," I say. "It's as simple as that."

"Jake," she says, "don't you think this is kind of sudden?"

"Sometimes impulsive decisions are the best kind," I say.

"Tell that to anyone who lived through the Bush years," she

jokes, but I'm too frantic to laugh at her humor. I merely feign a smile.

It takes quite a bit of coaxing, but eventually I wear her down. She agrees to let me move in with her. Now I'm closer to her and can keep a better eye on her in case Richard Sweeney were to strike.

I think back to Coralline and hear the old man's taunt; "Murderer! Heathen! Murderer!"

Maybe I inadvertently led to the death of one person. Maybe I accidentally killed Coralline Thomson. But I will not fail Adeline. This test is my redemption. Even if I have to kill again—wipe out that psychopathic fucker—I'm not going to let Adeline die. Never.

CH. 49

"Looks like a storm's a brewin'," a man leaning against the wall outside of a bar says to me. He's got his hands in his pockets and eyes fixed on the sky. He's a tall slender man with a couple days growth of facial hair on him and a thin hand-rolled cigarette resting between his lips. He shuffles a little back and forth. "This one looks like it's gonna be a bad one." That accent is so southern and so hick; he looks and sounds like a misplaced farmer from the Deep South. Maybe he is. I could ask him where he's from but I don't see the point.

I look up, enjoying a mutual cigarette break from a hard night of drinking, and nod my head, "Yeah it looks like you're right. I should probably head home soon. I don't have a car so it's probably wise to beat the storm."

He nods agreement with his eyes still on the clouds, "I reckon you should. There's no point in dillydallying. If you don't head out soon, you'll be trudgin' through water with a thunderstorm bearin' down on you. Would be wise to leave now."

I turn to him, "Guess I should leave then. Nice meeting you." I extend my hand. "The name's Jake."

He shakes my hand. "My friends call me Nasty."

I laugh, "I'd love to hear how you got that nickname."

"Kind of a simple story really," he says, his eyes half focused on me, half focused on nothing. "When I was young I used to make a bunch of predictions. Thought I had all that precog shit. Was jus' a narcissistic youth. But as always, you make enough predictions; some are bound to come true. So they used to call me Nostradamus after I predicted the score of a football game. O'er time, things are bound to shorten. So Nostradamus was too long; so out came Nasty. And the boys had fun with that name." He laughs in nostalgia.

"Interesting origin," I say. "Well anyway, keep well."

"And you the same." He nods and I head off.

I walk a few blocks in the direction of Adeline's before the rain starts to drizzle. I look up and Nasty was right; this one's going to be a bad one. I quicken my pace to a jog, but it's not fast enough to beat the storm. About a block away from Adeline's I'm soaking wet, with lightning piercing the sky and the booming sound of thunder cracking loud. Guess I'm stuck in it now.

I find my way to the door, fidget with my key for quite some time and finally enter the home I share with Adeline.

When I enter, Adeline looks at me dripping water all over and looking like I just jumped into a pool with all my clothes still on.

"You should really drive more often so this doesn't happen," she says. "Or at least check what the weather's going to be like."

I shrug, "Yeah, I guess you're right. This weather is freezing. If I waited any longer to get inside, you would have been stuck dating a popsicle."

She laughs that sweet laugh. "Go take a shower. I'll brew us some hot chocolate."

I oblige her willingly and hop in the shower. We've been living together for almost a week, and everything is going fine. The arguments have been minimal—practically nonexistent—and the spark in our relationship hasn't dimmed. Sure things have gotten a little bit more patterned and less surprising, but to be honest, I kind of like that.

I head downstairs and can hear the storm roaring. The thunder claps loudly and I sit in the kitchen sipping hot cocoa and chatting with Adeline. Afterward we watch a movie, make love, then fall asleep. The entire time the storm rages on; loud and fierce. The lightning brightens our room many times, but still we manage to sleep. Nasty was right. A storm was definitely 'a brewin'.'

The next day I'm at work; it's a typical day, just the same as always. I'm starting to love this refreshing repetition. No chaos: nothing. I go to work, I might go out somewhere depending on the day, and then I come home to Adeline. The only difference today is that I'm starting to sneeze. I hope I don't come down with a cold. I like the routine sex I'm experiencing with Adeline, and nothing is more of an effective form of birth control than a clammy, feverish, man with a runny nose.

I enter my car with Coralline's pistol in the glove box and start driving. If I don't have that gun in my car, I have it on me. Always be prepared; that's the Boy Scout motto.

I've hidden it from Adeline though. She is no fan of guns—neither am I really, but circumstances change everything—and she would flip out if she saw me with a firearm. Any time before we do anything remotely intimate, I hide the gun somewhere. If I keep it too long, she'll eventually find it. But it won't be long. Just as long as I figure out what to do regarding a certain psychopath. I've got to decide on a plan, but I've got time. He normally waits a good amount of time between selecting and killing his prey.

As I'm sitting at a red light, there's a group of wackos congregated on the corner. What looks like the leader of them is chanting, "The end is near! Repent! Repent your sins! The end is near! Heed my warning! The end is near!"

I always hate these particular types of nut-jobs. The reason why I hate them so much is because a part of me hates to hate them. Yes they're annoying and completely misled, but their intentions are good. They truly believe the apocalypse is coming and they really do want to save everyone around. I really wish there was a polite and respectful way of telling someone to shut the fuck up.

I continue driving and pass the religious warning. He continues chanting, "The end is near!" I just drive on past them. Back to the relic of sanity in this world. Back to Adeline Stewart. A block away I sneeze a couple of times. Damn this cold.

Four days pass. I called off work for this day and the previous three. This cold manifested itself to the flu. I stated earlier that nothing is as effective a form of birth control like a clammy, feverish man with a runny nose. Well, when you're glued to the toilet and making unholy sounds through your digestive system, it turns out that also isn't an aphrodisiac.

Luckily, I'm starting to get better. My bowel movements are starting to solidify, and the duration of breaks between running to the bathroom have lengthened. If it weren't for that night where I got stuck in the downpour of that freezing rain. Damn. If only.

Adeline comes home and I try to greet her with a hug. She puts a hand out in front of her and says, "Are you still sick?"

"I'm getting better," I say. "Honestly, I feel much better. I may not be a hundred percent, but I'm getting there."

"Well let's wait until you're a hundred percent." She smiles, "That way you can almost be half of what a real man is."

I laugh, "Smartass."

She walks over to the kitchen. "So, you think you can handle solid foods yet? Or is it soup again?"

"I think I have the strength to eat," I say.

"Well, what are you feeling?" she says, walking around.

"How about some takeout?" I ask.

She looks at me with mild irritation, "Care for specifics?"

"Chinese?" I say.

"Geez," she says, "you want more Chinese food than a Manhattan Jew."

"Well, that might be a tidbit racist." I smile.

"More than a tidbit," she says with a short chortle. "And anti-Semitic; not racist."

I look at her for a period of time. She's standing there just in regular work clothes, but still manages to look stunning. You could put anything on her and she'd make it look good. She might even be able to add style to a burka.

"You look wonderful," I say.

She's a little surprised with my sudden adoration of her and gives that sweet smile. "Thanks Jake." She pauses for a while. "It's actually nice you living here. Nicer than I thought it would be. You know I love-"

The door swings open and the cold air chills my spine and I spin around to see *him*. The devil himself is at my front door with a knife in hand. It's Richard Sweeney.

I freeze instantly. He looks at me as if I was unexpected, but quickly shakes this off and advances on me.

I stay frozen a little longer. I was not expecting this—I should have—but I didn't. I was sedated through the daily rituals and patterns and planned out days. The siren's song of monotony has lulled me to inaction. I should have killed him while I had the chance. I should have prepared better. I should have put a bullet in that fucker and let him disappear. But I didn't. That's all that matters now. I didn't.

My inaction lasts a little longer. The shock hasn't worn off. But as for him, a psychopath never is that surprised. They always know how to adapt to a situation.

He keeps walking towards me with that gleam of murder in his eyes. The knife in his hand getting closer with each step.

Finally I snap out of it and reach for my gun. I grab behind me and fumble with it in terror. Now's the time. I have to save her.

I grab the gun and whirl it around toward him. Before I can finish the arc with my arm, his long blade collides point-first hard into my wrist. The gun fires and barely scratches his left arm—making a mere flesh wound that can be rectified with a large band aid.

After that the gun flops out of my hand and I feel my wrist go limp. The tendons have been split and my right hand is useless—can't even hold on to a fucking gun.

Adeline lets out a blood-curdling scream, and Richard—only a couple of inches away—gives five quick jabs in my gut with his blade. I'm already dead. Time is all I have left—and not much of it at that. Adeline's still screaming, and Richard's still smiling. That smile. That fucking repulsive smile.

As if to make certain that I'm dead—or quicken my journey to the afterlife—he slashes his sharp blade across my throat and I feel the hot blood pour onto my chest.

I fall down to my knees. My mind playing over and over, *Must... save... Adeline.... Must... save... Adeline.*

But it's too late. I can't move. I'm useless. I'm dead and I can't move. There's no hope for me. I'm dead.

I fall face first onto the ground, trying to move but can't. I'm choking on blood and feeling a hot puddle start up underneath my face.

Must... save... Adeline.... Must... save... Adeline.

Adeline is screaming bloody murder as my weak eyes watch Richard close the gap between them. I know he's got that smile on his face. He walks slowly—taking his time—just enjoying his savagery. The sicko. The fucking scumbag.

Must... save... Adeline.... Must... save... Adeline.

Still Richard slowly trudges toward her—knife in hand. And still Adeline is backing up, screaming her brains out.

And then it all goes black.

CH. 50

My hands are clenched to my throat as I'm gasping for air. My mind is playing the same mantra: *Must save Adeline. Must save Adeline.* I toss and turn trying to get air; my eyes are closed and I'm feeling cold all over. My mind's still playing, *Must save Adeline. Must save Adeline.*

Finally, a little eureka moment wakes me from my catatonic state. I realize I can breathe. How can that be? I was choking on blood just a moment ago. I feel my shirt and the hot blood sticking to it has been replaced by cold sweat. My body is completely soaked; drenched in freezing perspiration and I'm wondering how this could all be. Did I dream that horror I witnessed? Have I just experienced a terrible nightmare? Then I realize that I'm neither laying face down in a pool of blood dying, nor am I laying on my back or side as if I had been sleeping; I'm sitting straight up. I'm bolt upright, presumably in a chair.

A little wary, I open my eyes and I realize with more anguish than relief where I am. I'm in my shabby home sitting in front of my computer with the almost completed manuscript of <u>The Mind of a Madman</u> open as a WORD document. More importantly, I'm back in reality.

Most people would prefer reality to the previous state I was in—coated in blood and fading into nothingness—but not me. For some reason this seems worse. I don't know if I can save her now. But I can save her, can't I? I *have to* save her. I have to find a way back into that nutty story and put Richard Sweeney's head on a silver platter. I have to save Adeline and then I can fall in love with her and live happily ever after. That's how all the stories they feed to us growing up end. If it's been ingrained into our mind since childhood then it has to be true. Doesn't it?

But what if it doesn't? What if that's not the case? What if the fact is that she's no longer with you and you can never see her again in your miserable life? What if-

"Shut up!" I shout to myself. "Shut the fuck up!"

Luckily this time there's nobody around to scold me with their confused looks. This time I'm alone. All alone. Completely alone. No Adeline, no nobody. She's gone.

"Shut the hell up, god damn it!" I shout again.

Unsure of what to do, I check my pockets for cigarettes. Luckily there's still one from I have no idea how long ago. I doubt I smoked while I was under this trance. This would be a prime time to quit if I weren't in mental agony. Most of the physical addiction is out of my system.

I decide to read the last little bit of what I wrote while under this hypnotic spell. I shudder at the way I had—willingly or not—callously disregarded the lives of the people of the story in lieu of strengthening the entertainment value of the story. I get to the last sentence on the screen and am stuck with it:

Richard advances on her with a knife in hand, walking slowly—but less of a snow leopard stalking its prey and more of a housecat playing with a doomed mouse—as Adeline fights her inevitable doom.

I start to feel a little physically sick. I wonder if I'm going to vomit again. I feel as physically nauseous as when I was swallowing the blood caused by Richard's knife, or maybe when I was disposing of Coralline's body. I try to choke back that horrific sickness. But still, I can't help but gag a little.

How could you say that, Henry? How could you word it like that? You sick son of a bitch. You're just as bad as Richard Sweeney.

But I didn't actually write it. It was my body on autopilot. I am not responsible for what came out of that body while I was under Coralline's spell. That witch poisoned me and made my body act in contradiction to my conscious willing.

But she said it was your subconscious that was in control of all this. Could that be what all this is? Could you—in your stripped down bare true form—have actually thought of this as callously as it is written? Could you really be more interested in literary clout and fame than you were in your 'devout' love for Adeline?

Of course not, god damn it! Leave me alone!

But I remember that conversation I had with Lindsey McClain right before Molly's death when I showed my true colors. I remember what I said to her: "I would be willing to die at the age of thirty if it would guarantee me a century of respect and fame. Hell, I'll die this week if I could be remembered for eternity." And how many times did I say that I would give anything for the kind of respect that Coralline had in the literary community. Anything, I said. Any goddamn thing.

I'm so tired, but I don't know if I can sleep tonight. I should try. Maybe I can figure out a game plan tomorrow. Don't stress yourself Henry, you'll figure all this out tomorrow. You can still save her. You can still be with her.

I look at the calendar on the computer and realize that it's been only a little over a week since I entered the story. I've spent well over the better part of a year in that world and it translates into reality time to just be about a week and a half? Jesus.

I walk over to the answering machine and hit play. First it's Jimmy:

"Hey Henry, this is Jimmy. I haven't seen you in a while, and I tried your house but didn't find you. Where are you man? I'd like to catch up."

Then there's a handful of telemarketers. Finally Jimmy left another message:

"Hey man… about the other day when I bumped into you. Is everything alright? I mean you looked like shit. If anything's bothering you, you can always talk to me. I saw that look in your eyes and it was just… well just kind of vacant. I'm honest man. Come and talk to me. You're starting to scare me a bit. Well, 'scare' isn't the right word. Fuck, I don't know what I'm saying. Give me a call when you can."

There's a few more telemarketers and then a call from my brother Mark:

"Hey this is Mark. I just talked to Jimmy, and he's kind of worried about you. He said that you almost looked like you were strung out on heroin or something. Please tell me you're not doing that shit. Anyway, you know my number. Call me when you can. I may be younger than you but we're still family. You're still my brother and I worry. We can always talk. See ya'."

There's another group of telemarketers and then a message from Carl Johnson:

"Hey, I haven't seen you in a while. I wrote a few more chapters and would appreciate some feedback. Also you think… maybe… I don't know… you think that maybe you could get Coralline Thomson to look at them. I don't know if that's asking too much. Anyway call me back…. Oh, this is Carl by the way…. But you probably already knew that. Haha."

Another two telemarketers and then—less than an hour ago—a call from Coralline Thomson:

"Henry, it's me, Coralline. Don't be worried about what you did to me. I understand. But I hope to God that you wised up and will exit the story soon. I really hope for your own good. Regardless of when you do get this message, please get back to me. Even if you've been in there for a long time, still get back to me. I'm concerned about you Henry. And I don't want you to take the wrong path. I want to help. I really do. Trust me Henry….."

Bye."

And that's all the messages.

I pick up the phone and dial Coralline's number hastily. It rings four times and I hear a tired, "Hello?" She must have just gone to sleep. But how could she sleep after all of that. I know I'm tired. Physically I'm completely exhausted, but mentally I'm wired.

"Coralline, it's me, Henry," I practically shout into the phone.

"Henry?" She's much more alert. "Thank God, you decided to leave the story sooner than I expected. Thank God."

"You have to let me back in," I say. "I need more of that medicine—or whatever the fuck it is. I need to save Adeline."

There's a long pause on the phone and then finally she says, "Henry, it doesn't work like that." She sounds tearful.

"What? Why?" I ask. "Of course it does! There's got to be a way. We'll find one out. Don't lie to me Jane. Don't lie."

"Damn it Henry, it's Coralline, not Jane," she says.

"Whatever, Coralline," I say. "Don't lie to me Coralline. Show me how to get back in the story. I know you know how."

There's another long pause and then she says, "Get some sleep Henry. We'll talk tomor-"

"Get some sleep?!" I say exasperated. "How the fuck do you expect me to do that?!"

She has a mix of agitation and sleep deprivation in her voice, "Just... try. Just try to sleep. I know you must be going through a lot right now. But-"

"You don't know shit!" I cut her off. "How could you know? How could you *possibly* know?"

"Trust me, Henry," she says. "I can barely think right now I'm so tired. You're exhausted too whether you know it or not. Just lay down and try to get some sleep and we'll talk tomorrow."

I'm pretty pissed but ultimately concede, "Fine."

"Alright," she says. "Meet me at my place at noon. I'll still be tired, but I'll be able to think clearer."

All I can say is, "Fine."

"Goodnight Henry," she says and I hang up the phone saying nothing.

How the hell could she possibly know? How could she know anything? Sleep? My ass, sleep. Yeah I'm exhausted, but there's no way of getting shut-eye.

Regardless of whether I can actually fall asleep or not, I go to lay in the bed. It's comfy, but for some reason I feel that if I sleep I've made a deal with the devil. My soul for sleep; that's what it feels like.

The last line plays in my head:

Richard advances on her with a knife in hand, walking slowly

Stop it Henry.

but less of a snow leopard stalking its prey and more of a housecat playing with a doomed mouse

You're only hurting yourself more Henry.

as Adeline fights her inevitable doom.

Shut up! Just stop it already!

Inevitable

Shut-

Doom

up!

What's the point of all this? What's the point of beating yourself up? But then again what's the point of trying to sleep? You'll never fall asleep. Not with all this insanity in your head. No way; no how.

But somehow during my conversation with myself of how I'll never fall to sleep, I drift off and taste the sweet forty winks.

I'm running—sprinting full force with sweat pouring down my body—but still they remain ten feet away, neither getting closer nor further. Richard Sweeney is holding that blood-soaked blade, advancing slowly on Adeline as she's shrieking in terror.

"Adeline!" I scream "Run!" But it's as if they can't hear me. None of them can hear me—or they choose not to acknowledge me.

I'm still sprinting—going nowhere—just remaining ten feet away.

Adeline's face is in horror as she's backed into the corner. She's screaming so loudly it's hurting my ears. In the background I hear a vague constant thudding. It's getting louder and clearer with each passing second.

Adeline strikes Richard in the face with her fist but this does presumably nothing. I can only imagine that Richard still has that insufferable grin plastered on his face. That slight smile that can sustain anything. Like a cockroach after a nuclear assault.

"Stop!" I scream. "Stop it Richard! For Christ's sake stop it!"

The faint thudding in the background becomes clearer and now it's more of a click. Accompanying this atrocious scene is the sound of *click, click, click, click, click, click, click, click,* moving faster and faster.

Richard plunges the blade into Adeline and she doubles over in pain—blood spewing out of her stomach. Her face turns white.

"No!" I scream, still running, but it's already too late.

She falls over and I notice what that clicking is. It's fingers striking a computer keyboard. The strikes are hard and loud.

Adeline falls to the floor as the life drains from her. Still that *click, click, click,* is in a constant loop.

Richard squats over her and does that sick ritual of removing the thumb and middle finger of each hand and draping it over each eyelid. The fingers mash the keyboard hard.

Richard finishes his ritual and looks at me with that smile. He looks directly at me—right into my eyes and walks towards me.

I charge at him, still going nowhere. I can't save her

anymore, but I want revenge. Cold-blooded revenge.

I'm pumping my legs and lowering my shoulders to tackle him down. Still I go nowhere, but he advances on me in his slow—'who gives a shit'—pace. The keyboard sound drowns out everything else.

He reaches me and keeps on walking; just passing right through me as if I were nothing. Just an apparition that cannot affect anything or anyone.

When he reaches the door, he turns around—still with that repulsive smile—and gives me a farewell wave and exits the house. The fingers smash that keyboard and the sound echoes throughout my head. Then everything fades into nothingness.

My eyes flutter open and the realization that it was all a dream hits me. I'm somewhat relieved, but I'm still plagued by that nightmare. I have that cold sweat again and I'm shivering, shaking like an epileptic.

The clock says that it's eight in the morning. I could probably start my way over to Coralline's at eleven. That gives me three hours to kill. What to do?

Figuring I can't be alone just bludgeoning myself with my own thoughts, I head over to the nearest gas station to buy a few packs of cigarettes. When I get home, I chain-smoke until eleven.

I exit the door and head to the bus stop which will bring me closer to Coralline's house. I feel like Frodo traveling to Mount Doom or like Tom Sawyer venturing into the unknown for an adventure. Maybe a more accurate analogy would be a Muslim journeying to Mecca having a vague hope of what I will find, but in all reality, uncertain of what I will actually discover on my Hajj.

Fuck the fancy metaphors. I enter the bus and head towards Coralline.

CH. 51

I knock hard on Coralline's door, taking out my subdued rage and hate on an inanimate object the way a frustrated child hits a pillow. After a good whacking on the door, I ring the doorbell twice and pace back and forth with my cigarette burned down to the butt.

I see her coming and I cash the smoke on her front porch and squash the ember out with my shoe as if it were a cockroach. She opens the door and has a mixture of wariness, guilt, sympathy, and reproach plastered on her tired face.

"Come on in," she says with a bit of caution. "I've got some iced tea in the fridge."

"Fuck the pleasantries." I stare at her with a cold glare.

"Alright," she says, not so surprised with my reaction. "Well at least come inside. If you're going to vent at me, at least have the decency to do it in private."

"Fuck decency," I say, but I walk inside anyway.

I sit on her couch as I did before but this time with hate brewing in me. She steps out of sight for a little bit and then returns with two glasses of iced tea.

"I know what you said," she says, "but I decided to bring some anyway. Anger can definitely make one thirsty."

I scoff at her peace offering. "Last time I saw you, you tried to kill me."

She looks back at me with a semi-smile, "Last time I saw you, you succeeded in killing me."

Outraged at her response, I say, "How can you be so callous? I know you don't know what I'm going through, but you should have some vague concept. You should be begging forgiveness and bending over backwards to help me out."

"You did say, 'fuck the pleasantries,' didn't you?" she says.

I don't respond. I just stare at her with a hard glance. My glare is enough of a response.

She backs up on what she said, "Alright, I'm sorry for the way that circumstances left us. But understand I was trying to help you out. I still am."

I take a sip of my tea—my eyes not leaving hers—and say, "So let's stop pussyfooting around. How do I get back in the story?"

She shakes her head sympathetically and says, "You can't."

"Of course I can," I say. "Don't bullshit me, Coralline."

"I'm not," she says.

"I said, 'don't bullshit me' and I meant it." I say. "I was able to get in there once. I've got to be able to get in there again. Just give me the serum and send me on my way."

"Let me tell you a story," she says.

"Fuck your stories," I say. "Just give me what I need and I'll leave."

"This will explain it, I swear," she says. "It's about Isaac Thorn."

I can tell that she's starting to get to that point where it's beginning to get hard to speak. The throat is getting dry and the eyes are wet. So out of curiosity I say, "Fine. Go on."

"Alright," she says and takes a large gulp of her iced tea. "I'll try to make it short." I nod and she continues, "Isaac had been retired for a good number of years when I met him. He asked me if

I would be willing to take one last journey with him into one of his stories. I was fairly established at this point, but figured I would oblige my mentor. He created a world that was almost utopic. The story was never published—I never could bring myself to publish it—and it was his last journey. He traveled into the subconscious, and we experienced it together in what he called our telepathic connection. But he found someone—like you did—who was his ideal woman personified. There's always a character like that, but most the time you're lucky enough not to find them. I'm sorry you found yours your first time in. I didn't count on that. I should have prepared better, and for that I'm sorry. But he found her—her name was Julia—and within the first couple meetings he was head-over-heals. I tried to tell him that he shouldn't see her anymore but he wouldn't—maybe *couldn't*—listen."

Her eyes are at the point where they're going to spill like waterfalls at any moment. She raises her glass and takes another hefty two gulps and continues, "He spent six years in the story—story time, not reality time obviously—and had married her. I knew things were getting out of hand and I tried to talk sense to him—I really did—but he wouldn't listen. He was under her spell." She sniffs back some mucus. "Finally—as if as a savior—a bus hit him and killed him on the spot. I committed suicide and was back in reality to talk to him in case he was losing it or anything."

She takes another couple of swallows from her drink to coat her dry throat. Then she continues, "But he wasn't taking it well. He had told me time and time again how you could only enter each world you create once. He said that it was impossible any other way. He said that if you were to drink the liquid after you have died and exited the story you would most certainly die. But after that particular instant, he claimed the contrary." She swallows some more of her drink, and she's choking on her words more so than before. "I tried to talk him out of it, but he wouldn't have any of it. He decided to write a resurrection of his character in the story. It was so out of place and unlike the story, it sickened me both as an author and someone who cared about him. His rationale was if the character was alive—even if he had been previously killed—he would still be able to be a host for the subconscious."

She coughs a little bit, takes a couple of deep breaths and finishes her tale, "But I should have known. I *did* know in a way. But he was the genius. He invented this concoction so what authority could I possibly have on how it works? But he wasn't thinking rationally. He was thinking like a man in love. So he downed the solution and then... and then..." a single tear falls down her cheek, "and then his heart immediately stopped. I knew right then that he was dead." A few more tears flow. "That's why I can't let you repeat the same mistake. I can't have your blood on my hands."

I'm distraught and shaking my head. I can't believe this. I can't! There has to be some way. Some other way. We haven't exhausted all possible options. Resurrection may be out, but there are still other possibilities, aren't there? There must be.

"No I don't accept that," I say, vehemently shaking my head. "No. There's other options, we just haven't thought of them yet."

"Henry," she says compassionately. "There isn't. If Isaac—the person who created this formula—couldn't find a loophole, what chance do you have?" She places her hand gently on my arm. "She's gone, Henry. I really am sorry. You may not believe me, but it's true. You have to accept it."

I just shake my head back and forth for a long time repeating "no" over and over again. Now *my* throat is getting dry. Now *my* eyes are starting to well up.

We sit in silence for a long time, and I say—mainly talking to myself, "So what do I do now?"

"The test of a book is how much good stuff you can throw away," Coralline says.

"What?" I ask in confusion.

"Ernest Hemingway," She says.

Now I'm really angry. "God damn it! What the hell does that have to do with anything?"

"Henry," she says, "you have to throw her away."

"Throw her away?!" I say in exasperation. "Throw her away?! How can you say that? How could you be so damn callous? Maybe—yeah—she isn't a real person, but my love for her was sure as shit real. I *really* loved her—still do in fact. And you're telling me to just throw her away as if she were a piece of trash? What the fuck is wrong with you?"

"Henry," she says, "I want you to do me a favor. Take some time to figure things out; a couple days, a week, a month, whatever. And then when you're thinking more rationally, read over everything you wrote with the knowledge that you'll never enter that story again. And once you're thinking clearer, finish the book. Write the finishing touches. She's gone. There's no changing that. But you can still have a potentially great book on your hands."

I start, "How could you-"

"Just promise me," Coralline says. "Promise me you'll take some time to clear your head and then read what you wrote so far. After all that, you can do what you choose. Okay?"

Incredibly hesitant, I say, "Okay."

She says goodbye and sends me on my way. She tells me to feel free to call her if I feel the urge. And I exit her house.

As I distance myself from Coralline's and walk towards the bus stop, I can't shake the feeling that I'm leaving the crossroads. A confused man that just made a deal with the devil. Trying to clear this thought from my mind, I keep on walking.

CH. 52

I take a long drag from my cigarette while finishing reading what I have of my story for the third time. The last line sticks with me:

Richard advances on her with a knife in hand, walking slowly—but less of a snow leopard stalking its prey and more of a housecat playing with a doomed mouse—as Adeline fights her inevitable doom.

I'm trying to think of the right noun to categorize what I am. Murderer? Not quite. Widower? That's not it either. Tool? Doesn't relay the right connotation. God? Assassin? Traitor? Heretic? Fool? Adulterer? Blasphemer? Victim? No, no, no, no, no, no, no, and no. No matter how much I try I can't find a suitable word. What am I?

I suck deeply on my smoke again. Who knows? Maybe if I die of cancer before I finish this I won't feel as bad. Maybe it'll be justice. Maybe what I need is a little bit of karma. What goes around comes around. Isn't that the saying?

Jimmy called me a couple of days ago asking how I was doing and appeared delighted that I was more loquacious than the last time we met.

"What was going on last time?" Jimmy said. "You gave me

a bit of a scare."

I paused for a while, contemplating if I should tell him the truth. But if I did, I would surely appear mad. "Yeah, sorry about that." I opted for the lie. "I had a bad mixture of the flu, lack of sleep, and some strong medication prescribed by the doctor. I was out of it, but I'm better now." Am I?

"Glad to hear," he said happily. "For a while I thought you started getting into the heroin scene. You looked really out of it. What meds did they give you? You were pretty messed up. Maybe if you have any leftover you can swing some my way," he joked.

I gave a terribly faked laugh, but I could probably have blamed it on my recovery. "Yeah, I don't think that's going to happen. I don't remember what he gave me... I think it started with a 'P'." I tried to think of some joke to tell him, but I wasn't in the mood to continue a friendly banter. "Anyway, I'm still recovering so I should probably get some sleep. I'll be pretty catatonic for I'm guessing a week, so I'll call you then." After that we said goodbye and he went back to living in his world and I went back to dying in mine.

Now a week has passed and I've just been reading over my manuscript. Almost a year that was spent in that world is condensed to four hundred and eighty-three pages of computer paper—less than that considering that much of the story preceded me entering it.

So much of what I wrote needs to be cut though. I've made some errors making myself into a main character and really threw things out of sync with some of the actions that were recorded in these pages. But that's for the editing process.

I puff away and reread that last line:

Richard advances on her with a knife in hand, walking slowly—but less of a snow leopard stalking its prey and more of a housecat playing with a doomed mouse—as Adeline fights her inevitable doom.

What do I do from here? Do I forfeit my integrity as an

author and let Adeline live—thus creating the weaker ending—or do I do away with the woman I've spent so many intimate moments with and was willing to give my life for only weeks ago?

I still love her. There's no doubt about that. She may never have been real, and I may never see her again, but that love is still there, and I believe it will always be there. It will last until the day I die.

She was everything I could have ever wanted. Beauty, brains, personality, sense of humor, unrelenting love; she had it all. She was my dream woman, and now she's gone. Anything I want in a woman; it was her.

So what do I do? The damned catch-22. Damned if I do; fucked if I don't. The limitless oxeye daisy. I kill her. I kill her not.

I know what I morally should do and I also know what would make the best story. The choice that would bring me fame, riches, and become a great addition to literature, clashes hard with what my heart tells me. Do I think with my heart or my brain? Which one has the best track record of not leading me astray? In all honesty, neither of them has served me all that well in the past.

Only semi-certain of what to do, I know I can't delay it anymore. I place my hands on the keyboard and sell my soul.

> **Adeline's eyes shift back and forth between Jake lying on the floor curled up in a warm puddle of blood and Richard armed with a long blade and a passive smile. Her mind is bouncing between trying to fight and accepting her fate.**
>
> **Richard still travels in that obnoxiously slow continual pace, scanning her body with his romanticized visions in his mind. The images of her dismembered body entering rigor mortis soothes him like a mothers song to a baby nuzzled in her bosom. She may be alive in her own concept of life and death, but Richard sees her differently. To him, he is not approaching a live frightened**

woman, but a corpse that is awaiting decomposition. He does not believe himself to be a murderer, but rather Death assuring a quicker trip to her destination.

Adeline knows there is not much time left. He is a mere two yards away from her and running will be futile. She has to attack, and attack now. Jake cannot save her anymore. She is on her own.

She scans the area, looking for something to use. She needs some weapon to fend off this monster. She's stopped screaming and is now thinking more coherently. But it's too late, Richard's less than a yard from her.

At last she catches sight of a butcher's knife in a container filled with other kitchen supplies to her right.

Richard is now on top of her, looking her square in the eyes with that slight smile as he rubs the knife on his pants. Having the blood of two people is unclean after all. He's a murderer, not a barbarian.

Adeline acts. She reaches over and grabs the knife, rears it back and plunges it deep into his gut. The blood slowly runs out of his body and within seconds is a continuous pour.

Richard looks down in disbelief. *This isn't supposed to happen. This never happens*, he thinks to himself. He grabs his stomach and leans over a bit. Could he actually be dying? Could his reign of sacrificial killings finally be at an end? No it can't be.

Still with the blade deep in his stomach, he yanks her hair back and sticks his blade through her soft neck with much force. He feels the click of metal colliding with spine. He savagely works the rest of the flesh out with his knife creating a deep hole in her neck. He may be dying, but Adeline is already dead.

When he releases her hair, she falls immediately to the ground with her lifeless eyes staring at him vacantly. He tries to take a step but immediately falls to his knees.

He may die, but he has to finish this. He's the bringer of death, but he's an artist. He's dying, but he's got a certain standard to keep. He's got a reputation. He's even got a fan base. Who is he to let them down?

Despite the pain, he hovers over her—one hand sustaining his weight and one holding the knife—trying to distinguish the middle finger through his blurry eyesight. The pain is overwhelming and his temples pulse with agony. He puts the edge of the knife on the center of her finger and pushes down, separating finger from knuckle.

The shift in his body twists his stomach and it's overwhelming. He can't help but cry out loud. He coughs, and a little blood shoots from his mouth to her shirt. The dizzy spells hit him and the world starts spinning. He's trying to find the thumb, but the world keeps moving and the pain distracts him.

Overcome with sensory failure and pain, his left arm gives out on him and he falls to her right side, dropping the knife in the process.

He must finish this, he thinks, he absolutely must.

He tries to sit up, but that attempted curl causes a wave of agony through his body. He grasps his stomach, and tries to remove the knife but is too weak. In a matter of minutes, his arms aren't even strong enough to lift an inch off the ground.

As time passes, the life fades from him, and the three people in that house are finally at peace.

As I type that last word, I feel a hot tear run down my cheek, followed by another one.

At peace?! At Peace?! Where's your fucking peace,

Henry?! Huh?! Are you peaceful now?! Did Richard deserve peace?! Do you, *Henry?! Well, do you, you evil fuck?!*

Some more hot tears sting my cheek as I wrap myself up in the well-deserved self-loathing.

The tears keep flowing even though I haven't cried since I was a child. They flow faster and faster. And within less than a minute, I'm starting to sob.

CH. 53

After you've separated your mind and your will to live from your physical host, time becomes a relative concept. The days turn into weeks, the weeks into months, and before you know it a year has passed—but you remain unaware of this. It doesn't feel like anything. A millisecond and an eternity are the same. Time flies too quickly and trudges by unbearably slow simultaneously. Has it been a full year? I don't know. I don't care.

<u>The Mind of a Madman</u> was released, and shortly after became number one on the charts with the help of Coralline Thomson's positive review. After that came the overwhelming praises. One magazine used my last book as an influence for the title of the review calling it, "Henry Riddick's Redemption."

It's all bullshit. I'm not redeemed. I never can be. I used to be a failed author; now I'm a failed human being—corroded to the core. If you peel away the skin and flesh, you'll find a moldy, rotten, soul still ripe with treachery.

I look down at the slip of paper—I've been doing this since I've finished the story. It's Lindsey McClain's phone number that I tore out of the phonebook. I wonder if I should call. Maybe even if

Adeline is forever gone, I can still rekindle what I had with her prototype. But for some reason—whether it's fear or shame or guilt or unworthiness—I can't bring myself to dial the number. I still stare at the number, like a religious man transfixed on a passage from the Bible that directly relates to his life.

I may have awoken from that long spell of catatonic writing while I believed that I lived and loved and died, but I'm still on autopilot. Sure I continue the motions. Just a few months ago at my brother's wedding, I was the best man and gave a toast. I laughed and joked and jived and smiled; but behind the eyes, no one was home. I am a mere combination of cloth and stuffing, being pulled to act this way and that by the strings of knowing what is socially acceptable.

I am not an author. I am an actor—a liar. I say my lines and give my performance, but there's no point. Nothing matters. Nothing ever will again. Maybe it never did. Who knows?

And what was the main goal of all this? What was the author's dream if everything goes successfully? To be read by uninterested students a hundred years from now? What's the point of writing? What's the point of trying?

I browse the numbers underneath Lindsey McClain's name on a stained and weathered sheet of paper. To call or not to call? That is the question. I take a long drag from my cigarette and ash it a little, missing the ash tray by an inch, but not giving a shit.

Carl Johnson has been nagging me about reading over his work. I've read it, but I can't give much advice. I merely state that it's good and try to switch the conversation. He asks if I can set up a meeting with him and Coralline—hopefully trying to attain the luck that he perceived that I got—but I can't do that. I may have separated myself from this world, but I'm not that much of a monster. I can't let Carl go through the same heartache that I endured. No way am I that cruel. Everyone may have a price for them to attain fame, but I got ripped off. I won't let Carl. I'm not cruel. I'm not Coralline.

A few weeks ago—maybe it was months, I don't know, like I said time's a relative concept—I got the notification that I had achieved the New York Times Best Seller status. I've made the transition to stardom and I feel like a murderer. I don't feel like a best seller. I feel like Judas; selling his savior for thirty silver coins.

You know that musician who started off with a group of his high school buddies? They started off small time and then built up some notoriety. Along the way he had suffered several tragedies and turned to hard drugs. He overdosed a couple of times, and his friends saved his life and helped him get clean. They turned his life around and were there for him when everybody else left him, diagnosing him as a lost cause. And right when they get a taste of fame, some big wig producer offers him a contract if he goes solo. "The others are small time, boy," the hotshot producer says, "but you're the real talent. You're gonna go far." And he takes that contract, sells out, gives his friends the big 'fuck you' and heads off on his own. That's what I am right now. That's what I'll always be. The sellout musician who told his friends that saved his life to fuck off in order to further his own selfish needs. That's me.

I sigh and take a long drag from my cigarette. Is this what life has left me? Depressed and chain-smoking, wrapped up in self-pity? Some life I've got. Some future is ahead of me. The spectacular life of a famous author. Isn't that grand?

My eyes continue the occasional glance at the slip of paper with Lindsey's name on it. The oxeye daisy is back again. I call her. I call her not. I call her. I call her not.

There's a knock on my door. I pause for a while. It's Jimmy. No shit, it's Jimmy. Normally I would love to talk with Jimmy—him more than anyone—especially in cases of emotional turbulence. But not since I left the story. I don't want to talk to anyone. And I'm not in the mood to put on my acting shoes—to smile and joke and do the happy dance; not now. Not again. Not *ever* again.

"Come in, Jimmy," I call to the door.

Jimmy opens the door, with his beard trimmed and looking a little healthier in his skin pigmentation and body weight. Maybe he's been getting lucky in the art world. Maybe he can finally afford a regular flow of food. Maybe, but I don't care enough to ask.

"I understood that you didn't lock the door before," he says, "but now that you actually have money, maybe it's time to lock your door. This still isn't Sesame Street."

"What are they going to do?" I ask.

"Rob you? Kill you? Those are just two possibilities," he says.

I cash my cigarette and fish out a new one. "Let them."

He's starting to grow accustomed to the new and depressed form of Henry Riddick. He doesn't like it, but he's still a loyal friend. The same way that a mother can't separate love from a psychopathic child who just went on a shooting spree, Jimmy still clings to his friendship with me despite my incredible decline.

"Well," he ignores my laconic self-pitying response, "I figured that since you've made the New York Times Best Seller, I'd give you a little present." He holds up his right hand and presents a bottle of scotch.

Normally I would give Jimmy a friendly jab about actually paying for the liquor but instead I only offer a weak smile.

To put some words in the silence I say, "You know where the glasses and ice are."

He shuffles his way over to the kitchen, puts the bottle on the counter and makes his way over to the glasses, "I saw Hank the other day. He's not doing too well. I hate to say it, but he's looking like he's on his way out."

"Oh," I say without much emotion, "that's awful."

I haven't thought much about Hank. Sure I saw him in passing since I've awoken from that trance, and realized that he was actually alive, but that's about the extent of it.

I think back to Ron Madsen's wake and wonder if Hank goes soon, how much it would coincide with Ron's. Then I shake it off and realize it doesn't matter. Not anymore. The epilogue I wrote doesn't matter, where Todd Reynolds finds the murder scene, comes to the conclusion that the cross-killer was in fact Richard Sweeney, but still finds no solace in that. Todd Reynolds doesn't matter. Howie Mumbles doesn't matter. Old Man Hackley doesn't matter. Even Adeline Stewart doesn't matter. That was another world. That epilogue doesn't matter, and neither does my life's epilogue. Both that world and this one are immaterial now. Now I just have to go through the motions.

Jimmy pours the ice and scotch into the glasses and asks, "What's that piece of paper?"

I realize that I'm still holding Lindsey's number in my hand. I figure I won't lie. Deception got me nowhere so far after all. "It's Lindsey's number," I say.

He smiles, "Thinking she might come back to you now that you're well established? Maybe you'll get a second chance?"

I give another weak smile, "Something like that."

I look down at the weathered yellow sheet of paper reading ten digits that I used to know by heart and call so often. Lindsey McClain: the only real woman that I ever loved. A part of me wants to call her. But a part of me feels sinful for even having that desire. The woman who begat—in some way—Adeline Stewart. I want Lindsey; but I *need* Adeline. But I can't. I'm a traitor—someone awful. But 'traitor' isn't the right word. Heretic? No, that's not right either. Murderer? No, that doesn't work. But then again, on second thought, 'murderer' may just be the most apt word.

Jimmy places my glass beside me and sits down on the couch, "So how does it feel achieving your dream? How does it feel to be a best seller?"

I take a long drag from my cigarette and say emotionlessly, "It's like how you felt when you let Molly die."

I fish my lighter out of my pocket and flick it, setting Lindsey's number ablaze. I put the burning sheet in the ash tray and watch it burn into nothingness.

And my longtime best friend, who I used to have a near telepathic relationship with, now looks at me hurt and confused.

ACKNOWLEDGEMENTS

I feel as though it would be disingenuous if I were to not thank the following people for their support in my creation of this book:

I would like to thank my father for not pulling punches when offering criticism—no matter how much it may have stung—and for taking the time out of his day to give me the first edits of my book. Even if sometimes his bluntness could get under my skin, I feel that it helped shaped this into a drastically better story.

I would like to thank my mother for always being in my corner and believing in me. Sometimes a kind word, after an especially trying day, was what it took to give me the motivation to write the next chapter. I would also like to thank her for a being a fervent reader, and for taking the time to discuss books with me after we had both read them.

I would like to thank my siblings, Sean, Matt, and Brigid, as well as my sister-in-law Sarah, for taking the time out of their busy lives to read all of those novels and short stories over the years, and being honest enough to let me know when one of them was a complete whiff.

I would like to thank Emmanuel Ventouris, Jonathon Young, and Alyssa Bostick, for being among the first of my friends to read my book and offer me feedback.

I would like to thank Andrew Tuchscherer for coming up with my favorite throwaway line that I used in chapter thirty-two.

I would like to thank Marissa Allbee, for being one of my earliest and most fervent supporters that never stopped believing in me.

I would like to thank Divyesh Bhatt for never forgetting to give me a kick in the pants to publish the damn thing already every time he saw me.

I would like to thank Jennifer McConahy and Mike Carter for everything.

And I would like to thank you, the reader, for giving this strange book a chance. I hope you enjoyed the ride.

Made in the USA
Coppell, TX
24 December 2025

67270600R00223